Advance Praise for *Red Helmet*

The latest from *Rocket Boys* author . . . takes an inside look at coalmining, from shoveling gob to negotiating international trade deals, through the lens of modern romance.

—Publishers Weekly

A new book by Homer Hickam is always a cause for celebration, and *Red Helmet* is no exception. Set in the Appalachian coal country that Hickam knows down to the bone, every line of this rousing tale of true love and underground adventure is filled with the author's huge heart and boundless energy. I loved riding the twists of both the plot and the relationship as Cable and Song explored all the depths two people can find when they enter dangerous, exciting places like a coal mine . . . or a marriage. By the time I closed the book, I'd been entertained as all get-out and had my faith in humanity bolstered. Homer Hickam is a national treasure.

—Joshilyn Jackson, author of *Gods in Alabama* and *Between, Georgia*

America's working men and women are Hickam's heroes; he is the Mark Twain of our age, and perhaps the best mainstream writer still tapping keys.

—Stephen Coonts, *New York Times* best-selling author of *The Traitor*

Red Helmet is a tremendously compelling read, and further proves what most of us know already: Homer Hickam is a born storyteller. He writes about real people, and what genuinely matters most— love. Song Hawkins and her precarious hold on life, both spiritually and physically, make this a truly memorable book.

Bret Lott, best-selling author of *Jewel* and *A Song I Knew By Heart*

Other books by Homer Hickam include

The Far Reaches

The Ambassador's Son

The Keeper's Son

We Are Not Afraid

Sky of Stone

The Coalwood Way

Back to the Moon

Rocket Boys / October Sky

Torpedo Junction

Red Helmet

HOMER
HICKAM

THOMAS NELSON
Since 1798

NASHVILLE   DALLAS   MEXICO CITY   RIO DE JANEIRO   BEIJING

Published in Nashville, Tennessee, by Thomas Nelson. Thomas Nelson is a registered trademark of Thomas Nelson, Inc.

Thomas Nelson, Inc. books may be purchased in bulk for educational, business, fund-raising, or sales promotional use. For information, please e-mail SpecialMarkets@ThomasNelson.com.

All Scripture quotations are taken from the King James Version of the Bible.

Library of Congress Cataloging-in-Publication Data

Hickam, Homer H., 1943-

    Red helmet / by Homer Hickam.
      p. cm.
    ISBN: 978-1-59554-214-4 (softcover)
     1. Married people--Fiction. 2. Businesswomen--Fiction. 3. Coalminers--Fiction. 4. New York--Fiction. 5. West Virginia--Fiction. 6. Domestic fiction. I. Title.
PS3558.I224R43 2008
813'.54--dc22

                2007043926

Printed in the United States of America

08 09 10 11 QW 5 4 3 2 1

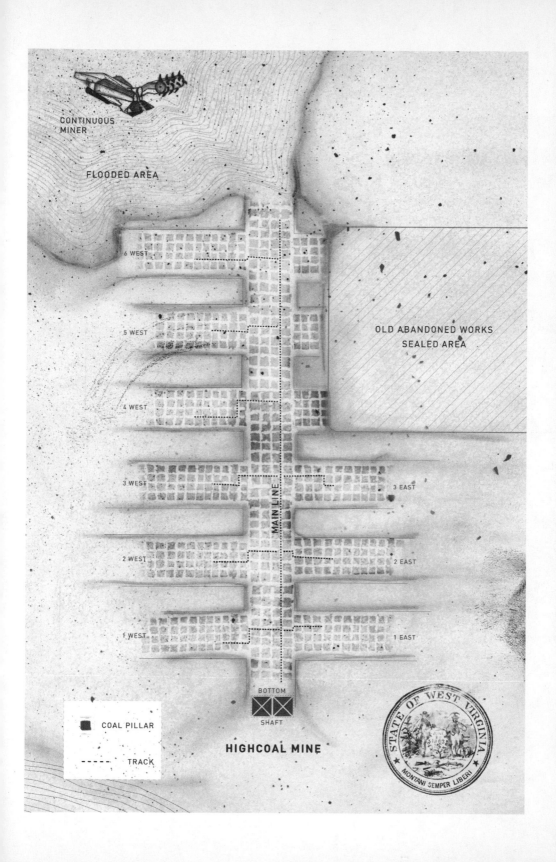

CONTINUOUS
MINER

FLOODED AREA

6 WEST

5 WEST

4 WEST

3 WEST   3 EAST

MAIN LINE

2 WEST   2 EAST

1 WEST   1 EAST

OLD ABANDONED WORKS
SEALED AREA

BOTTOM

SHAFT

COAL PILLAR

TRACK

HIGHCOAL MINE

STATE OF WEST VIRGINIA
MONTANI SEMPER LIBERI

To mine rescue teams everywhere.

Part One
HIGHCOAL

If you don't have love, buddy,
it don't matter what else you got—
house, car, all the money in the world,
because you ain't got a blame thing.

Overheard in a coal mine, not so long ago.

One

Listen to me, Norman. I'm not going to say this twice. You call Bill Roberts back and you tell him I said he'd better get his little business plan together or I'm going to do it for him and he won't like that, Norman, he won't like that at all!"

Song frowned deeply as she listened to her assistant's reply through the cell phone clipped on her ear. Norman could be such a wimp! When he was done whining on behalf of the owner of the latest company acquired by her father, a company headed toward failure without some serious reorganization, Song rolled her eyes and stamped her bare feet in the sand. "He'll do it, Norman, and he'll do it on time exactly the way I told him to do it unless he wants to be on the street looking for a new job. And Norman? You might be out there with him. Now, shut up and do what I tell you! *Now!*"

"Uh, Song?"

Song cut her eyes toward the man standing beside her. "What?"

"Well . . . ," the man drawled, "the preacher just asked you a question."

"Oh!" Song clutched the flowers in her hand and looked into the deer-caught-in-the-headlight eyes of the woman standing in front of her.

"Would you mind repeating that? *Not you, Norman!* I'm doing something here. Just hang on. Better yet, hang up!"

"Now?" the woman asked plaintively.

"Now," the man beside her said before Song could.

"Will you take this man, to have and hold . . ."

Song nodded. "Yeah. Got it. Sure thing. I do."

"Attagirl," he whispered to her.

Song looked up at him. "Cable, I'm sorry. I just had to take care of this. I told Norman not to call for the next hour. Norman, *hang up*! Don't call me back until you get this solved. Good-bye!"

Cable laughed. "I love you."

Song squared her shoulders. "I love you too."

The minister prattled on, rings were exchanged, and then she said, "I now pronounce you husband and . . ."

I'm married!

That was Song's astonished thought as she heard the final words from the barefoot minister. Her second thought was, *This is crazy*. She looked into the lake-blue eyes of her groom. "Boy, are you in trouble!" she said to Cable while inwardly, she said, *So am I*.

Her entire life, Song had wanted to love and be loved. Her smart tongue, her New York attitude—that's what she had shown the world. But now, here he was. This man, finally, at the right time and the right place, who saw through her, saw her as she really was, or at least as she thought she could be. Nothing else mattered at that moment but him. At long last. Her phone played its little song. She quickly turned it off.

Cable kissed her and she eagerly kissed him back while their fellow just-marrieds laughed and applauded. When they came up for air, Song threw herself on him in joyful abandon and, heedless of her white sarong, wrapped her legs around his hips and gave him another long, enthusiastic kiss. Whoops and cheers covered them like a wave. Song threw her head back and laughed. It was perfect. The sun was just dipping below the crystal blue sea. Love had finally reached her. It had taken long enough but, never mind, it was hers.

She whispered in his ear, "Do you really love me, Cable?"

"I surely do, Mrs. Jordan," he answered with an easy grin.

She still couldn't accept it. "Why?"

His killer dimple made an appearance. "Why do you think? Because you're you."

Which was exactly the reason Song had asked the question. Loving her, she believed, had to be a hard thing. She was a complicated woman and exuded toughness in a small, durable package. Men didn't like women who were complicated, and they didn't like a woman who was a fighter by trade and inclination. Yet there he was and here she was, standing together wiggling their toes in the sand on a lovely beach on the island of St. John, also known famously as Love City. It was that, and more. Perhaps due to the dangerous combination of romance and rum, St. John was also known as the isle of marriage, which, as had occurred between Song and Cable, sometimes happened between couples who had planned nothing more than a little fun time in the sun.

They were quite the pair.

She was Song Hawkins, the daughter of one of the richest men in the United States. He was Caleb "Cable" Jordan, the son of a coal miner who'd been killed in a mine. She was the "point man" for the acquisition of new properties in her father's company. He was the superintendent of a coal mine. She had been on the cover of *Fortune* magazine. The title of the piece was "You Think Joe Hawkins is Tough? Meet His Daughter." He had been on the cover of *Mining Equipment News*. The title of the article was "Ventilation and Brattice Curtains in the Modern Mine." Her mother, the heiress to a Hong Kong family fortune, had been an adventurer who had fallen to her death in the Himalayas in an attempt to be the first Chinese woman to climb K2. His mother lived in Panama City, Florida, in a double-wide trailer with her second husband, a retired plumber. Song lived in New York City. Cable lived in Highcoal, West Virginia.

Against any reasonable calculation of odds, they had met and fallen in love.

And now they were married.

He'd asked her in the most endearing and oh-so-Cable-like manner. It was right after her morning yoga. She was lolling in the hammock on the veranda of their cottage when Cable came and took her by her hand. "I want you to meet someone," he said.

"I can't meet anybody dressed like this," she'd protested, motioning to her string bikini.

"Aw, you look great, honey bunch," he drawled, and pulled her to her feet. She took the time to toss on a spaghetti-strap jersey and followed him to the open-air terrace. To Song's astonishment, at the piano sat someone she had never met but instantly recognized: Jim Brickman, her favorite romantic musician. Brickman was scheduled to sing at the resort the next day, an event Song had been keenly looking forward to, but here he was, the actual, real person, greeting Cable like he was an old friend. It turned out they had known each other for all of a half hour, but that was Cable. He liked people, so different from Song who always held back from strangers unless they were part of a company she was interested in buying.

Brickman nodded to her and said, "Cable asked me to sing a song especially for you," and, without further preamble, his fingers danced across the keys and he began singing a ballad "Destiny."

> *What if I never knew,*
> *What if I never found you,*
> *I'd never have this feeling in my heart.*
> *How did this come to be?*
> *I don't know how you found me.*
>
> *But from the moment I saw you,*
> *Deep inside my heart I knew,*
> *Baby, you're my destiny.*
> *You and I were meant to be.*
> *With all my heart and soul,*
> *I give my love to have and hold.*
> *And as far as I can see,*
> *You were always meant to be my destiny.*

Song's knees felt strangely weak, and she leaned against Cable. Brickman finished his song, then said, "My friend Cable has something he wants to ask you."

Cable went down on one knee and took her hands. "Song, will you marry me?" he asked.

"That's ridiculous!" Song blurted, but when she looked into Cable's eyes, she saw he was serious. She was utterly astonished.

"You want to marry *me*?"

"I do. Right here on this beach. I've already talked to the resort manager. She said she can make it happen in a day. It'll be fun, and the right thing to do too. We're gonna get married sooner or later, aren't we? You know it's true."

"You're crazy, Cable. I don't know any such thing."

"Never make an easy thing hard," he said. She rolled her eyes, having heard it all before.

"There are no easy things," she replied with the certainty of experience, "only things that appear easy but aren't."

Still holding her hands, he stood up. "I know that's what you think, but what a terrible opinion that is of this old world! I love you, you love me, and I don't see that changing. All we have to do is stand up on the beach like all the other couples we've seen at this resort, say I do a couple of times, and we're good to go for the rest of our lives. What could be easier than that?"

Brickman was signing autographs. Their new friends, mostly couples who had come to St. John to be married or to honeymoon, gathered around, urging Song to accept.

Song gave them a cold smile, then pulled Cable aside. "Marrying may be easy," she said, "but marriage isn't."

"Is that a no?"

Song did a quick check of her heart. It was giving her a steady signal.

"No, it's a yes," she said, almost sadly. "This is going to get complicated, Cable, very complicated."

Cable gave out a shout. "She said yes!"

Cheers followed, Brickman played triumphant chords on the piano, the other couples came up and hugged them, and Song was washed away in an emotional tsunami. When she came up for air, she looked into Cable's eyes, searching for even the slightest hint of doubt. She saw only a rock steady certainty.

"You're amazing," she marveled.

"Is that good?"

"Not always, Cable. Not always." She took his hand. "Let's go back to our cottage."

"I'll go back with you," he said. "But I'll be sleeping in the hammock tonight. Once you decide to get married, you got to start acting right."

She had never known a man like this. "All right," she said. "Does this mean I can wear white at the wedding?"

He laughed. "Just make sure you can get out of it in a hurry."

"You goofball. I guess Jim Brickman is right. You're my destiny whether I like it or not."

"Then I guess it's a good thing we're going to get married."

IT WAS THEIR wedding night. Cable was the most marvelous lover. His touches, his kisses, everything he did lifted her higher until at the top of an arc of passion, there was an amazing spontaneous combustion of raw, wild emotion. Song had never imagined such pleasure existed. After they'd made love, they lay quietly in the warm breeze coming through the open sliders. Gradually, the volcano within her subsided, and her rational self returned.

"What have we done, Cable?"

"We got married, that's what," he answered lazily. He nuzzled his nose into her neck and took a deep breath. "You smell fantastic. I wish I could bottle you up and carry you around everywhere I go. And you are one fantastic loving machine, lady."

Wheels were turning in Song's head, wheels she'd stopped to get married and then make love but were now fully engaged. Without realizing she was doing it, she twisted on her finger the thin gold band they'd bought at the resort gift shop.

"What are we going to do?"

"In the morning, we'll drive up to Francis Bay and do some snorkeling," Cable said. "I heard there's tarpon there."

Cable could be so obtuse at times. It was one of his more endearing traits, one of several that she looked forward to changing. "I mean after our honeymoon. How are we going to work this out? I mean, you in West Virginia, and me in New York?"

Cable's reply was instantaneous. "You'll move to West Virginia. Wait until you see our house. It's up on the mountain that overlooks Highcoal. You can see the mine from there and everything."

"I can't move to Highcoal," she replied in a firm tone. "My father depends on me too much. And I love my job. I couldn't possibly give it up. Why don't you transfer to New York?"

He removed his arm from around her, came up on one elbow, and looked at her with more than a little surprise. "I can't go up there. All they do is crunch numbers in that old office. I mine coal for a living. And I love Highcoal. It's my place. Always has been, always will be."

"You love it more than me?" The question just popped out of her. If she'd thought about it, she wouldn't have asked it, or at least phrased it quite that starkly, but there it was, asked and hanging in the air of the sweet Caribbean night, fragrant with frangipani and plumeria.

She watched him start to say one thing, then she could almost see him change his mind. "Never make an easy thing hard," he said, as if that settled everything.

"I told you there are no easy things . . ."

". . . only those that seem easy but aren't. I know." He gazed at her. "I think you're beautiful."

Song had been told she was beautiful by other men, all of whom had let her down. She chose to argue the point. "Beautiful? Hardly. My lips are too big, my nose is too small, and my eyes are too narrow. I'm a funny-faced girl. You know it's true."

He traced a finger across her forehead and down her nose and touched her lips. "Your face is perfect. I loved everything about it from the moment we met."

"I'm too skinny. I'm too short. And I'm flat-chested."

"You have a figure most women would die for," he said.

"My hair! It's so straight. There's not a bit of curl in it."

"I love your hair," Cable said, although now there was a touch of weariness in his tone. "Don't touch it, don't cut it, don't curl it, leave it alone. I love everything about you, I swan—!"

"I swan? You always say that but I never knew what it meant."

Cable explained, "Coal miners think it's bad luck to say 'I swear' in the mine. It's sort of like taking God's name in vain. So we say 'I swan.'"

She pondered him. "Am I going to have to learn a new language with you?"

"I swan you might," he said, allowing a smile, and his dimple appeared. But both vanished when he saw Song was not smiling. "You're really serious about all this, aren't you?"

She scrutinized him. "We've done the most romantic thing, Cable. We got married at sunset on one of the most beautiful beaches in the world, and we did it on the spur of the moment. But now we're having a business meeting to decide our proper course."

"A business meeting? In bed on the night of our honeymoon?"

"Yes, Cable. Now pay attention. In any business meeting, it's good to start with a little truth. Do you know what makes me happy? I mean besides you, of course."

"Not really," he confessed.

"My work. I crawl up inside a company for my father, see what makes it tick, then mentally take it apart. After I understand everything about it, I either recommend moving on or buying it. If we buy the company, we maximize its profits by making it better. Sometimes that means we fire everybody and start over."

Her job description didn't surprise him, but her attitude did. "You make yourself sound ruthless."

"I don't mean to be, but I have a job to do and that's to make my father money. It's a family business after all."

"A job is an important thing," he said. "My job is also my town. That's why I can't leave it. It's a responsibility I took on. I can't walk away."

They fell silent for a few moments.

"Well, I can't leave New York."

He rested his head on his pillow and looked at the ceiling where there were only shadows, not counting a stray gecko.

"Don't worry," he said, after what she considered too long a time. "We'll figure it out."

"*How* will we figure it out?" she pressed.

"We'll talk."

"When?"

"Soon. Not now. I'm sleepy. You know. We just made love and all."

Cable clearly didn't understand they were having a meeting, and Song knew it was important never to leave a meeting with a critical question unanswered. She was quiet for a long while, knowing he probably hoped she'd gone to sleep.

"Do you know who else got married on the same beach we did?" she asked, spoiling his hope.

"Well, I'd say about a million other folks," he answered. He made a show of yawning.

"Renée Zellwegger and Kenny Chesney."

"Who are they? Did we meet them?"

It didn't surprise Song that Cable wouldn't know who the actress was. He didn't seem to know anything about movies or the people who acted in them. But Kenny Chesney? Surely he knew country music. She identified the pair and said, "They had their marriage annulled, Cable. Some say it was because she wanted to live one place, he another."

That got his attention. He sat up. "Honey, don't talk like that! It's bad luck."

"I don't believe in luck—except what you make for yourself."

"Don't say that, either! Saying you don't believe in luck is bad luck all by itself."

"Cable—"

"No more," he shushed her. "Miners are the most superstitious of fellows. Don't you know that? Talking about annulments and such on the night of our marriage is like whistling in a coal mine. It just isn't done."

"All right, Cable," she said, shaking her head at his little rant.

"Things will be better in the morning. My mother always said that."

Song turned wistful. "I wish I'd known my mother. They say she was beautiful and brave. But why she chose to risk her life with a baby at home, I don't know. I've missed her my entire life. I know my father never really got over losing her."

"My daddy had something to say on that," Cable replied. "He told me—it wasn't too long before he got killed—you ever find yourself a good woman, son, don't you ever let her go, no matter what. Good women don't come around that often."

She crawled into his arms. "I am not a good woman," she said, resting her head against his chest. "I'm complicated."

"Daddy didn't say a good woman had to be simple," he answered, stroking her hair. He adored her long hair and tried to remember to tell her fairly often. Women were always cutting off their wonderful long hair, and men could never figure out why.

"Will it be okay, Cable?" she asked quietly. "Tell me it will be okay."

"It will be okay," he said. "I swan." His big hands began to explore her again, and she arched her back in pleasure.

"You're beautiful," he said.

"I almost believe it when I'm with you."

The business meeting was adjourned.

Two

It wasn't long ago that Song had been standing in Times Square watching some street dancers. She looked up and there he was, about as retro a man as she could imagine. A snap-brim hat right out of Indiana Jones, blue jeans, a plaid shirt, and work boots, a country boy in the big city if she'd ever seen one. He wore a bemused smile, as if what he was seeing, not just the dancers but everything and everybody around him, was strange and exotic. Their eyes met across the dancers, and something clicked. One of the dancers lost his balance and fell into her.

Cable pushed through the bystanders to pick her up. He did it so easily, as if she weighed nothing. To her astonishment, he doffed his hat, just like in an old movie.

"I hope you're okay, ma'am," he said in a twang that somehow spoke to her of coal mines and mountains. He smiled, and that's when she first got a look at the dimple in his right cheek. What is it about a dimple in a man that can fire the heart of a woman?

"I'm okay," was her answer, but it wasn't true. Her heart felt as if it were going to beat itself right out of her chest. "I was just going for a cup of coffee." It wasn't pertinent, just something to say.

He stuck out his hand. When she didn't grasp it, he reached down and took her hand anyway. His hand was vast and strong and warm and strangely potent. "My name is Cable Jordan, ma'am, and I'm from West Virginia. Coffee? Don't mind if I do."

And so they sat down together in a coffee shop, and it was as if they had been friends for life, desperately needing to catch up. She told him everything, of her lonely childhood without her mother, and of her father, whom she adored, and something of her education—MIT and Princeton—and a little of her job as property and acquisitions manager for Hawkins-Song, Inc.

He in turn told her about Highcoal, his hometown in southern West

Virginia, and his parents, and how his father, whose name was Wire, had been killed in a coal mine just before Cable graduated from high school, and how he'd joined the army, then gone to get his engineering degree at West Virginia University. Now, he said with pride, he was superintendent of the mine in Highcoal, a position he'd always wanted. Atlas Energy, Inc., the company that owned Cable's coal mine, had its headquarters in New York, and he was there for a meeting with his boss.

She wouldn't have much cared if he had told her he'd been raised on Mars by Martians. From that moment on, she wanted to be with him. Perhaps it had something to do with the fact that she'd recently been rejected by another man, and not for the first time, and now here was Cable with his charming but raw masculine energy. What was a woman supposed to do with a man like that? Run away? She was astonished that he even liked her, and in complete disbelief when he told her, after they'd known each other for a few months, "I've totaled things up, and I'm pretty sure I love you." She had laughed at the way he'd put it, but then she had sobered up. Fast. She could scarcely believe her response. "I'm pretty sure I love you too!"

Her friends made light of him after she'd brought him around. They called him "Garth Brooks," refusing to remember his real name and constantly imitating his mountain twang. Song acknowledged that Cable's cheerful demeanor, his big dimpled grin, and his easygoing attitude were mindful of the country singer, although with much better hair, of course.

She also agreed he wasn't much like the other men she'd fallen for. He seemed at times to be of another age. He opened doors for women. He even stood when a woman entered the room. He was unfailingly polite during conversation to everyone and could not be drawn into debate about much of anything, certainly not anything that had to do with the usual arguments of the city, of the decisions of the mayor, or the rudeness of taxi drivers, or the meaning of the latest play by a radically left (and therefore praised) playwright.

He did not, in fact, seem much curious about the world. Highcoal, the town where he'd been raised and the site of the coal mine he now managed, seemed to absorb his mind. When he spoke of either, Song noticed her friends would automatically roll their eyes, but he took no notice at all. These things worried her, not that her friends thought less of him, but that they might be right in their assessment. He was too different, yet seemed impervious to change.

But when Cable held her, Song wanted to melt into him, to be as one with his enormous strength. She wanted him, needed him, and adored him. That was all she knew. It was all she *cared* to know. Any flaws he might have could be changed. Over time, she would see to that. She would make the man into the man he could be. Wasn't that, after all, a woman's prerogative?

The morning after their wedding and their romance-interrupted business meeting, Song rose while Cable was still asleep. Just as she'd anticipated, the major problem left over from the night before still existed. She still lived in New York, and he still lived in West Virginia. She slipped out on the veranda of their beach cottage to use her cell phone to call her father, who was naturally astonished at the news of her marriage. When Cable came outside, anxious for coffee, she handed the phone to him.

"How you doing, Sir?" he said. "Pretty morning here. Sky's blue as a robin's egg, I swan. And you should just see this ocean—it's as clear as air."

"I don't care about the ocean," Joe Hawkins grumbled. "And I don't care about the sky. Or even the air. What I care about is my daughter. Cable, you idiot. You know I like you, but you've messed up now, son. What were you thinking? Did you get into the rum? Now, listen to me. Song isn't going to move to West Virginia. The only thing for you to do is move to New York."

"But I can't do that, sir," Cable protested. "I have a job to do in Highcoal and I've got to keep doing it. I'm not being selfish, not at all. The people there depend on me. Surely you understand."

"I should come down there and thrash you is what I understand."

"If I was in your place, I'd feel the same way," Cable acknowledged. "But I do love Song, I really do. That's why I married her, after all."

To Cable's surprise, Hawkins chuckled, and his voice dropped to a conspiratorial level. "I just wanted to yell at you a bit, son. You understand. Truth is, I'm glad you married her. I was afraid Song would end up with one of those girly men she's mostly dated. You at least strike me as a man's man."

"I'm happy that's your opinion, sir," Cable said. "So you agree she should live in West Virginia?"

"No, I don't!" Hawkins snapped. "I need her exactly where she is. She's made me a lot of money, and I want her to make me a bunch more. She's a sequential thinker, boy, which is rare in a woman. She does A, then she does B, and she keeps going until she's run through the alphabet and anybody standing in her way. Never met a man who could stand up to her. She's a bit cool and sharp-tongued with most people. Won't give them a chance. Maybe you can warm her up a little."

"She's warm enough already for me," Cable said, in defense of his wife who, he noticed, was wandering off alone on the beach, kicking at the sand, her head down. She didn't look very happy, not like a woman on her honeymoon should look. He wondered if he should be worried.

It was as if Hawkins was there beside him with his arm around Cable's shoulders, confiding in him. "Well, I'm glad you think she's warm, Cable. I don't know. Maybe it's because she lost her mother so young. She's kept to herself most of her life. She doesn't have many friends, just a few gal pals who live for business just like her. Most of them think men are weak and spineless. I was afraid Song would join them, be an old maid, get harder and tougher than she already is."

Hawkins barely paused for breath. "I can tell you this much," he went on. "You married an interesting woman. She's like her mother in that regard. That is not necessarily a good thing. In my experience, interesting women are a great deal of trouble. My daughter also generally gets what she wants. I would hate to be in your shoes right now. Surrender and get it over with, that's my advice." Then, after welcoming Cable into the family, he hung up.

"What did he say?" Song asked when she came back from her unhappy walk.

"He said he was going to thrash me."

She smiled. "How I love that man," she said. "You too, of course." She took her cell phone back. "Are you ready to talk?"

"About what?"

"Where we're going to live."

He picked up his mask, snorkel, and fins. "I'm ready to go snorkeling."

She scowled. "You're going to put this off, aren't you?"

Cable was honest. "Yes, ma'am, I sure am. We're on our honeymoon. Let's make it a good one. The last day will come soon enough. We'll decide then."

But when the last day of the vacation that became a honeymoon arrived, nothing had been decided. On the ferry from St. John to St. Thomas, Song and Cable stood on the outside deck watching their magical island shrink until it disappeared in the mist of an encroaching storm. Song wondered if the magic that had brought Cable to her was also disappearing in that mist.

"Cable . . . ," she began. "We have to talk."

"Not yet, honey," he said, gathering her in his arms. "Let's just savor our last moments here."

As the rain pattered down, they took a taxi to the airport. Her plane was the first one to leave, and when they called her to the gate, he held her until, after an awkward kiss, they parted with him promising to call her, to get everything settled. "It's all going to be okay," he said.

"But how?" she asked.

"You're my destiny," he answered. "It has to be okay."

She waved away the umbrella the attendant tried to hand her and walked through the rain across the apron to the airplane, allowing the raindrops to mix with her tears and hide them. She climbed the steps and looked back. He was there, holding his hat, watching her. He started to smile, but she turned away and walked inside the airplane. All the way home, she brooded and plotted and schemed, ultimately solving nothing but managing to make herself thoroughly miserable.

THREE WEEKS PASSED. Song and Cable talked every day on the phone. At first, their talks were long, detailed, but they began to get shorter. She was busy at work, and so was he. He became increasingly difficult to call. He had no cell phone, which struck Song as odd, and his home phone rang and rang. It was only at his work phone, usually answered by a man named (incredibly) Mole, that she had any chance of catching him. Though she kept bringing up their forced separation, he kept saying it was all going to work out because it had to. After a while, she realized he was trying to wear her down.

And to an extent, it worked. On a lonely day, after a string of lonely days, Song called Cable. "I miss you," she said, which she'd said before, too many times.

"Well, honey, I miss you too," he replied. "Tell you what. In a couple of weeks, if I'm running some good coal, I'll come up to New York for a day or two."

"No, Cable," Song retorted. "I want to see this little town you love more than me. I can visit for a week. How about if I fly in next Wednesday?"

"That new section is giving me fits," he said. "Time is somewhat limited."

It didn't matter what he said because she wasn't listening. She'd already made up her mind.

"I'll be there on Wednesday."

After a short pause, Cable said, "Well, come on then." It was scarcely a declaration of his aching need for her, but she let it pass.

Arrangements were made. Song would fly to Charleston, West Virginia's capital, and Cable would pick her up and drive her to Highcoal. She would stay for a week, get to know the town, and then they'd see what happened next. Everything was incremental—judgments would be made, understandings would be forged, love would be allowed to carry them like an inexorable river to where they needed to go. First there was A, then there would be B, and so on, until she and Cable lived wherever they were going to live, as long as it was together. What Song didn't expect, could not even imagine, was that she was embarking on a journey that would not be sequential, but as chaotic as the jumbled hills of West Virginia.

Three

There he is! She was so excited. It was like something out of a movie. Waiting for her at the airport gate was Cable, wearing his snap-brim hat, a blue denim work shirt, and khaki trousers tucked inside high brown leather boots, and a big *hey lady, I sure am glad to see you* grin. She ran to him and threw herself into his arms while her fellow Mountain Air passengers walked past with small smiles.

After a sweet kiss, she told him about the landing. "It was scary, Cable. The man beside me pointed at this little runway on top of a mountain and said that's where we were going to land. I thought he was joking!"

"Flat land is kind of rare in this state," Cable allowed. "Everything is either built on top of mountains or between them."

"Bulldozers and dynamite," she said. "Anybody ever heard of them?"

"Well, we don't much like knocking our mountains down," he said, conveniently ignoring the coal companies who did just that.

She had considered winging into West Virginia on one of her father's corporate jets but had decided that might be too pretentious. Now she knew she'd made a mistake. She'd packed two bags for her journey, and it soon became evident one was lost. Tired, hot, and still a little scared after the landing, the worst of her New Yorkiness came out as, "I can't believe you lost my bag!" Her face darkened as she slammed her hand down on the desk. "What kind of airline is this? The service is terrible. I expect you to make it up to me. A full refund, at least."

"Now, honey . . . ," Cable interceded. "It isn't this nice lady's fault. She's just trying to help."

"When we find your bag, we'll deliver it to you," the agent assured her.

Song was relentless. She did her own job with one hundred percent efficiency. She expected everyone else to do the same. "You act like I lost my own bag. But you lost it! I need what's in it. All my cosmetics, *and* some very expensive clothing." She shook her head. "This is ridiculous."

Cable tipped his hat to the agent and steered Song away. "I had more to say to her," Song protested.

"I think you got your point across."

"I doubt it. I have a feeling I'll never see that bag again." Cable loaded her remaining bag into his bright red Porsche roadster. She was a little surprised. She'd expected him to be driving something like a 1973 Chevrolet pickup.

"Don't worry about your bag," he said. "You can get what you need in Highcoal."

"Can I get Tracie Martyn products?" she demanded.

"I don't know what that is, but Omar has a little of everything."

"Omar?"

"He owns the store in town."

"*The* store?"

"You only need one store if it's got everything you need."

"That is so you, Cable," Song accused. "Do you not understand the difference between *need* and *want*? Or the thrill of shopping?"

He pushed his hat back. "Well, there's a Wal-Mart over toward Beckley," he offered.

"All my problems are solved."

Her sarcasm was lost on Cable. "That's great," he said, then made certain she was buckled up and drove the little car out of the airport. She reached into her large handbag and retrieved a scarf to cover her hair.

"What are you doing?" he asked. "I was looking forward to seeing your hair flying in the breeze."

She leaned over and let the wind blow her hair in his face. "Now do you see why?"

"Oh, baby," he said. "Keep doing that."

"Don't be obtuse, Cable," she said crossly, and bundled the scarf around her hair. She had a headache. Traveling by commercial air nearly always made her sick, one way or the other. Unbelievable. The little airplane she'd flown in on didn't even have a first class section. Everything was coach, with the seats crammed so close together there was hardly any room to breathe.

"I really do love your hair," Cable said.

"So you say." She kept the scarf in place.

Charleston was in a river basin nestled in hills, and Song thought the town was pleasant enough. There were no tall buildings; there was no particular architectural style, just concrete and brick, a town that could be anywhere in flyover country, she supposed. They crossed a wide, blue-green river, which Cable said was named the Kanawha.

"That's a pretty name," Song said. "What's it mean?"

"It means there were Indians that hunted around here a long time ago," he answered, "and now there's not."

Cable pointed across the river to a majestic white building with a glittering, golden dome. "Our capitol building," he said. "It's modeled after the one in Washington. The dome is covered with gold leaf. It should have been made out of coal. That's West Virginia's gold."

"Very nice," Song said absently. She needed her cosmetics. She was going to look like a witch if she didn't have them.

"Charleston's a pretty town," Cable went on, "but wait until you see Highcoal. It puts this place to shame."

Song searched for something salient to say. "When I told my friends I was going to Highcoal, they all got a good laugh out of it."

"Did they?" Cable glanced at her. "Why?"

"Well, because it's a funny name."

"It's not funny at all. High coal means the seam is thick enough that a man can stand up, or nearly so. In other words, a miner's happy when he's in high coal."

"I didn't know miners were ever happy. I thought they were all miserable. That's all I've ever seen on television or in the movies."

Cable's eyes narrowed, and his mouth turned down. "Coal miners are some of the happiest people in the world. That's because we're engaged in productive work."

It registered on Song that perhaps she had insulted her husband. "Did I say something wrong?"

"No."

"Are you sure?"

"Yes."

"Cable, tell me the truth. Are you sorry I came?"

"Not at all."

Song pondered his short answers, then asked, "Have you been thinking about us?"

He allowed a short sigh. "Song, the only thing I've had a second to think about is that old mine." He reached across and patted her on the knee. "But everything is going to be all right. You're going to love Highcoal."

"I'm just visiting," she reminded him.

"We'll see," he said. "More than one woman's come to visit Highcoal and never left. We coal miners have a pull on pretty women, you know."

"A pull? That doesn't sound too inviting."

"Trust me," he answered, then pressed his lips together, the way a man does when he doesn't want to talk anymore.

Song let it go. Her headache was getting worse. She opened her purse and took some ibuprofen, washed down by water from the bottle resting in the little car's console. The Porsche droned on, its tires thumping across the expansion joints of the highway, all the louder because of the sudden silence of its passengers. After a few miles on the four-lane that paralleled the river, Cable turned off at an exit ramp that led to a two-lane country road. "This isn't the fastest way to Highcoal," he said, "but it's got the most scenery."

Song sat back, took a long, cleansing yoga-inspired breath, and told herself to enjoy the drive. After all, summer was in full bloom, the air was warm and smoky, the sky a gorgeous blue, and there was a rainbow riot of happy little wildflowers on the hills. Although in truth all this nature made her a little nervous, she told herself to be content. She was with the man who, for no reason she could exactly discern, loved her. And she loved him. Love would take care of everything. It was their destiny. That's what Jim Brickman had promised, anyway. But did the singer of romantic songs know where Cable lived? Somehow she doubted it.

When the ibuprofen began to take hold and her yoga breathing began to work, she tried to make conversation above the noise of the blowing wind and the rumble of the powerful engine under the hood. She told Cable she'd heard from some of the people they'd met in St. John. Her father was doing well. Her job was stressful, as usual.

Cable didn't do much to keep up his end of the conversation except to occasionally point at the scenery, which was essentially hills on top of hills, all covered with a thick forest. For the next two hours, the road kept to the valleys, until it finally arrived at a bullet-riddled sign that said Powhatan County. Someone had added graffiti to the sign that said Coal Miners Do It Deeper. Past the sign, Song saw the road disappeared into the folds of a steep mountain. She removed a plastic bottle from her purse and began to spray her legs with it.

"What are you doing?" Cable asked.

"My doctor said these mountains are filled with ticks. He said if I didn't use this anti-bug spray, I'd be certain to catch Lyme disease."

"I guess a tick could bite you just as easy in Central Park," Cable grumped. "Are you ready?'

"For what?" She put the bottle back in her purse.

"The road gets a little curvy after this."

She thought the road had already been curvy. She faked a smile. "Don't worry about me. I'm a New York girl. I can take anything this place has to throw at me."

He shrugged. "All right. Here we go. Hang on."

She hung on. Up and over the first mountain they went, then through a narrow, convoluted valley, then up the next mountain, then the next. They began to meet huge trucks, their vast beds piled high with coal. Their massive radiators were like chromed tombstones, and they insisted on taking their side of the road and a good portion of the other. Cable expertly dodged them, while simultaneously dodging potholes and the occasional boulder. A number of deer were complacently grazing along the road. Every mile or so there were deer crossing signs along with other signs that read Dangerous Curves Ahead, Falling Rocks, and Look Out for Coal Trucks.

"Pull over, Cable." They were on the third mountain crossing, and her voice was barely a croak.

He was focused on accelerating through a curve. "What's that?"

"Pull over."

"Why?"

Song grabbed his arm, and her voice dropped in pitch but increased in volume. "I said, *pull over!*"

Cable pulled over at a scenic overlook but Song wasn't interested in the view. She flung open the door and ran for a ditch, falling to her knees just as her lunch made a reappearance. There she stayed, oblivious to the dirt besmirching her slacks, until her stomach stopped its spasms. Cable knelt beside her, offering paper napkins and water. She took them, washing her mouth out and wiping her lips.

"Cable," she said, after emitting a pathetic little groan, "I'm *sooo* sick! I not only threw up lunch, I think I threw up a kidney! Aren't there any straight roads in this county?"

Cable gave her question some thought. "Not really," he concluded.

She climbed back inside the Porsche and clutched her stomach while the world kept spinning. "How much farther?"

"Three more mountains to Highcoal. Four to our house."

"*Your* house."

"Yes. But yours too."

"I just need to sit very, very still for a while," she said. "I don't want to argue. Okay?"

Cable drummed his fingers on the steering wheel while Song sat still. Then she remembered she'd forgotten to call her father to tell him she was okay. She fumbled in her purse until she found her cell phone, then hit the speed dial. After a few seconds, she stared at the phone, which had remained stubbornly mute. "Cable," she said, "why doesn't my cell phone work?"

"Probably because there's no service," he replied.

Song's eyes widened. "Are you *serious?*"

"Serious as a muddy road. I suppose for you, this place seems a bit rural."

"Rural? Buffalo and Rochester are rural. This is *primitive.*"

"I'm sorry you feel that way."

"Please," she begged, "go slow or leave me behind as road kill."

Cable's face was a frozen mask as he eased out on the road just in time to dodge a gigantic coal truck that came roaring from around a blind curve fifty feet away. It swept past them with a jarring rumble, and its great horn blasted displeasure at being impeded. Cable just laughed.

"Get on, old son!" he called to the rapidly receding truck. "Get them black diamonds to market!"

Song closed her eyes and tried to think of something pleasant, like her apartment overlooking Central Park. She only lasted six more curves before she had to ask for another stop. Cable would have to pull over three more times before finally stopping at an overlook where there was a rusting metal sign attached to a wooden post. It read, in black letters on white:

HIGHCOAL

UNINCORPORATED

Population 624

"We're here," he said.

Song was still holding on to her stomach and her eyes were closed. "Just give me a minute. I'll come around." She lifted the bottle of water from the console and chugged, then squinted at the sign. "Six hundred and twenty-four? Is that a misprint?"

"It is now. You make six hundred and twenty five." He pointed through the bug-spattered windshield. "Now, look. Tell me the truth. Isn't that just about the prettiest town you ever saw?"

Song looked. What she saw was a row of tired old boxy houses with slate gray roofs lined up along a crooked valley between two steep mountains. She also saw a couple of shabby brick buildings and, slashed into one of the mountains, a nasty looking black area surrounded by a chain-link fence. Behind the fence was a tall derricklike structure from which a gray cloud was rising. Song had never seen a place that looked quite so sad or downtrodden.

"Welcome to Highcoal," Cable said, his pride evident. "Your new home."

If there had been anything left in her stomach, Song would have thrown up again. This ugly place wasn't about to be *her* home, not now, not ever. For one thing, the road to get to it was cruel and unusual punishment and she meant to cross it only one more time—leaving.

Four

Cable eased the roadster on down the road. Recalling the sign, Song asked, "What does unincorporated mean?"

"It means the town has no elected government."

"What *does* it have?"

"Me, I guess. Atlas Energy owns a good portion of the town, so I kind of run things, more or less, with the constable and the preacher, of course."

"The constable?"

"Hired company gun." He laughed. "I'm just joking. The constable is sort of a night watchman, although he also watches during the day too."

"How about the preacher?"

"Preachers are important men in coal towns, honey."

"I'm an agnostic, you know," she confided.

His expression reflected his astonishment. "You're a *what*?"

"An agnostic, Cable. You know, I'm not religious? Hello? I don't go to church. I thought about being a Buddhist like my mother, and also because Richard Gere is a hero of mine, but I kept falling asleep reading about it. Anyway, I do yoga. If you have to characterize my religion, call me a Yogist."

Cable scratched up under his hat. "Funny we never talked about any of this."

Song put a hand on her stomach. Talking was making her queasy again, but because it was important that Cable understand who she was, she forged ahead. "It's not funny at all. I don't know if we've ever had a *real* talk about anything personal. I listened while you talked about coal mining and I guess you listened while I talked about my job. Then, out of the blue, you said let's go have a vacation in St. John to have a little fun, and of course I agreed. A girl likes to have fun now and again, especially with a stud hillbilly like yourself."

"Well, we did have fun, didn't we?"

"We did, Cable," Song sighed. "We did. But what do we have now?"

"Each other," he said.

"Let's pray that will be enough."

"Do Yogists pray?"

"Shut up, Cable. You're not half as amusing as you think you are." Song looked at the approaching row of dilapidated houses and then she saw, walking along the street, her first coal miner—identified by his heavy black boots, filthy coveralls, and a white helmet.

Cable pulled over. "Hey, Bossman! Come over here and meet my new wife! Come on, honey. Get out and say hello to my mine foreman." He whispered, "Could you take your scarf off so he can admire your pretty hair?"

Song obligingly removed her scarf and climbed out, although her legs were still a bit shaky. She leaned on the car's fender while Cable brought the man over.

"Bossman, meet Song."

Song nodded to the man but he didn't nod back. Instead, he frankly studied her from head to toe, his thin face, small bright eyes, and hooked nose giving him the appearance of a big-beaked bird. Song felt like a bug beneath his steady gaze.

"Not bad, Cable," he concluded. "She's cute as a speckled puppy." Then, without warning, he peeled Song off the fender and gave her a big hug.

Song recoiled at the sour odor of dirt and sweat permeating Bossman's baggy coveralls. When he let her go, Song looked down at her blouse, appalled to see it smeared with a black, sticky substance.

"Look at what you've done!" she screeched. "Do you have any idea how much this blouse cost me?"

"Thirty dollars?" Bossman guessed.

"More like fifty," Cable said. "She shops in New York."

"Two hundred dollars and it was on sale!" Song angrily informed them both. "Now it's ruined!"

Bossman peered at the blouse, then turned and spat out a thick stream of dark liquid. Song watched its trajectory until it landed with a splash, then coagulated in a nasty brown pool in the dirt. She groaned and slapped her hand over her mouth as her stomach protested.

"You was robbed. You ought to go shopping with a Highcoal woman, ma'am," Bossman said. "They can show you how to get the bargains."

Song considered a biting reply, something along the lines that no mountain woman could outshop a New York girl, but she lacked the energy. Instead, she shook her head, then climbed back inside the roadster and closed her eyes. Cable and Bossman talked some more, then Cable sat down behind the wheel. "Carsick again, babe?"

Song took a deep breath. "What was that awful stuff that came out of that man's mouth? It looked like liquid poop!"

"Tobacco juice, honey. Lots of miners chew it. Keeps the dust out of their lungs, so they say. You'll get used to it."

"I can't imagine getting used to something that gross. And what's this stuff on my blouse?"

He studied the fabric. "Looks like gob," he concluded.

"I don't think I want to know what gob is."

"Stuff that comes out of a coal mine," he answered. "Coal dust, rock dust, grease, you know."

"No, I don't know. But I do know my blouse is ruined."

"Put it in the washing machine with a little Clorox and I bet it comes out white as rice," he suggested.

"That may be," she replied coldly, "but it happens to be a pale, translucent blue. Before your friend turned it black, that is."

"Well, maybe you could dye it back the way it was."

Song stared at him. "You know, Cable, it just occurred to me that sometimes you can be an idiot."

Cable arched an eyebrow. "Maybe I got bit by a tick with Lyme disease. Affected my brain."

All Song wanted was to get somewhere other than where she was. "Let's just go," she grumped.

"Bossman's a great fellow. You'll love him once you get to know him."

"Next time I see him, I'll wear a raincoat."

Cable frowned in confusion, then pulled the roadster back onto the road, if a narrow, pot-holed strip of cracked asphalt was worthy of the name. They continued past another row of depleted houses, where Song saw, strolling up the street with a lunch bucket, her second miner, a giant of a man with a flat nose and furtive eyes. He was wearing a black helmet. When he saw the car, he stopped and solemnly raised his middle finger.

"Hey, Cable!" he yelled. "Lookit what I got for you!"

"Who's that?" Song was astonished.

Cable ignored the miner's rude gesture and kept driving. "His name's Oswald Wilkes, but everybody calls him Bum. He has trouble with authority, mainly mine."

"He works for you?"

"He does."

"And you let him flip you the bird?"

"He does things like that to get my goat. If I reacted, it would only make his day."

"You should fire him," Song said. "My father would. For that matter, so would I."

Cable shook his head. "Can't. I need every miner I can get. Besides, he was a teammate on my high school football team. We almost won the championship."

"Loyalty to a poor employee is bad for business, Cable," Song lectured. "Surely you know that."

"Well, I guess I know the mining business a bit better than you do, honey," he replied. "Now, look there. It's Omar's! Where Highcoal shops."

Cable's point led Song to a grimy brick building set between weed-choked vacant lots. A sign above its front door read Omar's Dollar and Cents Store. Song saw two display windows. One had a selection of plastic lawn ornaments, with pink flamingos dominating, and the other a mannequin wearing blue coveralls, boots, and a black miner's helmet.

"That's not a store, Cable," she said. "It's a yard sale."

Cable's lips twitched, and his left eyebrow arched minutely, but he otherwise acted as if he hadn't heard her. "There's the mine," he said. "What do you think of it? Quite a complex, eh?"

Song had always imagined a coal mine would look something like a train tunnel in the side of a mountain where men with shovels and picks on their shoulders walked in and out. Instead, she saw an ugly slash in the side of a mountain that had produced a level area. It was covered with a grayish-black substance, and was dominated by a skeletal tower that had big wheels on top and thick, greasy cables dropping down its center. Beside the tower sat two huge dirt-streaked metal buildings perched on stilts. Beneath them were piles of a dark, glittery substance that Song assumed was coal. Big, grimy pipes went this way and that along the outside of the buildings, and steam rose from somewhere behind them. "It looks dirty," she concluded.

"It's a coal mine," Cable said heavily. "It's supposed to be dirty. I don't know how you could have a coal mine without it being dirty."

Song dropped her chin. "All I know is, I feel as dirty as it looks," she muttered.

Cable allowed a sigh, then turned the car. In contrast to the grimy, dilapidated structures she'd seen so far in Highcoal, the next structure they approached was so clean it sparkled in the bright summer sun. It was a snowy white church, just as pretty as a picture, with a peaked roof and a steeple with a cross on top. There was a sign in front of it that said The Highcoal Church of Christian Truth. Beneath it was the message: The First Step to Heaven Is Knowing You Are Lost. Standing up from putting the last "T" on the message was a pudgy, sweet-faced man in jeans and shirt sleeves. Cable tooted at him, and the man grinned and waved. "That's our preacher," Cable said. "And that's what we call him. Preacher. Every so often when I need an extra man, he also works in the mine. You want to meet him?"

"Aren't you listening, Cable? I need a bath!"

"What do you think of Preacher's sign?" he asked. "He makes up those sayings all by himself."

Song shook her head in exasperation at Cable's obtuseness. "I don't know about heaven, but I can tell you my first step to hell. That was landing on that postage stamp glued to the top of a mountain you West Virginians call an airport. It's been downhill from there. Literally. And uphill too."

"I take it you aren't happy," he said.

"My, aren't we perceptive?" she grumped. "I'll tell you what I am. I'm hot, tired, dirty, and I recently vomited several times. Therefore, yes, I am *not* happy."

"I'm sorry," he said.

"Then do something about it, Cable."

"I'm trying."

They passed another row of old houses. People were sitting on their porches, every man, woman, and child dressed in either blue jeans or bib overalls. The men favored ball caps and plaid shirts with the sleeves rolled up; the women and kids were mostly in T-shirts. They looked to Song like people she'd expect to see at a professional wrestling match or tractor pull. At least they were friendly, with everybody waving and nodding. Cable happily waved and nodded back. She just couldn't do it. Their stares made her too uncomfortable.

Around another curve, and there—no surprise—sat yet another mountain. Song had already seen enough West Virginia mountains to last a lifetime. Up they headed along its switchback curves. Just before she was going to demand he stop again to let her stomach do its work, he pulled the little car off at an overlook. "No more scenery," she pleaded.

"This is scenery I guess you need to see," he said. "There's Hillcrest."

Song sighed and dutifully looked across a deep valley to a ridge where a mansion sat with turrets and bay windows and a wide front porch, all surrounded by a lawn of the greenest grass she had ever seen. Even at that distance, she could see colorful flowers along a winding brick driveway, and behind the house was a green-and-white wooden structure, which she judged to be a stable, and behind that a big, glossy meadow surrounded by a bone-white fence. It was all lovely. "Cable, that is a truly beautiful estate," she conceded.

His dimple made an appearance. "I knew you'd like it. The house was built by Colonel Sam Fillmore, the man who founded Highcoal and dug the first coal mine around here. I bought it about this time last year and remodeled it and added a stable. I wanted you to have a nice place to live."

"But we didn't know each other then," she pointed out. When Cable looked sheepish, she asked, "Was it for another woman?"

"It was for you." He winked at her. "I just didn't know it at the time."

Before she could pursue the subject of another woman in his life before her, Cable pulled back on the highway, then turned off onto a dirt road. Soon they'd reached the driveway that led to the house. Beside the stable, Song observed two horses, both watching them with bright, intelligent eyes.

"What beautiful animals," she said.

"The mare's name is Trixie; the gelding is Ben. He's the one I ride, mostly.

There're trails everywhere on top of this mountain. We'll have a great time riding our property."

Song, feeling suddenly revitalized, got out and walked to the fence and slowly put out her hand. After a moment of hesitation, the mare rewarded her with a cautious nuzzle. "I'll have some carrots for you next time, girl," she promised, noting the obvious care and grooming of the horse. She called out, "Cable, who takes care of them?"

"I have a boy come by every day," Cable replied as he carried her bag up on the porch. "Stay there until I come back." He disappeared inside with her bag but soon returned, calling out, "Okay. Ready."

Song petted Trixie again, then walked to the house and up on the porch, whereupon Cable swept her into his arms and carried her through the open front door. She squeaked in delight. "Cable, that's so old-fashioned!"

He set her down, took off his hat, and bowed. "You married an old-fashioned fellow, honey."

Song was starting to feel better about everything. She looked down at the stunning parquet floor of the hallway. It was absolutely gorgeous.

"Solid oak," Cable said, stomping it. "All the floors in this house are of the finest West Virginia lumber."

"Lovely. How many bedrooms?"

"Six. Including the nursery."

"Nursery?"

He shrugged. "Well, we don't know what happened down in St. John, do we?"

Song knew very well what *had* and *hadn't* happened in St. John, and she'd no intention of having a baby any time soon, if ever. But this wasn't the time to tell him she'd been relieved to find out she wasn't pregnant a couple of weeks after returning to New York—and that she'd decided to go on the pill. She instead admired the grand curving staircase. Cable tossed his hat onto the banister post.

"Buying and remodeling this old place cost me a fortune. What do you think?"

"It's amazing, Cable," she said, and meant it.

Cable took her on a tour, pointing out the exquisite oak and maple furniture in the parlor, living room, and dining room. There were fresh-cut flowers on the dining room table. "Who did you hire to do the interior decorating?" she asked, since she was nearly certain Cable hadn't done it on his own.

"Her name's Rhonda," he confirmed. "She runs the Cardinal Hotel, which is a kind of a boarding house for bachelor miners and visitors." He grinned at her, obviously pleased that she liked the house and its furnishing. "I have an idea. You go upstairs, take a long, luxurious bath—wait'll you see your bathroom— and then we'll make mad, passionate love until Rhonda brings us supper."

Song gave the offer some thought, could see nothing wrong with it, and nodded toward the curving staircase. "The stairway to heaven, I take it?"

"It is, Mrs. Jordan. It certainly is!"

A bell rang, long and insistent. "That's the mine phone," Cable said, and walked into the parlor to pick it up. It proved to be a black rotary dial phone, the likes of which Song had never seen except in old movies.

Cable put the clunky receiver to his ear, listened, and then said, "Call Doctor K. Then wait for me. I'll be right there." He crossed quickly to the staircase and plucked his hat off the post. "Got to go to the mine," he said.

"You're leaving?" Song asked in disbelief.

"A pillar let go," he said. "Broke a man's arm."

"A *what* let go?"

"A pillar in the new section. If one gets mined too close . . . Look, I'll explain later. I'm truly sorry, but I've *got* to go. Rhonda will come by with a supper basket. Don't wait up for me. It could be hours. I'll take the truck."

"Cable, wait!" She ran to follow him, but he was out the front door without looking back. She stopped on the porch and watched as he hastily climbed into a battered pickup and tore down the driveway. In seconds, he had disappeared in a literal cloud of dust.

Song shook her head, then allowed a long sigh. "Bath, strong drink if I can find it, and a working telephone—in any order." She headed back inside for all three.

Five

Considering everything, Song decided getting clean was her first priority. She peeked into the bedrooms until she found where Cable had deposited her bag. It was a big room with a high ceiling dominated by a king-sized four-poster bed and a magnificently carved headboard. Looking closer, she saw the carvings were of grim-looking coal miners holding picks and shovels. *Appropriate*, she thought, *if going to bed with your wife is supposed to be work.*

The adjoining bathroom had twin marble sinks and a deep spa tub. "Thank you, Rhonda," she said to the decorator whom she presumed had also designed the bathroom.

Song opened her bag to retrieve her various bath potions, including shampoo and conditioner, and then remembered they were in the lost bag. She dug around in the bathroom closet and found a plain white bar of soap, an anti-dandruff shampoo, and an off-brand conditioner. She sighed. They would have to do.

She started filling the bathtub and was startled when a stream of amber liquid, punctuated by several ugly burps, erupted from the spigot. After a few seconds, the hydraulic grunts stopped, but the gushing water remained the same ugly brown. She filled the tub and climbed into the nasty, lukewarm water. The soap produced no suds and her skin began to itch. Feeling only mildly cleaner than when she'd climbed into it, she got out of the tub, toweled herself dry, and then tried to wash her hair in the sink. When she was finished, it felt like matted straw. "What's in this water?" she muttered. "Rock?"

Fortunately she carried an extra toothbrush in her purse. She brushed her teeth with an off-brand toothpaste also found in the closet, gargled with an off-brand mouthwash, and then got dressed, choosing from her surviving bag a comfortable skirt, blouse, and sandals. Now she was ready for that phone call to her father. He wasn't going to believe that such a backward place still existed in the United States. But he would listen, probably make a joke out of it, and make her feel better. She sat down on the edge of the bed and picked up the telephone on the bedside table. Like the one in the parlor, it was an old rotary device. "Dispatcher!" a man immediately yelled into her ear.

Song was so startled, she hung up. Tentatively, she lifted the receiver again. "Hey, who's this?" the same man demanded. "Is that you, Mrs. Jordan?"

Song realized it was Mole, Cable's secretary or whatever he was. "It's me, Mole," she said. "Where's Cable?"

"Don't matter where he is," the man said. "This phone is for mine business only. Welcome to Highcoal, ma'am, but you got to get off this phone." He abruptly hung up.

Song looked at the phone with some astonishment, then put the receiver in its cradle and went downstairs and poked around until she found another telephone, this one a relatively modern touch-tone attached to the wall in the kitchen. She picked up its receiver and was rewarded by a dial tone. Eagerly, she dialed her father's number only to receive an irritating series of beeps followed by a tinny voice that said, "All circuits are busy. Please try again later."

She dialed the number again and received the same message. "Time for a strong drink," she muttered and started searching. The cabinets were empty of anything alcoholic so she peered inside the double-door stainless steel refrigerator that contained a quart of milk, a loaf of white bread, a package of bologna, a box of Velveeta cheese, and three bottles of white wine—two chardonnays and one fumé blanc. It was a bachelor's refrigerator if she'd ever seen one. She next looked in the pantry and was pleased to find it contained a nice stock of reds, including a French pinot noir, which she chose.

After searching for wine glasses, she found a pretty set that appeared to be hand-blown crystal. She admired them, even though at that moment she would have settled for a plastic cup.

Song carried a glass of the dusky red to the front porch, where there were four white rocking chairs. She sat down in the nearest and contemplated the town, the black smear of the coal mine below, and the lush, green mountains that seemed to go on forever. She was distracted by cardinals, as scarlet as the reddest rose, chirping prettily as they fed from a bird feeder hanging from the porch. Squirrels also squawked and fussed as they gamboled through the magnificent oaks that grew along the driveway. Song was starting to wind down, feeling more comfortable as the wine settled happily on her empty stomach.

Her gaze went back to the mine. She wondered where Cable was, if he was already below the earth. She shuddered, unable to fully comprehend what it was like to be underground. Then, interrupting her thoughts, a battered gray pickup truck pulled into the driveway and a heavyset woman with short-cropped blonde hair emerged wearing a white sweatshirt that read I Love Myrtle Beach.

"Guess you'd be Song," she said. "I'm Rhonda—cook, hotel manager, interior decorator, and all-round Cable enabler. Come on, Young Henry. Bring the basket."

A boy climbed out of the bed of the truck and lifted a large wicker basket. He had a burr haircut and big ears that stuck out. Song guessed him to be around twelve years old. He shyly glanced at Song and she smiled at him. He quickly looked away.

"So you're the Rhonda Cable told me about," Song said.

Rhonda nodded. "That would be me."

Song stood while trying to think of something else to say. She was always awkward when she met someone new unless it was business—then she had plenty to say and she said it whether they wanted to hear it or not.

"I like what you've done with the house," she managed.

Rhonda's round face lit up. "Do you really?"

"Simply elegant. Where did you get the furniture?"

Rhonda was now beaming. "Let's get your food inside and I'll tell you!" She held open the screen door for the boy who carried the basket inside.

Song followed Rhonda to the kitchen. "Where's Cable?" Rhonda asked as she began to unpack the basket.

Song tried to remember what Cable had said before he'd rushed out. "Gone to the mine. I think he said a pillar fell down. Somebody got their arm broken."

Rhonda shook her head. "Fell down? Pillars don't fall down, honey. They explode." She clutched the boy by his arm and dragged him over. "Say hello to Mrs. Jordan, Young Henry."

"Hello, ma'am," the boy said glumly. "Pleased to meet you."

"He gets shy sometimes, don't you, Young Henry?"

"I used to be shy too," Song said, trying to coax a smile out of the boy. "Sometimes I still am."

"Get on out to the stable and go to work," Rhonda ordered, and the boy scurried out of the kitchen. Rhonda looked after him, then said, "I hope you like what I brung ya. Fried chicken, mashed potatoes, homemade rolls, and a fresh garden salad. I got the best vegetables this year, I swan."

Song mentally added up the calories and fat grams in that menu, including the salad dressing, which didn't appear to be the fat-free variety. She wrinkled up her nose. Rhonda must have noticed, since she frowned and asked, "It don't suit?"

"I'm sure it's all delicious," Song replied. "It's just that I'm not used to such rich food."

Rhonda put her hands on her ample hips. "This is just good old-fashioned West Virginia cooking, darlin'."

"Actually, I'd prefer something lighter," Song said. "And nothing fried. Ever."

Rhonda opened her mouth to say something, apparently thought better of it, and amiably nodded. "Well, all right, honey. I'll see what I can do."

"Thank you."

"Now, about decorating this place. Cable bought it and remodeled it, but then had no idea what to put in it, so he hired me for the job. Of course, Cable's always in the mine so I had to guess a lot on his tastes, presuming he has any. He's a man, you know? Besides, Cable's so busy he hardly has time to lace up his boots. The furniture I got mostly at a place called Tamarack in Beckley, which features West Virginia artisans. You'll have to visit it sometime."

"I'll do that," Song said, frowning. Rhonda's loud voice was making her head hurt.

Rhonda studied Song for a moment, then shrugged. "Well, enjoy what you can eat. I got to go. There are hungry bachelors at the Cardinal who'll likely tear down the place if their supper's two minutes late. You ought to come down some time, have supper with them. They're all coal miners. They'd go crazy for a pretty woman like you."

"I already met one coal miner and he made me sick."

"Who was that?"

"Cable called him Bossman."

"Bossman? Why, honey, there ain't a nicer man in town. How'd he make you sick?"

"Spitting."

Rhonda walked to the front porch with Song following. "Miners tend to spit. It ain't pretty, I swan, but that's what they do. They also work like the devil to keep their families from the poor house. Anyway, welcome to Highcoal. Hope you like living here, spitting and all."

"I'm only here for a week."

This stopped Rhonda. "Why only a week?"

"My job is in New York."

Rhonda was clearly astonished by her answer. "Honey, jobs are for quitting when you got a good man like Cable."

"A good man can live in New York too," Song replied. "Especially if his wife has important work there."

"Well, nobody has more important work than what Cable's got. He keeps this whole town going. Don't you know that?"

Song didn't want to discuss it, especially since she didn't care if the town kept going or not. "Do the phones ever work around here?" she asked instead.

Rhonda climbed into her truck. The window was rolled down and she let her arm hang out. "Squirrels ate through the lines a few days ago. Taking awhile to get up some new ones."

"I need to call my father," Song said.

"Maybe they'll be up by tomorrow morning."

Song was shocked. "Tomorrow? I have to wait until then?"

Rhonda shrugged. "That's Highcoal for you. Patience is a virtue around here. Anyway, here's the drill. Cable gets a covered dish every evening. Usually he picks it up, but while you're here, I'll bring supper by since he'll probably be home later than you'd care to eat. Just put the dishes in the sink when you're done. Rosita will be over every day to wash up and clean the house. She's my maid and yours too. Oh yeah, Old Roy—the gardener and fix-it man—will be by once a week to mow the lawn, spruce up the yard, do anything you want him to do. Like I said, we're Cable enablers. Man works hard for us, for the whole town. He ain't got time for all this silly domestic stuff." She cocked her head. "Say, I've been listening to your voice. It's a good one. Do you sing, by chance?"

"I was in my high school choir. Why?"

"You're a soprano, I think. We need a soprano in the church choir. If you lived here, I'd see if I could get you in. Being a member of the choir is a pretty big deal."

"I don't go to church," Song replied.

Rhonda's mouth fell open in astonishment. "You got to go to church, honey. It's the place where everybody meets and greets."

"I'm an agnostic," Song said. "It would be wrong for me to pretend otherwise."

"A what-nostic?" Rhonda laughed. "Oh, I get it. Honey, there ain't no such thing around here. Don't much matter what particular religion you are, or even if you ain't got no religion at all, best to get close to God in these old hills. It's His country, make no mistake, but that don't mean there's an end to trouble. Some folks think the Lord likes to throw fuel on the fire just to see how we'll do. Anyway, give it some thought. You want to meet people, it's the only way. Gotta go."

Song touched her stiff hair. "One more thing. What's wrong with the water? I took a bath and came out dirtier than when I got in."

"Water around here is hard as a rock," Rhonda explained. "Full of minerals like limestone and I don't know what all. Shampoo don't have a chance in that soup."

"It was cold too."

"I'm not surprised. Cable takes his baths at the mine so he don't much care about what comes out of the spigot here. Let's do this. I'll tell Old Roy to install you a new hot water heater and a water softener, and put it on Cable's bill. You just consider it done."

"Thank you," Song said.

"You bet, honey. I can enable you as well as I can enable Cable." She turned the ignition key and the old truck roared.

Song watched Rhonda drive away and felt a little abandoned and lonely. She walked to the stable where she found Young Henry mucking out the stalls with a shovel and a wheelbarrow. She tried to think of something to say. "It stinks," was what came out as she wrinkled up her nose.

"Horse manure generally does, ma'am," he answered and kept shoveling.

"Cable—Mr. Jordan—had to go to the mine," she said, making another attempt at conversation. "Wonder how long he'll be gone?"

Young Henry leaned on his shovel. "Hard to say. It takes a good hour to get to some places in the mine. I know what happened, by the by. One of our miners what lives in our hotel told me while Mom was putting together your basket. Navy Jones got his arm broke, you see."

"Navy Jones?"

"Yes, ma'am, that's right. Name's really Ernest. Served in the navy, you see, so that's how he got his nickname. Anyway, he'll be fine. Doctor K will fix him up."

"Doctor K?"

"Our doc. She goes inside the mine when a man's hurt, but likely Navy came out on his own."

"*She* goes inside the mine?"

"Yes, ma'am. Doctor K's a lady and, despite it, a dang good doctor. Naw, Navy's gonna be just fine."

"But the way Cable rushed off, he acted like it was serious."

The boy shrugged. "He's the superintendent so he's responsible for everything."

"Is your father a miner too?"

"Ain't no more."

"What does he do?"

"Plays a harp, I reckon. Up in heaven."

"Oh, I'm sorry!"

"Well, I don't know why. It weren't your fault. Anyway, I never knew him. He got killed in the mine when Ma was pee-gee with me." He saw her perplexed look. "Pregnant, you know? Anyway, piece of slate fell on him, just like Mr. Jordan's daddy. It happens. There's some rough roof in that old mine."

Song was saddened by the boy's obvious cover-up of his true feelings. "It's a dangerous place, isn't it?" she asked.

Young Henry only shrugged. "You got to watch yourself in there. But, ma'am, you don't need to worry about Cable. He runs a safe mine. Just about everybody says so. Now, if you'll excuse me, ma'am. Got to dump this 'barrow, then feed the horses."

Song waited until the horses were happily munching their oats in their stalls before asking, "Could you stay and have dinner with me, Young Henry? You can tell me all about coal mining."

"Thank you, ma'am, but no," he answered, politely. "I got chores to do at

37

home. But I'll be here tomorrow to make sure everything is done what needs to be done around the stable, and I guess you can ask me some more questions then."

Song saw the boy wanted to go and said, "Thank you, Young Henry."

"No problem, ma'am." He started walking down the driveway.

Song called after him. "How will you get home?"

"Hitchhike," he replied over his shoulder.

"Hitchhiking in this day and age? Aren't you afraid?"

Young Henry stopped and scratched his head. "Not unless I stand in the middle of the road. Them coal trucks will surely run over you." Then, whistling, he kicked an acorn down the driveway.

"Opie lives," Song said, shaking her head, then went inside the house and headed for the kitchen. More wine, that was the ticket.

IT WAS, ACCORDING to the glowing clock on the bedside table, nearly three in the morning before Cable climbed in bed beside her. She reached out and touched his arm, then walked her fingers onto his chest.

"I'm awfully tired, honey," he said, "and the alarm clock is going to go off in two hours."

She withdrew her hand. "You're going back to work?"

"Got to," he yawned. "Big mess to clean up."

"What happened?"

"It would take too much energy to explain it to you," he said, then rolled over on his side. Song stared at the high moonlit ceiling and listened to her husband breathe. She was still listening when she fell asleep. When she woke and felt for him, he was gone.

Six

Cable had been taught by his parents, Wire and Jensey Jordan, all the things a West Virginia boy needed to know for a good life: how not to get lost in the woods, how to drive a truck, and how to treat other people with respect, no matter how low or shiftless they might be. He'd learned to say "sir" to every adult male, and "ma'am" to every adult female. He was taught to protect the weak and not be intimidated by bullies. He was taught to be kind to defenseless creatures, as long as they weren't in season, and even then to respect game animals and aim for the heart so they wouldn't suffer. He'd also been taught the names of the trees and the plants that adorned the surrounding mountains and told that they were all part of God's blessings on the good people of West Virginia, which, despite the biased news accounts, was a wonderful place to live. With all that good teaching under his belt, not to mention his native intelligence and vigor, Cable had made his parents proud by being a good student and a tenacious, if not overly talented, football player on a team that had nearly won the state championship his senior year in high school.

His father had operated a continuous mining machine, a giant crablike machine that used spinning steel teeth to tear coal from the ancient underground seams. As a boy, Cable had been proud of what his father did and was intrigued by his stories of what it was like below. When he was fourteen years old, Cable begged his dad to take him inside, so he could see for himself. Wire consulted the mine superintendent, a man by the name of Carpenter Fillmore, and Mr. Fillmore said sure, let the boy have a look. The following Saturday, a day when only a few miners were working, down Cable went with his father into the earth.

From the first moments in the mine, Cable loved everything about it. He loved the great machines going about the business of cutting and loading coal, and he loved the complexity he saw in the ventilation plans required to channel air throughout the mine. The subtleties of mining had a strange pull on his intellect. When he came out that day, he said to his beaming father, "I want to mine coal." When Mr. Fillmore came out of his office to inquire how the visit had gone, Cable pointed to the mine superintendent's white helmet, and said, "I want to wear your hat someday." Mr. Fillmore laughed, and so did Wire. But Cable didn't laugh. He was serious. The best way to wear a white helmet, Mr. Fillmore told him, was to become a mining engineer. This became Cable's ambition.

A few months before Cable graduated from high school, his father stopped his continuous miner and walked to the front of it, "inby" as it was called, which meant he was beneath an unsupported roof. He had broken the first safety rule of the mine. Wire was usually the most careful of men and no one ever knew why he'd broken the rule. When he leaned over to inspect the teeth on the cutters, the roof fell on top of him. He was still alive when they brought him out, but he didn't stay that way long.

The church was crowded to overflowing at his funeral. The preacher of that day intoned, "We have lost a great man in a town filled with great men, they who dig the wealth of the nation. God knows them as His special people, for they are devout in the faith. It is not important how he died. What is important is how he *lived*." The preacher was the father of the preacher who now presided over Highcoal's church. There was a continuity in Highcoal. Preachers were part of it, and so was Cable.

After Wire's funeral, the people sang the old-timey songs of faith and healing, and the church bell tolled the passing of another miner, and then the men of Highcoal got up and went back to work in the mine. The preacher went inside his church to continue his work of spreading the gospel, the women went home to their work of raising their children, and the teachers stood up in front of their classrooms and did their work too. It was the way of the place, as it had always been, and so Cable thought it should always be.

As soon as Cable graduated from high school, he joined the army. Many boys and girls of Highcoal joined the military services. It just seemed the right thing to do, considering all the blessings their country had given them. Their parents had taught them that. Cable went into the infantry and fought against

Saddam Hussein during the first Gulf War. He did not kill any enemy soldiers, but he and his buddies captured quite a few. His prisoners knelt before him and kissed his hand while he told them they were going to be fine, that they were going to live, that they had nothing to worry about. The Iraqis naturally trusted him, as most people did.

Cable served out his enlistment, then went home. With the money he'd saved, and with the help of the G.I. Bill, he enrolled in West Virginia University's mining engineering school. When he graduated, he went to work for Atlas Energy, Inc., because they owned the Highcoal mine and it was still his ambition to wear the superintendent's white helmet. It wasn't long before he had the job.

This morning Cable was at the working face of one of the sections of his coal mine, a place where he had always been the happiest. But he was not happy, not with his worries about production, and certainly not after the events of the morning at the Cardinal Hotel. With barely two hours of sleep, he had slipped out of the house without disturbing Song, then swung by the Cardinal for breakfast. The old boarding house was a lovely neo-Georgian, two-story stone and brick structure with a wide front porch, a cozy parlor, and a huge dining room that had once served hundreds of miners old Mr. Fillmore had brought in from Poland, Italy, Hungary, Russia, and Ireland. Abandoned by the company in the 1970s, the building became Rhonda's when she bought it with the insurance money after her husband was killed. She extensively remodeled it, filled it with tasteful antiques, and made it her own. She was a good hostess and a great cook.

Cable entered the Cardinal, hungry for some of her special apple pancakes, and turned into the dining room just as George "Bashful" Puckett was holding forth on a most interesting subject: Cable's New York wife who, according to Bashful, was "full up with herself, snotty, and a pure little witch."

Cable and Bashful had been at odds for months. Bashful owned a well drilling company and worked under a contract from Atlas Energy headquarters, which meant he was outside Cable's purview. Since Atlas owned the mineral rights nearly everywhere in the county, Bashful had made a nuisance of himself by drilling on private property without asking permission of the owners. Cable had to field most of the complaints, though he could do little or nothing about it. Bashful seemed to enjoy the trouble he caused. He was a balding little man with a blonde moustache who fancied himself God's gift to women. He also had a big mouth. Cable walked up behind him just as he crowed, "Goes to figger Cable'd end up with some kind of little Chinese witch for a wife." This was followed by a choking sound because Cable had just plucked him out of his chair by his neck.

"Apologize!" Cable demanded, and then Rhonda had run in from the kitchen to break it up, and it had gone downhill from there.

Things were no better now that he was at work. Standing beside him, if standing was the word for being bent under a slab of dense rock, Bossman Carlisle eyed his superintendent, sensing Cable's unhappiness. He shifted the bulging tobacco chaw in his cheek.

"Six West is running good coal today, Cable."

Cable cut his eyes toward Bossman. "I guess you heard about me and Bashful."

Bossman shifted his chaw to his other cheek, then spat into the gob. "Yeah. I heard something about that."

"Best I can tell, he's not the only one who's been talking dirt about my wife."

Bossman pretended to be studying the men putting up a ventilation curtain, then said, "Sorry, Cable. I guess I opened my big mouth when I shouldn't have."

"I've never liked the way gossip gets going around here," Cable growled. "Turns out Rhonda added her two potatoes in the pot too. I got on Bashful's case about it, but he was only repeating what others had said—and it started with you!"

Bossman's helmet light rocked up and down. "You're right, Cable. I had no call to say anything about your wife."

Cable made no reply, lest his anger make him say something he didn't really mean. He depended on Bossman, and he knew the man was sorry for telling the story of how Song had gotten upset about her blamed mussed-up blouse. Bossman probably only told his wife, but women talked and so did men in Highcoal, and it didn't take long before everybody knew everybody else's business.

Cable turned his attention to the face. The spinning teeth of the continuous miner ground into an ebony layer, violently ripping the coal from where it had peacefully lain undisturbed for over three hundred million years. It was similar to the machine that Cable's father had operated but bigger and more powerful. Shuttle cars trundled in behind the monster digger to receive a load of the ancient treasure, then raced to dump it on a conveyor belt to be carried out of the mine. When the continuous miner backed out, the roof bolt crew moved in to brace the newly exposed roof, using a powerful hydraulic drill to pierce the roof in several strategic places, then inserting slender anchors with retaining plates called roof bolts. Working with the camaraderie and skill of a NASCAR pit crew, they backed out as the continuous miner roared into the seam to rip and tear it anew. It was the choreography of the working face, and Cable thought it as beautiful a thing as there was on the earth.

Cable raised his voice over the machinery. "It's a good section, Bossman. Real good. Give Vietnam my compliments."

Charles "Vietnam" Petroski was the foreman of the section. A miner for over thirty years, he'd passed his foreman's exam only a few months previously and was now proudly wearing his new white helmet, the mark of a mine supervisor. Almost as if he sensed Cable's comment, Vietnam looked up from where he'd been helping to hang a ventilation curtain and flashed his light across to the two watching bosses. They flashed their lights back.

"Vietnam's a good foreman, Cable, and he's got good men. But if one of them gets sick, his section's pretty much out of business. I got nobody to fill in."

"I know that," Cable replied. "I'm working on it."

"I'm just telling you." Bossman shrugged.

Cable *was* working on it, but without much success. He couldn't find any miners to hire. Coal was suddenly in demand across the world because of rising oil prices coupled with the rapid multiplication of steel mills in China and India. Orders for fuel coal and metallurgical coal had poured in, quickly exceeding the capacity of the coal industry in the United States. The coal from southern West Virginia was especially suitable for making steel, resulting in hot competition between the local coal companies to hire the few veteran miners around. Hiring and training new miners was the answer, but there weren't enough applicants. It didn't matter that the starting salary averaged over fifty thousand dollars. Today's miner's kids and grandkids, raised on iPods and computer games, just weren't interested. For the few who were, the drop-out rate was high because of unexpected claustrophobia or an aversion to what they quickly realized was hard and dangerous work. The small number who stuck it out were, as the Marines put it, the few and the proud. But mostly the few.

Cable withdrew a gas monitor from the holster on his belt and held it near the roof. The digital readout told him that the explosive methane gas seeping out of the coal was at a safe level, the oxygen content was normal, and carbon monoxide, the stealthy murderer of coal miners, was undetectable. As a final check, he licked his fingers and held them up within an inch of the stone roof. When they quickly cooled, he knew the air was moving along according to his plan. Satisfied, he turned to leave.

"Keep them safe, Bossman."

"I'll do my best, Cable," Bossman said, his grin wet from his chaw. He added, "I'm awful sorry I started the gossip about your wife."

Cable gripped his mine foreman's shoulder. "Forget it," he said. "When you get to know her, you'll see she's a great girl."

"She's a good lookin' one, that's for sure," Bossman said.

Cable nodded agreement, then walked away, bent beneath the roof, until he reached a small battery-powered car called a jeep. He energized the low-slung boxy vehicle and aimed it along the track toward the main line. Wooden support headers passed overhead and the rails clicked below. It was two and a half miles back to the manlift and then a short walk to his office where a mound of paperwork, including the latest MSHA inspection results, awaited him.

Em-Sha, as everyone in the industry called the federal Mine Safety and Health Administration, was all-powerful. It could shut down a mine or levy a stiff fine for a thousand and one different violations, big and small. Although many mine superintendents and owners resented the agency, Cable wasn't among them, even when he thought they were a little heavy-handed. Paying a fine was a way to keep everybody on their toes. Being shut down, however, was another matter. As competitive as it had become in the past year, closing even for a day could prove disastrous, especially since the Highcoal mine was already having difficulty meeting its orders.

There was a new steel mill in India that desperately needed an extremely pure metallurgical coal. Atlas headquarters had first signed a long-term contract to supply this coal, and then installed new equipment in the Highcoal processing plant to provide it. But, to date, the Highcoal mine had failed to meet the demand as specified in the contract. Cable could not figure out why. All the sections were nearly at peak production, and the seam they worked contained what was reputedly the finest metallurgical coal in the world. But when all the raw tonnage was separated into its different grades, he kept coming up short. He feared that the quality of the coal in the mine was decreasing, that they had already dug out most of the good stuff a long time ago. If so, the Indian steel mill would go elsewhere with their orders and Highcoal might be in danger of laying off miners, or even shutting down.

Cable's mind revolved around this concern for a while, but he was distracted by thoughts of Song, which didn't cheer him up. It wasn't just the gossip about her that worried him. After seeing so little of Highcoal, she wasn't happy, which was more than a little distressing. Highcoal was a beautiful town and the people were purely wonderful, not counting their propensity toward gossip. They gossiped in New York City too, right? He pondered what might make her happy and came up with not much, except he guessed he should spend more time with her while she was visiting. But when would that be, with all this bad coal being run?

Cable kept worrying about Song as the tracks clicked below the jeep. When no answer came, he went back to worrying over his mine. Both problems seemed to have unknowns he couldn't quite put his finger on. With his wife, she seemed to have a strange lens through which she observed Highcoal. With the mine, it simply made no sense that he couldn't meet the orders sent down from head-quarters. The overall tonnage was good, but the special high-grade tonnage stayed low. Why? And was it a permanent situation? Was there really that much rock mixed in with the coal? Visually it seemed fine, but when it emerged from the preparation plant, it just didn't add up. He had gone over the numbers with the plant manager, Stan Stanvic. He'd grown up with Stan, was on the football team with him, and he trusted him. Stan also loved Highcoal and would never do anything to hurt it. No, it had to be something else, probably just some bad coal they were passing through. It happened sometimes. But if they didn't get through it soon, Atlas headquarters was going to go into some kind of spasm that wouldn't be good for anybody.

He passed phosphorescent safety placards that presented safety messages. Danger High Voltage. Caution Low Roof. Phone One Hundred Yards. He had installed a hard-wired pager system throughout the mine, each station with a telephone and monitor inside a hardened, blast-proof box. He'd also had carbon monoxide sensors installed up and down the main escapeway and air return. A coal mine was an inherently dangerous place. Cable's men worked in the dark beneath hundreds of feet of densely packed earth and rock, much of it unstable, all of it hideously heavy. Methane leaked out of the prehistoric seams, and if the gas was allowed to pool, it only took a single spark to set it off in a massive explosion. Carbon monoxide was the silent killer, the result of a fire, sometimes so low and smoldering no one noticed. The roof, the tight confines of the face, the heavy equipment on the move, all could combine to crush or maim a miner with only a second's inattention. Every day a miner faced injury or death in too many ways to count.

A little past the midpoint of the main line, Cable caught sight of two lights toward Three West, an old section that had produced consistently for over forty years. In fact, his father had been killed at its face. The lights were flashing around, then one of them seemed to drop. Cable turned into the entry, but stopped when one of the lights flashed in his eyes. He climbed out of the jeep and walked bent beneath the low roof. The light stayed in his eyes. "Look away. You're blinding me!" he yelled at the miscreant.

The light moved off him and he saw, with a sinking sensation in the pit of his stomach, that it belonged to Bum Wilkes, who only yesterday had gleefully given him and Song the finger. He was crouched next to a power plant that fed electricity to the machines working the face. "What are you doing, Bum?" Cable asked.

Bum didn't answer, but then another helmet light came on. Cable saw it belonged to a miner sitting in the gob and recognized him—Pinky Wilson, a young man who'd recently completed his red cap training. Pinky had a bloody nose.

"What's going on here?" Cable demanded.

"Nothing, Cable," Bum said. "Ain't that right, Pinky-winky?"

Pinky ran his arm across his nose, leaving a scarlet trail on his shirt sleeve. "That's right, Mr. Jordan," he said in a shaky voice. "Nothing going on here, no, sir."

Cable knew the answer already, but he had to ask it. "Did Bum hit you?"

"No, sir. I tripped."

Cable turned back to Bum. "I asked you what you're doing."

Bum held up a screwdriver. "Foreman said for us to check the power plant. Circuit breaker keeps tripping. I'm fixing it."

Cable inspected the substation. "You've disconnected the ground."

Bum grinned his gap-toothed grin. "Sure did. That circuit breaker ain't gonna trip no more."

"Are you crazy, Bum? You could electrocute somebody with a stunt like that!"

Bum's grin vanished. "It's been done before, ain't nobody got hurt. You pushing everybody around here to load coal, what do you expect us to do?"

"I told him it was wrong, Mr. Jordan," Pinky said. He had his hand over his nose. "That's why he hit me."

"You shut your mouth or you gonna swallow some teeth," Bum growled.

Cable turned to Bum. "Bum, I'm fining you one hundred dollars for this stunt. Pinky, you're fined fifty for not going after the foreman. As for your foreman, you tell him to come see me. *Move!*"

Pinky instantly started walking toward the section, but Bum stayed put and put his light in Cable's eyes. "Aw, Cable. I'm your old teammate, ain't I?" he said. "We got to stick together, right?"

"We were teammates awhile ago, Bum. Now I have a job to do. And get your light out of my eyes."

Bum looked away. "It ain't right, you fining me," he rumbled. "It ain't right at all."

"Just get back to work, Bum. I'll think about the fine, but this brawling has got to stop. I've been fielding complaints on you ever since I took over. You're either fighting or sleeping on the job. I've taken up for you a lot more than I should."

"Yeah, right," Bum said. "Big man now, ain'tcha? How'd you get up so high, anyway?"

"I got an education, Bum. You could have too."

"And how was that going to happen, with my daddy all busted up and my ma so sick all the time? I had to go to work."

Cable didn't bother to remind Bum that his own father had been killed in the mine, and his mom also had to struggle until she married her plumber in Florida. Bum knew all that. He was just baiting him.

"Go back to work, Bum," he said. "And stay out of trouble. That's all I'm asking."

Bum's light flashed insolently into his eyes again, then the big miner turned and stomped off, passing the foreman, Harry "Poker" Williams, who was actually running bent beneath the low roof.

"Sorry, Cable," he panted as he arrived. "I was up to my neck in alligators. The coal's getting mighty low and the roof's working something fierce."

Cable was not impressed with the excuse. "Poker, you sent Bum with an inexperienced man to look at a power plant. What were you thinking? You should have called an electrician."

Poker's mouth opened to answer, then closed as he took another moment to think. "You're right, Cable," he concluded. "It was stupid."

"I know you're undermanned and I'm pushing you to mine coal, but you've got to use some common sense. Now, go call that electrician."

"You going to fine me?"

"I'm not going to fine anybody if you do your job for a change."

Poker hastily withdrew, heading toward one of the hardened telephones to make the call for an outside electrician. Disgusted, Cable aimed his jeep back down the track to the bottom and the manlift, which would carry him back to where the sky wasn't made of stone.

On the surface, Mole Phillips, his clerk and dispatcher, was waiting for him. Mole looked worried, and for good reason. "Einstein's in your office, Cable," he announced even before Cable stepped off the lift.

"Einstein" was Ian Stein, the meticulous and ruthless MSHA inspector who apparently thought the Highcoal mine was his personal project. When you talked to Einstein, about the only words he wanted to hear out of your mouth were, "Yes, sir!" That was mostly what he got.

"What's he doing?" Cable demanded.

"Studying your mine map."

"Trouble on top of trouble," Cable groaned, and headed for his office.

Seven

When Song awoke, she lay in bed for a while to think about the situation. She'd come all this way, taken a week out of her busy schedule to be with her husband, and now he was somewhere else. She contemplated his empty pillow, then reached over and tossed it off the bed.

"Thanks, Cable," she muttered.

She was angry and hurt, and she was also not used to being ignored. "Reality has sharp teeth," her father always told her. "If you turn away from it, it'll bite you in the butt." Crudely put, but it reminded Song that her father was, after all, famous for his ruthlessness in business, and devoted to his only child. She knew he liked Cable, but she also knew he'd bury the man if she wanted him to. But Song didn't want to bury Cable. She loved him, even if she wasn't absolutely sure, based on his performance yesterday, if he loved her anymore.

Song needed to talk to her father. She tried her cell, receiving the same message she'd gotten the day before: "No service." Shaking her head, she went into the bathroom, only to remember she had no makeup, except what she had carried in her purse, which wasn't much. She did a few things, some light powder, some lipstick, then put on jeans, a chambray shirt, and running shoes. She headed downstairs to try the kitchen telephone. When she dialed her father's number, the recording told her the circuits were still down. The squirrels were apparently still in charge at the local telephone company.

After looking in various cabinets for something she could eat, she discovered some cereal in the pantry. With the milk in the refrigerator—unhappily not low-fat—breakfast was solved. She also made a pot of strong coffee. Carrying a cup outside, she walked to the edge of the yard, which ended abruptly at a cliff that had a vertical drop of about a hundred feet. With all the trees lower than the yard,

49

the result was an unimpeded view of the town and the mine. From that elevation, she could see every house. They were almost all uniformly gray in color, which made the white church stand out all the more. Its steeple seemed to reach for the sunlit sky. Its bell began to toll, and Song wondered what it was announcing on a Tuesday morning.

She recalled Rhonda's advice, that the church was the place to "meet and greet," but Song knew she'd never go there. As far as she was concerned, religion and superstition were one and the same. There had to be other ways to meet people, not that she was particularly interested. Cable was the only person in Highcoal she cared anything about. Well, maybe Young Henry. He seemed like a nice kid.

She turned her attention to the ugly black scar of the mine. She studied its layout and tried to figure out what its various structures were for. The wheels atop the black tower were turning. She recalled there were cables attached to it, so perhaps it was lifting or lowering something. Maybe, she divined, the tower was just an elevator. But what did it lift and lower? Miners? Coal? Equipment? Her intellect was stirred.

She saw a big truck crawling along until it reached three silolike structures on stilts. When it stopped at one of the silos, the acoustics of the valley were such that she clearly heard what sounded like a rumble of rocks down a metal chute. She suspected the truck was probably receiving a load of coal from the silo. But why were there three of them? Did they hold different kinds of coal? *Were* there different kinds of coal? The mine complex was mysterious, but she was confident it would all make perfect sense if she studied it long enough. As the property and acquisitions manager for her father, she was required to understand what companies did, sometimes even better than their own employees. Now she wondered what it would take to learn about coal mining, even to know as much as Cable knew. This made her smile, though it was somewhat grim. That would surprise him, wouldn't it?

But she didn't want to learn about coal mining. What she wanted to do, what she *had* to do, was to get Cable out of Highcoal. It was not possible for her to live in the grimy little town. She had already seen enough to convince her of that.

Song sat in one of the rockers on the porch and wondered what she was going to do with herself for the rest of the day. She looked at Cable's roadster parked outside the garage. Presuming she could drive it, where would she go? To visit Cable at the mine? He hadn't invited her there. She could cruise through town, but she'd already done that coming in, and what good would that do? Somebody might spit chewing tobacco at her and she couldn't take any more of that! Horseback riding appealed to her. She could saddle Trixie and take a turn around the pasture. It would pass a little time, at least. She was thinking about that when a battered brown pickup truck rattled up the driveway. Every truck Song had seen so far in Highcoal had been beat-up. She wondered if they came that way.

A woman in blue jeans, a plaid shirt, and a wide-brimmed canvas hat, not to mention a confident air, stepped out of the truck.

"Mrs. Jordan, I presume," she said, then without waiting for an invitation, climbed the steps to the porch and stuck out her hand. "I'm Doctor Gloria Kaminsky, or Doctor K, as they call me around here. Welcome to Highcoal. I must say, you are a lovely young woman, and I am pleased that Cable has done so well. Surprised, but pleased."

Doctor K shook Song's hand vigorously, then took off her hat to wipe the sweat from her forehead, revealing a mop of bright red hair that looked as if it had been cut by a dull knife. Song presumed the doctor didn't care much about her looks, although she had an interesting face, and a lot could be done with her hair. Her figure was a bit pear-shaped, but a little work in the gym could probably solve that.

"Young Henry told me about you," Song said. "He says you go inside the mine."

"I do, indeed," Doctor K confirmed, plopping her hat back on, "and take care of everybody around here who'll let me. It's a full-time job. No, *two* full-time jobs. I've long since given up on the sleep cycle entirely."

"May I offer you a cup of coffee?" Song asked.

The suggestion was greeted with an agreeable nod of the doctor's head. "That would be much appreciated."

Song went to the kitchen, poured a cup for the doctor, refilled hers, and brought them back to the porch. By then, Doctor K was sprawled in one of the rockers, fanning herself with her big hat. The sun was already making itself felt, and the day was going to be a hot one. The doctor took the cup from Song, then greedily drank from it.

"Ah. Elixir of the gods. I needed that."

Song's job often required her to sit across a table from an executive and decipher, sometimes based on body language or facial expressions, the person's characteristics, especially, their strengths and weaknesses. She saw in the doctor's blue-green eyes a strong intellect, and in her Romanesque nose a certain nobility. But her lips twitched with what Song suspected was a sardonic sense of humor. The doctor reminded Song, in a vague way, of the actress Meryl Streep. Song suspected that here was a woman who would be interesting to have as a friend, not that she intended being in Highcoal long enough for that to happen.

The doctor didn't say anything, just sat there sipping her coffee with obvious pleasure.

"It's good of you to visit," Song said after the silence had stretched on. "What's it like to be a doctor here?"

Doctor K eyed Song over the rim of the cup. "Crazy, insane, maddening—but ultimately satisfying," she said. "I'd be pleased to wax on about it, believe me, but my time is limited. I have my rounds to make. I have an office in the back of Omar's, but around here, a doctor still makes house calls. Anyhoo, to cases. I'm here to talk about you, not me."

While Song absorbed the doctor's intention, Doctor K took another sip of coffee, then said, "I thought you should know something. There was—how shall I put it?—an event at the Cardinal Hotel this morning. Cable was involved. Don't worry. He's fine. So is Bashful. George Puckett's his real name. Everybody around here has a nickname. Bashful is what he's called because he's anything but. Always bragging about this and that. Hits on every female in town, even me, who's old enough to be his mother. Owns a couple of gas drilling rigs and he thinks that makes him a big man. Cable came into the Cardinal this morning for breakfast just as Bashful was holding forth on—ta-da—you. There were no punches thrown, but some pretty loud words were spoken." Doctor K leaned forward and looked Song in the eye. "Bashful said you were snotty and a pure little witch."

Song frowned. "I don't understand."

"Well, snotty means aloof. Pure means one hundred percent. Little in your case means, ah, diminutive. Witch means . . ."

"I know what the words mean! But I've only met a miner named Bossman, a cook named Rhonda, and her son, Young Henry! How did this Bashful person decide I was one hundred percent or fifty percent or even ten percent a snotty little witch?"

"I understand your confusion," Doctor K said. "You have to understand in a town like Highcoal, anything anyone does is almost instantly disseminated to nearly everyone else. And, of course, a new someone in town is even more intensely studied. So, here's the gossip on you. Bossman said he accidentally got your blouse dirty and you went on and on about it to him, then sulked in Cable's car. Wouldn't even say good-bye, kiss my foot, or anything else. People around here don't like it when a newbie insults the top foreman of the mine, and that would be Bossman."

Song provided a defense. "But I just told him how much my blouse cost. And I didn't sulk. He spit tobacco juice and it made me sick."

Doctor K provided an encouraging smile. "I believe you, honey. I'm just telling you what's being said. Part two of the gossip. Rhonda said you didn't like her food and griped about it."

Song was getting angry. "I didn't gripe. I told her it was too rich for me. Am I supposed to be dishonest?" She shook her head. "So Bossman and Rhonda hate me."

"No, honey," Doctor K said. "They don't hate you at all. This is just the way Highcoal works. People tell stories on other people. It's a major part of what passes for entertainment."

Song absorbed the information, then asked, "How about Young Henry? What did he say about me?"

"Oh, he said you were nice. But he's just a boy. His opinion doesn't count."

Song processed the situation. "All of a sudden, I feel like I'm under a microscope."

Doctor K vigorously nodded. "You are! Being married to Cable, you're like Caesar's wife. He's the most important man in this town and that means you have to be perfect in every way or gossip is going to ensue."

"This is *so* not fair."

"Gossip is never fair, or it wouldn't be gossip. Now, if you'll indulge me, I have a few questions for you. Do you mind telling me where you went to college?"

"MIT, then Princeton. But what—?"

"Degree?"

Song shrugged. "Bachelor's in physics. Master's in business administration. How about you?"

"Virginia Tech for premed, Johns Hopkins Medical School. What did you do before you became Cable's wife?"

"It's what I still do. I'm the property and acquisitions manager for Hawkins-Song. That's my father's investment company. He buys and sells companies, and I choose which ones."

"Everybody's heard of Joe Hawkins. Are you any good at your job or just a beneficiary of his nepotism?"

"Within two years of taking over I streamlined the division, oversaw a dozen new acquisitions, and made my father a lot richer."

"How did you and Cable meet?"

Song studied the woman. "Why the interrogation, Doctor?"

"Cable's pretty tight-lipped. The people of Highcoal don't know much about you. I want to carry a good report back, get the ball rolling in your favor."

"Why? What's your interest in helping me?"

"I like Cable."

"You don't like me?" Song was a little plaintive.

"I don't know yet. You come across as tough, New York–style, but I think there's a softer side of you hiding out."

"I'm complicated," Song confessed. "I always have been."

"Here in Highcoal, it's best not to be too combative over little things that don't suit. You have to kind of roll with the punches, if you get my meaning."

"You're saying I have to keep my mouth zipped. That's hard for a New York girl, Doctor."

"Honey will catch more West Virginia flies than vinegar, Song."

"I'll try to keep that in mind."

"How did you and our mine superintendent get together?"

"We met in Times Square. I was bowled over by a street dancer and Cable picked me up off the sidewalk."

"Cute way to meet," the doctor said. "When was that?"

"About six months ago."

The doctor gave Song's answer some thought. "That must have been right after he broke up with the governor."

Song blinked. "What does that mean?"

"Cable and the governor. Michelle Godfrey. You know."

"Honestly, I have no clue."

Doctor K took on a worried expression. "It seems I'm in a dangerous area here. It would be better if you talked to Cable."

"Finish your story," Song demanded.

Doctor K drummed her fingers on the arm of the rocking chair, then provided a shrug. "Well, I guess you'll hear about it from somebody. Might as well be old busy-body Doctor K. Governor Michelle Godfrey and Cable were an item until about six months ago. I guess that's when you entered the picture. You sure Cable never mentioned her?"

"This is the first I've heard." A sense of foreboding was creeping up Song's spine.

"Huh," the doctor grunted. "Slipped his mind, I guess. Men have minds like steel sieves when it come to former girlfriends. Do you know anything about our governor?"

"Until this moment, I only suspected West Virginia might have one."

"You've heard of Birch Godfrey, maybe? He represented West Virginia for about a thousand years in the U.S. Senate. Ten years ago, Godfrey's wife died and a year later, he met and married Michelle, who at the time owned a big real estate company near Washington. She moved to Charleston, whereupon she became the instant leader of everything cultural in our capital city. The symphony, opera, all the arts, it didn't matter. She was always there with her checkbook out. She became extremely popular. When the senator died three years ago, she was urged to run for his seat. The way I understand it, she didn't want to leave Charleston, so she announced for governor. Then, even though all the pundits said she didn't have a chance, she won in a landslide! As they say in these hills, whoda thunk it?"

Song absorbed the account, then went to the heart of the matter. "What does she look like and did Cable sleep with her?"

"Looks? Great figure if you like the hourglass variety, blonde from a bottle, and big blue eyes. Sleep? From what I hear, a man probably doesn't get much sleep around her. Oops. There I go. More Highcoal gossip. It's contagious, I fear."

"I think I hate her," Song said, the truth too strong to hold back. "And, at this moment, maybe Cable too."

Doctor K shrugged. "Hate Cable? For what? He's a man, honey, that's all. For about a year, she and Cable were in the paper all the time, going here and there around the state for this and that. Most folks in Highcoal were certain they were going to get married, and it made the locals plenty proud. Michelle is very popular here. But then she pulled the plug on Cable. It's just what she does. She's gone through a string of handsome men. Maybe she found a new one. Anyhoo, Cable's time was up." She glanced at Song. "But now he's done better, hasn't he?"

"It seems I don't know my husband very well," Song said in a voice as small as she felt.

Doctor K cocked her head and smiled encouragingly. "Oh, come now. That all happened before he met you. He didn't marry Governor Godfrey. He married you, and that's all that matters."

"I need to talk to my husband." Song abruptly rose from the rocker, dropping her cup, which broke into pieces. She ignored it, even though it was a metaphor for her heart at that moment. "I need to clear this up between us. The gossip about me, the governor, everything."

"Cable's in the mine by now," Doctor K replied gently. "Won't be out until late in the afternoon."

"I don't care. I'll go to the mine and wait for him." She looked at Cable's car. "If I can drive that thing."

The doctor placed her cup on the banister and stood up. "Look, I'm headed back to town, then going on my rounds. I'll give you a lift to the mine. You can wait in Cable's office. Might be a good idea, anyway. You'll meet some of his men. When they get a look at you, I think they'll like what they see."

"I don't care what they like," Song growled. She thought about that for a second, then said, "Was that snotty of me to say?"

Doctor K smiled. "I've decided I like you. You ready to go?"

Song went straight to the doctor's truck and climbed in. The floor on the passenger side was littered with crunched cola cans and candy bar wrappers. She also had to straddle Doctor K's big black medical bag. She didn't care. She needed to see Cable. She strapped on her seatbelt while the doctor turned the truck around, steered it down the driveway to the access road, then turned onto the highway. "I got sick on the drive in yesterday," Song warned.

"Look in my glove compartment," the doctor said. "You'll find some chewing gum. It'll help. When I first came here and started driving around these hills, I might as well have been bulimic I threw up so much. You'll get used to it."

"I won't be here long enough to get used to anything," Song said, popping the gum in her mouth. Then she looked at the doctor. "Snotty again, huh?"

The doctor's radio crackled. "Hey, Doctor K," a rich male voice intoned. "You out there with your ears on?"

The doctor plucked the mike off its holder. "That you, Constable?"

"Sure enough, Doc," came the laconic reply. "Got a situation up on Harper Mountain. Seems Bashful decided to drill in Squirrel's front yard this morning and got some bullet holes in his rig for his trouble. The state po-lice are on their way loaded for bear, and Squirrel's the bear. Might be somebody's going to get themselves hurt before this is done. Can you come by like right now?"

"Be there in a few," Doctor K replied. She hung up the mike, then looked at Song. "Hang on."

"For what?" Song asked, just as the doctor jammed on the brake and twisted the steering wheel hard over at the same time, whipping the truck completely around, end for end, with blue smoke erupting from its tires as they shrieked in protest. Then she stomped on the accelerator, which produced more screams from the spinning tires.

"What are you doing?" Song yelled over the cries of the tortured rubber and the thunder of the truck's big engine.

"Duty calls," the doctor said calmly, as she steered madly through a series of curves going back up the mountain.

"Let me out!"

"No time. If there's going to be shooting, I've got to get there ASAP."

"But I don't want to go where there's shooting!"

Doctor K gave Song's objection some thought. "That's reasonable," she said, but she didn't slow down.

Eight

Doctor K's truck flew over the crest of the mountain, skidded around yet another bend, then into a series of curves, bottoming out into a twisting, narrow valley and soaring up another mountain. Despite the wild gyrations, Song didn't get sick, mainly because she was absorbed in her thinking and generally being miserable about Cable's infidelity before they met. It was something of a surprise when at last the doctor hit the brakes and the truck slid to a stop.

"We're here."

Song peered through the truck's bug-splattered windshield. In a patch of raw brown dirt was a ramshackle, unpainted shack with a sagging porch. Beside it sat a rusty pickup truck, perched atop cinder blocks, and behind it, she saw the boom of a tow truck sticking above the patched roof. Lawn ornaments decorated the dirt in the front yard, including plaster gnomes, windmills, birdhouses, and a statue of Jesus with hands pressed together, his eyes toward the sky, a resigned expression on his bearded face. There was another vehicle in the yard, a big blue truck with a great deal of complicated machinery on its bed. A plastic pink flamingo was flattened beneath one of its front tires.

On the other side of the road was a black and white police car, the lights flashing blue and red. A heavyset man in a gray-green uniform was leaning against its fender. He had his hands jammed in his pockets and was pondering the house.

"That would be the constable," Doctor K said. "The town sheriff, you might say, but paid by the coal company. And this would be the Harper place." She nodded toward the shack. "The Harpers have lived on this mountain for about two hundred years and they're fanatic about it. Bashful should have known better than to drill in Squirrel's yard."

"Why is he called Squirrel?"

"I have no idea. He's a good old fellow, although a little short-tempered. Used to run a lot of moonshine. Now he has a tow-truck business. His boys, Ford and Chevrolet, have been fighting in some God-forsaken desert somewhere for the army. I think they're due home any day. Be nice if we kept their father alive for them."

Song noticed three men wearing yellow helmets crouched in a ditch behind the constable's car. "Who are they?"

"Bashful and a couple of his drillers."

"So now what?"

"That's up to the constable. Would you like to meet him?"

"Does he think I'm a one-hundred-percent snotty little witch?"

"Pure."

"What?"

"You should say pure, not one hundred percent, if you want to get the mountain vernacular down pat."

Song rolled her eyes. "Does the constable think I'm a snotty little witch, pure or otherwise?"

"The constable tends to make up his own mind about people and things."

"Then, yes. I would like to meet him."

Doctor K led her to the constable. "Constable Petrie, this is Song, Cable's fresh wife."

The constable scrutinized her, then shook Song's hand and said, "Hidy, little lady. Welcome to Highcoal. How do you like our fair city so far?"

"It's been an illuminating experience," Song replied.

A warm smile creased the constable's wide, intelligent face. "Illuminating. Haw. That's for sure."

"What's the situation?" Doctor K asked.

The constable shrugged. "The situation is that Squirrel Harper might have the moral right to chase the drillers out of his yard, but the law's not on his side, and he definitely didn't have the right to shoot at them. The state's on their way. Most likely, knowing Squirrel, there's going to be a shoot-out. That's why I called you."

"Why do they want to drill here anyway?" Song asked.

The constable clucked his tongue. "Atlas owns the mineral rights for just about the whole county and, legally, they can drill wherever they want. See that fellow over there, the one looking this way with the smirk? That would be Bashful. He owns this drill rig and called the state po-lice. They called me."

"Have you tried talking to Squirrel?" Song asked.

The constable lifted a bullhorn off the roof of his car and showed it to her. "Until this thing about melted down. No result. Squirrel's pretty stubborn."

Song gave that some thought. "Negotiating with stubborn males is part of my job. I'm good at it."

"Well, I'm not averse to being helped, little lady. Hypothetically, how would you negotiate in this case?"

"Can I talk to the boss of the drillers before I answer?"

"Sure. Why not?" The constable aimed the bullhorn at the ditch. "Bashful, get your tailbone over here, boy. Need to talk to you and I mean right now!"

Upon arrival, Bashful proved to be a ferret-faced man with a thin moustache. He studied Song appreciatively, then pushed his yellow helmet back on his head while flashing a toothy grin.

"My! Cable done good for himself, ain't he? You are one hot chick! You get tired of that old coal miner, just remember, well diggers do it deeper'n anybody and straight down too. Ain't that right, boys?" His men crouching in the ditch stared at him, then looked away.

Song ignored his comments and demanded, "Who do you work for?"

Bashful's grin cracked. "What's it to you?"

"Answer her, Bashful," the constable ordered.

After a moment of hesitation, Bashful shrugged and said, "Atlas Energy. Like everybody else around here."

"Then Cable is your boss?"

"No way, lady. I'm a contractor. I answer to Atlas headquarters, not your husband."

"Did Atlas headquarters tell you to drill in this man's front yard?"

Bashful shook his head. "Naw. If Atlas owns the mineral rights, I have the right to drill where I think there's gas. And Atlas owns the mineral rights on this whole mountain."

"It's a big mountain," Song pointed out. "Why not go a few hundred yards down the road and drill there?"

"Because I chose to set up here."

Song put everything together, Bashful's comments, his body language, and the natural expression of villainy that played across his face. "Here's what I think, Mr. Bashful," she said. "I think you've come here entirely for the purpose of causing trouble for Mr. Harper. What I want to know is—why?"

Bashful's face closed down. "That's none of your business."

"There's always been bad blood between the Harpers and Bashful's family," the constable said.

"The Harpers are a low bunch," Bashful growled. "And one of his boys, that varmit no good for nothing lowlife Ford, did my sister wrong. They were engaged, then he and Chevrolet up and joined the army. Sarah Sue still ain't over it."

"Last I heard," the constable said, "Sarah Sue was seeing some man over in Fox Run. Owner of the Dairy Queen, as I recall."

"She is, but she cried a river over that Harper scamp," Bashful retorted. "But that's got nothing to do with this. I'm just here after the gas. That's all."

Song thought a bit, then turned to the constable. "Is there a law about serving notice on private property before drilling?"

The constable nodded. "Law says the owner has to be notified by letter," he said.

"I done better than that," Bashful interjected. "I nailed a notice on their door."

"When?" Song asked.

"Last week. No, two weeks ago."

Song turned back to the constable. "Is there anything in the law about the number of days notice has to be given before drilling?"

The constable smiled. "Why, now that you mention it, yes it does! Ninety days. Bashful, my boy, she has you there. You're here illegally by about two and a half months!"

"Nobody pays any attention to that stupid law," Bashful retorted.

"We're paying attention to it today," Song said. "Aren't we, Constable?"

"Yes, ma'am, we are. Bashful, consider yourself under arrest unless you move your rig forthwith."

"You can't arrest me," Bashful spat. "You're not a real policeman, just a hired hand."

The constable roughly turned Bashful around and twisted his arms behind him. "I'm real enough until the state gets here." He got out a pair of handcuffs and started to slap them on Bashful's wrists.

"Wait, Constable," Song said. "I think he understands the situation better now. Isn't that right, Mr. Bashful?"

The constable let the driller go, and grimacing, Bashful rubbed his arms. "I guess I do," he sniffed. "But I can't move my truck. Squirrel will shoot me if I try."

"I think perhaps it's time to talk to Mr. Squirrel again, Constable," Song said. "We now have a negotiating point."

The constable nodded appreciatively to Song, then aimed his bullhorn at the house. "Squirrel!" he called. "Turns out Bashful and these old boys have broken the law. They're going to move. So don't shoot them. Come on out on the porch, old son, or give me a sign you hear me and agree not to shoot."

There was no response. All was quiet in the little house. "He could be asleep," the constable said, just as the first wails of sirens could be heard in the distance. "Here comes the state SWAT team. Helmets, flak vests, M-16s, the works. They won't even slow down. They'll kick in the doors and go in shooting."

Song gave that some thought, then said, "All right. We have no choice. Let's go knock on his door."

The constable frowned. "We?"

"I don't see anybody else who's going to do it."

He smiled at her, then shook his head. "You got some guts, lady."

"You saw what happened on 9/11. Give us a challenge, and we New Yorkers do what has to be done."

The constable lifted the bullhorn again "Squirrel? I got Cable's new wife here. She'd like to say hello. Promise not to shoot, and we'll come on the porch."

There was a protracted silence, then, through a broken window, a hoarse voice yelled, "Bring her on, then. I'd like a look at her, sure enough."

"Try not to get me shot, okay?" Song asked, her bravado melting a little. "My father spent a fortune straightening my teeth. I'd hate for him to lose his investment."

"Squirrel probably won't shoot if he says he's not going to."

"*Probably?*"

"Life in these hills, ma'am, is a series of probabilities," the constable said.

Song nodded, then walked beside the constable across the muddy yard. When they stepped up on the porch, the front door swung open and a man in bib overalls stepped out. He had a round, pink face, a white beard, and a big tub belly. He also had crisp blue eyes narrowed with suspicion, and a shotgun with his finger on the trigger.

"Squirrel," the constable said, "this is Cable's wife. She's from New York City."

Squirrel looked her over, pulled the door shut behind him, then said, "They sure make 'em pretty in the city of New York, don't they?"

"Thank you," Song said.

"Not atall. Why, if I was thirty years younger, I'd give old Cable a run for his money." He chuckled. "What can I do for you today, ma'am?"

"You can let those drillers remove their truck and leave."

Squirrel cocked his ear at the approaching sirens. "What about the state?"

"I'll explain it's all been a misunderstanding," the constable said. "Anyhoo, the law's on your side today."

Squirrel scratched his ear with the barrel of his shotgun. "I'd like to oblige, I really would. But I think I need to shoot Bashful while I got the chance. He's not only trespassed on my land, but he makes a habit of trespassing on other people's land too. Shooting him is about the only way to make him stop."

Song pretended she hadn't heard the threat, a negotiating technique her father had taught her. "He won't come into your yard again. That's my promise. I'll talk to Cable and make certain of it."

"Who is it, Daddy?" came a sleepy voice from inside the house. The thin face of a young man appeared in one of the broken windows. He was wearing desert camouflage fatigues and holding a rifle.

"Go back to sleep, Chevrolet," Squirrel said. "It's all right. The drillers are leaving. We ain't gonna shoot nobody today. Tell Ford too."

"Okay, Daddy," Chevrolet said, then moved out of sight.

"I didn't know your boys were back," the constable said.

"Came in yesterday. When I saw that hateful drill rig in my yard this morning, I thought to myself, here my boys are heroes back from the war and first thing ol' Bashful does is plunk his rig in our front yard. Made me so mad, I had to do something."

"How did your sons get their names?" Song asked.

I liked Chevies; their maw liked Fords. You know how it is."

Song nodded, though she feared for her sanity if she *really* knew how it was.

Squirrel lowered the shotgun. "If that truck leaves in the next five minutes," he said to the constable, "I promise I won't shoot Bashful, at least not today."

"That's a deal," the constable said quickly.

"Thank you, Mr. Harper," Song added.

Squirrel beamed. "Ol' Wire—that would be Cable's daddy, ma'am—surely would be proud to see his son did so good in the woman department. I just hope my boys find somebody like you, sweet lady, and there's the truth of it." He glared at Bashful, who was peeking over the roof of the constable's car. "I sure am glad Ford got away from that Sarah Sue. She's sorry as a drunk possum. That feller owns the Dairy Queen over at Fox Run is welcome to her."

Squirrel kicked the door with his heel. "Open up, boys!" The door opened behind him, and Squirrel backed inside, then the door slowly closed.

"You done good, Mrs. Jordan," the constable said as they walked past the drilling rig.

"You didn't do too bad yourself, Constable."

"We're a good team. Want a job? I could use an assistant."

Song laughed. "Don't tempt me. This was fun."

Doctor K came out from behind the constable's car and gave Song a hug. "I think you just made yourself a lot of friends in Highcoal, young lady."

This brought Song crashing back to earth. There was only one friend she wanted in Highcoal and that was her husband, the exalted Cable who had enjoyed the pleasures of the governor of the state but somehow neglected to mention it. She needed to either punish him for that, or love him so much he'd forget all about West Virginia's chief executive forever. At that moment, Song was uncertain which one she was going to do. But she was going to do something.

Nine

Cable hurried up the wooden steps of the brick building that housed his office. Mole made a hand gesture like a hangman's noose as Cable passed his office. He found the MSHA inspector at his desk, writing in a notebook.

"Cable," he said, closing the notebook with a snap, "I've been waiting for you." He had an edge in his voice that sounded threatening, but then Einstein always sounded threatening.

"Einstein, I'm glad you waited," Cable lied as he hung his helmet on the hat rack by the door. "I wanted to get your advice on mine operations."

Einstein was a prissy man but tough, the Napoleon of inspectors. He smirked. "That'll be the day when a mine superintendent asks an MSHA inspector for advice about mine operations." He got up and walked over to the big map of the Highcoal mine pinned to the wall and put his hands behind his back. "Tell me about Six West, Cable. It evokes my curiosity."

"Opened three months ago. Been running some good coal out of it. What else do you want to know?"

"How's the roof?"

"Silty shale. Not the best, but I have a roof bolt plan I'm confident should support it."

"The seam?"

"Six to seven feet of soft, friable coal, much of it of high metallurgical quality."

"Heard Navy Jones got his arm broke on that section yesterday. A pillar let go. I'm looking forward to your report so I can write my criticism of it."

Cable nodded toward the stack of paper in his in-box. "The pillar didn't completely let go, just a corner of it. You can see my backlog. I'll file a report as soon as I can."

"Addressing safety violations always comes first," Einstein lectured. "Now, either your boys cut that pillar too close or there's some other reason why it collapsed, even if it was only partially."

Cable ran a hand over his grimy face. "I'm looking into it."

Einstein consulted his notebook. "You have a new foreman, and all the operators on that section are new too. Are they trained adequately?"

"Yes, of course they are," Cable grumbled. He didn't like being interrogated as if he had committed a crime.

Einstein rocked in his boots for a while. "Vietnam Petroski is a good man, and your operators seem competent enough from the little I've observed. So I think there's another reason that pillar crumbled. The old works just north of Six West. Much of them are flooded, are they not?"

"So I'm told."

"You ever heard of Quecreek in Pennsylvania?"

Cable knew where Einstein was headed, and it was nothing but trouble. "I saw it on television," he allowed.

"What happened there? Refresh my memory."

Cable sighed. "As you well know, since you went up there with the MSHA team, they mined into old works filled with water. It flooded the mine, nearly drowned the miners. But they all got out safely."

Einstein nodded. "They were lucky. For one thing, their mine wasn't very deep, so rescue came quickly. Six West is eight hundred and fifty feet deep. If it flooded, you'd have a crew of dead miners."

"There's no reason for it to flood," Cable argued. "It's a long way from those old works." He pointed out the area on the map. "I had a couple of boreholes put in here and here. I found water to the north, and that's why I changed the direction of the face to head west."

"I know about those boreholes and I know the results. I approve of your action there. Still, I worry that you just lied to me. I asked you about the water and you said you'd been told it was there when, in reality, you were concerned enough to drill to find out. And now I learn you've changed the direction of the face."

When Cable didn't say anything, Einstein continued. "That's what I thought. You're as worried about it as I am. And anytime you start working near an old area, there's more than water to worry about. What about methane? You know it has to be accumulating. How are those old sections isolated from the working mine?"

"They're sealed off," Cable answered. "Concrete block construction."

"What if there's an ignition and the seals don't hold?"

Cable shook his head. "Hell, Einstein, what if the sun doesn't come up in the morning?"

Einstein was not impressed with Cable's argument, or lack of one. "I want you to close down Six West, Cable. I believe it to be dangerous."

"If I did that, I would be so far behind on my orders for high-grade metallurgical, I'd never catch up."

Einstein looked disappointed. "The audacity of you mine superintendents never ceases to amaze me. Production means more to you than the safety of your own men. Scandalous."

"That's not fair."

"I don't care if it's fair or not," Einstein retorted. "My job is to keep you on your toes and your mine safe. Now, let me tell you why that pillar collapsed. I think water is leaking in from the old area."

"There's no proof of that."

"My theory is as likely as any. And what if I'm right? Eventually, the entire section could come down."

"Look, I'll put down some more boreholes to see if you're right. Just let me keep working the section until I get the results back. Even if it's happening, you know it's a slow process. I'll put some pumps in there too."

Though Einstein looked dubious, he said, "All right. You can keep the section open for now. But I want to see the test results as soon as you get them. By the way, your man at the manlift gate didn't pat me down. You will be fined."

Cable knew it was best to let it go, but he couldn't help arguing a little. "Everyone knows who you are. You're MSHA. You're not going to carry anything inside you're not supposed to."

"For that opinion, you will pay one thousand dollars," Einstein said, and walked out.

Sighing at the unfairness of it all, Cable sat down on the edge of his desk and worried over his mine map. He knew Einstein was right about everything, but especially right about Six West. It was dangerous to mine so close to those old works. If it wasn't for that big order from India, Cable would have never gone after that coal. But he was also confident in his ability to keep his men safe. He would do what needed to be done, including those new boreholes.

Cable headed for the bathhouse, Mole again giving him the hangman's signal as he walked by the dispatcher's office. Cable stopped at the manlift to have a word with Elbow Johnson, the gate guard.

"Elbow, were you here when Einstein went down?"

Elbow gulped. "Yes, sir. And I know why you're asking. I didn't pat him down. That man scares the bejeebers out of me."

"You know the rule. Anybody who doesn't work at this mine gets patted down before he gets on the manlift. He fined us because you didn't do your job. Next time, turn him inside out."

Elbow nodded. "I'll pat him down so hard, he'll think he's been in the ring with Rocky Marciano."

"You do that," Cable said, reflecting on the fact that Elbow and a lot of Highcoal's miners were ancient enough to recall who Rocky Marciano was. He *had* to find some young miners!

Cable handed over his lamp battery to the lamp house man for recharging, then hung his brass identification tag on the board marked Outside. At the bathhouse, he pulled the chains to bring his basket down from the ceiling. Such baskets were common in West Virginia coal company bathhouses. They eliminated the need for lockers and used space efficiently by storing the miners' clothing, helmet, and other necessities in baskets drawn up against the ceiling.

Cable took his clean clothes out of his basket and put them on a bench, then stripped, put his work clothes in the basket, pulled the chain to run it back up, then headed for a shower stall. There were so many things running through his mind he was having trouble sorting them all out and putting them in their proper perspective and priority sequence. Six West, Einstein, flooding, ventilation problems, roof control, Bum, and the stack of paperwork on his desk.

Then, he recalled, there was also Song. Which problem should he solve first? How disappointing that she'd become a problem. A man's wife, after all, should be his pleasure, at least until there were kids. After that, she was put up on a pedestal for life and if Mama wasn't happy, nobody was happy. That was what Wire had taught him. It was the West Virginia way.

He turned the shower on wide open and let it beat down on his weary back. As the coal was washed off, a black puddle formed at his feet, and he got back to worrying about the mine and especially Six West. *If I didn't love this job so much*, he thought, *I'd hate it.*

"Uh, Cable?"

It was Mole standing outside the shower stall. Cable poked his head out and saw his clerk/dispatcher wearing his usual gloomy expression, except it seemed even gloomier. "What's going on, Mole?"

"Well, sir, it's about your wife. I just heard about something she did. She like to got herself killed, you see."

Cable's jaw fell. "What?"

"Yes, sir," Mole said. He allowed the glimmer of a smile. "Seems like she's done decided to be the new constable."

WHEN CABLE GOT home, he found Song asleep, wrapped in a quilt on the couch in the parlor. "Why are you not upstairs in bed?" he asked.

Song wiped the sleep from her eyes. It had been a deep sleep, and she'd been home, truly home, safe in her New York apartment. "I wanted to see you the moment you came home."

"Why?"

"We need to talk, Cable."

"We are talking, best I can tell."

"So we are, although you've been gone practically from the moment I arrived here. I was coming to see you at the mine, but then I was required to solve a little problem."

"I heard," he cut in. "I've already had some words with Doctor K and the constable. They got an earful, I can tell you that. What were you thinking? You could have been killed!"

Song fought a strong desire to pick up one of Rhonda's tasteful lamps and break it over Cable's head. "I was coming to see you," she said with precision, "because I heard what happened between you and Bashful this morning. I felt that we should talk about it. Doctor K was visiting me—actually she was the one who told me about the gossip and how you nearly beat up Bashful over it—and agreed to drive me to your office. That was when the constable called about Squirrel Harper. I didn't have any choice but to go with her. Once there, I did what I could to help out. I know how to negotiate, Cable. It's one of the things I do in my job."

Cable had listened intently, all the while turning a shade of purple. "What you did was *stupid*!" he erupted, then worked to control his anger. That was something else his father had taught him. No matter how provoked, a real man never yelled at a woman. He allowed a moment more to cool down, and then said, in the most reasonable of tones, "Look, honey, this isn't New York. You don't know anything about my people. Until you do, you can't charge off without letting me know. Do you understand?"

Song stood and handed Cable the quilt. "This is for you," she said. "Use it on the couch, the floor, or one of the other bedrooms, I don't care. 'Stupid' here is going to bed. *Alone.*"

Cable stared at the quilt with some astonishment, then carelessly threw it down. "It's my bed too! I will sleep there tonight, tomorrow night, any night I choose."

Song was wearing the sheer gown that had driven Cable wild in St. John. She knew he loved the way she looked in it, and even better when she shed it. She allowed it to drop to the floor and Cable's mouth went ajar.

"Mercy," he said, his tongue suddenly thick. He took a step in her direction, but she took a step back. "What's wrong?" he all but begged.

"What's wrong? Hmm. What could possibly be wrong?" She snapped her fingers. "I have it. Let me just say this name and see if you recognize it. Governor Michelle Godfrey." She lifted her eyebrows. "Do you know her, Cable? As in *know* in the biblical sense?"

Cable opened his mouth, then closed it. "It's a long story," he said. "But I swan—"

"You can swan on the couch. I'm going to bed."

"You're not going to let me explain?"

"Would I like the explanation?"

His face was pinched. "What you might like is a complete mystery to me."

"All the more reason for you to sleep alone." Tears filling her eyes, she started up the steps, hoping he would call her back.

But he didn't. Instead, he said, "You know what? This old couch is real comfy."

Song was certain now she knew the truth. Her husband had slept with the governor of West Virginia (not that sleep had anything to do with it). It didn't matter that it had occured before they met and married. The fact he hadn't confessed it to her was all she needed to know. Her tears flowing across her cheeks, she ran to the bedroom and slammed the door.

Ten

When Song came downstairs the next morning, the couch was empty except for the quilt. After fixing coffee, she tried the kitchen telephone again. To her everlasting joy, this time it worked, and her father—her wonderful, dear, though sometimes ruthless, father, Joe Hawkins himself—answered his phone.

"Song!" She imagined his handsome face, his silver fox hair and moustache, and his delighted grin. "So good to hear from you! But where've you been? I've left a dozen messages on your cell. How goes it, daughter? What's it like in wild and wonderful West Virginia? I believe that's their slogan down there."

"Wild, but not wonderful," Song replied, then gave her father a quick rundown of all that had transpired. "Maybe I made a big mistake with Cable, Daddy," she concluded, on the verge of tears.

Her father was silent for a long second, then said, "Listen, honey. You know I like Cable, but this marriage . . . well, it *was* quite a surprise to everybody. More than one person has asked me what you were thinking."

Song put a hand across her eyes. "I know, I know."

"I can have a car and a driver pick you up in a matter of hours. What's the closest town of any size?"

"I have no idea."

"Well, I'll find out. Just give me the word and you'll be on your way home."

Song considered the offer, which was tempting. "I promised Cable I'd stay a week. Anyway, I don't think I should run away. I've got to figure things out."

Hawkins got to the heart of the matter. "The question, it seems to me, is can you give him up?"

"I can't live here. That much I know. The town hates me. Not only that, it's ugly and backwards. Cell phones don't even work here."

"So what's your next step?"

"I've got to convince him to transfer to New York."

"And if you can't, what then?"

Song pressed the phone hard against her ear and lowered her head. "I don't know, I don't know," she moaned. "It's such a mess."

"There is such a thing as an annulment," Joe Hawkins said.

"I know, Daddy," she whispered.

"I can fix it for you, daughter. Hell, if it comes to it, I can kidnap Cable and drag him up here. You just name it and I'll see it done."

"I love you, Daddy."

"And I love you, pretty girl. Never doubt it."

"And who else do you love?" she teased. "Are you still going out with that redhead?"

"Monique? No, she didn't have enough energy to keep up with me."

Song laughed and it felt good. "Let's see. I think you're thirty years older than her, right?"

"Thirty-two, actually."

"You're amazing, Daddy."

"Yeah, maybe. So many women, so little time."

"You're a rogue, that's what you are."

"Well, Song, I love women. I can't help it. But if your mother was still alive, I wouldn't look at anyone else. She was a fantastic woman in every way. She filled my heart the way I hoped Cable would fill yours."

"Cable always says I shouldn't make easy things hard. But this isn't easy. I don't care what he says."

Hawkins chuckled. "You two are quite the pair."

"I guess we are." It was a lament.

Their talk shifted to business—her office was struggling without her—then Song told him how much she loved him again, and he told her he loved her even more, and they hung up. Nothing had been solved, but at least she'd been able to get a few things off her chest.

"Now what?" Song asked herself, but she had no real answer. "A mess, a mess, it's all a mess."

She poured herself a fresh cup of coffee, then went out onto the porch and sank into a rocker to contemplate the view, which unfortunately hadn't changed. It was still Highcoal, the mine, and the mountains. She was studying the montage when Young Henry came whistling up the driveway.

"Morning, missus." He tipped his baseball cap to her. "Pretty day, ain't it?"

"Pretty day, isn't it?" she corrected him, as matter of course.

"Oh, I know," the boy said. "I was just using the West Virginia vernacular."

Young Henry went on while Song laughed at herself. The boy was cute and clever, and she really liked him.

She went upstairs and looked in the bathroom mirror and was startled at her appearance. She was looking decidedly tired and drawn. If she and Cable were going to talk and settle things, she supposed it might go better if she didn't look like a hag. There had been no word of her missing luggage. *Cosmetics*, she thought. *I need cosmetics.* But where to get them? There seemed but one answer—the store that, according to Cable, had everything. Omar's Dollar and Cents Store.

Song changed into a chic blue skirt, a white blouse, and strappy heels, figuring she might as well take a turn at impressing the townsfolk. She didn't care what they thought, but Cable did. The whole idea was to lure him to her bidding, especially now that he'd had a night of sleeping alone.

She went out, climbed into the Porsche, and stared at the instrument panel, the stick shift, and the three pedals on the floor. It looked like the cockpit of a jet plane. She was flummoxed. There was no way she could drive it. She sought out Young Henry and found him manning a shovel in the stable.

"I need to go to the store. Any idea how I could do that?"

The boy gawked at her. "Go-oll-ee," he said. "You sure are pretty, ma'am."

"Why, thank you, Young Henry," Song said, quite pleased.

Young Henry mulled over her question. "If you want to go to Omar's, you should take Mr. Jordan's car," he concluded.

"Yes, but I don't know how to drive it."

Young Henry mulled some more. "Folks that don't have a car usually just hitchhike. If you call them, the constable or Preacher will come get you if they got a minute. Of course, you usually have to listen to Preacher preach. Come to think on it, he's working in the mine today, anyway. The constable, he might come. Good thing about him is he tends to be quiet unless he thinks you been busting out streetlights with a BB gun or something like that. Then he's likely to fuss at you."

"I don't think I want to hitchhike, and I don't want to call the constable either, even though I've never even seen a real BB gun. Any other ideas?"

"Well, first off, I don't understand why you can't drive Mr. Jordan's car."

"In the city we have taxis, subways, buses, and trains," she explained. "I don't have to drive, so it's been awhile, and then only with an automatic."

Young Henry puzzled over that, then said, "Mom lets me drive her truck all the time. She gets busy and there's nobody else to pick up stuff for the hotel. I drove all the way to Bluefield a month ago. Surely that little car can't be no harder to drive than the old truck."

"Do you have a driver's license?"

"I'm only twelve, but a West Virginia boy does what a West Virginia boy has to do."

Song gave his proposition some thought and concluded she had no choice. "Young Henry," she said, "consider yourself my chauffeur!"

In all her life, Song thought she'd never seen anyone grin so large as Young Henry. His face split, jug ear to jug ear. "Dale Earnhardt, Junior and Senior," he said to the sky and heaven, where little boys keep their dreams of adventure and conquest, "eat your heart out!"

YOUNG HENRY SAT on a pillow to see over the steering wheel, and he had to stretch his legs to reach the pedals, but he was a smooth shifter and soon had Cable's roadster sailing along the mountain road, heading for Highcoal.

"Aren't we going a bit fast, Young Henry?" Song asked after the boy steered through a number of curves and made the tires shriek. She wrapped her scarf tighter around her head.

"Oh, no, ma'am!" Young Henry said. "These cars are made to go fast. If you go too slow, the engine gets all full of crud and stuff."

"Um . . . well, I trust you, I guess."

"That's a good thing, ma'am."

At the bottom of the mountain, there was a straight stretch, and Young

Henry floored the accelerator. As the needle flicked past eighty miles an hour, he dodged an especially large pothole and lost control. The little car jumped a ditch, knocked down a wooden fence, then skittered across a meadow of slick, green grass until finally stopping beside a startled milk cow. The cow mooed irritably, emptied its large intestine, and walked away, its head held aloft in bovine dignity.

Young Henry's bloodless fingers were wrapped like claws around the steering wheel. "I didn't really mean to do that," he said.

During the unexpected detour, Song had been so terrified her mind had gone blank. Now she crawled out of the car and sat on what she thought was grass, but was actually a fresh and steaming cow patty, which she didn't see and was too shaken to smell. Somehow she had lost her scarf and her hair was in her eyes. Young Henry knelt beside her, carefully keeping out of the cow patty. Song looked at him, her eyes wild and wide.

"Now, just breathe easy, ma'am," he said. "There you go. Breathe in and out. Good! Oh, that's so much better. Maybe you'd like to get up? You're sitting in cow poo, you see."

Song found her voice. "Cow poo?"

"Yes, ma'am. Like the stuff that comes out of cows."

Song tried to gather her wits, a difficult project after looking death in the face. "You know, Young Henry," she finally managed, "I don't believe I've ever sat in cow poo before. West Virginia certainly is wild and wonderful."

"Yes, ma'am. I reckon it is."

Song took Young Henry's hand and the boy drew her to her feet. She looked at the cow dung on her skirt and wrinkled up her nose at both its appearance and stink.

"It's really awful stuff, isn't it?"

"I guess that's why cows like to get it out of them. But come look at the car. It's hardly scratched, I swan."

Song wobbled over to the roadster. There was indeed only a scratch on its bumper. "Thank goodness. Cable loves this car," she said. Her wits returning, she looked around for a source of water. "I've got to wash the stink off me," she said.

"There's a creek not far away." Young Henry motioned with his hand.

Song considered the creek, then changed her mind about the washing. "I should go home," she concluded.

"No problem," Young Henry said. "All I have to do is get the car back on the road and I'll have you back in no time atall. You just stand over there. No ma'am, not there! Oh, look, you've stepped in the cow poo with your nice shoes."

"Only a couple hundred dollars," she said faintly.

"Really, ma'am? You can buy a pair just like them in Omar's store for about thirty bucks."

"Young Henry, let's discuss the price of shoes at a later time."

"Yes, ma'am."

Young Henry climbed into the car, revved its engine, popped its clutch, and went for it, wheels throwing up clumps of turf as he steered it through the hole in the fence, across the ditch, and back up on the road.

Song watched from her place on the grass as a massive coal truck rounded the curve and roared relentlessly toward Young Henry and the car. Brakes squealed and smoke erupted from the truck's tires as Young Henry dived out of the car just seconds before the collision that, miraculously, did not occur. The huge steel bumper of the truck, nearly as big as the car, stopped only inches away from it.

"Oh, thank goodness!" Song cried, although her relief was short-lived. Several tons of coal, its momentum unchecked, erupted from the truck and fell like a black tidal wave on top of Cable's car. Song ran toward the buried vehicle, but slipped at the edge of the ditch and went sprawling face-first into mud. Young Henry helped her up and then supported her as she limped to the road.

"Them coal trucks sure can build up a head of steam," the boy marveled.

The truck driver, a mountain of a man in bib overalls, climbed out of the cab and lumbered over. He grinned in recognition when he saw Young Henry.

"Hey, boy! Where'd you get that little car I done buried under my coal?"

"It's Mr. Jordan's. And this is his wife, Mrs. Jordan."

The driver peered at Song through coke-bottle glasses. "I'm Foureyes, ma'am," he said, then put his hand over his nose. "Par'm me, but you kinda stink."

"I'm sorry. I think I sat on a cow . . . thing."

"Ten-four, ma'am. You surely did. You really married to Cable? I got to say you ain't much like I pictured a wife of his'n."

"Because I'm Asian-American?"

"Uh-uh." He patted his chest. "The way I heard it, Cable likes 'em big along here."

Song, rising above her despair, lifted her muddy chin. "Are you hurt in any way, Mr. Foureyes?"

"Not yet, but I probably will be. Cable's gonna kick my tail for dumping coal on his car."

"I got an idea!" Young Henry chirped. "Squirrel Harper details cars and he owes Mrs. Jordan a favor. He could clean that car up, sure as spit."

"Might work," Foureyes agreed. "If you had a way of calling him." He looked at Song. "Cell phones don't work around here, you know."

"Really?" Song rolled her eyes.

Young Henry was momentarily stymied, but then he brightened. "You could tow it yourself. That big old truck oughta be able to tow a battleship."

"Oh, would you please, Mr. Foureyes?" Song begged. It was her only hope. She was having enough trouble with Cable without him finding out she had buried his car beneath several tons of coal.

Foureyes gave it some thought, then shrugged. "All right, ma'am, I'll do it. But you have to do one thing for me."

"What is it, Mr. Foureyes?" Song asked, in her sweetest voice.

"Stand downwind. I can hardly breathe, you smell so bad."

WHILE SONG, CHAGRINED and mortified, stood some distance away, Foureyes and Young Henry dug out Cable's car from beneath most of the coal and found a length of chain in the coal truck suitable for towing.

"Aren't we going with him?" Song asked as the truck trundled away with the roadster rolling behind.

"No, ma'am. We have to fix Mr. Spratt's fence. We busted it down, after all."

"*You* busted it down."

"You were with me."

"I could just pay him for the damage."

"Yes, but that's not the way we do it in West Virginia. You break something, you fix it. You don't just throw money at it. That ain't considered polite."

"An interesting philosophy." Song shrugged, then chuckled. Sometimes, when everything goes wrong, it's best to laugh. Her father had taught her that. Of course, he'd also taught her that after laughing, figure out how to end up ahead. "All right," she said. "Let's fix the fence."

The fence, though in pieces, fit back together like a jigsaw puzzle, so it didn't take long. When they were done, the cow wandered over and produced another cow pie as commentary.

"Well, that's done," Song said, wiping the muddy sweat from her brow with the back of her hand, leaving a long smear. "But how are we going to get home?"

"I reckon we put out our thumb, ma'am. Somebody will pick us up."

Song considered his plan. "Other than Foureyes and us, there's been no traffic," she pointed out.

"That's because most folks are at work."

"We can't stand beside the road all day, Young Henry."

"We could walk," he said, "but it's four miles to your house, and pretty much straight up that there mountain."

"I'm discovering there's always a mountain to cross around here," Song sighed.

"But Highcoal's not far," Young Henry said thoughtfully. "And I know a shortcut. If we go there, Mom will loan me her truck and I can drive you home. Simple as pie."

Song shook her head. "There's no way I'm going into Highcoal where everybody will see me looking and smelling like this."

"Nobody will see us."

"How so?"

"We'll sneak through backyards and stuff."

Song considered her options. She really didn't have any, except the one. "All right. But nobody sees me or even gets close to me, got it?"

"Got it."

Young Henry led her across the meadow where the milk cow had gone back to grazing. Along the way, Song stopped and broke the heels off her shoes, which she'd seen somebody do in a movie. Surprisingly, it helped. They soon reached a creek, where Song insisted she wash out her skirt while Young Henry went behind some bushes and hid his eyes. She got her skirt as clean as she could, then wrung it out, and put it back on.

"How do I look?" she asked Young Henry. He perused her, and his expression told her everything.

"That bad?"

"You look kind of rumpled, you might say."

"Thanks, Young Henry," she grumped. "How else am I supposed to look after being in a wreck? One that you caused by driving too fast, by the way."

The boy's lower lip went out. It was trembling. "I already said I was sorry."

"I know you are," she said. "It's okay. Honest. Nobody sees me in Highcoal, right?"

His lip stopped trembling. "Right."

"Okay, let's go."

Young Henry led her through the woods, then across another meadow, another creek, and then up a rocky cliff where she slipped and fell, scraping her knees.

"Are you all right, ma'am?"

"I seem to be bleeding, Young Henry."

He inspected her scraped legs. "They're not bad. I get scabs on my knees all the time."

"Yes, but you're not a newlywed."

"What difference does that make?"

"Never mind. Lead on."

Young Henry led on until finally he led her across a ditch and Song saw they were on the outskirts of Highcoal, marked by a row of houses. Young Henry climbed out of the ditch with Song doggedly behind him, and they sneaked through backyards until they finally reached the rear of the church where there was a small graveled parking lot. In it sat several cars, one of them a black limousine.

"Just over there's the Cardinal Hotel, ma'am," Young Henry said, pointing across the road. "Ma's truck's in the back. I'll go get it. You hide here, maybe behind one of those cars until I get back."

"A good plan."

"Thank you, ma'am."

It would have indeed been a good plan if they'd time to execute it, but before they could take a step, the back door of the church opened and three women stepped out. They were laughing heartily, but the laughter stopped when they saw Song and Young Henry, both staring back at them like startled cats.

Young Henry instantly chirped, "Hidy, Mrs. Carlisle, Mrs. Petroski, Mrs. Williams! How y'all doing?"

"Well, hello, Young Henry," one of the women greeted him. "And who's your playmate? Looks like she's been playing in the mud!"

"Why, this is Mrs. Jordan, ma'am!"

Song cringed.

"Mrs. Jordan?"

"Yes, ma'am, she is, I swan." Young Henry turned to Song. "Ma'am, this is Mrs. Carlisle in the blue dress, Mrs. Petroski in the other blue dress, and Mrs. Williams in the, ah, bluest dress."

"I'm going to kill you," Song muttered.

"We're on the church board," the woman introduced as Mrs. Williams said. "You're the woman who married our Cable?"

"That would be me," Song confessed. "I'm sorry for how I look, but I've just been in a wreck."

"Very nice to meet you, I'm sure," Mrs. Carlisle said uncertainly. "A wreck, you say? Are you all right?"

"Yes, but I need to go home. Young Henry was just going after his mother's truck."

"Well, we won't hold you then," Mrs. Carlisle said. "I expect we'll see you and Cable in church on Sunday?"

"Oh, sure. I'll be there." Anything to get away from these women.

It was then that another woman stepped out on the porch. Impeccably dressed in a chic suit, the woman was tall, blonde, and had an impossibly small waist balanced by large, perfectly formed breasts highlighted by a low-cut blouse. (Song immediately wondered who her surgeon was.) Her big eyes, so blue Song was certain they had to be contacts, inspected Song and Young Henry, then asked, with a smile demonstrating very white teeth, "Who are these delightful children?"

"That one is Young Henry," Mrs. Williams said. "He's Rhonda's son. The other . . . well, that would be Cable's wife."

The woman's eyes widened. She cocked her head and her blonde, lustrous hair (surely enhanced) fell across her perfectly sculpted cheek. Although she was obviously curious, no querulous lines appeared in her forehead. *Botox,* Song immediately thought.

"Did you say Cable's wife?" the dazzling woman asked.

"She and Young Henry have been in an accident," Mrs. Williams explained.

The woman walked down the steps. "Your first name, dear?" she asked, smiling faintly before her perfect nostrils flared. She had apparently detected the remnants of cow still clinging to Song.

"Song."

"What nationality are you, dear?"

"American. What nationality are you?"

"Presently West Virginian." She turned to the trio of women. "I enjoyed our meeting. I believe your activities will make a difference. Let me know how my office can assist."

"Oh, indeed! Yes! Thank you! By all means!" came the chorus.

The woman gave a final glance at Song before walking regally to the limo. A driver hopped out and opened the door for her. She didn't acknowledge him, just sat in the back seat, then gracefully swung her lovely legs inside. She looked straight ahead as he closed the door.

Song watched the show, then asked, "Who was that?"

Mrs. Carlisle answered, "That's Governor Godfrey, Mrs. Jordan. Here on a visit. She's a wonderful woman."

Song watched the limo turn onto the road. "So I hear."

And she's also tall, blonde, and surgically enhanced in all the right places, apparently just the way my husband likes his women!

Eleven

After saying good-bye to the three friendly but bemused church ladies, Song decided she might as well go to the store and see to her cosmetics. How, after all, could anything worse happen to her now?

Young Henry led her along a fortunately empty street. She went inside the store and walked up to the counter where a bald man with warm brown eyes and a neatly trimmed beard awaited her. He wore an expectant expression, and she introduced herself.

He replied, "My name is Omar Kedra, Mrs. Jordan. May I be so bold as to ask if perhaps you have been in some sort of recent accident?"

"Actually, I was in a car wreck, then I sat in cow poo. Later, I fell in a ditch and then off a cliff."

"I see. Then everything is perfectly explained. May I offer you perhaps a drink of a most excellent drink known as ouzo? You seem to have need of a bracer."

"Thank you, Omar." Finally—someone who understood the travails of the day. "You may, indeed."

"I fear it has a kick," Omar apologized as he drew from beneath the counter a bottle that held a clear liquid. He filled a crystal glass and slid it across to her.

Song tossed back the contents, then slid the glass back. "Hit me again," she said, and he did. She took a swallow. "Very nice."

"Now," Omar said, "I believe I see some color returning to your cheeks. That is a good thing. What else might you need? Laundry detergent, perhaps? Or bath salts?"

Song went for broke. "Do you by any chance have Tracie Martyn skin products? Or Clinique?"

Omar chuckled deeply. "Ah, extremely nice choices, indeed. Clinique is known the world over for its quality. And Madonna herself uses Tracie Martyn. I have heard that Susan Sarandon uses those products as well."

"I adore Susan Sur, uh, sur . . . Sarandon and all she stands for," Song said, surprised at the difficulty in pronouncing the woman's name. She was also feeling warm and oddly benevolent. The world, it seemed to her, was a fine place, where nothing bad could possibly occur.

Omar perused her. "So you admire Miss Sarandon? Her philosophy too, I presume? That must mean you are of the liberal persuasion. I am president of the Highcoal Patriotic Club and your husband was president last year."

"What is the Patter, uh, oddick Club?" she slurred.

"In a very short fashion, we are a group of conservative men and women who, I tremble to tell you, consistently vote Republican."

Song finished the glass of ouzo, then stared at Omar. "Cable is a *Republican*?"

"Oh yes, indeed, madam. A loyal Republican, indeed. Although I must say he does stray a little to vote for Senator Jay Rockefeller, who is a big Democrat. He knows the senator personally, and so believes in his good quality."

"My husband is a Republican! I can't believe it!" Song had to grip the counter to hold herself up, her knees suddenly weak. "This is, well . . . astonishing!"

"Oh, madam. I have distressed you! May I pour you another little finger?"

Song nodded, then took another swallow of the fiery liquid. She had married a Republican. On top of everything else, why had she and Cable never discussed politics?

"Madam?" Omar said, interrupting Song's fuzzy thoughts. "May I assist you further?"

Song tried to get back on track. "What cosmetics do you have, Omar?"

"I have a product known as Coal Country Woman. It is made right here in West Virginia."

"You're kidding, right?"

"Oh, my dear. You must understand. Coal Country Woman is all the rage amongst the women of Highcoal and is a most excellent line of cosmetics. But if it does not suit, perhaps you could visit Susan, the preacher's wife, who represents the line of cosmetics known as Mary Kay." Omar searched under his counter and produced a business card. "If you call this most enterprising woman, she will attend to you in your very home."

Song took the card. "I'm sorry we do not see eye to eye politically," she said, every word perfectly slurred.

Omar grinned, displaying an excellent set of healthy teeth. "Yet we are friends! And you are married to someone who does not believe anything that you believe! Only in America is such a thing possible!"

Song realized she was exhausted and possibly somewhat drunk. "You have been most helpful," she replied, carefully enunciating since her tongue seemed to have thickened to the size of the milk cow in the pasture. Then, thinking to salvage at least something of her encounter with Omar, she added, "I just want you to know I respect and admire the Muslim faith."

"Do you? I am a Lebanese Christian," Omar replied. "A Muslim man murdered my grandfather. Of course, my grandfather murdered that man's brother. It is so nice to live in Highcoal where hardly anyone murders anyone else. May I show you perhaps some shampoo for your hair?"

A few minutes later, Song exited the store carrying a brown paper bag that contained a large bottle of Coal Country Woman shampoo, Coal Country Woman soap, Coal Country Woman deodorant, and Coal Country Woman Guaranteed to Make Your Skin Soft as a Calf lotion. At the curb, Young Henry was waiting for her in his mother's truck. Between Song and the truck was a crowd of townsfolk, including several off-duty miners identified by their black helmets. They gawked at her, and some held their noses.

"Don't pay them no mind, ma'am!" Young Henry cried. "Hop in!"

Song threaded her way through the townsfolk, listening to their buzz: "That's Cable's new wife? I heard she's snotty. But why's she so dirty? What's that smell? She ain't like I pictured. She looks more like a boy. Is she Oriental? She looks Oriental. She's Japanese, I think. No, Chinese! I bet four days, how about you?"

Song climbed into the truck, pulled the door shut, and vaguely waved down the road. "Take me home, Young Henry." Then she giggled. "You know, I think I'm a little drunk."

"Yes, ma'am," Young Henry replied, waving away the fumes of the ouzo mixed with the odor of cow.

"What did that man mean when he said I bet four days?"

"It's stupid," Young Henry said. "People are betting how many days you're going to stay."

"But I'm here for a week. Why didn't you tell them?"

Young Henry shrugged. "I told you it was stupid."

As they passed the mine, Song spotted Cable walking across the grounds, his head down, his hands behind his back. He was in an obvious hurry to get wherever he was going. "Stop, Young Henry!" Song commanded.

Startled, the boy hit the brakes. "What's wrong?"

"Gotta talk with my husband. Right now. Not gonna wait!" Song flung open the door. "You know why?" When the boy didn't say anything, she said, "'Cause I love him. What do you think of that, Young Henry?"

"I don't think now's the time, ma'am," Young Henry replied.

"Oh, what do you know?" Song demanded, and slammed the door shut. "You're just a boy!"

Song walked unsteadily through the gate and headed for the low brick building she'd seen Cable enter. All of a sudden, everything was crystal clear. She loved Cable and he loved her. He was absolutely right. Why make an easy thing hard? This problem of location could be worked out. Maybe they'd share their time between New York and Highcoal. *Yes, that was it!* Why hadn't she thought of that before? She also realized that she was, well, very, very needful for Cable in a quite physical way. With tears of joy, sudden knowledge, and wifely lust, not to mention ouzo, filling every fiber of her being, she ran up the steps and burst inside. In a room to the right was a little man in a white helmet pecking at the keyboard of a desktop computer. At her sudden appearance, a shocked expression crossed his molelike face. Song knew instantly who it was.

"Mole! It's you. It's me. Song. Where's my hubby? Where's that Cable man?"

"Cable? Why, he's in his office, ma'am. You're Mrs. Cable? Hello, good to see you at last. But are you well? You look a little peaked."

"I'm wonderful, Mole!" Song cried, and threw open the door. Cable was sitting at a big desk. He looked up and, for some reason, his eyes widened. She only had eyes for him too.

"Sweetheart!" She ran to him and threw herself into his arms, which almost tipped him out of his chair. She began to cover his face with kisses. "I love you, love you, *love you*! Need you too. Take me now, Cable, right here on this desk!" She threw herself back and began to unbutton her blouse.

"Song . . . ," Cable said, easing her off his lap. "Um . . . this isn't the time."

Song felt no warmth from Cable. In fact, she sensed that she somehow had made him unhappy. Then she knew what it was, and laughed.

"Oh, 'cause I stink!" she cried. "I'm earthy, that's all. You like your women earthy, don't you, Cable? I wrecked your car—well, I didn't, Young Henry did— and then I sat in this cow poo . . . it's all so messed up in my mind, but . . . *what is it*? Why are you looking at me like that?"

The expression on Cable's face was so severe and unyielding, it was nearly enough to sober her up. Nearly.

Cable cleared his throat, and said, "We're having a meeting, Song."

" *We?*"

"My foremen, my engineers, the owners of the mine, and Governor Godfrey."

It was as if an alien world had suddenly coalesced out of a fog. Song turned and saw the grimy and thoroughly astonished faces of a dozen men wearing white helmets, plus those of several men in dark suits and the oh-so-perfect con-descending, Botoxed face of the governor of West Virginia.

"You'd better go now. Get yourself cleaned up," Cable said.

Song lifted her chin and blinked at the faces. "I'd like to 'pologize for my 'pearance and for what I jus' said and also for being alive. I jus' wanted a word with my husband, y'see."

Then Young Henry was there to take her by her hand. "She was in a bad accident," he explained to the assembly as he led her out of the office and down the steps and into the dirt. Faintly she heard Cable ask, "Did she say she wrecked my car?"

"How deep is the mine, Young Henry?" Song asked.

"About eight hundred feet down the shaft, ma'am."

"Should be enough," she said. "'Scuse me while I throw myself down it."

Young Henry tugged her toward the gate just as Bum stepped out of the bathhouse. "Hey, girl. I heard you were born rich. What's that like?"

Even through the muddle of drink and chagrin, Song's New York smarts clicked into gear. "Pretty nice. I heard you were born stupid. What's that like?"

Bum reddened as a storm of guffaws erupted from the bathhouse. "Guess she got you told, Bum!" someone yelled.

His mouth pinched, his small eyes burning into Song, he said, "You go on now, girl. You'll hear from ol' Bum one of these days."

"Cable should fire that man," Song muttered as Young Henry steered her through the gate.

"Bum and Mr. Jordan were best friends in high school," Young Henry said.

"He's still a monster."

"Yes, ma'am. And now you done got him mad at you. Anything else you want to do in town today?"

"Guess I've done it all. Take me home, Young Henry."

"That's what I've been trying to do the last hour, ma'am. I surely have."

THAT NIGHT WHEN Cable came home, Song had gone to bed, sleeping the sleep that ouzo provides. When she rose, bleary-eyed from drink and teary-eyed with shame, she saw evidence that he'd slept on the couch again, but there was otherwise no sign of him. A quick check revealed his truck was gone.

But it's Saturday. Song lurched into the kitchen and consulted the calendar for confirmation. When she picked up the mine phone, Mole answered.

"Where's Cable?" she demanded.

"In the mine."

"It's Saturday."

"We run a shift on Saturday, ma'am."

"Tell me, Mole, what do the women in this town do since their men are always at work?"

"Why, I guess they take care of their kids, ma'am."

"And if they don't have kids?"

Mole was silent for a long second, then said, "Wives around here either got kids or are working to get some."

"So they just stay at home?"

"They also go to church."

"Is that any kind of life?"

"I ain't heard no complaints lately."

Song slammed down the phone, the sound making her head feel like it was going to burst.

"I hate this place," she whimpered, sinking to the floor. "I really, really do."

Twelve

They next person to visit Song arrived in a pink Cadillac with fins that looked like they belonged on a giant shark and enough shiny chrome to cause temporary blindness. When it stopped, the smell of burnt oil wafted across the porch where Song was sitting. She had been moping there since her call to Mole. While she waved the vapors out of her eyes, the man Song had last seen working on the sign in front of the church stepped out of the Cadillac. He identified himself, with a slight bow, as the Reverend Theodore Edwards. "They call me Preacher," he said. "The inevitable nickname."

Song winced in pain with every word, regretting yesterday's encounter with Omar's ouzo.

Preacher was short, portly, and had a face the same color as his car. He also had sad but hopeful eyes. He looked up at Song, who was standing on the porch with her hand on one of its columns, mainly to stabilize herself. Despite a night's sleep, many ibuprofen tablets, water, and coffee, the effects of the ouzo were still pronounced. It was vicious stuff.

Preacher doffed his hat, which was actually a black miner's helmet. He was wearing khaki work clothes, a thick leather belt, and heavy boots.

"Mrs. Jordan, as you surely know, I lead the Highcoal church. I trust I'm not disturbing you."

Song fully expected to be preached at, and she wasn't in the mood, not even close. When she didn't reply, he said, "I'm off to work shortly, so I swan I won't take more than a minute of your time." He held aloft a brown paper bag and then handed it up to her. "My wife sent along this complimentary sample set of cosmetic products."

Pleased, Song accepted the bag, then nodded toward the pink Cadillac. "Did your wife win that Cadillac by selling Mary Kay?"

Preacher chuckled. "Oh no, ma'am. The missus would never be able to sell enough in a little town like Highcoal. But to show her how much I appreciate her enterprise, I went out and bought this Cadillac for her. It was white, but Squirrel painted it pink."

"Well," Song said, "that was sweet of you, and I'm certain your wife appreciated it. Now, Preacher, I must confess I don't feel very well, so, if you don't mind, I think I'll go lie down for an hour. Or the rest of the day."

Preacher nodded toward the rocking chairs. "I understand, I really do, but do you mind if we sit and talk for a spell? I promise to be brief."

Song hesitated. Then, recognizing the futility of putting the preacher off, she said, "Okay. Five minutes. No more."

Preacher nodded, then climbed up the steps and sat down in one of the rockers, taking a red bandana from his back pocket and mopping the sweat from his forehead. Obviously the Cadillac did not have air conditioning. Song sat down on an adjoining rocker and held her head while waiting for whatever came next.

"May I call you Song?" Preacher asked, "or would you prefer Mrs. Jordan?"

"Song will do," she sighed.

"I like your name. It sounds, well, musical."

Song lifted her head. "I used to sing a lot when I was little," she confessed. "My dad couldn't shut me up."

"Is that why you're called Song?"

"No. It's my mother's family name."

Preacher nodded and smiled agreeably. "Anyway, I should like to hear you sing some time. When you're feeling better."

Song couldn't resist a question. "Tell me, Preacher, do you actually work in the mine or do you just go inside to preach?"

"Not much time for preaching, I fear. Today they need somebody on the rock dust crew, and I can use the money. The missus and I have six children, three boys and three girls. It would be difficult to make it on a preacher's pay. As for the mine, the men think I'm lucky to have around. They figure the Lord will keep me safe, and them too. I hope they're right."

"I hope they're right too," Song said. "Now, Preacher, you promised to be brief."

"Indeed I did, and I shall. People here use me as a resource in many ways, not just for spiritual matters. Do you understand what I'm getting at?"

Song raised her eyebrows, which also hurt. "You're Highcoal's version of Doctor Phil?"

"Precisely! If there's anything I can perhaps help you with . . ."

Song slowly shook her head, lest her brain shatter. "Nothing immediately comes to mind."

"I heard you were a bit unsettled yesterday."

"Unsettled? Yes, I suppose I was. Let's see. I was in a wreck, sat in cow poo, and Omar got me drunk. Then I embarrassed myself in front of Cable's foremen, the mine owners, and the governor of this great state who, shall we say, has known my husband in the biblical sense. Yes, I guess you could say I was unsettled, Preacher. And your point would be?"

Preacher had the pained expression of a man who knew his plans were not going well. "I've counseled Omar on the strong drink he keeps under his counter. It's wicked stuff. Not that it isn't good, mind, but it's not for everybody and certainly not in the middle of the day."

"I applaud you for your wisdom," Song said, settling into the rocker with her eyes closed. A fly landed on her nose and she could not summon the energy to wave it away. Surreptitiously, Preacher did it for her.

"About the meeting you interrupted," Preacher went on, then waited until Song opened one rather bloodshot eye. "There's something I think you should know. After the governor left, the owners in attendance thoroughly chastised Cable and his foremen. It had nothing to do with you, dear lady. The mine, you see, has not been producing enough of a certain kind of coal."

Song allowed Preacher's words to filter through her foggy brain. When it finally did, she opened both of her eyes, and said, "Wonderful news. Let me tell you a secret, Preacher. I'm going to do everything in my power to convince Cable to move to New York City. If he manages to get himself fired, I would be a happy woman."

"But, my dear, Cable *must* stay here! The people of Highcoal depend on him. If Cable was to be sent packing, Atlas would bring in another manager who would push production and forget safety entirely. Men might die, families would be broken, the town would suffer in so many ways beyond counting. I prayed about this and the answer was for me to come and speak to you."

"Let me see if I've got this straight. God sent you to me so that I would keep Cable in Highcoal?" She would have laughed, but it would have hurt her head too much. "I'm sorry to have to tell you this, Preacher, but apparently the Big Guy Upstairs hasn't been paying attention to the situation. Cable and I aren't agreeing on much of anything right now."

"He loves you, you know," Preacher said.

"Then he has a funny way of showing it."

"God?"

"Cable. Stay focused, Preacher."

"So you won't help him?" Preacher asked.

"God?"

"Cable."

"Well, sure. I'll help him move."

"Oh, that is so sad!"

Song allowed a patient sigh. "Preacher, be reasonable. I don't like this place and the people here don't like me. I just don't fit in. You've heard the gossip, haven't you?"

"I never believe gossip."

"But you've heard it, right? I'm a pure snotty little witch, correct? That was yesterday. Today I'm probably being called a pure drunken, snotty little witch who rolls around in cow poo. How do you expect me to recover from that?"

Preacher shook his head and stood up. "I have failed in my mission."

Song also stood, though slowly so as to not move her head too quickly. "I'm sorry."

"May I suggest something, Song? I have discovered it works nearly every time when a marriage is in trouble."

"Prayer?" she supposed.

"Makeup sex."

This time Song couldn't help it. She laughed, even though it hurt her head to do it. "I like you, Preacher, even if you do hear heavenly voices telling you to do strange things."

"Those heavenly voices are the result of prayer. You should try it. When's the last time you prayed?"

"I can't remember. Do you think God would get rid of this hangover if I asked Him?"

"Probably not. Hangovers are like rainbows. They exist to remind you of something important."

"Oh, believe me, Preacher. It's working."

"But you can pray for other things. Your marriage, for instance, and perhaps the grace to give the people of Highcoal another chance. We're not so bad, once you get to know us. We all have our little idiosyncrasies, but, for the most part, we're not completely crazy."

"Good-bye, Preacher."

"Good-bye, Song. Remember, when life deals you a bad hand, don't throw it in. Play it like it's four aces."

"Sounds like a sure way to lose, Preacher."

Preacher shrugged. "That depends on how bad you want to win."

"Thanks for the cosmetics."

"Don't forget my advice about the makeup you-know-what. And the prayer. God would like to hear from you. He has a plan for you, you know. He has a plan for all of us."

"If so, I think I'd like for Him to change it. So far, it's not working."

"Give it a chance. Put Him in the lead."

"I'll give that some thought. Thank you for coming, Preacher," Song said, and meant it.

IT WAS LATER that afternoon that Song rose from her bed at the honk of a horn and looked out the window. It was Squirrel Harper driving his tow truck with Cable's roadster behind, Young Henry in its driver's seat. When Song came outside, Squirrel doffed his battered old hat.

"All cleaned up, ma'am. I even got that scratch off the bumper."

While Squirrel beamed at her and Young Henry watched, Song inspected Cable's car and was amazed at its restored, pristine condition.

"I had Chevrolet and Ford scrub on her good," Squirrel said. "Does it please you?"

"Absolutely," Song said. "Just tell me how much. Whatever it is, it's worth it."

"Why, there's no charge, ma'am. My boys and me, we were happy to do it for you."

Squirrel and Young Henry disconnected the tow bar on the roadster, and Squirrel climbed in his truck. He gave her a thoughtful look. "If there's anything else I can do for you, ma'am, you got it. All you need to do is ask and me and my boys, we'll be along to help you."

Song was a bit astonished. "Squirrel, why are you being so nice to me?"

"Why, because you're a nice lady. You're about as nice a lady as I reckon I ever knowed, outside of my boys' mother. Cable is surely lucky to have you. You take care, now, you hear?"

"You too, Squirrel."

"I reckon I will," he said. "Just like I know Cable will take care of me. I'm going back to work in the mine."

"Aren't you a little too . . ." Song stopped herself before she completed the question, which she realized was impertinent.

But Squirrel finished it for her. "Too old?" He grinned. "Well, Cable needs help, so I reckon I'll load some coal for him, at least until he gets some youngsters trained. My boys are thinking about taking a red cap class so's they can learn to mine some coal too. Coal mining's honest work, Mrs. Jordan. Truth is, I've missed it. It gets in your blood, I reckon." He gave her a little salute. "I'm glad you came to Highcoal, ma'am. You're good for us, you might say. You've shook things up and that, like Martha Stewart says, is a good thing."

"You know who Martha Stewart is?"

"Sure. She spent a little time in one of our jails, you see. I think she halfway liked it. We sure liked her being here. It was an honor, just like having you here."

And with that, Squirrel drove off, his tow truck rattling until it was out of sight. A tear trickled down Song's cheek and she wiped it with the back of her hand. Young Henry eyed her curiously.

"Are you sick, ma'am?"

"Oh, I don't know, Young Henry. Maybe I'm just feeling sorry for myself, and maybe angry at myself too. Lots of people have been nice to me here and

I've been trashing them left and right. I don't know what's gotten into me. I'm not a bad person. I guess I'm just sad—nothing's what I expected."

"Yes, ma'am. But things will get better, I swan. I mean, if you try to make them better."

Song gave that some thought. "You're a wise man, Young Henry."

"I played one in the Christmas play, ma'am. A wise man, that is. I brought the gold to the baby Jesus."

"Typecasting," Song said, then headed inside to use the makeup Preacher had brought her and to get ready to make things better between a West Virginia man and a New York woman.

Thirteen

Cable returned just before eight p.m. Song had called Mole on the mine phone and asked him to let her know when her husband left the mine. Mole suggested twenty dollars ought to do it, and Song agreed to his extortion.

The dining room table was set with fine china, wildflowers in a vase, candles, and food from Rhonda's basket. This time it was fried chicken, hush puppies, baked beans, and coleslaw. Not exactly romantic dinner fare and laden with carbs, but Song put aside her misgivings and treated it like it was a meal from the finest restaurant in New York. She'd also opened the bottle of fumé blanc.

"What's this—" Cable began, dropping his hat on the banister post.

Song put her finger on his lips, then kissed him. "My way of apologizing for what happened yesterday," she said.

He wrapped his arms around her and sank his nose into her hair. "Mmm . . . you smell good."

She laughed. "You didn't like my perfume yesterday, eau de cow poo?"

"You are the only woman I know who could make even cow poo smell good." He touched her hair. "So soft," he marveled.

"Old Roy installed a water softener and a hot water heater today. I'm in business in the bathroom. And Preacher's wife sent me some Mary Kay."

Cable took her in his arms and kissed her again, delicately at first, then with passion. She responded, running her hands across his back, pulling him into her before stepping back. "I'm as hungry for you as you are for me, Cable," she said. "But first, let's eat, drink, and talk."

"Talk," he said. "All right."

"It won't be bad, I swan," she promised as they sat down.

Cable was pensive during the meal, no matter the topics Song brought up, such as a discussion of the crystal stemware Rhonda had purchased for the house, which were exquisite and obviously handmade.

"They have glassblowers at Tamarack," Cable said. "That's where she got them, probably." He fell into silence, then looked at her. "Are you really going back to New York Wednesday?"

"I have to, Cable."

"I'm sorry about nearly everything."

"I know. So am I. It's all right."

"This is a good place to live," he said fervently. "Won't you give it a chance?"

"I have given it a chance, Cable. Mostly alone."

Cable looked away and shook his head. "I won't make excuses. I had a choice all week. Be with you or do my job. I chose to do my job. It's part of who I am."

Song reached across the table and took his hand. "I heard about the orders you can't meet. Tell Atlas Energy to go to blazes, Cable. We can live in New York. You can go to work for Hawkins-Song. We can have a wonderful life."

"I can't leave my miners. They depend on me."

"You'll leave them if they fire you."

He pulled his hands away. "They're not going to fire me because I'm going to deliver that coal."

"And in the process, you're going to wear yourself out."

"No, I won't." He closed his eyes and took a breath. "I will confess I'm tired. It's been a tough month."

Song stood and walked around the table. She made him turn his chair around, then crawled into his lap and wrapped her arms around him. "I love you with all my heart and soul," she said simply. "That's the truth."

He kissed her hard, then swept her into his arms and carried her upstairs. He gently placed her on the bed and began to undress her. She stopped him with a hand on his chest.

"I thought you were tired," she said.

"Not for this," he said, and proved it.

Afterward, she curled into his arms and wept tears of confusion. He turned her face to his and gently kissed her. "I love you so much."

"What are we to do, Cable? Tell me. What?"

"All I know is I can't live without you."

She held him as tightly as she could. They kissed, then made love again. Later while Cable slept, Song looked up into the darkness and wondered what had just happened.

Fourteen

Her luggage finally arrived, and for the church service, Song chose a gold silk shantung ensemble she'd brought in case she might be attending a party. How idiotic that was, she now realized. There were no swanky parties in Highcoal, only work and church. Still, she knew she would look dazzling in it.

But when Cable saw her, he frowned. "A bit fancy for Highcoal. Preacher's eyes will pop out of his head during the sermon, I can tell you that."

"Are you saying I should change?"

"Not at all. Come on or we'll be late."

In the church, the pews were packed, and men swiveled their heads as she walked arm in arm with Cable down the aisle to the front. The women looked too, and then they looked around the church to catch each other's eyes. Rhonda was in a back pew with Young Henry.

"Gol-lee," Young Henry said, loud enough to be heard three pews away. "She is *hot*!"

"You're in enough trouble as it is, Young Henry," Rhonda growled. "Don't push it."

"Why? What did I do?"

"Let's see. You wrecked Cable's car, you got Mrs. Jordan drunk, and you stole my truck."

"It was Omar who got Mrs. Jordan drunk," Young Henry pointed out.

Rhonda pinched his arm. "Don't argue with me, boy."

Omar and his wife were sitting nearby. "I was only trying to steady her nerves," he defended himself while his eyes were riveted on Song. "I must say. That is a most wonderful dress Mrs. Jordan is wearing this morning."

"Take care, husband," his wife said, "that it is only the dress you are admiring."

"All you husbands best put your eyeballs back in your heads," a woman growled low, but audible enough that most of the church assembly could hear her. A hundred or more female heads vigorously nodded in agreement.

The choir, dressed in maroon robes, regally marched down the aisle, and then Bossman entered the pulpit and offered a prayer. A spirited hymn by the choir followed. Everyone swayed to the music, while the piano player in front, a woman in a big red hat, banged away. Song stood close to Cable, feeling out of place, holding the hymnal but not joining in with the boisterous joy that seemed to fill the church. There was another hymn, another prayer from Bossman, and then Preacher entered in grand fashion. He was dressed in a maroon and gold robe, and armed with a big black Bible and his sermon.

Preacher's message proved to be on the responsibilities of marriage, and Song had little doubt it was aimed like an arrow directly at her.

"My text today comes from First John, chapter three, verse eighteen," he intoned. "'Let us not love in word, neither in tongue; but in deed and in truth.' Husbands, wives, how often have you said to your spouse, 'I love you,' without any thought other than to fill a lapse in your conversation, or as a temporary farewell, or sometimes—don't say it's never happened!—to avoid having to talk about something you'd just as soon not talk about?"

Preacher smiled down at his wife and six children, the oldest ten years old. The children were squirmy but attentive. His wife, a plump young woman who wore carefully applied makeup, was a beam of sunshine. Song envied her role within a happy family.

Preacher went on. "Oh, Lordy. If there's one of you married folks here today who has never strayed, either in thought or deed, in your marriage, who has never said words of love to your partner simply out of habit, you have my permission to stand up and walk out right this second, and God be with you."

There was a murmur from the congregation, but no one walked out. Preacher tapped his Bible. "There's a lot of trouble in the Good Book—God doesn't shy from it—so marriage is naturally included. Proverbs says a virtuous woman is a crown to her husband, but she that shames him is as rottenness in his bones. Now, ladies, you know what that means. When you go out while your man is in the mine, and you're dressed like you belong in the Bunny House in

Beckley, even though you're only going to Omar's or even the Wal-Mart, why he'll hear about it and it's going to make him ashamed in front of his buddies. There's no reason to do that. Take a look at Mrs. Jordan here. That's what you should aim for. Elegance, not looking like trash."

"Amen, Preacher!" a man cried out, followed by a rumble of masculine approval leavened by a few hissed words of feminine objection. Song smiled, unaware of the gender gap she had created by her appearance that morning.

Preacher's sermon went on, the subject still marriage, and his delivery became ever more passionate. "Women, honor your husbands with your chasteness. Men, honor your wives with your devotion. God has sanctified marriage from heaven. It is His institution, all part of His plan for your salvation. Marriage is holy!"

Preacher continued in that vein, receiving numerous amens and yes sirs and uh-huhs for his trouble, mostly from the men. The women remained subdued. When he was finished, Preacher smiled and said, "Well, that's my two cents worth on marriage this Sunday. Nobody's perfect is the bottom line. God doesn't expect you to be. He just expects you to keep trying. Amen to that, amen to you all. I'll turn it over to you now, Cable."

Cable stood up. Song thought he was going to affirm to Preacher what a fine sermon he'd just delivered, or perhaps even give a prayer or maybe add his praise of marriage, but instead he looked around the assembly and tapped his watch. "Time to go, boys." Then, to Song's astonishment, he bent down and kissed her on the cheek. "I'll see you later."

"Where are you going?"

He looked at her with a perplexed expression, then leaned in close to her ear. "Didn't I tell you? The mine's starting a half shift at noon, then we're all going to double back to do an evening shift. I've got a hoot-owl shift coming in too. I'm going to meet those orders."

"Cable, I can't believe this. You're really going to work on a Sunday? And leaving me alone again?" She tried to keep her voice low, but it came out a bit higher than she intended.

"I have to. All the other men are going to work. I can't take the day off."

"Even for us? What about that sermon Preacher just gave?"

Cable took her hands. "It was a good sermon. But this isn't a matter of choosing between you and my work."

"Yes, Cable. Yes, it is!"

Preacher was still in the pulpit. "There's men here who have to get their oxen out of the ditch, folks. God bless all you miners. Go dig yourself some good coal even if it's on Sunday. Amen!"

Bossman stood up. "Thank you, Preacher. We'll do it, I swan!"

The congregation started to applaud. Song wouldn't let go of Cable's hands. "How am I supposed to get home?"

"I lined up the constable to drive you. Look over there. See? He's waving."

"Cable, you can't spring something like this on me! I'm supposed to be part of your life!"

"I was going to tell you," he said sheepishly. "But then last night, it was so good to hold you again, I didn't want to spoil it. But, honey, listen to me. I've solved our problem."

Song stopped herself from saying the harsh words already in her mouth. "I'm all ears," she said dubiously.

"Let's have a baby. Then another one. Up to three, I think. Hillcrest would be such a great place to raise children. What do you say?"

Song opened her mouth but was momentarily at a loss for words. She sorted through a number of responses, including picking up one of the hymnals and hitting her husband over the head with it. After a few seconds of cooling down, she said, "Cable, pay attention to me very carefully." Her next words were enunciated one after the other. "We are not going to have children anytime soon, if ever, especially because you think they will solve our problems."

"Well, I just thought . . ."

"No. You didn't think. You're just trying to take the easy way out. Didn't I tell you there is nothing easy?"

"But, honey, it would be so much fun getting there." He whispered into her ear. "We would be in bed all the time."

"I'm not your slut, Cable!" Song erupted. "I'm your wife!"

As luck would have it, there was a pause in the congregation's excited buzz just in time for Song's words to ring loud and clear throughout the church. Song thought she even detected an echo. One and all turned to stare at her. She blushed and Cable mumbled, "I have to go."

Cable and his miners marched out of the church to cheers and tears like soldiers going off to war. Women waved, and little children chased after them. Shaken and angry, Song trailed along behind. Young Henry came up to her. "You all right, ma'am?"

"No, I'm not. But I don't want to talk about it."

Young Henry crept off and Constable Petrie stepped up beside her. He was in his constable uniform, his hat in his hands. "I'm your ride, ma'am. Anytime you're ready."

Song watched Cable and his miners trooping down the street toward the mine. "I don't know what to do," she confessed. "Should I follow after Cable and see him go below?"

"The tipple grounds are no place for that fancy suit, ma'am, nor those pretty pumps."

Song sighed. "No, I guess not."

The three women Song had met behind the church—Mrs. Carlisle, Mrs. Petroski, and Mrs. Williams—formed a phalanx between her and the constable's car.

"Mrs. Jordan, a word, please," Mrs. Carlisle said. "Not you, please, Constable. Girl talk."

The constable took a step aside.

"This is difficult for us, dear," Mrs. Carlisle began.

"You mean all the miners going off to work on Sunday?" Song asked.

"Of course not!" Mrs. Williams waved it away. "They have a job to do. No, someone must say something to you. As much as it hurts us to do it."

"You look wonderful in your fine outfit, Mrs. Jordan," Mrs. Petroski added. "But, I mean, really. What were you thinking wearing it to church?"

"You see, Mrs. Jordan," Mrs. Carlisle said, "there's a fine line around here between being well dressed and . . ."

"Overdoing it!" Mrs. Petroski blurted.

"Putting on airs," Mrs. Williams filled in.

"Being puffed up," Mrs. Carlisle completed. "Do you understand what we're getting at?"

"All the men think you're beautiful," Mrs. Petroski noted. "But all the women think you're trying to make the rest of us look bad. You must dress down, dear."

The constable stepped back in. "You ladies are out of line. Mrs. Jordan's ensemble is quite tasteful."

"Shut up, Constable," Mrs. Carlisle said. "This is between us women."

The constable looked straight at Song, who had been stricken into silence. "You ready to go home, ma'am?"

Song looked into the constable's cool, brown eyes and found her voice. "I don't belong here, Constable," she said.

"No, ma'am. Not with these hypocrites, that's for sure."

He tipped his hat to the trio of women and offered Song his arm. Song took it and numbly walked beside him to his car. She stopped and looked back at the women, then at the miners trooping off to work and their families heading in all directions, and the ugly black tower of the mine.

She squared her shoulders. "Take me back to Hillcrest, Constable," she said, and he did.

WHEN CABLE CAME home near midnight, he went straight upstairs to their bedroom. He pushed the door open and peeked inside, then switched on the light. The bed was neatly made and on the nightstand was an envelope with his name written in Song's handwriting. He opened the envelope and read the note inside:

Cable. I've gone back to New York. Don't call. Don't write. Don't follow. We need time apart. A lot of time. I have so much to think about, and so do you.

—Song

P.S. Whoever bet on four days wins. Wednesday was a half day and so was Sunday.

Cable sat down on the bed, holding the note. Then he let it drop to the floor. He lowered his head and put a hand over his eyes.

Don't call. Don't write. Don't follow. There had been nothing said of love, or affection, or even anger. Cable took a breath.

What have I done? He sat quietly for a time and thought about many things, rationalized them all, and allowed his heart to harden against the woman he had loved so much he had honored her with a marriage. *I've done only what I had to do*, he concluded.

After mulling it all over some more, Cable said aloud—just so he could hear the words and make them real, "She can just stay in New York. It's for the best. She doesn't belong here, and she was never going to fit in."

Then Cable reached over and turned out the light in the bedroom and in his heart. It was not an easy thing, but he pretended it was.

PART 2
THE RED HELMET

To wear your heart on your sleeve
isn't a very good plan;
you should wear it inside,
where it functions best.

—Margaret Thatcher

Fifteen

The party thrown by Charles and Miranda Delgossi at their New York apartment was at that stage when its host and hostess—and everyone present—knew they had yet another grand success on their hands. Charles and Miranda were inveterate party-pitchers, willing to throw one for nearly any excuse. To receive an invitation to a Delgossi party was to be handed a ticket to fun, to be seen by the in-crowd of the city, and perhaps to be considered part of the in-crowd yourself. The Delgossis knew a successful party depended on who was on the invitation list. Tonight, the attendees were clearly compatible, the hum of conversation at just the right pitch, and the laughter breaking out at perfect intervals. The hors d'oeuvres were disappearing at an appropriate rate, and the wine had received compliments by two of the most pompous *connoisseurs de vino* among them. It was a party certain to make the *Times*.

Fall was when the big books came out and the art and theater scene turned interesting. The Delgossi autumnal party was a herald for that special season and there was always a clamor to get on the invitee list. Many called and begged to come to the party, but few were chosen.

Among those chosen this year was Song. She suspected she was of interest to the Delgossis not only because she was the daughter of Joe Hawkins, or even for her rather remarkable achievements in the business and financial world, but because party-team Delgossi was aware of her surprise marriage to a coal miner and her subsequent dreadful experiences in deepest Appalachia. Such a story, if teased out of her, could by itself raise their party to another level. It was so deliciously amusing, the moneyed half-Chinese daughter of Joe Hawkins going ga-ga over a backwoods, moonshine-swilling mountaineer. She'd gotten exactly what she deserved, of course, and scooted home after only four days. That made the fun all the better.

Song was grateful for the diversion despite the fact that she was part of the entertainment. She had just sustained a period of astonishing creativity and productivity. She had convinced her father to acquire two companies, one holding an obscure patent for a lithium ion/polymer battery, the other holding patents for electronic polyswitches, thermistors, and connectors. Song had overseen the merger of the two companies and the subsequent production of the smartest little batteries ever known, and at a competitive price too. The orders had rolled in from nearly every electronics manufacturer in the world, with bids to buy the company in the general area of two billion dollars. Once again, Song's photo was scheduled to appear on the cover of *Fortune*. The title of the article was "Daring to Dream Small—How Song Hawkins Changed Our World." She was on a roll.

But for all her success since she had come back from West Virginia, Song was not happy. She had never quit anything in her life, yet she had run from Highcoal. It gnawed at her. Although she had buried herself in her work, she kept going over the events of her short stay in the hills. It was as if she was stuck in some awful repetitive memory loop: getting sick during the drive over the mountains, Bossman and his chewing tobacco, Hillcrest, the dirty water, the fatty food, Doctor K, and the dreary gossip. Then there was the idiot well-digger who'd tried to drill in Squirrel's front yard. She'd resolved that situation— the one thing she was proud about—but then there was the day she'd gone to the store to buy makeup. She'd been wrecked by a twelve-year-old, sat in cow poo, and snockered by the hardest liquor she'd ever drunk, given to her by a Lebanese so-called Christian! Then she'd embarrassed herself in front of Cable's foremen, his supervisors, and the governor of the entire state who, oh, by the way, was a former lover of her erstwhile dear husband. After that, Song had done everything she could to get her marriage back on track, including seducing Cable and then going to church with him, only to be abandoned again and graded by the local church ladies as improperly dressed. Was it any wonder she'd given up and decamped for New York City?

Yes? No? Song wasn't certain. All she knew was that she had been left unsettled by the experience. Somehow she needed to come to terms with it.

But never mind, she was at the Delgossis' party and determined to enjoy herself. She was dressed smartly in her most flattering black New York dress, set off with red stilettos and ruby jewelry (a gift to herself), which coincidentally matched the rather large glass of red wine she was holding. Her hair was shiny and swinging free rather than pinned up as she wore it at work. She knew she looked good and was irritated when she found herself wondering what Cable would think if he saw her. A picture of her soon-to-be-annulled-forever husband formed in her mind. He was wearing his ridiculous hat. *Go away, Cable.* She drank more wine.

Song looked around the room, filled with her fellow New Yorkers and a few out-of-town guests. When she had occasionally listened in, she was aware that the partygoers were all abuzz over the number one best-selling memoir titled *It Takes a Prison*, written by an unfairly jailed, rights-deprived man named Shazmaz Caliph, who incidentally also happened to be a murderer, serial rapist, child abuser, wife beater, drug dealer, and homegrown terrorist with a rap sheet that stretched for miles. *Prison* described in graphic profanity Shazmaz's life in a federal lockup, which was, according to his account, operated by fanatical Christians. Song made a mental note to purchase the book.

Song idly wondered if Omar would carry Caliph's book in his store, or if anyone in Highcoal would order it off the Internet, and she had to smile to herself and shake her head. The ravings of a lunatic professional criminal might be of interest to these sophisticated New Yorkers, but not to the mining families in Highcoal. Except perhaps the constable. In the short time she'd spent with him, it seemed to Song that Constable Petrie had a powerful intellect combined with a great deal of common sense. She considered what her fellow partygoers would make of the constable. Likely, they'd put him down as a hillbilly cop not worth their time or interest. Yet there they were, fascinated by the opinions of a lowlife loser and believing everything he had to say! Now that she'd given it more thought, Song decided she wouldn't buy the book. She was thinking she might like to read a history of the coalfields of Appalachia instead.

She was thinking about Highcoal again! *Just stop it. It's in the past. You'll never go back there. What's done is done.* She swore to herself that she would not read about the coalfields.

Kitty Franks, author of a best-selling novel titled *The President Sucks*, about a vampire who sucked the blood from a president, then became president himself, pressed into Song's hands the advance reading copy of her newest, *The Last Christians (Thank God)*.

"You'll love it, Song," she said, "especially considering your recent experience."

"What experience would that be?" Song asked.

"I'm sorry, dear, but your recent foray into Appalachia is very much part of the conversation in this room. How horrible was it?"

Before Song could reply, Franks went on. "I can just imagine how crushing it must have been in a place rife with ignorance and right-wing religious zealotry. My novel takes place in those same hills where you were almost trapped. It's about the religious screwballs who live there."

"Did you go there to research it?" Song asked.

"Go to that nasty place? No, I have better things to do with my time."

"I see." Song looked at the cover of the book, which showed a bullet-riddled wooden cross lying in a pool of blood.

"To summarize the plot," Franks went on, "the hillbilly children rise up and murder their parents."

"They do *what*?"

Frank's smile diminished, then widened. "Good. I've shocked you. Shock guarantees sales. The story begins with a schoolteacher from New York who finds herself assigned to a nasty, run-down school in Appalachia. She meets a man, a Latino, who is supporting himself as a carpenter. His backstory is that he was a hero of the revolution from Cuba who defected, but now after seeing the atrocious life of people in the United States, has come to regret it. He and the teacher become lovers. At her invitation, he instructs her students on the glorious lessons of Cuban socialism. Inspired, the children rebel against their parents, using their own guns against them. The parents are all slaughtered, then the repressive federal government comes in and kills all the children. It's a metaphor. I know you will identify with the teacher, dear," she said, then flitted off to collar another partygoer with her books.

Deliberately and with a great sense of satisfaction, Song dropped the novel behind a potted plant. She wondered what Preacher would say about the novel. Probably, she thought, he'd only shrug and go about his business. Novels were novels, and life was real, and Preacher had real work to do. Song allowed herself to recall Preacher for a moment. She'd liked the man, and thought she might have liked his wife and children as well, if she'd taken the time to get to know them. But now it was too late. She would never see any of them again, of that she was certain, and that realization made her sad. It also made her think of Cable. *Again.*

After Song had left Highcoal, she hadn't heard from her temporary husband for three long and miserable weeks. Sure, her note had ordered him not to contact her, but she never thought he'd take it so literally! That demonstrated more than anything else how he didn't really care about her. When his letter came, its contents, so cold and distant, were a shock:

Dear Song,

I've been thinking about what I did or we did, however you want to put it. It was all my fault from the get-go, getting married down in St. John and then bringing you to Highcoal and expecting you to want to stay here and have kids and all that. I grew up in this town and I love it, but how could I expect a New Yorker like you to like it? It was just plain foolish. I know that now and I'm sorry. I can't blame you for leaving ~~because~~. Maybe I'm hardwired or something, but I have to stay here and do my job as long as they'll let me. Anyway, the long and the short of it is if you want to take care of the paperwork, I guess I'm saying you can send it on.

With honest and true respect,

Cable

P.S. The constable told me what the church women said about your clothes. That wasn't fair. I got on their case and they said they were sorry.

Song had read the letter dozens of times, putting every word under her feminine mental microscope. She keyed in on the crossed-out word *because. Because what, Cable?* She had probably spent more hours worrying over Cable's missive than the acquisition of the two battery companies. At once enraged and heartbroken, she had called Saul Tollberg, the family attorney, and told him to get cracking with an annulment. Saul had asked her what she wanted the grounds to be, and then gave her a list of possibilities. She'd picked fraud, just like Chesney and Zellwegger, but told him to put her down as at fault.

"That's not wise, Song," Saul replied, but she told him to do it anyway. She knew Cable well enough to know he'd never sign anything that said he was dishonest. She'd take the hit, just to get the thing done.

How she hated that man! But then, when she least expected it, during a meeting, when she was on the phone, or walking down the street, she would recall him again, and that sweet dimple in his cheek. Who was seeing his dimple now? The divine Governor Michelle Godfrey? She took another drink, not even bothering to taste the wine, just getting it down her throat. She wished it was Omar's ouzo.

"A penny for your thoughts." Song looked up to find none other than Michael Carr, the man who had been her love interest before Cable, the man who'd stopped calling her, the man who'd thrown her out of his life like a dead mouse.

"A penny would be too much," she answered as she forced the image of Cable out of her mind—*poof*—like vapor.

"Why don't you let me be the judge of that?" Michael asked, in his smooth, dulcet tone, so unlike Cable's twang.

Michael steered her onto the balcony where the city lay beneath their feet. "I've missed you," he said.

"Then I suppose you should have returned my calls," came her clipped reply. "Or maybe you shouldn't have left the voice mail you finally did."

He took away her empty glass, then took her hands. Her immediate thought was that Michael's hands were weak and cool, not strong and warm like Cable's. She berated herself for making the comparison. Michael was here and now; Cable was there and yesterday.

"You can't know how much I regret that call," Michael said, his eyes turned puppy dog. "I was overwhelmed with work and was nearly out of my mind. It was all so oppressive, and I was angry at the world and lashed out at you. It was the dumbest thing I've ever done. Please let me make it up to you."

"You can start by getting me another glass of wine," she said, to buy time while she thought about where this was likely heading. Cable's face flashed in her mind again, his big dumb face. That stupid dimple. That crooked smile. *Go away, you dumb coal miner!*

"Hello? Song?" Michael was back with two glasses of wine. He peered quizzically at her. "Are you all right? You were far, far away."

She smiled. "I'm sorry, Michael. Lately I've been having trouble focusing. It's nothing, really." She accepted the glass of wine he was holding out to her. "Thank you."

"A delightful Sancerre," he said. "The Delgossis do not stint."

It was indeed good wine, and she appreciated it. Cable didn't have the slightest concept of what good wine tasted like. He just tended to toss whatever was in his glass down his stupid throat. *Stupid man. Stupid, stupid man!*

"Hello?" Michael said. "I think you were slipping away again."

She blinked back. "No, I'm here. How have you been, Michael?"

Michael clinked their glasses together. "A little lonely, I'll confess. But, no matter, here's to us, darling."

"Us?" she asked. "Is there an us?"

He produced his sad little-boy smile, which she had once thought was so endearing. That was before she'd seen Cable's smile. "Tell me everything," Michael said. "I've heard all the gossip, of course, and believed little of it. I'm on your side, Song. I always have been, even when you thought I wasn't. Tell me what happened to you in that awful hog wallow of a place and let me be your strong shoulder."

She started to deny him the pleasure, considering how he'd jilted her, but then she took a healthy swallow of wine and told him some of it—of the mine and the miners, of Doctor K and Squirrel Harper, and also about Young Henry, Rhonda, and Preacher. She was feeling just a little unsteady on her feet now. *Too much wine, girl*, she told herself. *You're vulnerable. Take it easy.*

Michael's response was, "If I may say so, it sounds like the makings of an excellent memoir. It has everything—pathos, humor, hillbilly rustics, and you, a bright city-fish dunked into dark coal country water."

Song giggled. "Michael, I'm just telling you about the people I met, not pitching a book."

He lowered his head in pretentious modesty. "You'll have to pardon me. As senior editor of Variant Press, everyone is always suggesting a book to me. My heartfelt apologies. Still, it would be a funny, clever book in the right hands, similar to the novels of Garrison Keillor where he slyly puts down country folk while pretending to praise them."

"I'm not a writer," she said firmly. "And I don't want to be one."

He looked at her through his soft brown eyes, so unlike Cable's hard blue orbs that could look right through you.

"What are you, Song?" Michael's eyes bored into hers. "Besides being drop-dead gorgeous, of course, and impossibly intelligent."

She looked out over the city. "I'm just me. You ought to know; we spent a lot of time together. Maybe you've forgotten."

"I haven't forgotten. I know I grossly underestimated you."

"Most men do."

"You're marvelous. What more can I say?"

Song had once lived for Michael's praise. "Thank you, sir, for your good opinion," she said. She felt as if she had climbed onto some kind of emotional roller coaster. Cable had never praised her, not like that. He probably saved all his praise for one of his mining machines. Or perhaps the governor!

"When I heard you had married that bumpkin," Michael continued, his voice going low, "I *knew* it wouldn't work. Trailer trash is not my Song's style. I told everybody that. For a penny, I would go to West Virginia and soundly berate that man even now."

Song imagined Cable being "berated" by the pompous editor. She also imagined Michael flying through the air after Cable tossed him like a human glider. It was imagination enough to make her smile. Michael, uncertain what her smile meant, frowned, then put down his glass, took her glass away from her, and slipped his arms around her. His cologne had a musky aroma. Cable never wore cologne, but he still had an intoxicating scent. It was, Song had decided, pure *man.*

But it wasn't Cable here with her, no. It was Michael Carr, her ex-boyfriend who'd dropped her like she was something nasty and distasteful, and not so long ago. Yet here he was, kissing her, his lips so gentle, with nothing of Cable's eagerness.

Song kissed Michael back, her needs propelling her.

"Mmmm," she said, as their lips parted. "Wow."

Michael instantly moved his hand to cup her breast, and she felt a thrill travel up her spine at his familiar touch. He whispered into her ear, "Why don't we go back to my place and use each other like we used to do? No strings attached. I sense you want that, and so do I."

She looked at Michael, and it all came back to her, the heartsick days waiting for him to call, and how she'd felt when she'd gone for a walk in Central Park and seen him arm in arm with another woman she recognized as a young, blonde intern at Michael's publishing house. They could scarcely keep their hands off one another, and she assumed they were headed to an afternoon tryst.

Then she thought of Cable and that first night they'd made love beneath the stars of St. John. Could anything *ever* top that? No. Nothing. Never.

Before Cable, she might have simply laughed Michael's tawdry suggestion off, or maybe even gone along just for the pure physical pleasure of it. But now, equating sex with utility was repellant. Cable, she realized with an arc of joy, had changed her and her expectations of the physical act of love, even including how it was described. She and Cable had soared, flowed, merged, even morphed in the arms of one another, but never had she felt *used.*

Song peeled Michael's hand from her breast and stepped out of his arms, allowing her anger to build until it was exactly where she wanted it. No matter the wine, she was completely in control.

"I have a better idea, Michael," she said carefully. "Why don't you go back to your place and do whatever you like with the person you love the most? *Yourself.*"

SONG WAS RETRIEVING her coat from the closet when she heard a familiar voice.

"Hello, darling. How *good* it is to see you again!"

She turned around and there was none other than the glorious governor of West Virginia, Michelle Godfrey, spilling out the top of a form-fitting red dress. Diamonds sparkled around her throat and on her fingers, and her platinum blonde hair was coiffed in a poufy style reminiscent of Marie Antoinette.

"I never expected to see you here," the governor said, flashing her perfect pearly whites.

"I think that's my line," Song replied while pulling on her coat. "This is where I live. You live in the hills of West Virginia. Yes?"

The governor's smile was locked in place, like an ivory trap that had been sprung. "Of course, darling. But I always come up for the Delgossis' autumnal party. It's a little reward I give myself."

"Good for you."

The governor sniffed the air. "I must say your perfume has improved."

Song thought of a cutting reply about the governor's perfect, no doubt surgically bobbed nose, but dismissed it as unworthy of her wit. "If you'll excuse me . . ." Song tried to brush by her to get to the door.

"The Delgossis told me all about you," the governor said, moving to stand in the way. She clearly wanted a confrontation.

Song raised her eyebrows. "Did they?"

"I received your entire bio. Your ups and downs, in business as well as romance. I must say I was quite surprised. And here I thought you were some college-aged trollop Cable had picked up on the rebound from me! You Orientals have such wonderful genes. It's nearly impossible to tell how old you are."

"I could say the same for you," Song replied. "But it would have nothing to do with your genes."

Godfrey laughed a big open-mouthed laugh. "The surgeon is a white girl's best friend, darling. Now, is what I was told true? You are the daughter of the great silver fox himself, Joe Hawkins? Such a life of privilege you've known!"

"I've made my own way. You might want to read *Fortune* magazine next month. I'll be on the cover."

"Too bad my subscription ran out. Shall I tell Cable you said hello? We've recently been spending a great deal of time together. He is such a lovely man, but sometimes, like all men, he can be foolish. I mean, marrying someone such as yourself so unsuitable to West Virginia, after all! It was obviously a cry for help. And Cable is so cute when he gets that hangdog look about him, don't you agree?" She opened her hands, better to reveal her voluptuous body. "It just makes me want to give him . . . well, whatever I have to give. As often as I can."

"I guess Cable's developed a taste for big women," Song replied

The governor was not fazed. "No, honey, that's not it. Unhappily for you, West Virginia men simply don't like runts."

"This conversation is useless. I'm leaving now," Song said.

The governor opened the door for her. "I suggest you stay in New York from now on, dear. Tough places like West Virginia, and strong men like Cable, are simply too much for you young, pampered city girls."

Song slammed the door behind her, then jabbed the elevator button repeatedly until its doors opened. Visions of Cable and Michelle Godfrey flitted through her mind. She imagined them at Hillcrest, in the high-ceilinged bedroom where she and Cable had made the sweetest love. How could he have betrayed her so, and with such a woman? She wanted to go to Highcoal, confront him, make him look at her as she really was, a strong woman, not the one who'd run away.

Once on the street, Song hailed a cab as only a seasoned New Yorker could, then climbed inside. When the driver asked her where she wanted to go, she burst into tears. Where she wanted to go was one thing. Where she *could* go was quite another.

Sixteen

Song stared through the rain-streaked window in her office and watched the sky and the streets and the buildings blend into the nasty gray paste that meant New York was having a bad weather day. She was holding a telephone to her ear, talking to her lawyer. It was two weeks since the Delgossi party and Cable still had not signed and returned the annulment papers. If he and Michelle Godfrey were such a hot couple again, she did not understand why he was dragging things out.

"I'd be happy to light a fire under him," lawyer Saul was saying. "One of my associates can call him every hour, or I can even send someone to West Virginia to stand over him until he signs. Have you ever thought he might be holding out in the hopes of getting his mitts on some of your money?"

Song considered that idea, then dismissed it. "Cable's got his flaws but a gold digger he isn't. As for sending someone to Highcoal, I'm not ready to harass him. Let's wait awhile longer."

Song could imagine Saul rolling his eyes. "All right. If that's what you want. But I wouldn't give him more than another week. After that we need to force the issue."

Song reluctantly agreed, then hung up. She looked at the stacks of paperwork she needed to wade through, and it made her angry that Cable's failure to sign the annulment was keeping her off balance. *What was wrong with that coal mining idiot?*

"There are some things a woman simply has to do for herself," she declared and picked up the phone and dialed the number at Cable's mine. As expected,

Mole answered and Song pictured him in his office as she'd last seen him, his pristine black helmet perched on the back of his head, a sardonic expression on his face.

"Let me speak to Cable," she barked. "This is Song. His wife, as you may recall."

"Oh, hey, ma'am," Mole cheerfully replied. "Cable's inside the mine. Can I take a message?"

Song's eyes narrowed. "Here's my message, Mole." She still couldn't quite get over the fact she was talking to a man named Mole. She took a breath and continued. "You tell him to sign the annulment papers or I'm going to send a man named Vinny to fit him into a pair of concrete boots."

There was a slight pause, then Mole chuckled, and said, "Oh, I get it. Like *The Sopranos*, huh? I think I seen the annulment on his desk. I'm pretty sure he hasn't read it yet."

"How about you? Have you read it?"

"Sure have! It's pretty dull, mostly, but there are some good parts too. Just like a Grisham novel."

Song held her head. "I'll tell my lawyer. Maybe it will encourage him to moonlight as a novelist. Who else has read it?"

Mole produced a giggle that had the effect on Song of someone dragging their fingernails over a blackboard. "Nobody, just me," he said, "but I told nearly everybody in town what was in it. Well, I told Mrs. Williams, which is like telling everybody. Fraud as grounds is interesting. You got that from Renée Zellweger and Kenny Chesney, right? Considering they also got themselves married in St. John, there is more than a little irony in your choice."

Talking to Mole was like talking to a backwoods frat boy. "Do me a favor, Mole. Tell Cable to stop wasting time and sign!"

"Well, ma'am," he replied, lowering his voice to a confidential level, "if you want me to do some work for you, I mean with Cable and all, I guess I could. I mean, for a consideration."

Song sighed. "You want me to pay you?"

"A man usually gets paid when he does something for somebody else what ain't necessarily a friend, if you get my meaning."

"Blackmail," Song muttered.

HOMER HICKAM

"Technically, I'd put it closer to extortion," Mole replied, after a moment of thought.

Song had to chuckle. "Consider myself extorted. There's a hundred dollars in it if you get Cable to sign within a week."

"One thousand dollars," Mole instantly counteroffered. "It ought to be worth that much to you."

"I don't think I want to do business with you after all, Mole."

"Suit yourself, ma'am. Have a nice day." He hung up.

Song angrily thumbed the off button on her phone, then, after looking it up on her computer, punched in the number for the Cardinal Hotel, got Rosita, and asked for Rhonda. "Well, ain't this a surprise!" Rhonda said as soon as she picked up. "How you doing, honey?"

"Fine," Song said. "No, better than fine. In fact, I'm living the life of the rich and famous up here in the big city. Every day is nothing but limos, love, and laughter."

"That bad, huh?" Rhonda chuckled. "What's up?"

"Nothing, really. It's just that I left so quickly . . . I should have at least thanked the people who were nice to me. That's been on my mind lately. You were one of them, Rhonda. So, from me to you, thank you."

"Well, thanks, sweetie, but I wasn't nice to you at all. I gossiped about you, even called you snotty. That wasn't even close to true. You showed that by going up against Bashful and standin' up for Squirrel on Harper Mountain. I was impressed by that, and I should have told you. I'm real sorry about what I said, and if it had anything to do with you leaving, I'll never forgive myself."

"It wasn't you or anybody else. It was just me and Cable."

"Ah, the travails of romance. That Cable. He can be, well, such a man."

"You can say that again. How's Young Henry?"

"Getting taller, mostly. I can't keep him in pants, he's growing so fast. He's outside, playing touch football, only I think they're doing some tackle too."

"Sounds rough."

"It is. He might come in with a bloody nose, but that's what happens to boys. It's good for them. Do you want to hear about what Cable's up to these days?"

Song stared through the window as the rain beat harder on it. "No," she said. "I don't care anything about him."

"Lady, you don't fib too good," Rhonda replied. "He's working too much, of course. He's still missing his quota on that coal bound for India. But he has lots of orders besides that one. Gosh, the world is hungry for West Virginia coal these days. Who'd a thunk it? Anyway, most of the miners are doubling back nearly every shift. Old Squirrel even started mining coal again, only it turned out his back hurt too much to go inside and work under that low roof. So Cable put him in the preparation plant. That freed up a man to go underground. Here's some news. Cable's going to start a red cap class soon. He's only got four applicants, so I heard, which is too bad. He could use about twenty new miners."

Song watched the lowering clouds of the storm. The tops of the buildings just across the city canyon were obscured with a gray, ugly mist, and a cold wind was blowing raindrops sideways across her window. They sounded like wet bullets. "I'm sorry he's having such a tough time."

"Want me to tell him you called?" Rhonda asked.

"Rhonda," Song said, "this is a lot to ask, but is there some way you could get Cable to sign our annulment papers?"

"He hasn't signed them yet? And you claiming it was all your fault too!"

"Mrs. Williams told you, right?"

"Actually it was Mrs. Carlisle, but she heard it from Mrs. Williams who heard it from Mole. Anyway, I'll tell Cable to sign, but I imagine it's nothing he wants to hear. Truth is, I ain't seen him smiling much since you left. I do believe you broke his heart, darlin'."

"The only thing that could break Cable's heart is his coal mine." Then, letting her guard down for an instant, she said, "I guess I haven't been smiling much either."

"Well, there you go," Rhonda said. "What you ought to do, you want Cable's attention, you come back down here and get in that red cap class."

Song's laugh was bitter. "You might be onto something."

"I was just joking, honey."

"I know. Would you tell Young Henry I miss him? It's funny. I was only there for a few days, but I often think of him and Preacher and Doctor K and Squirrel. Even Omar, though he got me drunk."

"Well, I guess Highcoal's got its share of memorable characters," Rhonda said. "By the by, I've been working on recipes for low-fat, low-calorie meals. You ever come back, I'll try them out on you."

"I'm never coming back." The fury of the storm rattled Song's window. "I can't," she added in a small voice.

Rhonda was quiet for a moment, then said, "Governor Godfrey roared back into town the other day. She's been here quite a bit. She surely has an interest in this town. Or someone in it."

Song felt as if she'd been punched in the stomach. "Good for her," she managed.

"Sorry, honey. Just so you know the situation. You want to do something about it? Get your butt down here."

"I just can't," Song said.

"Suit yourself. Got to feed some hungry miners now. I'll tell Cable to do the right thing and sign those papers. Anything else I can do for you?"

"How about taking a baseball bat to the governor's bleached teeth?"

Song hung up to Rhonda's chuckle, then sat with her heart aching as she imagined Cable and the pneumatic blonde politician together. She looked at the paperwork on her desk, then swept it all away, the papers fluttering to her carpet. Norman, her assistant, stuck his head in, gawked at the mess, then said, "Your father called while you were on the phone. He'd like for you to visit him today if you can spare the time."

Song considered the litter on the floor. She needed cheering up, and there was no one who could do that so well as her father. "Call my driver; tell him to meet me at the door right away."

"Yes, ma'am."

"Then clean this mess up."

It felt good to order a man around, even if it was only Norman. She rose from her desk, grabbed her coat and umbrella, and swept majestically out of her office. Then she stopped and went back. Norman was crouched by her desk, carefully picking up the documents and sorting them as he went along.

"Thank you, Norman."

He looked up at her and smiled. "You're welcome, Miss Hawkins."

Song headed out again. Cable had broken her heart; Michael had broken her heart; every man she'd ever gotten close to except her father had broken her heart. But she wasn't going to let past history cause her to hate all men. Song was going to endure, and somewhere out there, she was certain there was a man for her, one that would love her for who she really was. She just needed to hang on and not settle for less of a man than she deserved. "Good-bye, Cable," she muttered in the elevator on the way down to the street. "Good-bye, good-bye, good-bye, and good riddance!" This, she swore, would be her mantra until that man's undeniably handsome face disappeared forever from her mind. She recalled the song Jim Brickman had sung for her and Cable on the beach at St. John:

> You and I were meant to be.
> With all my heart and soul,
> I give my love to have and hold.
> And as far as I can see,
> You were always meant to be . . . my destiny.

"Oh, sure, Jim," she growled. "Easy for you to say."

She hit the street and her limo pulled up to the curb, right on time. The driver must have been reading her mind because as soon as she slid into the back seat, he asked, "Want to hear some Brickman on the way out, Miss Hawkins?" She often requested him on longer drives. It always relaxed her.

But not today. Perhaps never again.

"I don't want to listen to anything. Just drive." She slumped into the seat and stared morosely at the gray rain.

JOE HAWKINS'S ESTATE was in Long Island's toniest neighborhood, locally known as the Gold Coast. She considered calling him on the way out, then decided to give herself some quiet time. The gray clouds matched her mood, and she settled down to wallow in a little honest misery.

Her father met her at the door, hugged her, then walked with her into the great room and had her sit down, while snapping his fingers at the beautiful young maid who whisked out of sight, quickly returning with two steaming cups of coffee, well laced with brandy. "Thank you, Miranda," he said, and provided her a wink as she curtsied and fled the room.

"You old dog," Song said, to her father's healthy laugh.

"She's a very good maid," he said, with an eyebrow cocked toward the door through which she'd disappeared.

"Russian?" Song asked.

"Hungarian, actually," Hawkins said. "She hopes to make it on Broadway. She's also quite a good singer and dancer."

"I'm sure," Song said dryly. The coffee and brandy were excellent, perfect in the midst of the raging storm outside.

Through a huge, reinforced double-paned window, Song could see the ocean rolling beneath the wind, foam flying off the waves and hurtling across the sand. Song had a feeling that her father had something to tell her that was going to be as tumultuous as the sea. Something was up. Something big.

Hawkins sat across from her, smiled, and ran a finger across his silver mustache, then cleared his throat a couple of times.

"What is it, Dad?"

He cleared his throat again. He was nervous, something rare for him. "Rumor has it you're going through a tough time," he said.

"Who've you been talking to?"

"The Delgossis."

Song puffed her disdain. "Ah. I just had a little dust-up with Michael, that's all, and then the governor of West Virginia. It made their party that much more interesting, I'm sure."

Her father rubbed his chin in a thoughtful manner. He did that long enough she was about to tell him to stop it. Then he abruptly said, "I love you, Song."

Song studied him. "Well, I love you too, Daddy. So what's this all about? You've got something to tell me. I'm here. I'm ready. Let's hear it."

Hawkins stopped rubbing his chin. "Since you came back from West Virginia, you've been more successful than ever. It's amazing what you've done, all the money you've made our company. I'd like to celebrate. Stay for dinner. We'll have champagne."

"I left a lot of work at the office," she said. "I need to get back to it."

"All work and no play makes my Song off-key."

She smiled. It was something he used to say when she was a child. She was always so serious about everything she did, her studies, her violin lessons, her chemistry set.

"I'm not off-key," she replied. "If you'd like to get into it—which I don't, really—I just feel unhappy with myself about what happened in Highcoal. I didn't handle it very well. Cable didn't handle it very well either, but . . ." She shook her head. "You know me, Dad, I understand business. But there I was, in a company town, and I not only didn't understand it, I made no attempt to figure it out. I just let my marriage unravel."

Hawkins nodded. "I liked Cable. I liked him from the moment I met him. He struck me as strong and sincere, but I could tell he was not street smart. I think it would be pretty easy to pull the wool over his eyes and cheat him. Still, I was happy you married him. I looked forward to getting to know him better, then I was going to toughen him up mentally, maybe even get him involved in our business, and let him make some real money."

"I'm sorry I messed up your plans for him."

"So you're just going to let him go? I had hoped this annulment business was to force him to leave Highcoal."

She leaned forward. "Daddy, please understand something. Cable doesn't want me. The only things that are important to him are his town and that coal mine. I don't even enter into his thinking. Better to just end this mistake now and get it over with."

"But you still love him . . . ?"

The rain drummed on the roof, and the mist that had obscured the city was now hiding the sea. "He had my heart," she said. "Completely had it. Nobody ever had it like that before. But he betrayed me."

"Maybe he didn't see it as a betrayal. Maybe he thought you would understand what he had to do."

"Stop taking up for him!" Song complained. "When I was with him in Highcoal, he treated me like I was nothing. He's never going to leave those hills, and I'm never going to leave New York. No amount of talk is ever going to change that. It's over. It's just over."

"Still . . . ," Hawkins began.

Song released a deep, exasperated sigh. "Still what, Daddy?"

There was a gleam in his eye. "There's Atlas Energy."

"What about it?"

"It wasn't easy, since you're the one in charge of property and acquisitions, but I went out and bought it."

Song thought she hadn't heard her father correctly. The storm was awfully loud. Thunder crashed around the old estate, and jagged lightning plunged into the sea. "You did *what*?"

"Atlas consists of three coal mines—two in West Virginia, one in Kentucky—and a number of natural gas wells. One of the two mines in West Virginia is the Highcoal operation." He smiled with satisfaction. "So I bought the company. It is my gift to you. You are now Cable's boss."

Song could only hope she was having a nightmare. "No!" she wailed at her father. "*Sell it back!*"

Hawkins's smile faded. "What? I couldn't do that. I'd lose too much money. I paid top dollar. It was the only way they'd sell."

"Daddy, why?" Song bleated.

Hawkins reddened at his daughter's obvious displeasure. "Because I got tired of seeing you mope around. That's why. Did you expect me to do nothing? Don't you get it? This way you can order Cable to New York. Or fire him, or do whatever you want with him. You're in the catbird's seat, darling girl. I did that for you."

Song wasn't sure if the thunder she heard was real or just in her head. She commanded herself to settle down. Even this could be fixed if she kept a level head. "Does Cable know?" she demanded.

"No, I figured I'd give you the fun of telling him. Nobody at Atlas knows. The company was owned by a consortium of energy companies called Taurus. I happen to be a friend of the owner—Frank Stewart's his name, lives in Montana—and he agreed to let me quietly peel Atlas out of his holdings. Atlas has operated independently of Taurus for years, so its managers don't have to know for a few weeks anyway. So, what do you think?"

She nodded toward the fireplace. "I think if I didn't love you so much and didn't know this was well intended, I'd use that poker on you."

"By purchasing Atlas, I've given you options," Hawkins replied, defensively. "But hitting me with a poker isn't one of them."

Song kept working to remain calm. "What you've done is your usual attempt to run and *ruin* the life of everybody who works for you." She sat back. "Look, I don't want to have anything to do with this. Just don't fire Cable, that's all I ask. Agreed?"

"Song," he said gently, "the truth is Cable is about to be fired anyway. Frank told me. Atlas headquarters intends to replace him with another man at the end of the quarter. Right now they're trying to find the meanest, most cold-hearted executive they can get to go to Highcoal and tear it apart and put it back together again. They intend to meet their orders, *all* their orders, even if they have to get rid of every man in that mine and start over."

Hawkins shrugged. "You know what? My first thought was, too bad for Atlas my daughter's not available for the job."

"That's not funny, Daddy."

"I guess not. But it made me laugh anyway."

Song puffed out an exasperated breath. "What a mess you've caused!"

Hawkins jutted out his chin. "No, you caused it by marrying Cable and then running away from him and coming back here where you've managed to depress nearly everyone in the company. Poor Norman is so nervous he tells me he has trouble sleeping. Since it was clear you intended to stay down in the dumps more or less forever, it was up to me to fix things. That's what I've done. I've given you power over Cable. So now I'm asking you, what are you going to do with it?"

"Nothing. I told you I want no part in this. You're on your own."

Hawkins, clearly angry now, reddened even more. "I'll take that answer as my spoiled, ungrateful daughter's reply. But as my employee, I'm going to ask you something and I want a response. What in your considered, professional opinion, should I do with Atlas?"

"Don't tempt me to say something crude," Song replied, then gave her father's question some thought. "All right. As your employee, I will tell you that your options are these. Do nothing, and let Atlas go about their business with uncertain results. Or send someone to Highcoal to figure out what the problem is, then fix it. In any case, my advice is to sell Atlas as quickly as you can. It's a turkey."

"If it's a turkey, it's your fault I bought it," Joe Hawkins growled.

Song stood up. "No, Daddy. You will not blame me for this."

Hawkins jumped to his feet. "I'm president of Hawkins-Song and I'm your father. I'll blame you if I want!"

"Good-bye, Dad," Song said over her shoulder as she strode to the front door. "I'm going back to work. Let me know what you want to do with Atlas. In the meantime, I'll be working on some projects that might make us some money, not lose it."

Hawkins went to the window to watch her climb inside her limo. After a few seconds, her window rolled down and a silvery disc came sailing out of it, splashing into a mud puddle. Then the limo pulled away, disappearing into the gray rain.

Curious, Hawkins got an umbrella from the stand beside the front door and went outside and retrieved the disk. It proved to be a Jim Brickman CD titled *Destiny*.

ALONE IN HER apartment overlooking Central Park, Song suffered through the night. She kept looking at the telephone, wondering if she should call Cable and warn him his head was on the chopping block. But in the end, she just couldn't do it. Likely, it would only precipitate Cable's doing something stupid like flying to New York and confronting his bosses. *Men belong in a zoo.* Evolution had done them no favors. Modern life required a vastly more complex approach to problems than bulling your way through them. Maybe it came from prehistory, when men had to go out to slay the mammoth for meat while women stayed in the cave. Killing something was direct and brutal while taking care of the fire, the meals, and the children required more sophisticated thinking. The women who couldn't do it were chased off by the other women. The men, on the other hand, kept the simplest of their fellows in the clan, if for no other reason than because they were amusing and were good at telling dirty jokes while waiting for the animal herd to walk into an ambush. The result had been a dichotomy of the sexes, with women seeing every facet of a problem and a desire to fix it, while men sometimes couldn't see a problem at all, and if they did, they tried to fix it with a stone ax or its modern-day equivalent.

That morning she had shared the elevator with Woody and Soon Allen. Soon had smiled shyly at her and said something in what Song suspected was Korean. Perhaps she had mistaken Song for a fellow countrywoman. In any case, Song smiled and nodded. Afterward, as Allen and Soon walked into Central Park, Song watched them. Where else but the city could you ride an elevator with a famous director and his wife/daughter? But it also made her chuckle. New Yorkers made fun of Appalachia and its kissing cousins but Woody and Soon, *no problem.*

Song checked her cell phone. There were three apologetic messages from her father. At her office, there was a big bouquet of roses on her settee as more evidence of her father's remorse. Song had decided to let him stew, then she'd call in her team and figure out how to unload Atlas on some unsuspecting investor. Norman buzzed her. There was a call from West Virginia, he said, a doctor. Song picked up and heard Doctor K's familiar voice.

"What a lovely surprise!" Song chirped.

"Song," Doctor K said grimly, "this is not a social call."

"More gossip about me, is there? At least this time you can't shanghai me to Harper Mountain." The doctor paused long enough for Song to be concerned. "Are you still there, Doctor K?"

"I have to tell you something," she said heavily. "There's been an accident at the mine."

Song had a sudden vision of Cable, his crushed body beneath tons of rock. She held on to the phone, her mouth gone dry, her breath caught in her throat, the scent of her father's roses suddenly funereal. *I loved him,* she realized while she waited for Doctor K to tell her how, even though she'd never really been a wife, she had become a widow.

Seventeen

The stately hymns had been sung, and now a hushed stillness filled the Highcoal Church and its pews of bowed heads and tear-streaked faces. Preacher mounted the pulpit and looked down at the flag-draped coffin surrounded by flowers.

"This much we know," he said with a sad smile. "As our dearly departed lived his life, so will there be a place for him in heaven. 'Let not your heart be troubled,' that's what Jesus said. 'In My Father's house are many mansions. If it were not so, I would have told you. I go to prepare a place for you.'"

Preacher looked into the bright sunbeams streaming through the stained glass windows, and rainbow colors played across his face. "Squirrel Harper lived and died with the assurance of this promise. Oh, it's true when he was a younger man, sometimes he ran a little 'shine. And I guess there were a number of women in the roadhouse on the way to Fox Run who knew his company back then. But Squirrel found his faith in time. He also raised a couple of good boys, Chevrolet and Ford, who, when their country called, weren't afraid to go across the ocean to fight for us. You know a man by his sons, I have always believed."

Preacher looked at Squirrel's sons, who were sitting together on the front pew. "You boys want to say a few words?"

A lanky youth with a shaved head stood and looked around the congregation. He was wearing jeans and a desert camouflage shirt. It was the eldest son, Chevrolet. "I appreciate what you had to say, Preacher, and you're right. My pa weren't no angel, but when we was little, he never beat Ford and me as much as we deserved, and anytime I ever got in a scrape, I knew my daddy was going to be there, taking my side. When Ford and me joined up, I swan if Daddy didn't try to join up too. They said he was too old, but he said he'd taken the measure of them blamed Viet

Cong and he reckoned he could do the same with them A-rabs. But the recruiter sergeant sent him on home. Still, weren't hardly a day me and Ford were over there we didn't get something from him—a letter, a box of Girl Scout cookies, whatever. We had the best daddy in the world."

Chevrolet sat down, and Ford stood up. He was a little shorter than his older brother, and a little thinner, but otherwise they looked much alike. "Daddy always said to me, Ford, don't you worry what other folks think about us. All them other folks, they can just go to . . . well, you know. Daddy wanted Chevrolet and me to know we were as good as anybody else. Thank you for that, Daddy. Now, you go on and be with Jesus. We'll do as good as we can down here until we get to come up to heaven and be with you and Mama too. I hope she fixes you her special cornbread you always liked so much."

Ford sat down. There was much sniffling going on in the church, and Song was one of the chief snifflers. "That's so sad," she whispered to Rhonda, who was sitting beside her. Young Henry was on her other side. He was bawling into a red bandana.

Cable was sitting in the front row with the two brothers. Governor Godfrey was sitting in all her blonde glory beside him. She wore a black turtleneck and a black Versace leather coat. Song had to admit the woman at least had some style. When Cable looked up and turned his head, Song saw that he looked tired and drawn. Still, as much as she wished it weren't so, her heart sped up at the sight of him. As far as she knew, he hadn't yet realized she had come to the funeral. She had ordered Rhonda not to say a word. Remarkably for Highcoal, it appeared her secret was being kept.

There was an explosive sob behind Song. Startled, she looked over her shoulder and saw Burn stand up. "He was a good old boy, Squirrel was!" Bum cried. "And now Cable done kilt him deader'n a hammer!"

"Hush now, Bum," Chevrolet called out.

"I ain't gonna! Somebody got to tell the truth around here."

"Stop making a fuss," Ford said. "Daddy and you never got along."

"That ain't so!" Bum stood up and pointed at Cable with a trembling finger. "You better stop killing us, Cable!"

Cable stood and, facing the back pews, calmly said, "Bum, this isn't the time."

"Why the hell not?" Bum pushed his way into the aisle. He balled his big fists and started toward Cable, who stepped out to meet him. Bum stopped short, and then whined, "Some day you'll get yours, teammate!"

"Go home, Bum," Cable said gently. "And sleep it off."

Bum stormed out of the church, leaving the congregation shaking their heads. Preacher interrupted the silence, saying, "Since you're up, Cable. Maybe now would be the time for you to say a few words."

Cable nodded and rested his hand on Squirrel's casket before climbing into the pulpit. His eyes slid past Song, then came back to her. Surprise registered in his expression, then he looked past her, into some other place, and said, "There was never a better man than Squirrel Harper. My daddy sure loved him. They were buddies in the mine. Dad ran a miner, Squirrel a shuttle car. Boy, they sure loaded some good coal in their day."

Cable took a breath and went on. "Maybe Bum's right about something. I don't run as safe a mine as I should. I already said it privately, but now I want to say it where everybody can hear. Chevrolet and Ford, I want you to know I take full responsibility for your daddy's death. I'm the mine superintendent. If any man is hurt in my mine or, in this case, at the preparation plant, it's because I didn't do something right."

"No, Cable," Bossman said, standing up midway back in the pews. "This ain't your fault. You didn't kill Squirrel. Sometimes bad things happen, that's all." He looked around until he saw the MSHA inspector. "We all know Einstein—I mean Mr. Stein—is the best investigator in the world. If he says Squirrel tripped coming down those steps on the outside of the preparation plant, then that's what happened."

Einstein stood up, and his angry little eyes glared at Bossman. "My report reflects the facts as far I know them. That's all. Nothing more."

"Well, sure, Einstein," Bossman said, "we all know you ain't gonna land on Cable's side too often. But I reckon you got my meaning, sir. Squirrel died in an accident, nothing for Cable to be beating himself up over."

"That I will stipulate," Einstein said, and sat down.

Cable nodded toward both men. "Thanks, Bossman. And thank you too, Mr. Stein. Squirrel Harper was a man of honor and a man you could trust. In short, he was a coal miner. A coal miner may die, but death can never destroy how he lived, or why. God in His wisdom provided this country with the

American coal miner who glories in loading good coal! Sure, it's hard work, but there is a beauty in anything that's hard if it's well done. We know this much for certain about Squirrel. He loved his family. He was a man of integrity. And he was a man who laughed and knew how to tell a good story. Of course he could. He was a West Virginian!"

Some people chuckled and there were a few amens.

Cable looked across the people in the pews. Once more his eyes landed on Song, lingered on her momentarily, then roved on. "Here, in this glorious and beautiful and sometimes fearsome place of mountains and mines, there are still people like Squirrel, people who yet believe in the old ways, the old virtues, the old truths. They still lift their heads from the darkness to the light and say for the nation and all the world to hear: We are proud of who we are. We stand up for what we believe. We keep our families together. We trust in God." He took a deep breath. "And we are not afraid."

Cable went back to his seat. Preacher climbed into the pulpit while the choir stood and, with the congregation in full throat, began singing anthems of joy. When Young Henry handed her a hymnal, Song sang her heart out too.

The funeral was done and Song walked out, the constable suddenly appearing by her side. She saw why. Just as the last time she had attended the church, the trio of church women awaited her—Mrs. Carlisle, Mrs. Petroski, and Mrs. Williams. They did not look happy.

"We don't know what to call you," Mrs. Williams said. "Are you still Mrs. Jordan?"

Song was tempted to walk right by them, but she didn't. She didn't want to give them the satisfaction. "Just call me Song," she said. "And I'm sorry if I didn't wear the right clothes again. It doesn't matter. I'm not staying. I'll be leaving in a couple of hours."

"Preacher gave us what-for because of what we said to you the last time," Mrs. Petroski said. "So did Cable."

"Can you forgive us for being so catty?" Mrs. Carlisle asked. "It weren't right. We were raised better than that."

"What it was, we was jealous," Mrs. Williams said. "Our men were breaking their necks looking at you. But that was their fault, not yours."

"Preacher told us to read our Bible and we did," Mrs. Petroski went on.

"Proverbs says anger is cruel and fury overwhelming, but who can stand before jealousy?"

"We're awful sorry!" the trio bawled in unison.

Song couldn't think of a snappy reply. "Thank you. I accept your apology."

The church women all required a hug and Song gave it to them. "We wish you would come and live amongst us," Mrs. Williams said, wiping at a tear. "I swan."

"Maybe if I'd been a little stronger . . ." Song began, then shook her head. "Good-bye, good-bye, and good-bye."

"Please come back and visit us any time," Mrs. Carlisle called after her, while the two other ladies eagerly nodded their heads in agreement. One of them also said very softly, "You look real pretty today, honey."

The constable escorted Song to the Cardinal Hotel, where she'd taken a room. "Them church ladies are nice, pretty much," he said, "if they can keep their mouths away from mean gossip. They work hard for the poor families in the county, and, let me tell you, there's a bunch that ain't doing too well, especially with meth and OxyContin eating so many folks up these days."

"Drugs here?" Song was a bit startled.

The constable shrugged. "I'm the boy at the dike with his finger in the hole, only there ain't no hole and there ain't no dike. It fell down a long time ago. These hills got flooded with drugs when the mines started closing back in the 1970s. People were just desperate and wanted to get numb, I guess."

"But now the mines are back."

"Yes, the thing is, people don't trust them to stay back. Generation after generation around here, it's all boom or bust." The constable wearily shook his head. "When I read about how Congress and the president are worrying about making sure the country has enough energy, or wringing their hands over Social Security, or proposing free medical care for everybody, I just get mad. None of that is ever going to happen if the coal miners in this country one day decide they've had enough. They're close to that now. Washington better start paying some attention to the folks down here or the economy is going to turn into an even bigger mess than it already is."

"You should run for office, Constable Petrie," Song said, impressed by his little speech.

The constable chuckled mirthlessly. "Aw, I'm just shooting my mouth off.

As long as I'm doing that, I have to tell you something. I'm not so sure Squirrel died in an accident."

Song stopped and stared at the constable. "What do you mean?"

"Squirrel was sure-footed for an old coot. It was raining that day and maybe the steps were a little slippery, but to go over a rail like that . . . I think Einstein was a little suspicious too."

"Why are you telling me this, Constable?"

The constable scratched up under his cap. "People around here would go a little crazy if I said to them what I just said to you. They'd start accusing everybody under the sun. You know how Highcoal is. But you're from the outside, and I guess I just had to tell somebody what I was thinking."

"Thanks, I guess," Song said, frowning. "So what are you going to do?"

The constable puffed a short, exasperated breath, then shook his head. "Nothing I can do, I don't reckon, except stay on the lookout for anything suspicious."

"Do you suspect anybody in particular?"

"No. Squirrel worked alone, tending to the equipment, which runs pretty much automatically. Cable used to require two men in there, but he's so shorthanded, he doesn't have that flexibility. Stan Stanvic's the supervisor in the plant and mostly mans the computers that operate the place. He weighs nearly three hundred pounds. I doubt if he could climb up to where Squirrel fell, not without a heart attack, anyway."

"Who found Squirrel?"

"A truck driver who was there to pick up a load. Foureyes. I think you know him. My guess, Squirrel had been dead for a couple of hours when Foureyes spotted him lying in the dirt back behind the coal bins. Foureyes is a pretty simple soul, so I don't think he had anything to do with it. Stan said he hadn't seen Squirrel most of the day, but that wasn't unusual. Squirrel just did his thing, keeping everything rolling along. And now he's dead."

Song thought it over. "Did Squirrel have enemies?"

The constable cocked his head, then nodded. "I guess he had a few. The Harpers have been in these hills for a long time. You surely recall Bashful the well driller? He and his family have no love for the Harpers. They've been arguing about this and that for a long time. Squirrel said he thought Bashful needed killing, and Bashful called the state boys to swat him away. But I checked it out and Bashful was nowhere near the mine that day. He was out trying to drill in somebody's apple orchard or some such. Anyway, he never struck me as a killer, just sneaky and dumb."

Song considered telling Constable Petrie her father was the proud new owner of Atlas and maybe he could send someone to help the constable look further into Squirrel's death. But she held back. If the constable said there was no evidence, just his suspicions, then she thought there was probably little or nothing an investigator from the outside could do.

"Well, good luck, Constable," she said at the door to the hotel. "I hope you catch your killer or at least find out for certain it was an accident."

He studied her. "I apologize for dropping all this on you, ma'am. It'll all come out, one way or the other. Highcoal isn't a place to keep secrets for long. Anyway, I hope you find some happiness back there in New York. I surely do."

She smiled a sad smile. "Sometimes happiness is to be found in our work, Constable. That's how I see things these days."

He tipped his hat to her. "If I can ever do anything, big or small, for you, just let me know. You're one of my favorite people in this world, ma'am, and that's the truth."

"Really?" Song sounded and felt like a little girl around the big cop.

"Really," the constable said, smiling.

"Maybe you can do something for me. Watch out for Young Henry. Don't let him get into any trouble."

"Oh, he'll do fine, ma'am," the constable said. "Most boys around here do fine if we can keep them off the drugs."

"That's what I mean."

"You can count on me," he said, then tipped his hat again and walked away. Song already missed him.

WHILE SHE WAS packing, there was a rap on Song's door. It was Rhonda. "There's somebody downstairs to see you, hon'. It's Cable."

Song forced herself to be resolute. "I don't want to see him. Tell him I'm sorry."

Rhonda looked at her, opened her mouth as if to argue, then closed it. "I'll tell him."

CABLE WAS IN the parlor, still in his black funeral suit. "She said she doesn't want to see you," Rhonda said from the stairs. When Cable tried to go past her, she put her hand on his chest and gently pushed him back. "Let her be, Cable. You had your chance with her. Let her go."

Cable's eyes changed from determined to sad. Rhonda patted him on the arm. "Go on home, now. You gave a great speech in church today. Squirrel would have been proud. But go on home, Cable, or you'll ruin what's turned out to be a pretty good day, all things considering."

CABLE WAS OFF the Cardinal's porch and walking toward his truck when the door of the hotel opened.

"I just have a minute."

Cable whirled about, then whipped off his hat. His eyes soaked in the sight of Song, then he walked to the bottom of the porch steps and looked up at her. "I just wanted to tell you I'm glad you came. The first day after he came back to work, Squirrel told me how much he liked you. He said I was a pure fool to let you get away."

"Well, I liked him too," Song said. She waited, and when Cable didn't say anything else, she said, "Well, good to see you, Cable. Take care of yourself. I have a car coming. Got to finish packing."

"Sorry you had to come all this way for a funeral," he said.

She inspected his weary eyes, his hair ruffled by the breeze coming down the hollow, his face filled with an emotion she couldn't identify. "I'd appreciate it if you'd sign the annulment papers," she said.

He tapped his hat against his leg. She was starting to recognize the gesture— it was when he was uncomfortable.

"I haven't had time," was his answer.

"Take the time."

"I will. Don't worry."

"I'm not worried. But there's no reason to stretch this out."

He fiddled with his hat. "Well, like I said, I'm glad you came."

She knew this was probably going to be the last time she saw him, and she hesitated before going inside.

"What's next for you, Cable?"

He scratched the back of his neck. "I'll keep mining coal and try to run as safe a mine as I can."

You're going to be fired, she thought. She ached to tell him, to somehow make it easier for him, but she didn't know how. "Somebody told me you were working too hard and too much," she managed.

"Naw. I'm fine. I just can't figure out why we keep missing our quota for refined coal."

"Is your mine playing out?" she probed.

"Seems so, but I can't believe it. I sent some samples over to MSHA in Beckley for them to study, and they pronounced it the finest metallurgical grade they ever saw."

"Your tonnage is adequate?"

"Yes. But the percentage of high grade is too low, so getting the tonnage up hasn't helped enough. I can't figure out why it's so low though."

"How about a consultant to study your operation?" she suggested.

Cable's expression registered deep disapproval. "That would be a waste of money. I know that mine like I know the back of my hand."

"Some men would say 'like I know my wife.' Too bad you can't say the same."

"I didn't mean to hurt you. I still care. You know?"

"No, Cable. I don't know." She marched down the steps and stuck out her hand. "This is good-bye. I don't believe we will meet again. Sign those papers and let's be done with it."

Her hand was lost in his. He hung on to it. "I will," he promised.

"It's best," she said in a soft voice, then withdrew her hand from his. "For both of us."

Cable looked as if he had something to say, but he put on his hat and walked away without another word. Song watched him and alternated between sadness and relief. But then, from somewhere deep inside her, there came a message: *You're here now. Do something. Fix this situation or regret it for the rest of your life.*

Song looked around, looked at the Cardinal Hotel, the church, and the mine. She looked at Highcoal and its people. She looked at Cable as he slowly drove his truck away, his dream of being the mine superintendent in his town about to be taken away. God only knew what would happen to him then. From within her came the message: *You're here. Fix it. You're the only one who can.*

Song recalled what Rhonda had suggested, if only tongue-in-cheek. Could she do it? How outrageous a thing that would be! Perhaps as outrageous as a small woman wanting to climb K2 nearly thirty years ago. She was her mother's daughter. She was the daughter of Joe Hawkins. She was made of stern stuff. She could do what needed to be done.

It was enough to make her laugh at the irony of the entire thing. If Preacher was right and life was all part of a heavenly script, then hers had been written by an angelic comedian.

Young Henry, carrying a football, came walking up and Song hugged him. As much as he squirmed, she wouldn't let him go. "I have missed you so much, so much, *so much*!"

Young Henry was astonished. "Are you okay, ma'am? Hey, you're crying!"

"Cable gave such a beautiful talk today, didn't he, Young Henry?"

"Why, yes, ma'am. Everybody said so."

"What would happen if he left Highcoal?"

Young Henry looked puzzled, then scratched his head. "I don't guess folks around here would know what to do without Mr. Jordan. He kind of bucks us up all the time, I reckon. Looks after the miners as best he can too."

"Thank you."

"For what, ma'am?"

"Just for being you. And for helping me make up my mind about something."

"Like what?" he asked suspiciously.

"Oh, nothing. Well, something. It's crazy, but I'm going to do it."

"Can I help?"

"You already have, Young Henry. You already have!"

INSIDE THE CARDINAL, Song asked Rhonda if she could use the telephone in her office.

"Sure, hon'. Your ride to Charleston will be here in about thirty minutes. You all packed?"

"No. And cancel that ride."

"*What?*"

"You heard me."

SONG CALLED HER father.

"Song! How's it going?" She heard a lathe winding down. He was in his workshop. Building bird houses was his hobby. Birds didn't care much for them. They were mostly inhabited by squirrels.

"I don't know, Daddy," she answered. Song closed the door. She pressed the telephone to her ear, really leaned into it. "It hurts to be here." She was quiet for a moment, then said, "Daddy, do we still own Atlas Energy? You didn't sell it, did you?"

"If I could find a buyer, I would have, but unfortunately it's still ours. Why do you ask?"

"I've decided to stay here for a while. I want to study Cable's mine. If I can figure out what's wrong with it, maybe we can get it back on its feet."

Hawkins gave that some thought, then asked, "What if Cable is the problem?"

Song mentally crossed her fingers and said, "Then he has to go."

"I knew you were tough but not *that* tough," Hawkins replied in a dubious tone.

"I guess the acorn doesn't fall far from the tree."

"Apparently not. Do you really think you can figure out what's wrong with Cable's mine?"

"Yes."

"And you'd fire Cable if he's not doing his job?"

"Yes."

After an interval, Hawkins said, "Sorry, this just doesn't add up. Tell me what's really going on. I know there has to be more."

Song considered sticking with her story but knew her father was too sharp for her. She twisted the telephone cord around her hand until it hurt. This was going to be difficult to explain. "The people here, Daddy, they need Cable. And he needs them. I'm sure now that I don't love him, not like a wife should love her husband. He hurt me too much for that. But it just so happens, as crazy as it seems, I am the one person in this world who can save him. I want to do that if, for no other reason, he'll finally understand who and what I am."

"In other words, what he's lost," Hawkins interjected.

"Yes. But at the same time, I believe I can save our company a great deal of money. That's my reasoning. Now, tell me I'm wrong and I'll come home."

Song could almost feel her father smile. "I'm proud of you, honey, more than you can possibly know. I think your reasoning is perfectly sound, especially the part about saving our company's money. So what can I do to help?"

"I want to join what they call a red cap class. It starts in just a few days and will give me a crash course on coal mining. Get Atlas headquarters to approve me as a member of that class."

"Would you go into the mine?"

"Yes. But I'll be careful."

"You'd better. What happens when Cable finds out?"

"I'm sure he'll make a fuss, but with headquarters' approval, he won't be able to do anything about it."

"Consider it done. But are you sure of this, sweetheart? Really sure?"

"I'm sure. Do you know how much I love you, Daddy?"

"No need to butter me up, young lady. Just stay safe. Frankly, this situation takes me back to when your mother told me she was going to climb K2. She thought it was going to be a great adventure and I supported her one hundred percent. I'd give anything now if only I had stopped her."

"Could you have?" Song asked. "Stopped her, I mean?"

He was silent for a long second, then said, "No. Just like I suppose I can't stop you."

Song reassured her father, told him again how much she loved him, then hung up. She remained at Rhonda's desk while giving herself a gut check. "Yes," she said to herself. "I'm going to do this." *Why?* the question came back. *For Cable? For the town? For the company? What's the real reason?*

I guess I'm my mother's daughter. That was the answer. The red cap class was her K2, a challenge that she needed to overcome, not for anyone or anything but herself.

And across time and forever, she could almost feel her mother's proud, loving arms around her. Song had only been a year old when her mother died, so they were arms she had known only in her dreams. She leaned back in the chair and closed her eyes. Soon a tear formed and rolled down her cheek. "I miss you, Mommy," she whispered toward heaven. "I miss you so much."

Eighteen

The class was to be taught in what had been a storeroom in the little brick building behind the mine superintendent's office. The room was swept out and mopped, and ersatz wood panels tacked up to give the place at least the semblance of a classroom. Fluorescent lights were hung, and a dozen student chairs set up to face a plain wooden table. Behind the table was a white marker-board that could also be used for slides and viewgraphs.

The teacher of the class was Henry "Square" Block, retired from mining for three years but urged back by a wife tired of having him underfoot. Belying his nickname, he had turned softly round in leisure, acquiring a couch potato's gut and the full jowls of too many chips and cans of beer while watching football and basketball and every other sport on television. For exercise, he had tried walking but got tired of seeing the same old neighborhood. Hunting was no longer fun, he'd never cared for golf, and gardening was just digging in the dirt. Then one evening Cable had called and asked him to teach his red cap boys. At first Square said no, but his wife, Hildy, said yes, and so here he was in the Highcoal mine classroom, nervous as a cat but prepared to teach his first class.

Square stacked his lesson manuals on the table, wrote his name on the whiteboard, and took a deep breath, releasing it slowly. He had never been afraid of much in his life, but now, just an hour away from teaching his first class of red caps, he found his stomach in knots. What if his students laughed at him? He considered walking out the door and heading home, but he knew Hildy would chase him out of the house with a broom if he did. No, he'd teach this one class, see how it went. If it was too bad, then he'd quit and go back to loafing.

After writing his name, Square thought about his students. Mole had given him the list and he'd glanced at the names. He figured they were going to be just like his grandkids and great-grandkids, who mostly sat around and played computer games. Not one of them seemed to care about working for a living. Likely these newbie red cap miners would be the same and that would mean Square would have to push them, more than a little.

On the positive side, kids of today might be a bit lazy, but they were also plugged into the future. He recalled an afternoon of frustration trying to figure out how to make a DVD player work. His great-grandson, diagnosed as ADD and all that nonsense, took the remote out of his hands and had the movie playing in seconds. The kid even came up with a split screen where he could watch the movie and keep track of a ball game at the same time. The youth of today weren't stupid. Mostly, he reasoned, they were just unmotivated. It would be up to him to provide that motivation.

Cable stuck his head in the door. "Square, you ready for tonight?"

Square ran a hand across his thatch of snowy white hair. "I reckon, Cable. How many you say I got again?"

"Only four. I hope to get more for you next time."

"If there is a next time," Square answered. "I just don't know if I'm cut out for this."

Cable came over and slapped Square on the shoulder. "You'll do fine. I hired you because I remembered how you always took the time to explain things to new miners. They always came to you for help. It didn't have anything to do with the fact that Hildy called me and ordered me to get you out of the house."

Square chuckled. "She does say I tend to get underfoot."

Cable looked around. "How do you like your classroom?"

"No complaints," Square said.

Cable nodded. "Good. Well, just enjoy yourself tonight. I'm not sure who's coming. I've been so busy I had to let Mole do the hiring. Maybe I'll pop in a little later, see how things are going and meet them."

"I'll do my best for you, Cable."

"Your best is twice as good as anyone else's," Cable replied. Then he was off, leaving Square with multiplying butterflies inside his stomach.

Square was a bit surprised when five, not four students showed up, and one of them was a woman. The first thing about her that Square noticed, and it was hard not to, was she was a pretty little thing. No, the truth was she was drop-dead gorgeous. There were going to be some jaws hanging in the gob when the boys in the mine got a load of her, that was for certain, and, considering the age of some of them, maybe their false teeth too!

Square told the red caps to take a seat, and they did and stared back at him with the expectant faces of new students the world over.

"My name's Square Block," he said. "I have more than forty years experience mining coal. I've done a little of everything inside, from shoveling gob to operating long wall machinery. You may not know what that all means, but you will. You're going to shovel a lot of gob, and maybe one of you will end up operating a long wall, or a continuous miner, or a shuttle car, or some other kind of complicated machinery. There's going to be more things for you to learn than you can imagine. Most of all, I want you to start thinking about being safe. There's no reason for any man—or woman—to get hurt or killed in the mine, if you follow all the rules. Now, I got something for you to see."

Square placed four bright red helmets on this table. "I'm sorry, miss, but you weren't on my list. I'll get you a helmet, though. Don't you worry. These helmets represent your entry into the profession of mining coal. You have a whole lot to learn, and it's my job to teach it to you. If I don't do my job right, you could get yourself hurt or hurt somebody else. And coal won't get mined. That's what we do, gents . . . uh, and ma'am. We mine coal, dig it out, and send it to the surface. Other men—and women—take it from there to carry it across the world. The whole world would just about stop if it wasn't for coal. Steel wouldn't get made, this country would lose half its electricity, and a whole bunch of other industries would grind to a halt. What we do is important. We ain't paid much attention, unless we get ourselves killed, or trapped, or some-such. Only then do the television crews come a-running. Our job is to keep them TV folks away. We accept the world ignores us. We just go ahead and do what has to be done to keep things going. That's always been what coal miners do."

Square passed out the helmets. One of the students, who looked Mexican, handed the girl his red helmet and smiled at her. She took it, fiddled with it, then looked up. Her eyes were filled with questions.

"I want you to start wearing your helmet wherever you go," Square said, "so you'll get the feel of it. In the days ahead, if you slack off, or prove too stupid to learn, or give me any kind of grief, I'll take that helmet back. Out you'll go, no second chances. Questions?"

"Why is it red?" the girl asked.

"So you can be identified as a trainee and kept out of trouble."

The girl nodded her understanding. Square picked up a clipboard. "Let's find out who you are. First, let's hear from Chevrolet Harper. I was sorry to hear about your father, son. He was a great miner. Wished I could have made the funeral, but my wife's uncle died about the same time. Tell you the truth, since I moved across the mountain I haven't seen Squirrel, but he was a fine man, a fine man indeed. We mined some good coal together."

Chevrolet stood. He was just over six feet tall and wore a mischievous expression. He nodded toward another young man who had a similar expression. "That's Ford, Mr. Block," he said. "He's my younger brother. From what you just said, I reckon you know all about us. Our family's lived up on Harper Mountain for a coon's age. With Daddy gone, and Ford and me out of the army, guess we need to learn how to mine some coal." He nodded to his brother again, and they grinned at one another. "We're gonna be the best coal miners you ever saw."

Square looked the boys over and thought they might be a bit tall for the mine. He kept it to himself. They'd find out for themselves soon enough. "All right, Chevrolet. You can sit down. No, Ford, you don't need to stand up. Chevrolet told enough for the two of you." Square scanned his clipboard. "All right. Who's next? How about you? Your name is . . ."

Gilberto Guiterrez was his name. He was a stout young man with a droopy moustache and dark, sad eyes. He rose and said, in accented English, "I come from Mexico. I have the green card. I want to mine coal and make some money. That's it."

"You don't need a red cap. You need a red sombrero," Ford said, which made Chevrolet laugh. "Hey, Pancho, why don't you go back to Mexico?"

"Chevrolet, Ford, stand up!" Square ordered. The boys, looking sheepish, did as he ordered. "Now, put on your helmets and come here."

Chevrolet and Ford came forward, and Square slapped them both on the sides of their helmets. "Owww!" they cried in unison.

"Quit your whining. That didn't hurt two hardheads like you, especially with your helmets on. But I hope it got your attention. We don't make fun of anybody in this class. Now, sit down."

The brothers, for no apparent reason, limped back to their chairs and crawled into them.

"You can sit down as well, Gilberto," Square said. "I've not met too many Mexican miners, but I'm sure you're going to do just fine. Chevrolet and Ford are going to help you every step of the way. Aren't you, boys?"

The Harper boys looked up with contrite expressions. "Yes, sir," they said.

"All right. Who's next? Justin? I know you, don't I?"

A painfully thin young man stood up. He was in baggy jeans, and an overlarge plaid shirt hung on him like a tent. "My name's Justin Brown, Mr. Block. You know me, I guess. I used to be quarterback on the high school team."

"Yes. I recall. Didn't you win a football scholarship?"

"Yes, sir. I lost it."

"I see. What've you been doing lately?"

Justin scratched his head. "I got nothing to say about what I been doing. I'm here to work. That's all."

"If you want to stay in this class, you'll answer my question," Square ordered.

Justin stared at him, then shrugged. "I been in trouble with the law for drugs. My son got took away from me. My wife—well, she committed suicide. Ate Drano with a spoon while in the county jail. The state says if I can find a job and hold it, I might get my boy back. Mining coal's about the only way I can get him."

"What kinda drugs did you take?" Square asked.

"Meth, mostly, sometimes OxyContin."

"You wanted to get high, you shoulda just bought some 'shine," Chevrolet said.

"I didn't want to get high," Justin said. "I wanted to get dead."

"You can sit down, Justin," Square said. "Thank you for being honest with us. You have a clean slate in this class. Nothing you did will work for or against you. It's what you do from here on that matters."

Justin sat down. Both Ford and Chevrolet reached over and patted his shoulder. After hesitating, so did Gilberto.

Square put his clipboard down. "All right, gentlemen, we have another student. Would you stand, young lady, and tell us something about yourself?"

"Aw, everybody knows who she is," Chevrolet said, and Ford and Justin nodded in agreement.

"Well, I don't," Square answered. "And I reckon Gilberto don't neither."

"I know who she is too," came an angry voice from the doorway.

"Cable," Square greeted the mine superintendent.

"I'm sorry to interrupt your class, Square, but I would like a word with Mrs. Jordan, if you don't mind."

Square's eyebrows shot up. "Mrs. Jordan?"

"Sure enough, Square," Chevrolet said gleefully. "She's his wife."

Song stood. "It's all right, Mr. Block. Let me talk to Cable. It won't take long."

"SONG, ARE YOU crazy? What do you think you're doing?" They were outside, standing in the lights of the tipple.

"My permission to enter the red cap class is from Atlas headquarters in New York," she said, a lot more calmly than she felt. "I'm in this class for my own reasons. It shouldn't concern you."

"Everything that happens in this mine is my business," he growled. "Is this some ploy to get us back together?"

"Listen to me, you moron," Song hissed. "Wild horses couldn't drag me back to you. You want to know why I'm taking this class? Fine. Without telling me, my father bought your stupid company."

Such was his astonishment, Cable's mouth opened and his eyes went wide. He whipped off his hat and took a step back. "He did *what*?"

"He bought Atlas, including your mine. He went around me when he did it. Now Hawkins-Song has a big turkey on its hands, and I don't just mean this mine." She nodded toward him.

"I'm not a turkey," Cable grumped, slapping his hat against his leg. He had the look of a man who needed to think, but without a decent thought to be had.

"From a business point of view, that's debatable," Song retorted. "The reason I'm taking this red cap class is so I can learn enough to fix your idiotic mine."

"What do you mean?"

"Since you can't meet your orders, I'm going to be the consultant you claimed you didn't need."

This was too much. Cable threw his hat down. "That's crazy! You don't know the first thing about mining coal. We're just going through a bad spot that has too much rock in it. It happens. Of course, you wouldn't understand that."

"Which explains why I'm taking the red cap class," Song replied.

Cable glowered. "I have years of experience and a college degree in mining, Song! This red cap class won't teach you anywhere near what you'd need to know to solve this problem. What are you thinking?"

"It doesn't matter what I'm thinking. My father is your boss now and you'll do as you're told."

When Cable just stared at her in stricken silence, Song softened her voice. "Look, you might not believe me, but I'm going to figure out what's wrong with your mine. Don't take it personally. It's just business."

Cable's mouth was compressed into a flat, hard line. He broke the line long enough to ask, "How come nobody at Atlas seems to know they're part of the Joe Hawkins empire?"

"Because he chooses to be silent about it for now. That doesn't concern you. You just keep doing your job, as best you can, and don't get in my way."

After a moment more of reflection, Cable picked up his hat. "It seems you and your father have me over a barrel."

"Finally, you understand. Now, if you'll excuse me, I've got a class to attend."

"Look," Cable said, "there's no need for you to take this class. You want to learn about coal mining, I'll take you for a tour of the mine, tell you everything you want to know."

"No, thanks, Cable. If you want to occupy your time, why don't you sign our annulment papers?"

"I'm looking them over but they're complicated," he glumly replied. "Ticks keep biting me, giving me new forms of Lyme's disease, making me too stupid to figure out your lawyer's tricks."

Song almost laughed. "There are no tricks. Sign them, Cable."

"I will," Cable promised. "But I'm asking you, Song. As a friend. Stay out of my mine."

"You are *not* my friend, Cable. You are my ex-husband, or will be soon. You are also my father's employee. Don't forget that. I'm going back to my class now. *Good night.*"

Song walked back to the little brick building. Cable dourly watched her, then huffed out a little laugh. She'd soon learn how difficult it was to work in a coal mine.

Cable trudged back to his office and looked in on Mole. He and the evening shift dispatcher, J.C. Flannery, were studying the monitors that showed data from the carbon monoxide sensors Cable had installed throughout the mine. Cable had also installed a seismograph in Mole's office to detect tremors in the mine. If a pillar let go, or anything else that caused the earth to heave, Mole or J.C. would know about it, and soon after, so would he. There was also a bank of lights that showed when any of the telephone pager systems were in use. The pagers were all "permissible," meaning they were shielded and grounded, safe in even methane-rich air. By punching the right button, the dispatcher could listen in on what was being said on the pagers, or call one to talk to a section foreman or any miner. With a few flipped switches and punched buttons, anything that was wrong in the mine would be quickly evident.

But Atlas headquarters was always complaining about the money he'd spent on the monitors. Cable knew very well his head was on the chopping block for overspending as well as not meeting the quotas for India. But, never mind, he believed he had done the right thing, and if a man did the right thing, Cable believed all would be well. It had to be. The world could be unfair in spurts, that was his sense of things, but in the long run, it was mostly fair. He would depend on the long run to see him through, and maybe Preacher's prayers.

There was paperwork to be done, including responding to another punitive fine from Einstein, this time for having too much grease on the rollers of a conveyor belt in Two East. If it wasn't one thing, it was another. As for Joe and Song Hawkins, he'd worry about them later. It didn't matter who owned his mine. As long as he was superintendent, he'd run it the way it needed to be run.

Cable sat heavily in his chair and looked at the stack of documents on his desk, then drew a paper from the bottom of the stack and tried to focus on it. He didn't succeed.

He opened the back door to his office for a breath of fresh, cool West Virginia autumn air. He listened to the sounds of the tipple, the low thrum of the bull wheel as it raised and lowered the cages, the squeals and thumps of the coal cars being pushed along the tracks, the rumble of the coal dropping through the chutes from the preparation plant. He loved the sounds of the mine. To him, they were pure music, the finest kind. This evening's symphony told him all was well.

Just across the way was the red cap classroom. He wondered what was going on in there and then imagined Song wearing a red helmet. That image made him shake his head. "She won't last a day," he assured himself, then went back to the paperwork on his desk.

Nineteen

Song woke, blinking into the darkness, disoriented and a little frightened. She had to think for a moment to recall where she was. The Cardinal Hotel was dark and silent except for the occasional creak of a floorboard. Rhonda had explained to her about those creaks. They weren't ghosts, or at least she didn't think they were. The floors creaked because the Cardinal was always settling as the ground beneath it shifted on the old mine works a thousand feet or so below. Song detected the faint scent of mothballs. There were a number of them scattered in the tiny closet and she didn't want to think about what they were supposed to ward off. Her bed was an antique four-poster, ridiculously high off the wooden floor, with a step stool required to get in and out of it. Rhonda had explained that in the old days, the bed had to make room for a chamber pot.

Song was beneath a soft cotton comforter, but it gave her little comfort. She felt out of place. She rose and crossed to the window and looked down on Main Street, lit by a single light post. She drew up a chair. A block away sat the church on its little hillock, a faint glow in one of its back windows. Song wondered if Preacher was in there writing a sermon. She supposed he'd heard that she was in the red cap class. Surely everyone in Highcoal knew it! Cable had probably let everybody know what he thought about it too.

Not that she cared what Cable thought. "Sign the papers," she whispered to him, wherever he was. At Hillcrest, she supposed, and maybe with Michelle Godfrey. She gritted her teeth.

Her mind was filled with contradictions on how she felt, and why she was in the red cap class. No matter. When it was all done, however it turned out, she'd leave Highcoal and not look back, though she hoped Young Henry might some day visit her in New York. She would enjoy showing him her city, and perhaps even finding him a job with Hawkins-Song. The others, even Doctor K, she couldn't imagine outside of Highcoal. They were as much a part of it as it was of them. She realized at that moment she envied them, their sense of place, and knowing where they belonged. *I'm pathetic,* she told herself, then climbed back in bed and pulled the comforter over her head and finally fell asleep.

BREAKFAST AT THE Cardinal was served at five a.m. Song dressed in jeans, a long-sleeve T-shirt, and running shoes, and carrying her shiny red helmet, headed downstairs. She was the first of her classmates to arrive in the dining room although there were a few day-shift black-cap miners already there. They glanced at her, nodded, and went back to eating. They knew who she was, but had nothing to say about it. That was a good thing. Song didn't want to fight with anyone.

Rhonda came through the swinging kitchen door with a stack of pancakes, Young Henry behind her, balancing a dish of scrambled eggs, a platter of ham slices, and another with a pyramid of sizzling bacon. Rosita followed with trays of biscuits, toast, and homemade muffins with plenty of butter and jam. Coffee was self-serve from a big chrome urn. A stack of real coffee mugs was beside it. No Styrofoam cups were ever in evidence in the dining room of the Cardinal.

Song felt out of place, just as she had been the first time she came to Highcoal. She inspected the serving table, mentally adding up the calories in the buttered biscuits and muffins, and rejected them along with the ham, bacon, and eggs. All that was left was cold cereal and skim milk, a slice of plain toast (which was, unhappily, white bread), and the robust, flavorful coffee. She had just sat down with her meager food when the Harper boys, their eyes squinting against the overhead lights, strolled into the dining room. Rhonda took a look at them and hooted. "I heard you boys come in about two o'clock. You can't stay out all hours and mine coal."

They ignored her and made for the coffee urn, then the food. With their plates piled high with something from every serving tray, they sat down at Song's table and began to stuff themselves. Justin came in next, silently served himself, and sat beside Chevrolet.

"Good morning, fellow coal miners," Song finally said.

Justin and the Harpers morosely glanced up at her, then without pause went back to eating. Chevrolet had a swollen eye, and Ford a bruise on his cheek.

"Were you two in a fight?" she asked.

"They called Gilberto a name after class last night," Justin said.

Chevrolet shrugged. "I seen it on TV. They called this Mexican a taco-head. So I called Gilberto that to see what he'd do."

Song smiled. "I see he didn't like it. Good for him."

"Gilberto didn't do this. Ford did."

Ford piped up. "We're all part of the same team now, right? Gotta be nice to each other and all that. Chevrolet needed to be hit."

"You got me good, brother."

"You got me good back," Ford replied, with honest admiration.

Gilberto strolled in looking sleepy, gathered up his food and coffee, and sat down after kissing Rosita.

"I see you've met Rosita," Song said.

"*Sí. Naturalmente.* She is my wife." He looked at the Harper brothers, who were pretending they were in another universe. "You boys hokay?"

The brothers sheepishly acknowledged his question. "We're good. You?" Chevrolet asked.

"I'm good." Then he chuckled. "Taco-head. That is so *idiota.*"

"Well, hell, we don't know no good words for Mexicans," Chevrolet complained. "Tell us one, Gilberto, and we'll call you that. You got to have a nickname if you're going to work in the mine."

"But you don't have a nickname," Gilberto pointed out.

The brothers were startled by the accusation. Ford rallied first. "Our names are already kinda nicknames. Now, come on, Gilberto, give us something to work with. A Mexican skunk or something."

"Hokay," Gilberto said. "Call me *gran hombre.* It's *mofa,* how do you say it? You make fun of me with such a name."

Chevrolet and Ford squinted in suspicion, then Ford said, "Okay, your nickname is Granny."

"No, no! *Gran hombre!*"

"Granny, Granny, Granny," the brothers chanted, knowing they had struck pay dirt.

Gilberto hung his head. "You have filled me with disgrace."

"We sure have and proud of it too," Ford said. "Hey, Rhonda, Gilberto's name is Granny!"

"Shut up, Ford," Rhonda growled, as she set more plates of food on the dining table. "His name is Gilberto. You call him anything else, you answer to me. Now, all of you hurry up and eat. Square won't like it if you're late."

Song ate her bowl of cereal while the other red caps at the table wolfed down yet another heaping plate of food. She thought about saying something to them about their meals. They were surely going to get fat on Rhonda's food. But, upon reflection, Song said nothing. They were all adults. If they wanted to be obese, that was their problem.

THE RED CAPS gathered in the classroom, all wearing their red helmets except Gilberto, who had given his to Song. Square handed Gilberto a helmet.

"All right, boys—and, uh, girl . . ."

"I'm just one of the boys, Mr. Block," Song interrupted. "You don't have to keep making allowances for me."

Square nodded to her gratefully, then said, "All right, boys, here's what we're going to do. You can't go inside unless you at least look like a coal miner. You Harper boys, them fatigue shirts and tight jeans ain't gonna do. Justin, them slouchy pants ain't gonna cut it, with your drawers showing when your shirt ain't hanging over it all. That's the weirdest way to dress I ever seen. Any one of you boys care to explain how looking like that came about?"

When Justin and the brothers didn't say anything, Song raised her hand and advised, "I read where the fashion came from prisons. Pulling down your pants so your drawers could be seen is a signal you're available for homosexual relations. The shirt pulled over it was to fool the guards."

Justin climbed quickly out of his chair and hitched up his pants, which simply sagged down again. Blushing furiously, he sat down, careful to avoid eye contact, while the Harper boys laughed.

Square couldn't help but chuckle himself. "Gilberto, your khaki pants and shirt are okay, but you'll need some steel toe boots."

"His name is Granny, Mr. Block," Ford said.

"No, it's not," Gilberto retorted.

Square pondered the Mexican, then shook his head. "Naw. That nickname don't feel right. We'll stick with Gilberto until something better comes along."

"What about giving Song a nickname?" Chevrolet asked.

"Song is already a nickname," she defended herself. "Like you say Ford and Chevrolet are."

Square held up his hands. "Look, boys, a miner's nickname has to come about more or less natural. Understand? Like your daddy was called Squirrel, for instance. I was there the day he got that name. We was just kids together. He came to school with a squirrel sandwich your grandmother made for him. We all liked to busted a gut laughing. He fought everyone of us, but it didn't keep us from calling him Squirrel for the rest of his life. He liked it, I think."

Ford and Chevrolet looked at one another, then shrugged.

Song was next in Square's clothing appraisal. "You look right fetching, of course, ma'am, but you'll likely split them tight jeans when you start duckwalking under a low roof. And running shoes ain't particularly good footwear in a mine. If you should accidentally drop a sledgehammer on your toes, why, it's liable to hurt. So, what we got to do is get over to Omar's and buy you some decent mining clothes and boots. That goes for everybody."

"I don't have any money, Square," Justin advised.

"Not to worry, son," Square answered gently. "When you're hired on with the mine, you have an automatic line of credit with Omar."

"Can we drink some of his ouzo?" Ford asked.

"No, you cannot," Square answered. "That stuff can kill you."

"Amen to that," Song said with emphasis.

Square looked at her appraisingly, then smiled and nodded. "All right, gents. Let's go to Omar's."

THE FIRST THING Song noticed at Omar's was that the displays in the windows were the same as when she'd arrived in Highcoal months before. There was still a plastic pink flamingo in one window, a mannequin dressed like a miner in the other. The red caps went inside where Omar waited for them with an expectant expression. Beside him stood a trim middle-aged woman with large black eyes and black hair pulled back into a bun. She had gold rings on nearly all her fingers, many golden bracelets jangling from her wrists, and was wearing a gray pantsuit. Square introduced his class. Song noticed that Justin was staring at the couple with an odd expression. Then he lowered his head and didn't look at them anymore.

"My name is Omar, just as you say, Mr. Block," Omar responded with a slight inclination of his head and a familiar nod to Song. He glanced at Justin, then away. "Welcome to my establishment, gentlemen and gentle lady. My wife, Marla, and I will be pleased to outfit you according to your needs. May I be so bold as to ask if any one of you has worked in a coal mine before? No? It is just as well. We will start with a clean sheet of paper. Or a clean set of working clothes, as it may be."

Marla also made a slight bow. "Mrs. Jordan, how nice to see you," she said. "That was a lovely silk suit you wore in church that day last summer."

"Thank you," Song responded gratefully.

"I heard what the church women said. It was most spitful of them."

"Spitful?"

"Spiteful," Omar translated.

"They've since apologized," Song replied.

"Good. And well they should."

Marla reached under the counter and withdrew a pair of bib coveralls, a pair of khaki pants, a khaki shirt, and a full-bodied jumpsuit. She placed them all on the counter. "These are your choices," she said. "The jumpsuits are most popular for women these days, the bib overalls somewhat out of favor for men, the khaki pants and shirt a fine combination for either."

Omar produced a pair of boots, which he also placed on the counter. "Full grain leather, hard-toe mining boots. They will last many years in the roughest of conditions."

Square said, "You can't go wrong, boys, if you'll let Omar and Marla lead you."

Omar took the male red caps off to a corner to try on their clothes, while Marla led Song to a rack of jumpsuits on the other side of the store. "Something in a pastel, I am thinking," she said. "Such as Governor Godfrey favors." She slyly looked at Song out of the corners of her eyes.

"No pastels, please, Mrs. Kedra," Song replied. "Just a basic color. The navy blue is nice."

"Indeed, it is. And it shan't show the dirt. An excellent choice. And call me Marla, please."

"Yes, all right, Marla. Tell me something. Do you know Justin?"

Marla looked a little embarrassed. "Oh, yes. We are foster parents for his son, Tommy. When he and his wife were sent to jail, and then his wife died by her own hand, the court judged that he could not raise the child. He is a very nice boy, Tommy is, and a healthy four years old. Omar and I love him very much. Of course, we hope Justin is able to turn his life around. A son belongs with his father."

Song nodded agreement.

"And a wife with her husband," Marla added significantly.

"Don't start on me, Marla," Song replied when she realized where the woman was heading. "I did my best with Cable."

Marla dropped her voice so low Song had to strain to hear it. "Please, Mrs. Jordan, tell me true because everyone in town will ask me when they know we've had a moment alone. Why are you doing this thing, this going into the mine?"

"It's what I do. I consult. The owner of Atlas hired me to study this mine. It is only a coincidence that Cable is its supervisor."

Marla frowned. "Is this so? It sounds very much made up."

Song looked into the woman's clear eyes, so guileless and honest that it made her feel ashamed to tell the lie. "It isn't exactly so," she confessed, "but I can't tell you everything. It's not for me to get back with Cable, but it is to help him."

"I see. Thank you for telling me that much, Mrs. Jordan."

"Please. It's Song."

"All right, Song. Would you like to try the navy blue jumpsuit on?"

Song did. It fit perfectly. "I'll take two," she said.

"Now, the boots," Marla said.

"I'm sure you won't have anything small enough. I wear a size five."

"Here you are," Marla said after an excursion to the back of the store. "Size five, with steel toes and waterproofing. They are also insulated against electrical hazards. They will feel quite stiff at first, but I believe you'll break them in over time. You will also need these." She was holding a pair of soft, gray socks. "It gets cold in the mine sometimes, or so I am told."

Song tried the boots and socks on. They fit perfectly, although the boots were indeed stiff. "Why do you have boots in such a small size?" she asked as she walked in them.

"Ordinarily we would not carry such tiny boots. But these were a special order for another woman. She did not work at the Highcoal mine but another, the Fox Run mine, twenty miles away."

"Why doesn't she want her boots?"

"Oh, she doesn't want anything now. She died, run over by a shuttle car, so we were told."

Song was not particularly pleased to be wearing a dead woman's boots, but there was nothing that could be done. She took another practice turn around the room. The boots felt like wearing concrete blocks. She worried about blisters. "I am told talcum powder helps," Marla said. "But the only thing that can truly help is to spend as much time in them as possible to break them in."

"I don't know how much I'll be walking in them," Song confessed. "I don't know much of anything I'll be doing in the mine."

"Then it is good that you are with Square," Marla replied with certainty. "For he is a good man and will look after you."

Marla strapped a wide black belt around Song's waist. "For your lamp battery and safety gear," she said.

Fully outfitted, Song looked at herself in the mirror, from her shiny red helmet down to her heavy black boots, with the wide belt cinched at her waist over the navy blue jumpsuit. "I look like Batwoman," she said.

"With a red helmet," Marla added, giggling.

"What a woman has to do sometimes . . ."

"For love?" Marla asked.

Song frowned at the woman. "For work," she firmly corrected her.

SQUARE APPRAISED EACH red cap in turn, approving the choices Song had made. Gilberto elected to stay in khakis, with Square's approval, but the brothers in their bib overalls were sent back.

"Our granddaddy wore a pair just like this in the mine!" Ford said.

"Because he couldn't find anything better," Square replied. "Those things will get stiff as a board when they get coated with gob and then get wet, either by you sweating in them or the water that's everywhere in the mine. What you want is material that's strong and light. I suggest you take a look at the khakis or the jumpsuits."

Justin walked out of the dressing alcove. He was dressed in a crisp, bone white jumpsuit. "Go back," Square ordered. "The coal mine is not a place for an Elvis impersonation."

It took a couple of hours, but finally Omar had the red caps dressed to Square's satisfaction. The Harper boys and Justin had settled on brown jumpsuits. "I want you to wear your work boots from here on everywhere you go," Square told them. "Everywhere, you hear?"

"In bed too?" Chevrolet asked sincerely.

Square couldn't resist. "Yes," he said. "And in the shower too."

Chevrolet and Ford looked at one another, then at Justin. Justin laughed. "He's yanking your chains," he said.

Omar stepped in. "Mr. Block, you forgot your lunch buckets."

"Why, so I did," Square said, slapping his forehead. "Bring 'em out for the boys to see. There they are. Just plain old lunch buckets with a place for a thermos. Not like the round ones your daddies carried in the old days, boys. Those are antiques now, but they served, they surely did. The bottom was filled with water, the top held the food. We're a bit fancier now. There's plastic bottles of water down there when you want it. That's something Mr. Cable started. When you get back to the Cardinal, sign up for Rhonda to pack your lunch every day. Just give her your buckets and she'll take care of everything. I swan she makes the best sandwiches anywhere. And, trust me, you're going to get hungry in the mine, and when you get home, you're still going to be hungry. You'll burn a lot of calories down there."

Square led his students back to the classroom, all of them walking stiffly in their heavy new boots. They walked past the mine superintendent's office where Cable watched them parade by. Song squared her shoulders and showed off in her red helmet. Mole came out on the porch and said something, and then he and Cable laughed and went back inside. Song's lip went out a bit, but she kept marching.

In the classroom, Square began his prepared lessons. There was so much to teach. He began with how a mine was laid out and some of the terms miners used to describe the geological features, such as ribs, the roof, and the face. He also reminded them there were hazards everywhere and nearly an infinite number of ways miners could get themselves killed or seriously injured. Coal miners, he said, could be electrocuted, crushed beneath roof falls, poisoned by carbon monoxide, blown up by methane, run over by any number of machines, cut to pieces by continuous miners, and eviscerated by exploding pillars, not to mention all the knocks and contusions inevitable in tight spaces.

Over time, coal miners were prey to rock dust silicosis, coal dust pneumoconiosis—black lung—sprung backs, busted knees, amputations, broken legs, broken arms, broken heads, and crushed fingers, toes, and nearly every other part of the anatomy. Square did not hold back from using examples. He named names of miners he'd known who had suffered each of the awful possibilities. "Your daddy," he told the Harper brothers, "wasn't in the mine, but he was high up on a steel walkway that was slick from rain. One false step . . ."

"Daddy was always so sure-footed too," Chevrolet said sadly.

Song recalled Constable Petrie's suspicions about Squirrel's death. As far as she knew, he hadn't investigated further. The next time she saw him, she would have to ask him about that.

Square went on. "You Highcoal boys all know Mr. Tolliver. He's got a wooden leg. He lost his real leg when a bunch of coal cars ran away on the main line. That was before we started using conveyor belts."

"His peg leg don't seem to slow him down none," Ford said.

"He nearly bled to death before we could get him out," Square said. "And he was in pain for a long time. That's why he started drinking 'shine."

"Guess that's why he started making it too," Chevrolet put in.

Square took off his shirt to display a pink scar about two inches long on his back. "Roof bolt got me bad," he said. "You get tired when you're walking, you straighten up, and they take a piece out of your hide."

"I ain't never gonna get tired down there," Ford piped. "The army got me in good shape. Ain't no roof bolt gonna get hold of me."

"The army got you in shape in one way, but not the mining way," Square said. "You'll see what I mean once you're down there."

In the next nine working days, Square taught his red caps the basics of ventilation, and how to read mine maps, and how to set timbers and build cribs to support the roof and the ribs. They learned about the different kinds of underground coal mining, the traditional but obsolete way of undercutting the face, drilling it, and shooting it with dynamite, and the modern methods of continuous mining machines with spinning cutting heads. They learned about computerized long wall and short wall hardware that tore through vast lengths of coal. They learned to recognize shuttle cars, loaders, cutting machines, drilling machines, scoops, rock dusters, locomotives, and the little electric cars called jeeps.

Then Square loaded them up in his SUV and took them along a dirt road back into a hollow where there was a small mine in the side of a mountain. He called it a "punch mine," and the three miners who were working it were outside, sitting on benches having lunch. "Y'all be careful with them shiny new red caps," one of them called as Square led his students inside. Since they weren't wearing helmet lamps, they didn't go very far, but Square used a flashlight to point out roof bolts, timbers, and cribs. He tapped on the rock overhead with a brass-capped stick, telling them what to listen for when trying to find out if it was a good or bad roof. He walked them over to an entry where the coal was low so they could get a sense of what it was like. Song had always loved to learn new things. "I think I'm looking forward to going inside the mine," she told Gilberto.

"Not me," he answered, looking at the roof with worried eyes. "Not with a whole mountain on top of me. I'm plenty scared."

"You'll be all right," Song answered.

"I keep thinking about all the ways there is to get hurt."

"Then don't think about it."

"But Mr. Block said we should think about safety all the time."

He had her there.

On Thursday afternoon, Square's lesson was on the use of the self-contained self-rescuers, which he called by its initials SCSR. *Ess-See-Ess-Are.*

"This is the first line of defense when air becomes bad," Square explained, holding up a small aluminum box with a belt clip on it. "Carbon monoxide is a killer gas in a mine. Sometimes miners just call it See-Oh. No matter what it's called, it's a silent killer that will put you to sleep and you never wake up. You can't see it, and you can't smell it. That's why your foreman carries with him what they call a spotter or gas monitor. They're electronic devices that can detect the percentages of the various gases in the air. He'll be checking it all the time, to make sure there's not too much CO. He'll also check for methane, which is an explosive gas."

Song raised her hand. "What causes methane and CO to get into the air?"

"Good question—I was just getting to it. Methane naturally seeps out of the coal. It's part of the same process that created the coal out of dead plants. CO is caused by something burning. Methane, maybe. Sometimes—and this is the worst thing that can happen in a mine because it's so hard to put out—the coal itself catches on fire." He lifted a pair of goggles from the table. "Where there's anything burning, there's going to be smoke. In that case, wearing goggles like these will help you see where you're going. A pair is included in every SCSR pack."

Square showed them how to flip the lever on the SCSR pack and remove the cover. He took out the flimsy goggles and set them aside and then held up a gray plastic module with a white plastic bag hanging from it. Attached to the module was a mouthpiece and nose clips with a thin cloth strap. To demonstrate how to use it, Square put the strap over his neck, then put the mouthpiece in his mouth and clipped on the nose clips.

After removing the mouthpiece, Square said, "An SCSR is a self-contained oxygen breathing apparatus. It'll last about an hour if you're resting. The harder you work, the more oxygen you use, so it goes faster. You'll be issued a SCSR and attach it to your belt. You'll go nowhere in the mine without it. Everybody with me on this?"

When all nodded, Square asked Song to come up and try on the apparatus.

Song took the canister and flipped the lever on top. It was not easy to open, but she managed and drew out the assembly inside. She slipped its strap over her head, twisted the mouthpiece, and put on the nose clips, then took a breath. "It doesn't work," she complained.

Square chuckled. "That's because it's empty. I just want you to be able to operate it. Here, put your goggles on."

Song put the goggles on and put the mouthpiece back into her mouth and breathed around its edges.

"You look like a fish," Chevrolet said and the others laughed.

One by one, each student tried on the rebreathers and each got laughed at. Gilberto had the most difficulty. "It makes me feel sick," he confessed.

"If you ever have to use one of these for real, you'll do it," Square assured him. "Your instincts for survival will take over."

Gilberto hastily unstrapped the rebreather and put it down on the table. "I am afraid of it," he said. "I am starting to be afraid of everything."

"That's okay," Square said. "I want you to be a little afraid. I also want you to remember being afraid later on, because after a while, you won't be afraid at all, and you'll start thinking nothing can happen to you in the mine. That's when you'll get hurt."

When no one commented, Square continued. "Tomorrow, you'll go into the mine. I'll go with you for orientation. Then Monday through Friday for the next month, you'll put in a regular shift with the day miners. During that time, you'll be moved around to the various sections, do a lot of jobs, always under the supervision of experienced miners and foremen. After your probation period is over, and if you've done well, you'll be able to paint your helmets black. What I'm saying is tomorrow's the first real day of your career as coal miners. Show up here at five thirty so I can get you ready to go in. Any questions?"

"Can I operate a continuous miner tomorrow?" Chevrolet asked. "It looks like fun."

"No. But you'll see one."

"Can I operate *anything*?"

Square smiled. "Sure. How does a number four shovel sound?"

Chevrolet narrowed his eyes. "Like work."

Twenty

Song stood with the other students on the porch of the Cardinal and watched the trucks and cars containing the miners of the hoot-owl shift passing by, bound for home. Several of the veterans tooted their horns at them and called out rude comments such as "You'll be sor-r-r-y!" and "Don't get them pretty helmets all dirty now!"

The time had come for Square Block's students to walk in their new hard-toe boots to the mine. Song had worn them everywhere, but they were still stiff. The other red caps complained theirs were too. Now it didn't matter. They were going inside the mine, stiff boots or not.

It was still dark, and their breath made little clouds of steam in the cold air. Day-shift miners were driving or walking past in the direction of the mine. Rhonda came out on the porch. "You red caps gonna just stand here all day or are you going to work?"

"We're trying to get up the nerve," Justin confessed.

Rhonda crossed her arms and looked up the street to the tipple grounds. "My husband was killed in that hole."

"Thanks for the encouragement," Ford said.

Rhonda laughed. "Honey, I'm just reminding you what you're about to do. You go inside; you hold hands with death all day. That's just the way of it. But Henry, that would be Old Henry, used to tell me he'd rather mine coal than anything in the world. So you take the bad and you take the good. Some folks believe your days are numbered anyhow, so you might as well do something you love until you step up to heaven."

Gilberto swallowed, his Adam's apple bobbing. "I don't know if I can do this," he confessed. "Having an entire mountain on top of me. That is *muy asustadizo*, very scary." He looked with stricken eyes at his classmates. "I might need some help today."

"If you get scared, just reach out and hold my hand, Gilberto," Song said. "And don't any of you boys say a thing about it!"

"I ain't sayin' nothing," Chevrolet said. "Hell, I might want to hold your hand myself."

"I wouldn't mind holding your hand now," Justin said with a shy smile.

Song smiled encouragingly. "Anytime you need to."

"Okay, that's our plan," Ford said. "We hold Song's hand if we get scared."

"Agreed," Justin said.

"Remember, I've only got two hands," Song reminded them.

Rhonda checked her watch. "Don't make me get my broom and chase y'all off my porch. Get on with you! Time to go to work!"

GO TO WORK they did, feeling self-conscious as they walked onto the tipple grounds and caught the eye of the day shifters. "Nice clean clothes," one of the miners said with a knowing grin. "That ain't gonna last long!"

"Welcome, red caps," Square said in the classroom. "Take a seat. I'm gonna tell you what we're gonna do and then we're gonna go do it." He quickly reviewed the steps every miner took before descending into the mine.

"Any questions? You boys look a mite trepidacious."

"I keep thinking about an old well in my village," Gilberto confessed. "Our parents used to warn us about it. They said there were demons in it."

"Relax, son," Square said. "There ain't no monsters in the coal mine. Nothing's going to happen to you. I'll be with you all day."

"Square," Ford said, "how low a roof are we gonna get into today?"

"Don't worry about it. I want you boys to start thinking positive." When all he got was more wide-eyed stares, Square said, "All right, let's pray." Everybody, including Song, bowed their heads. Today she figured she could use all the help she could get. "Heavenly Father, please look after these red caps and keep them out of trouble. Help them not to do anything *too* stupid, like bump their heads, or trip over things. Help them come out of the deep dark with a new understanding of what coal mining is all about. But most of all, keep them safe. That's all, Lord. You know what's in our hearts. All right, boys. Let's hear an amen."

"Amen!" the red caps echoed.

AFTER THE VETERAN miners had descended down the shaft, Square and his students went through the procedures necessary to enter the mine. In the bathhouse, the boys drew down empty baskets to see how they worked. "Why don't they just have lockers?" Justin asked.

"Takes up less room, these baskets. Song, though, she's got a locker in her room."

There were actually two lockers in the tiny bathroom with a separate door allotted for women, and one had a padlock on it. It had a sticker of the great seal of West Virginia on it. The locker was surely assigned to Governor Michelle Godfrey. There was but one shower stall, and Song hoped she and Michelle would never have to compete for it. It wouldn't be today, at least. Rhonda had told her Michelle was having to deal with a particularly rambunctious state legislature and would be in Charleston for a while. That was good news. If Song could figure out why the mine wasn't meeting its quota, she could be out of town before the voluptuous governor returned. She never wanted to see her triumphant face again. As far as Song was concerned, if the governor wanted Cable, then she could have him. They'd make a fine pair, anyway. She could be the brains in the family, and he could stupidly mine stupid coal to his stupid heart's content.

Square tapped on her helmet. "Pay attention, please," he said.

Song blushed while the other red caps laughed. "Sorry," she mumbled.

"What were you thinking about?" Square asked.

"Um. Methane. I wondered why it burns."

"Because it does," Square said, frowning. "God made it that way."

Song plunged on. "But why?"

"That's a question for Preacher, I reckon."

"I'll be sure to ask him," Song said dryly.

"You sure are philosophical," Chevrolet said.

"I don't mean to be," Song answered, then glanced at the young man. He was practically swooning. His puppy love in her direction was all too evident.

The next step, Square said, was to go to the lamp house to receive helmet lamps and SCSRs. The lamps consisted of a light that clipped on the front of the helmet with an electrical cord leading to a thick, heavy battery with belt clips. On the battery was a brass tag with a number on it. Song's number was 415. The lamp house supervisor, called the lamp man, took another tag just like it and hung it from a peg beneath the number 415 on a dark green board.

"It just takes a glance at the board to see who's in the mine," Square explained. "They see that tag hung next to 415, it means you're inside. When you turn in your battery, the lamp man will take your tag off the board. It's a simple system and it works."

They next received an SCSR. Added to the weight of the lamp battery, Song now had nearly eight pounds tugging on her miner's belt. When she clipped the light on her red helmet, the extra ounces pressed down on her head like a circular vise. She suspected a headache would soon be on its way. She walked a few steps to get the feel of the new equipment hanging on her, then glanced at Cable's office, half hoping to see him watching her from the door. He wasn't there but Mole was. He was wearing a big grin and gave her a thumb's up. Song ignored him.

Square led them to the manlift, but it was in transition, the left side heading down with the right side coming up. When the right lift reached ground level, Song saw its freight was Cable and Bossman. Their faces were soot black. Cable's eyes cut toward her, then looked away. He said something to Bossman who smiled, and then they trudged toward the office, their heads down in deep conversation. Song again told herself to wipe Cable from her mind. She would deal with him later, after she'd figured out what was wrong with his mine.

"Okay, red caps," Square said. "It's time to go below."

The gate was open, the gate attendant smiling at the nervous novices. After being patted down by the attendant, the boys filed aboard with Song bringing up the rear. "Um, ma'am, I should pat you down for matches or lighters," the gate attendant said.

"She doesn't have either one, Elbow," Square put in. "Do you, Song?"

Song shook her head but said, "If the boys get patted down, then I should too. I don't want to be any different."

Elbow raised his hands, then put them down. "Ma'am, I trust you. You go right ahead."

"If Einstein's watching, he could fine the company," Square said.

"I'll take that chance, Square," Elbow said, his face crimson. "If my mrs. heard I patted Mrs. Jordan down, I guess the fine would be a little higher. If you get my meaning."

Square laughed, as did several other men standing around pretending not to be listening.

It was time for Song to go beneath the mountains of Highcoal to learn how to be a coal miner. It seemed like a dream. *Get it done*, Song told herself, and stepped aboard the manlift. Chevrolet stuck out his hand and she shook it.

A bell rang, the platform jerked, Song gasped, and she and the others were on their way down, and down, and down. Song looked up at the sky, then at the gray rock of the shaft sliding past. There was a wet, earthy odor in the shaft, and the air was cool and damp. She glanced at the sky again and saw that it had turned into a square of light, framed by the shaft, which kept growing, getting longer and longer as the light got smaller and smaller. Finally, the sky had turned into a bright little star that winked out. "Turn your lights on, boys," Square said.

Song reached up and turned the knob on the lamp attached to her helmet. The result was a spoke of light. She turned to look at her fellow red caps just as they all turned to look at one another. "Try not to put your light into your buddy's eyes," Square admonished.

Song pointed her light at the shaft, which was still sliding past as the manlift kept dropping. Her heart began to slow as she became accustomed to the strange sensation of descending into darkness. She was surprised when a hand sought hers. She didn't turn to see who it was. Gilberto. He was mumbling something in Spanish, and she supposed it was a prayer. She gave his hand a squeeze, and he let go and took a deep breath.

"Hey, this is fun!" Ford said.

"Yeah, like Disney World or something," Chevrolet said.

"All you boys doing okay?" Square asked.

"No problem," Justin said.

"Gilberto and I are doing great," Song said, and heard the Mexican take a deep breath. Very low, Song said to him, "Easy, now."

The manlift began to slow. A few seconds later, they were lowered into a vast, bustling cavern filled with lights, men, and machinery. The platform beneath their boots shuddered, then stopped. An attendant opened the gate, and Square and his red caps stepped out onto a concrete landing.

Square did a quick orientation. "This area is called the bottom. That little brick building there is the motor barn. It's got a small machine shop in it so equipment doesn't have to be hauled out of the mine to get fixed unless it's something truly major. See the tracks? They head down the main line, which is also an airway. That means fresh air blows through it. Most of the miners on the day shift have already caught a mantrip down the main line to their sections."

Song saw that there were still some black-helmeted miners standing in knots of twos or threes, talking or laughing at some joke. Others sat on the ground, heads leaned back, fast asleep. Then a mantrip arrived, its electric motor humming. The remaining miners crawled inside and it started up, followed a circular track, and then trundled off into the darkness. Square beckoned his students to another mantrip. "This is ours for the day. Mr. Jordan was mighty generous to let us have it too. This way we'll be able to cover a lot of territory without having to wait for somebody to give us a lift. Y'all go ahead. Hop in."

Chevrolet peered into the low steel interior of the machine. "How do you squeeze in there?"

Square demonstrated, squirming into the tiny compartment. When his students still held back, he barked out, "You're not going to get an engraved invitation. Climb in!"

Song looked around for Gilberto, but he was nowhere to be seen. She shined her light back toward the manlift where she spotted him, staring up into the empty shaft. She quickly walked to him. "They're waiting, Gilberto," she said.

Droplets of sweat were streaming down his cheeks and dripping off his chin. "I can't do it. I want to go up. I *have* to go up." His voice was on the edge of hysteria. "I can't breathe!"

She touched his arm. "It's okay."

"My heart is pounding so hard I feel like it is coming out of my chest."

"I'm scared too, Gilberto. We all are."

"I tell you I can't breathe." He moved a hand to his throat. "I try, but I just can't get any air into my lungs."

"Let it out," she said, after noticing his expanded chest. "Exhale. Come on. You have to let the air out to breathe it back in."

Gilberto leaned over, his hands on his thighs. He blew out, then stood up, and tested his breathing several times.

"Better now?" Song gently asked.

"*Sí.* Yes. Thank you."

"Hey, you two, let's go!" Square called. He had climbed out of the mantrip. His light flashed over them, then made quick circles.

"Gilberto, do you know what it means when Mr. Block makes a circle with his light?" Song asked.

"He's saying we are to come to him."

"That's right. You learned that. Think of all the other things you've learned. It would be wrong to learn something and not use it, wouldn't it?"

Gilberto gave that some thought. "I guess so."

She took his arm. "Then, come on. Just keep breathing and walk with me. Let's go use what we've learned. That's it. You're doing fine."

It was slow going, Gilberto taking small shuffling steps, but Song managed to get him inside the mantrip. Square didn't say anything, just gave her an approving nod. The mantrip's steel seat was hard, and Song's hip bones jabbed like knives when she settled down.

"For the first time in my life," she quipped, "I wish I had a bigger butt."

That earned a laugh from the red caps, even Gilberto. Square thumped the roof with his fist. "Let's go, Early!" he yelled to the driver and, with a lurch and grinding wheels, the mantrip eased forward. "Sit back, boys," Square said. "We're going to Six West, the far end of the mine. It'll take about half an hour. Any time you're on a mantrip, you can talk, sleep, do whatever you want to do, but don't eat your lunch. Save it for when you really need it."

The mantrip picked up speed and Song shined her light at the strange world passing by. Instead of everything being black as she expected, a white, powdery crust covered the profusion of vertical posts and crosshatched cribs that held up the gray rock of the roof. "Rock dust," Square said to Justin's question about it. "It's sprayed to keep the coal dust down."

There were placards with numbers on them attached to the posts, pointing this way and that, a confusing directory of destinations. "A mine is like a city with streets and boulevards," Square explained. "Only there ain't no buildings, just big square blocks of coal. The main line is like an interstate cutting through the city. The entries are like off ramps. Once you get into them, you'll see the crosscuts, which are like side roads. It's easy to get lost, so you have to pay attention to where you are all the time."

The mantrip roared past myriad equipment and Square did his best to yell out what it all was—electrical switch points, oil storage areas, telephone/pagers, belt lines, welders, SCSR stockpiles, first-aid stations, rock-dusting hardware, water lines, stacks of posts and headers and concrete block stoppers. Every turn, every corner, there was something that needed explanation.

"I'll never be able to figure out all this stuff," Justin said.

"Sure you will," Square answered. "A couple of weeks down here, it'll all make sense."

The mantrip slowed, then stopped, its wheels squalling, steel on steel. Square ordered his students out. Their lights swept around like individual lighthouses. "Now, be quiet for a second," Square said. "Turn your face back down the track. Tell me what you feel."

Song was the first to report it. "Air," she said. "A breeze."

"Very good, Song. Air, boys. Life, in other words. In this mine, the main line is one of the primary intakes. Big fans on the surface pull air down this line and then throughout the mine. When we get to a working face, you'll see it's not as easy to keep the air moving because there isn't much room. Figuring out where to hang curtains and brattices for airflow is one of the things Mr. Jordan does. On top of everything else, he's the main ventilation engineer. That means he spends a lot of his time figuring it all out because if the flow of air stops, it won't be too long before there's a buildup of gas and dust. One spark and it blows up."

Educated a little more, the red caps crawled back inside the mantrip and it started up again. Song shifted around on the steel seat, trying to get comfortable. She wondered if anyone would mind if next time she brought a pillow along.

Then she thought what she had learned about Cable, and what he did for the mine besides supervise. Figuring out how to ventilate a mine, she perceived, required more than engineering skill. It took a great deal of experience and a high level of confidence since even a tiny error could cost lives.

But another question on a different subject formed in her mind. "There's a lot of lost time just getting to work," she said to Square, raising her voice over the grinding wheels of the mantrip.

Square looked at her with approval. "That's right. Some mines sink another shaft so the men can get to their sections quicker. It's an expensive proposition, though. The shaft itself, and the new track that has to be laid, and everything else. It's a trade-off."

"Would it help production in this mine?"

Square shrugged. "Don't know. Somebody would have to study it."

Song salted the information away. Was the long run to the working faces part of the problem with this mine? Could it be that simple? Surely Cable had thought of it. But maybe not. She smiled. It was going to be fun solving Cable's problem for him. Then she could go back to New York and be happy. In fact, she was already happy. Being a red cap was just the adventure she'd needed. It had already made her feel closer to her mother. At every clack of the wheels beneath her, Song was beginning to understand what K2 was all about.

AT THE SURFACE, the red caps stepped blinking into the light. Cable was there talking to Elbow. He ignored Song as she walked by, so she tapped him on the shoulder.

"Good job, Cable," she said. "You've done a first-class job of ventilating your mine."

Startled, he managed a stuttered thank you. Then he took her in. "You almost look like a coal miner," he said.

"Why, thank you, sir," she answered, inordinately pleased.

He turned away from her. "Too bad you'll never actually be one."

Gilberto had to restrain her from kicking him in the leg with her hard-toe boot.

Twenty-One

The red caps were back in their classroom. Gilberto was aglow with success. The coal dirt that had stuck to their faces was scrubbed off. They were in clean clothes. In short, it had been a good day, they had watched coal miners in action, and they had learned.

Square, looking proud, sat on the edge of his table. "You red caps acted right good down there. Gilberto, you get a big attaboy. I was worried for a while, but I think you're gonna do fine from here on. Y'all got homework to do over the weekend, but it won't take long. Just read the chapters in the book I gave you. First thing Monday morning, you show up for work at five thirty sharp. I'm not gonna be there because you don't need me. The foremen will take care of you. From here on in, you work a regular shift. Tuesdays and Thursdays, though, we meet here after work to talk about what you've done, what you learned, and I'll cover some more things you need to know. Any questions?"

"When do we get paid?" Justin asked.

"End of the month. You got credit in Omar's store until then."

"Thank you for a good day, Square," Song said. "We couldn't have done it without you."

"Yeah, you got us down there and back in one piece," Ford said with a big grin.

"My pleasure, boys, I swan." Square looked away to cough. "I have to confess the dust at the face was hard on me. I'll be paying for it tonight, I expect. You just remember to keep your masks on when you're in a dusty situation. Don't end up like me."

The red caps strolled back to the Cardinal, happy within their cocoon of accomplishment. "Boy, miners work hard," Chevrolet said. "They never seemed to stop."

"Guess we'll find out what that's like on Monday," Justin said.

"We didn't talk to hardly nobody," Ford noted.

"Well, them miners kept looking us over. My eyes were full of their lights all the time," Ford recalled.

"I heard they can be pretty rough on new miners," Justin worried.

"Aw, we can take it," Ford replied. "How bad can they make it?"

Gilberto took a deep breath and let it out. "I just can't believe I did it. Song got me through it."

Song took Gilberto by his arm. She *had* gotten him through and she was proud of it.

"I weren't scared none," Chevrolet said. "Not at all."

"Oh yeah?" Ford demanded. "How come you wouldn't go back into the gob to take a pee unless I went with you?"

"Hell, I kept looking for the porta-potty but then Square said there weren't none. Never knew miners just went in the dirt like that. Seems nasty."

"I guess we'll get used to it," Ford replied. "Don't seem like we got any choice. Did it bother you, Song?"

It had, but she wasn't about to admit it. "Nope." She left it at that. Learning how to mine coal was strange enough. Discussing toilet habits with a group of men—well, she'd rather not go there.

Still, she already sensed she was going to miss her fellow red caps after this was all over. And Square. And Rhonda and Young Henry and Preacher, all of them. But she still eagerly looked forward to going home. New York was her home and nothing was about to change that. Even friendship.

SATURDAY DRAGGED BY for Song since she was essentially alone. The Harper boys had gone home to their mountain, Justin was holed up in the parlor watching football with the other bachelor miners, and Gilberto and Rosita had borrowed an old truck from somebody and headed out to visit Mexican friends who had settled elsewhere in West Virginia. Song sat at the little table in her room and read the handouts Square had given them as homework, and then looked out the window. Unable to be alone a minute longer, she went downstairs to see if she could find Young Henry and ask him if he'd take her to the movies in Beckley or Bluefield. When she didn't find the boy in the parlor, she sought out Rhonda in the kitchen.

"He's playing touch football," Rhonda reported. She guessed Song didn't much want to play touch football with Young Henry and his friends. "You look lost as a bird dog in the city," she concluded.

"I guess I'm at loose ends," Song confessed.

"Well, I'm going to choir practice. You wanna go?"

"No. Yes."

"Make up your mind."

"Yes. Just to listen."

Rhonda nodded. "Get your coat."

THE CHURCH FELT warm and inviting, a refuge from the cold wind that had blown into town. The choirmaster was Mrs. Carlisle. Mrs. Williams and Mrs. Petroski were also in the choir. Their full names, as now introduced by Rhonda, were Trudy Carlisle, Billie Petroski, and Dreama Williams. There were six other ladies in the choir and they were all introduced. Song felt like a specimen on a glass slide as they stared at her.

"Why don't you sing something for us, Song?" Trudy Carlisle asked. She was Bossman's wife. "That way we can see how you might fit in."

"I don't want to join the choir," Song said. "I just came to listen."

Frowning, Trudy said, "Nonsense. You're not going to get off that easy. Sing something for us."

Song gave in, not seeing any harm, and sang "Silent Night," even if it was a little early in the season for a Christmas carol. At the end, she waited to be laughed at, but the choir members were all nodding with approval.

"Very nice," Dreama said. "I think I speak for all of us. You can join the choir. We need a soprano."

"But I'm not here to join." When there was suddenly a solid wall of choir lady frowns directed at her, she sighed and gave in. What was the harm? She was lonely. The women were all potential friends and she reasoned she needed all the friends she could get.

"Well, all right—I mean, if you really need me."

"Of course we need you," Dreama said, "or we wouldn't have asked you. By the by, did you enjoy your day in the mine?"

"I did, actually," Song answered. "It's an interesting world down there. Have any of you ever been inside?"

All shook their heads. "Used to be, miners thought a woman in the mine was bad luck," Billie said. "But I guess I'd go inside and work if I had to. Thank God I don't have to. The way I see it, raising our kids and keeping the house is my job. My Chester thinks so too. He does the mining, I do the kids."

Rhonda said, "That's the way most ladies in Highcoal see things."

An elegant black woman named Serena spoke up. "Why are you working in the mine, honey? Are you after a man down there in the dark?"

Song laughed. "No. I didn't know what to do with the one I had."

"Ladies, it's time to practice," Trudy said, interrupting the grilling. "Song, we like to warm up with a—" she smiled at the repetition "—a song. It don't have to be religious. You got something you like?"

Song was feeling mischievous. She was no longer bored or lonely. She liked the women of the choir, and she did have a song. "When I was at Princeton, my room-mate and I used to sing something that was guaranteed to relieve all our tensions. We called it "the lion sleeps tonight song." Do you know it?"

"Hell, yes!" Trudy cried. Then looked up at the rafters. "Sorry, Lord. Didn't mean to cuss in Your house." She lowered her eyes and her voice. "I used to love to sing that song with my sister. Used to drive my daddy nuts, we'd sing it so much. Ladies? What say we sing and keep that lion asleep tonight?"

Soon the choir ladies of the Highcoal Church of Christian Truth were singing at full voice with joyful "aweemaways" while Song sang the main stanza about the jungle, the mighty jungle, and the lion sleeping in the night. Preacher popped in from his office to see what was going on. Laughing, he came over to join in. Soon his wife and kids charged inside too. Preacher's family put their arms around one another and sang as loud as they could.

Then the front door of the church opened and there stood Cable in his khaki work clothes, his fedora in hand. He had a smile that faded when he saw Song. Her happy expression also waned, and she stopped singing while the choir and Preacher roared on. For a few seconds that seemed to Song a long time, she and Cable held each other's eyes. Finally, to break the spell between them, Song pretended to write in the air, and silently mouthed: "Have you signed?"

Cable shrugged, tapped on his watch, and shook his head. Then, without further pantomime, he put on his hat and walked out, closing the door behind him. Song slowly picked up the song again and was ready when it was her turn to sing of the sleeping lion in the jungle, the mighty jungle. This time, however, her heart wasn't as much into it.

Twenty-Two

On Monday morning, the red caps showed up at the tipple, their lunch buckets heavy with two sandwiches, an apple, a bag of cookies, a bag of chips, and a thermos of orange juice. Song had taken her bucket, a pink one Marla had said was perfect for her, to her changing room and taken out one of the sandwiches and the cookies and the bag of chips and stored them in her locker. She had to shake her head in exasperation while she did it. Rhonda had packed enough food for a man who weighed two hundred and fifty pounds, or a woman who wanted to be that heavy! Rhonda was never going to get it when it came to food.

In the men's bathhouse, the practical jokes had begun and the red caps were the targets. When Gilberto placed his work clothes, helmet, and gloves on a bench to lower his basket, somebody took them while his back was turned. Then his red helmet came sailing in from nowhere, nearly hitting him. While he was picking up the helmet, his clothing was dumped on his back, and his gloves too. There was uproarious laughter, but when Gilberto stood up and looked around, all the veteran miners were innocently looking in different directions, minding their own business.

When Chevrolet pulled on his boots, he found one filled with soft soap. Ford discovered his helmet had a placard stuck to its front with chewing gum that said Baby on Board. A supposedly friendly miner distracted Justin with an article about West Virginia football. When he picked up his lunch bucket, Justin found it was filled to the brim with nuts and bolts.

When the red caps stood in line for their lamps and SCSRs, they were the brunt of a running barrage of comments by passing veterans. "Last time you'll be clean again for a long time, boys!" "What's that on your head, a strawberry? Naw, it's a cherry!" "Look, fresh meat for the foremen!" "Child, what you got in that lunch bucket? Animal crackers?"

On the manlift, as soon as the sunlight of the surface dimmed, every black helmeted miner on it gleefully yelled at the red caps, "Turn your lights on, boys!"

Song and the others fumbled with their helmets to turn on their lights, then everything fell silent. There was something about descending down an eight-hundred-foot-deep shaft that tended to make everyone quiet, even those trying to have fun at the expense of the novices.

At the bottom, the red caps gawked at the crowd of milling miners. Some of them were standing around talking; some were sitting on equipment brought down to be taken into the recesses of the mine; others were busy filling out paper-work. Three white helmets came over. Justin went with Brown Mule Williams, who was the foreman at Three East. The Harper boys both went with Hunky Jones to Three West. Song was called over by Vietnam Petroski, foreman of Six West.

"Mrs. Jordan," he greeted, touching his helmet. "I drew you but I don't like it."

"Because I'm a woman?" Song demanded. "You don't have to worry. I'll work as hard as any man."

"It ain't that, ma'am. It's who you have to work with."

About then there was a big shout, and Bum walked out of the crowd of miners. He had Justin by his shoulder, dragging him along toward a thick copper wire strung along the roof. "You ain't gotta be afraid of no juice, boy! Look here!"

"What's going on?" Petroski demanded.

"Aw, somebody told Justin to watch out for the trolley wire, it would kill him," a black cap answered. "You know Bum. He's gotta show off."

"Now you watch, boy," Bum said. "This can't hurt you." He stuck out his tongue and put it on the high voltage wire. As soon as he did, his eyes bugged out, he screamed, his knees shook, and his boots scrabbled a chaotic dance. Then he fell backward into the gob, his tongue lolling from his mouth, and his arms stretched out. He shuddered and jerked a couple of times, then went still.

Song couldn't believe it. Her first hour on the job and she'd already seen a man killed! But Bum wasn't killed. He got up and threw back his head and shrieked laughter. Petroski came up to him. "That was stupid, Bum!"

"Aw, boss, I was just having some fun," Bum replied, then strolled past the foreman and elbowed his way through the gathered miners.

"What just happened?" Song asked Petroski.

Petroski shrugged. "Ma'am, I got no choice but to work you with Bum. I can't trust him to run machinery, so he gets the odd jobs. That's what you'll be doing too. You watch your step with him, you hear? He gives you any trouble, you come find me." He stared angrily at the trolley wire. "That wire's been dead for three years. We need to take it out. Cable left it on the bottom just so we could remember what one looked like. These days we use diesel motors or batteries for our mantrips."

"I guess Cable's a bit sentimental, at least about mine equipment," Song replied ironically.

Petroski grinned at her. "I admire you for being down here, ma'am."

"Please call me Song," she said. "Why do they call you Vietnam?"

"Oh, I got some medals over there. Guys like to kid me about them."

"Thank you for what you did in Vietnam," Song said.

Petroski touched his white helmet. "I think that's the first time anybody ever thanked me. You're welcome." He flashed his light around the assembly of miners. "We're all sort of like soldiers in the mine, you know. We go off every day to a dangerous place, and sometimes we don't make it home. Most of the fellows down here are brave and honorable, even though they don't think of themselves that way. It's good to be here with them." His light sought out Bum. "Except him. You be careful around him, ma'am, that's all I can tell you."

"I will," Song promised.

After pointing her toward her mantrip, Petroski was pulled away by an engineer and Song crawled inside the steel box. She was glad to see she hadn't picked the compartment that contained Bum. Three black cap miners stared at her as she crawled over their legs. One of them said, "Hey, buddy. Appreciate it if you'd turn your light off on the ride in. We like to snooze a bit."

Song turned her light off and settled back on the steel bench. Before long, the mantrip lurched and started moving. The miners let their heads drop, and soon they were asleep. Feeling alone and nervous, Song thought back to choir practice, how much fun that had been. She'd sung in the choir the very next day and that had been fun too. Preacher had beamed at her from the pulpit. She only wished Cable had been there. Though she scanned the congregation for him, he never appeared.

Afterward in the choir dressing room, Rhonda said, "Cable went off to New York. Be up there for the next week. Lots of meetings."

"Whatever," Song said, shrugging.

"That's what I thought you'd say," Rhonda replied, not even trying to hide her smirk.

The mantrip trundled on, its wheels squealing and grinding at every curve, its headlight providing an arc of light that revealed posts and ribs sliding by, then disappearing beneath the black cloak that the car seemed to be dragging along behind it. When the mantrip stopped to let men off, the three in her compartment kept sleeping. Song hoped she wasn't supposed to get off too. The mantrip started up again, taking a sharp turn that caused the man beside her to slump against her shoulder. He dozed on while she shifted to get his weight off her, with only marginal success. His dirty work clothes stunk of sweat and tobacco juice, and Song's nose wrinkled with disdain. The mantrip gathered speed. At any moment, Song expected it to jump the track and roll over and smash them all. She didn't see how anybody could sleep through all the noise and lurching, but the three miners never stirred. After a while, she couldn't smell the man leaning against her. She could get used to anything, she supposed, even stinky miners.

Thirty minutes later, the mantrip slowed, then stopped. The men in the compartment raised their heads and turned on their lights, then silently crawled through the openings on both sides. Song slithered out while Petroski, somewhere up ahead, yelled, "Everybody pick up some roof bolts."

Song followed her fellow passengers to a wooden pallet laden with stacks of bundled roof bolts, each about four feet long. There were also several stacks of base plates. The miners picked up as many bolts and plates as they could carry and stuck them under their arms, then trudged on in a crouch beneath the low roof. Song picked up three of the bolts, but they were too hard to handle while also carrying her lunch bucket. She settled for two.

"That all you gonna carry, girl?" Bum demanded, then laughed. He shined his light in her eyes. "Vietnam's gonna be mad at you if that's the best you can do." He turned and crabbed off with a huge load of bolts and plates under his arms.

Chastened, Song picked up another bolt, shoved it under her arm, and hurried to catch up with the miners who were all moving in the same direction. Even though she was six inches shorter than most of them, she still had to bend over at her waist to keep her head from hitting the roof. Fearful of getting lost, Song scrambled to keep up. She kept craning her neck to catch sight of the lights up ahead and before long she had a painful crick in her neck. When she reached an opening with a higher roof, she was relieved to find the black cap miners were there. Petroski's light flashed toward her.

"Looks like we're all here, *finally.*" His light lingered on her for a long second, then dropped away. "Let's have a prayer, boys."

When the other miners turned their helmet lights off, Song reached up to turn hers off too, losing control of her load of roof bolts, plates, and her lunch bucket, which crashed noisily to the floor. Petroski's light flashed toward her again, then he sighed, shook his head, and said, "Heavenly Father, you know why we're here, to put food on the table of our families, and dig a little coal for the company and the country too. Help us all to stay safe while we do it. We have a red cap with us today, Lord. Look after her, and don't let her do nothing too dumb that gets herself or somebody else hurt. You know we believe in You and Your Son and the Holy Ghost, just like it says in the Bible. It don't matter what happens, that ain't gonna change. Amen."

There was a chorus of amens and the helmet lights were turned back on. Petroski said, "Y'all look after the red cap, all of y'all. No funny business, you hear? I won't have no jokers on my section. Now, boys, let's go mine us some good coal!"

The black caps headed off while Song picked up the roof bolts and plates and her lunch bucket. Clumsily, she waddled her way in the direction the miners had gone. By the time she caught up with them, the continuous mining machine had already started to grind into the seam, and the shuttle cars were moving into place, ready to catch the coal from the miner and carry it to the conveyor belt. The roof bolt crew watched with interest as she struggled by, but made no move to assist her. It was her first inkling that she was going to have prove herself worthy of help from the others.

Song swiveled her head until her spot of light landed on a stack of bolts and plates. Here, she judged, was where she could put down her load. With some relief, she dropped her bolts and plates on the pile, then took a moment for some quick yoga to stretch her back and legs. She sat down, took a deep, cleansing breath, and put her boot nearly behind her ear. The lights of the roof bolters swept in her direction, then she heard laughter. She ignored them, lying down in the gob on her back and stretching like a cat. When she stood up, she slammed her helmet into the overhead rock. Her knees buckled, and she would have fallen except for a hand that was thrust out of the darkness to catch her. It was Petroski's.

"Go back and fetch the rest of the bolts and plates," he ordered. "And try to keep your boots in the gob, not around your neck. You're distracting my boys." He moved away, his light flashing toward the continuous miner.

Song had no idea how to get back to where the bolts and plates were stacked. She chose a random direction that took her behind a shuttle car. She carefully stepped over its power cable just as the car shot forward, causing the cable to lift off the floor. It caught her in the crotch, picked her up, and slammed her against the roof. Her helmet went one way and she went another.

Petroski came over, picked her up, and handed her her helmet, now deeply scratched in several places. "Don't never step over a power cable!" he yelled. "Didn't Square tell you that? Always step *on* it. You just found out why. When are you going after those bolts and plates? Won't be long before the roof bolt crew needs 'em. Get on now, and stop fooling around!"

"I don't know where to go," she confessed. Her legs had been bruised by the cable and her head hurt from being slammed against the roof, but she tried not to show it.

"Go the way you came in," Petroski said, then pointed with his light. "Right over there. See the entry? When you're done, come see me and we'll get you going on the posts."

Song had no idea what "get you going on the posts" meant, but she headed into the darkness in the direction of the foreman's point. She saw a light ahead, which coalesced out of the gloom and proved to be Bum with another armload of bolts and plates. He didn't say anything, just pushed by her, breathing hard. Song kept going until she reached the pallet, loaded up as many bolts and plates as she could, then realized she had no idea what she'd done with her lunch bucket. While lurching bent over toward the face, she tried to recall exactly where she'd last seen it. She dropped her load with the other bolts and plates, then looked around and spied her pink bucket lying in the gob just seconds before a shuttle car ran over it. After the big steel vehicle rumbled on, she picked the crunched bucket up, then ran to get out of the way of another roaring shuttle. With some relief, she saw the bucket was just badly bent. She found a place in the gob where other buckets had been left and put hers down beside them. There was a flash of light across her, and when it flashed away, she saw it was Petroski again, watching her. He was talking to a miner and she saw both of them laugh. She was certain they were laughing at her.

Determinedly, Song made her way to the pallet, picked up as many bolts and plates as she could, and headed back toward the face. This time, she didn't pass Bum or anyone else. He had disappeared. There was no other option, so she kept going back and forth until the pallet was empty. Gasping for breath, she knelt beside the stack of hardware and tried to straighten her back. Petroski's light flashed over her again. While pushing her fist into the small of her back, she walked over to him.

"You done?" he demanded.

"Yes, sir," she replied.

"Got them all, every bolt, every plate?"

"Yes, sir."

"You put the plates on the bolts?"

"No, sir."

"Well then, you ain't done." Petroski turned away.

Song started sliding a plate over each bolt. It wasn't long before her fingers were bleeding. She pulled her gloves from her back pocket, put them on, and kept working. A man on the roof bolt crew hurried over, picked up an impossible armload of the bolts and plates, and headed back to the face. The continuous miner roared out of the cut and the roof bolters charged in, drilling, tamping, and bolting. It was all terribly loud, and dust filled the air. Some of the men wore paper masks, but most didn't. Song put hers on, but when she felt like she wasn't getting enough air through it, she took it off. She wished she had ear plugs. But then she realized ear plugs were probably not a good idea. In the darkness, the whine of an electric motor was sometimes the only way she could tell to get out of the way of something big that could crush her.

The roof bolters kept working until the roof was safely pinned, then clambered out so that the continuous miner could move back in. Its operator lunged it forward to knock down more coal, while its mechanical claws gathered up the spoil and transferred it via its conveyor to the shuttle cars. Then the mining machine backed out and the roof bolters charged in again, laden with the hardware Song had provided them. It made her a little proud to see her work being used productively.

The shuttle cars kept howling in and out, their operators expertly guiding them behind the continuous miners to catch the spewing coal from their booms. As soon as they were full, they were off, their big headlights lighting up the nearly rectangular tunnel, revealing the ghostly gray posts that lined it, the rugged gray roof of rock, and the dusty gray floor. The working area of the face smelt of coal dust and electricity. It was energetic and dynamic. Song realized she kind of liked it. It made her feel, well, alive.

Just as Song put the last plate on the last roof bolt, the foreman's light flashed over her again. She got up and went to him.

"See over there, that cross-cut?" Petroski demanded. "There's a stack of posts there. I want you to move them down to where there's a placard the engineers put up. Says Danger on it. If you look, you'll see where they've marked the old posts with some chalk. You take them old posts out, put the new ones in. There's shims in the pile."

Song looked in the direction Petroski was pointing. "By myself?"

"Bum's there already. Don't let him give you any crap."

Petroski abruptly moved off, and Song bowed her head beneath the rock and headed in the direction he had pointed. A shuttle car came howling out of the darkness and she ran from it, her helmet bouncing against the roof. Her headache deepened.

She found Bum sitting on a stack of wooden posts, each about five feet long and eight inches square. "Petroski sent me to put up posts with you," she said.

His light went into her eyes and stayed there. "You know how to timber, girl?"

"Square showed us. Raise the post against the roof, tap shims at the top to wedge it in."

Bum's smile was cold. "Pick up a post and let's go. We got to move them all before we start."

"Can't we carry one together?"

Bum didn't answer, just climbed off the pile and picked up a post, put it under his arm, and waddled off. Song did another yoga maneuver, a forward fold, to stretch her back again, wished at the same time she had some ibuprofen, then put her arms around one of the posts. It was all she could do to lift it, much less carry it. She took a few steps in a contorted posture, but the forward end of the post jammed into the roof, driving her to her knees. "Come on, girl!" Bum yelled from somewhere ahead.

Song gritted her teeth, picked up the post again, and staggered on. Petroski's light flashed across her as she disappeared into the darkness.

Song reverted to crabbing backward, dragging the post with both hands. This resulted in her head slamming into the roof again, knocking her helmet forward with the lip painfully cutting her nose. She felt the trickle of blood. She awkwardly turned and went back to dragging the post beneath her armpit, finally reaching Bum. She dropped the post and leaned over, her hands on her knees, to catch her breath.

"Well?" Bum growled. "Go get another one."

She followed Bum back to the stack of posts. He picked one up and lurched past her. Song also picked up a post and started dragging it. After she had gone back and forth four times, she didn't see Bum anymore. Still, she kept dragging posts, her jumpsuit soaked with sweat, her head throbbing like something inside it was busting to get out. Finally, she dropped the last post on the pile and sat down to rest. A light flashed over her. It was Petroski. "What are you doing?" he demanded. "You just sitting here? You were supposed to knock out the old posts and put the new ones up."

"Well . . . uh . . . you see . . ." Song stammered, trying to form some cogent thought around her monster headache.

"Look, lady," Petroski growled, "you can't expect no favors down here. You got that red cap on to work, and I expect a full day of sweat. You can't just sit around. Where's Bum?"

"I don't know," Song replied, her eyes squinted in pain from her headache.

"It's your job to keep up with your buddy," Petroski growled. "If he went off and left you, you should have come to me, not lounge around on this stack of posts."

"I wasn't lounging!" Song protested.

"You could have fooled me." His light struck her in the eyes, and her head felt like it was going to explode. He turned and left, called back to the face by flashing lights seeking him out.

Song looked at her watch. It was getting close to noon. She realized she was starving and thirsty. She hurried to her bucket. When she opened it, she discovered it was empty and the thermos bottle inside smashed. The shuttle car had probably crushed the thermos and then someone had stolen her food. Was it a joke or was she to starve?

She tossed the bucket aside and started walking, finding some miners tucked away near the now-empty pallet. All their lights flashed toward her. "Somebody stole my sandwich," she said, "and my thermos got busted."

"Sit down here, little lady," someone said. She sat on the pallet and a plastic water bottle was passed to her.

"You want one of my sandwiches?" another miner asked. She recognized him as the passenger in the mantrip who had used her shoulder as a pillow.

"If you don't mind," she said.

He passed over a sandwich, wrapped in wax paper, which looked suspiciously like the one Rhonda had packed for her. She didn't care. She needed food. It was peanut butter and jelly. She unwrapped it and took a big bite. But it didn't taste right. In fact, it tasted like grease. She spat it out while the miners roared with laughter. She stared at them, then spied a shovel. She grabbed it, scrambled to her feet, and smashed one of their thermos bottles to bits.

The grins on their faces quickly evaporated. "What did you do that for?" the owner of the thermos asked.

"I thought I saw a snake under it."

"There ain't no snakes in the mine, lady."

She shrugged. "You could have fooled me."

Then the grease that coated her mouth and throat and the gorge in her stomach would not be denied. She dropped to her knees and threw up. There was a stunned silence, then, "We always pull tricks on the red caps, ma'am."

"Ain't just you."

"Here's some water."

Song drank and felt better. "I'm still starving," she confessed. Instantly, sandwiches, apples, and cookies were passed her way. She ate two sandwiches, then a bag of cookies, then an apple, then drank some more water. She looked at her watch.

"Ain't no use looking at that watch, ma'am. You ain't going nowhere until the mantrip comes."

Song thought it couldn't come fast enough. A few minutes later, the miners abruptly rose and moved back to the face. Song had an urgent need to visit the toilet. She found a place, did her business, kicked gob over it, and then, hunched over beneath the roof, went back to the stack of posts. There was still no sign of Bum, but there were two five-pound sledge hammers and a miner named Pennsylvania.

"Let's go," he said brusquely, and used his sledge to knock out the first post. Song backed up. What if the roof caved in?

"Well?" Pennsylvania demanded, his light resting on her face. "Pick up some shims and a post, and stand it up so I can knock it into place."

Song felt in her back pocket for her gloves and discovered she'd lost them. She grabbed a post and a splinter sank into the fleshy palm of her right hand. She cried out and dropped the post on her foot. Luckily, it hit the hardened toe of her boot and rolled off. She sank to her knees.

"I can't do this." She hadn't meant to speak it aloud.

"You work the rest of the shift," Petroski growled, appearing out of nowhere. "Then you can quit at the end of it."

"I'm not going to quit," she hissed.

"You said you can't do this."

"You heard me wrong. I said, I *can* do this."

"Then I want to see you working."

Song took a breath, then grabbed a post. She ignored the sharp pain of the splinter in her hand and her splitting head. She ignored her back, which was sore, and her leg muscles, which were screaming. She even ignored her rational thoughts that kept telling her, in no uncertain terms, to crawl off somewhere until the mantrip came and never, ever do this again.

Twenty-Three

Rhonda and Rosita were working as fast as they could go to deliver food to the ravenous miners. Young Henry was even dragged away from his homework to carry heaping platters of chicken fried steak, baked potatoes, biscuits, corn on the cob, plus pitchers of sugar-laden punch and sweet tea to the table. Except for Song, the red caps were ensconced at their own table, devouring everything set before them. When Rhonda asked about Song, they reported the last they'd seen her was when she'd limped off the manlift.

"She looked pretty beat up to me," Ford said.

"I waited around for her," Chevrolet added, "but she was taking her time in the bathhouse, I guess."

Rhonda put her hands on her hips and frowned over the red caps. "If you'd been gentlemen," she lectured, "all of you would have waited for her, no matter how long it took."

Gilberto ducked his head. "*Sí.* You are right. But I was hungry." He looked around the table. "We all were."

Rhonda shook her head. "You men. There are only two parts of your body you pay attention to. And neither one of them is your brain."

Chevrolet gave that some thought. "Okay, our stomachs would be one of them. Not our brains . . ." He shook his head. "Can't figure out what the other one is."

Gilberto watched Rosita sashay by. "Ah. My lovely desert flower."

The other red caps watched her too, as did every man in the place. "You are one lucky man, Gilberto," Ford said. "Does she have a sister?"

Rhonda rolled her eyes and stalked off.

It was during a brief interlude between servings, when the only sounds were chewing, smacking, grunts, gulps, and belches, that Rhonda heard a thump against the front door. When she opened it, she saw a scratched red helmet resting on the welcome mat. Song was slumped on the porch steps, one arm flung toward the door.

"Girl, what's happened to you?" Rhonda gasped.

"I couldn't go any farther so I threw my helmet at the door," Song squeaked.

Rhonda helped her up. "What hurts?" Rhonda asked.

Song hung limply in Rhonda's arms. "Everything."

"What happened?"

"Vietnam Petroski said we mined some good coal today."

Young Henry appeared, and Rhonda handed Song off to him.

"Take her upstairs," she ordered. "Quick now before these yahoos in the dining room see her and start making fun."

Young Henry helped Song up the steps and into her room. She took off her boots, then flopped onto her bed, sighing.

"What can I do for you, ma'am?" The boy eyed her bloody socks.

Song showed him her hands. They were also bloody. "I have splinters. Can you get them out?"

"I'll call Doctor K."

"No. I don't want to start a lot of gossip. What do you do when you get a splinter?"

"I usually use a pocket knife to pry it out." He took a folded knife out of his pocket and showed it to her.

Song struggled into a sitting position. "Wash it in my sink, then get to work."

Young Henry washed the knife, then inspected Song's hands, whistling at the number of splinters. He got to work while Song gritted her teeth. "Easy, Young Henry," she begged.

"I have to go deep to get some of them," he said. "I'm sorry."

Rhonda came in with a tray. "I made you a fresh salad with low-cal dressing," she said, placing the tray on the bedside table.

Song looked at the bowl of vegetables. "What else do you have?" she asked.

"Chicken fried steak, potatoes, and biscuits soaked in butter. Sweet tea."

"Bring it all. I'm starving."

Rhonda scurried out.

Song yelped when Young Henry dug too deep.

"Sorry," he apologized. "But why didn't you wear your gloves?"

"Lost them," she gasped.

"I'll get you another pair," he swore, then sat back, and said, "I got all I could."

"Thank you, Young Henry." She smiled at him. "I couldn't do without you."

Young Henry blushed crimson. "Sure you could, ma'am," he said.

"Never turn down a compliment from a pretty woman, Young Henry," Rhonda said as she arrived with a tray loaded with food. Song dug into it while Rhonda and Young Henry left to allow her some privacy. When they returned, Song had cleaned the plates. "What's for dessert?" she asked.

"It's a really rich pecan pie," Rhonda said. "Loads of calories."

"Bring it on, please, and make it a big slice!"

Young Henry went off at a run to get the pie while Rhonda helped Song lie back. "What else is wrong?"

"Blisters on my feet."

Rhonda took a look, then whistled. "You have a few nasty ones, all right. Anything else?"

"I can't get the coal from around my eyes. I look like Cleopatra on a really, really bad day."

"It takes swabs and cold cream to get the coal out of the folds of your eyes."

Young Henry burst into the room carrying a plate with a huge slice of pecan pie. "Gimme it!" Song begged.

Song ate her pie, then there was a tap at the door. The trio of church women, Trudy Carlisle, Billie Petroski, and Dreama Williams, popped their heads in.

"We heard you were hurt some," Trudy said, holding up a bottle of clear liquid and barging in. "Take off your clothes. I'm going to rub on some liniment."

"And I'm going to get that coal dirt out of your eyes," Billie said, brandishing cotton swabs and cold cream.

"I'll work on your fingernails," Dreama said. "We'll get that gunk out from beneath them, have them all pretty again, I swan."

Song started to argue, saw it was useless, and gave in. She was too exhausted to fight. Young Henry was banished out into the hall, and, with the women's help, Song took off all her clothes except her underwear and stretched out on her stomach. Trudy got to work with the liniment. "I have to do this for my mister every so often," she said, ladling on the foul-smelling liquid and kneading it into Song's back.

"Vietnam said you worked for him," Billie said. "He told me you didn't do anything but sit around all day. I can see that was a lie."

"Didn't sit once," Song protested, her voice muffled by the pillows.

"I know, honey," Billie said. "It's what passes for humor with these crazy miners of ours."

After the massage came the eye cleansing and the fingernails. "Don't forget to wear gloves, girl," Dreama said, as she put the finishing touches with an emery board on Song's broken nails.

"I already got you another pair!" Young Henry cried from deep in the hall.

Doctor K appeared after stomping up the steps and making all kinds of noise and commotion.

"What's all this?" she bellowed. "How come I wasn't called? Oh, my stars, Song, what's happened to you?"

Song painfully turned her head to look at Doctor K. "I told Rhonda not to call you. Who did?"

There was the sound of someone running down the stairs. It was Young Henry. "Well, he always has my best interest at heart, doesn't he?" Song said. She would have smiled but it hurt too much.

Doctor K gave her a quick once-over and pronounced her diagnosis. "Dehydrated, bruised, and generally busted like most first-day miners. My initial prescription is water, and lots of it. It's best to drink it as you work. It's hard to catch up once you get behind."

"I will. I promise." Song flexed her arms. "It all hurts."

"Uh-huh." Doctor K smiled knowingly. "You're using muscles you've never used much before. I could give you some fancy prescription painkillers, but aspirin or ibuprofen will do for what ails you. What I *am* going to prescribe is rest. Tomorrow, take the day off."

"I can't do that!"

Doctor K was not impressed by Song's objection. "As the company doctor, I can make you stay home. Just one phone call, that's all it will take."

Song clutched Doctor K's hand. "Please, Doctor K! Don't do that! If they think I've weakened, they'll be on me like a pack of wolves."

Doctor K caught the aroma of the liniment slathered over Song. She wrinkled her nose. "You smell like a Christmas tree in a bucket of vinegar."

"My patented recipe," Billie said proudly.

"It smells bad enough to work," Doctor K grumbled. "All right, Song. If you think you can work, go ahead. But try to take it easy tomorrow, okay? You're pretty beat up."

"I will. I swan."

"I'm going to work on your foot blisters now, honey," Rhonda said. "Okay, Doc?"

Doctor K nodded. "You coal miner's wives are better at this kind of thing than I am anyway." She packed up her black bag and went out the door.

The red caps were in the hall. "How is she?" Justin asked.

"She's going to live," Doctor K reported.

"Is she going to work tomorrow?" Chevrolet asked.

"She says she is, so I guess so."

"If she says she's going to do something, she's gonna do it," Gilberto said.

"That's one tough lady," Ford put in. He rolled his head and straightened his back, his bones cracking. "Lord knows, my back don't feel none too good, neither."

"You boys better get to bed," Doctor K advised.

"What time is it?" Chevrolet asked.

"You've had supper. For a miner, that means bedtime or sleep in front of the TV, take your choice."

The red caps made their choice, heading for their rooms and their soft mattresses to snore through the night.

Song was also sleepy, but there was no dozing while Rhonda worked on her feet, opening the blisters, covering them with salve, and placing protective patches over them. Then, when all the work was done, her blisters repaired, the dirt from around her eyes removed, her fingernails cleaned, her back and legs rubbed, Rhonda saw the little coal miner was asleep. She covered Song up with a blanket, and the women tiptoed from the room. Song did not stir once during the night until her alarm clock rang the next morning. She reached for it, knocked it off the nightstand, and then stared at it until the spring inside ran all the way down. There was a knock on the door, and when Song didn't answer, it swung open. Young Henry, an anxious look on his face, entered, carrying a package.

"You okay, ma'am? I got you some new gloves."

Song started to crawl out of bed, noticed she was naked, and pulled the covers around her. "I hurt, Young Henry."

"I'll get the doc again!"

"No. Close the door behind you. I'll be fine."

Reluctantly, Young Henry closed the door behind him, and Song crawled out of bed. Literally. Down the step stool and onto the floor. She then crawled toward the bathroom. When she found her red helmet on the floor, she put it on, an act of defiance, and kept crawling. She was going to work.

Twenty-Four

Cable hung up the phone, then sat back on the couch in the governor's office and gave the conversation he'd just had some thought. Vietnam Petroski had supervised Song on her first day and wanted Cable to know she'd managed to finish the shift, but was battered and bruised.

"She won't be back tomorrow, Cable," Petroski said confidently. "She could barely walk to the bathhouse."

Cable tried to judge how he felt about the news. True, it had met his expectations. Song might be tough-minded, but her body was too small and frail for coal mining. Miners required extraordinary upper-body strength and she just didn't have it. On the other hand, he was impressed that she had managed to complete a full shift. As hard as Petroski worked any man under him, he had no doubt she'd been fully occupied throughout the shift with red cap work, which was typically dirty, hard, and monotonous.

But now Song was through, and that was good. Cable supposed Song would be back with her father by the time he returned to Highcoal. That meant, he realized, there was every chance he'd never see her again. He took a sip of the gin and tonic Michelle had mixed for him when he'd arrived at her office.

He took another drink. *I'll never see Song again.* The prospect was disheartening. But, *come on, Cable*, he thought. It was just as well, both for him and for her. They were never meant to be together. Why on God's green earth he had thought they were, he now could not imagine.

One thing he did know for sure, he was glad to be back in West Virginia after visiting New York. The visit to Atlas headquarters had been rough. He thought he was there for some routine meetings, but instead he'd been raked over the coals, the metallurgical bituminous coals, as it were. In the conference room, Helen Duvalle, Atlas's chief financial officer, had shown a series of viewgraphs detailing the Highcoal operation's tonnage targets. The numbers were all green at the bottom of her graphs and columns except for one, the most important one according to her, the special high-grade metallurgical coal desperately needed by the Indian steel mill that had contracted with Atlas. She pointed at that number and reminded Cable of his failure.

Cable had protested the implications. "Look, we're not missing it by much. A few hundred tons over six months is nothing."

"It may be nothing to you, but our Indian buyers are screaming. If we don't deliver precisely what they order, they'll find someone else who will."

Bob Hernandez, president of Atlas, leaned over and asked, "So, Cable. What are we going to do?"

Cable told them he was working on it. It all took time, and he needed more of it. Duvalle and Hernandez had traded glances. Cable knew very well he was being set up to be fired, whether he produced enough metallurgical coal or not. He was out of favor and they wanted a new man. He wondered now if Joe Hawkins was behind the scenes, pulling their strings. He recklessly asked them about it.

"I heard Atlas got bought," he said.

The expression on their faces told Cable that Hernandez and Duvalle were unaware of the change.

"That's ridiculous," Hernandez said. "We're part of the Taurus group, and have been for years."

"Guess my sources are wrong," Cable allowed.

"They certainly are," Duvalle snapped.

Hernandez and Duvalle moved on to review Cable's requests for new equipment, all of which were denied. Among them was a purchase order for electronic identification tags, designed to pinpoint where a miner was in the mine at all times.

"They've been mandated by the West Virginia legislature," Cable pointed out. "During the Sago rescue, nobody could figure out where the trapped miners were."

"How many other mines have them?" Duvalle asked.

"Only a few."

"Do they work?"

"So far, not reliably. We need to test them."

"We'll let somebody else test them," Hernandez concluded.

Hernandez next brought up drilling for natural gas on the Highcoal property. "Now, there's a successful operation, Cable. You should take a lesson from it. Bashful Puckett makes us a solid profit."

Cable nodded his agreement. "Yes, sir. Bashful punches a lot of holes. It's hard to miss all the natural gas that's in the area. But he's made a lot of problems for me. He's hated in Highcoal and needs to come under my control."

"Your control, Cable?" Duvalle demanded, his eyebrows rising in dismay. "I don't think so. We'll keep managing the gas drilling operations from here. That way, we know it will stay profitable."

Cable took a patient breath. "Bashful knocks down fences and tears up the forest."

"I'm sure he only goes where we own mineral rights."

"That's most of Highcoal and the surrounding mountains. Look, Bob, Helen, I'm not saying we shouldn't drill. It's just that it can be done without tearing up half the county."

Hernandez folded his hands atop the table, a signal he had made up his mind. The meeting was over. Hernandez and Duvalle strode out, leaving Cable to fume.

Now, sitting in the governor's office waiting for Michelle, he tried to shake off the memory of the meeting. Finally, Michelle swept in, dressed in a silver-sequined evening dress. They were on their way to the Charleston Symphony. She had just stopped in to sign some new laws. Cable put down his empty glass, stood, and admired her.

"You're beautiful," he said, and it was the truth.

The governor regarded him, a twinkle in her eyes. "You're not bad yourself, handsome man." She kissed him, a light peck on the lips. "Look what I've done. I've left a little bit of me on you."

Cable used his handkerchief to blot away her lipstick. Then he held her hands. "You are such a good friend, Michelle."

Her eyes reflected hurt. "Maybe we should be more than just good friends."

"Maybe. But I'm not the kind of man who can lose his marriage, then just start up with someone else right away. Even someone as wonderful as you."

"Have you signed the annulment papers?"

"Not yet."

She pulled away and pouted. "You are the most exasperating man I've ever known." She sighed, made a tsking sound with her gorgeous lips, then provided an understanding smile. "Take me to the symphony, my dear friend. Take me there and hold my hand while my heart beats just for you. Then send me home alone while you return to Highcoal."

"You make me sound heartless."

"Heartless? You, Cable? Nonsense. You have more heart than a dozen men. A hundred!"

Then, with a determined flip of her hair, the governor took Cable's hand and drew him along behind her.

Twenty-Five

Song stood in the crowd of miners waiting at the manlift gate. Petroski came over. "I'm surprised to see you back." He appeared to be studying her—for signs of weakness, she supposed.

Song was fully outfitted. Her lamp was attached to her helmet, her miner's belt was loaded down with an SCSR and a battery, her jumpsuit was still dirty from the day before, and she was wearing leather gloves. Except for the color of her helmet, she was the picture of a small but veteran coal miner. She gave her foreman a determined grin.

"I got up this morning and couldn't wait to get to work." The truth was every muscle in her body hurt, but Petroski didn't need to know that.

"Well, one thing you can count on in a coal mine, little lady, is work," Petroski said. "And a dang sight lot of it."

"I can't wait." She kept smiling, ignoring the ache in her back.

Petroski touched the bill of his helmet to her, then walked off to join the other white helmets.

"Good morning, Song," someone said. Song was surprised when it proved to be Preacher. He was in work clothes and a black helmet. "Bossman called me in to work today. You and I will be working together."

"That's wonderful," she said, and meant it.

"How was your first day at work?"

"I'm beat up," she confessed. She looked around and put a finger to her lips. "Don't tell anybody."

"I'll pray for your joints and bones."

"Pray for my head too. It hurts."

"Let me see your helmet."

Song handed it over, and Preacher fiddled with it. "I think it was too tight. Try it now."

Song did, and the helmet felt better. The four ibuprofen she'd taken that morning along with about a quart of water was helping too. "Just the ticket, Preacher. Thanks!"

He chuckled. "We try to be helpful to everyone in our congregation. Even," he added, "agnostics. But it don't matter whether you believe in God or not, just as long as He believes in you."

She puzzled over that. "What does that mean?"

"I have no idea," he confessed, just as the manlift bell rang.

The gang of white caps, black caps, red caps, Song, and Preacher stepped aboard. "Turn your lights on, you red caps," somebody growled. Sheepishly, they did.

"Good to see you here today, Preacher," a black cap said. "Guess I don't have to worry about the roof falling on top of me."

Preacher shined his light on the man. "Harvey," he said, "I don't recall you at services last Sunday. You'd best stand under a roof bolt all day. Otherwise, the Lord might let His presence be known."

"Don't say that, Preacher!" Harvey cried. "It's bad luck."

Preacher raised his hand. "I beseech thee, dear Lord Jesus Christ, to spare this poor sinner who I'm sure had important work to do, his oxen in a ditch or something."

"He went hunting," another black cap reported.

"You went with me," Harvey snapped.

"Bless all of us sinners on this manlift cage," Preacher intoned, "and let us see us, everyone, in Your house this Sunday, Lord, and maybe Wednesday night too."

"Amen!" all on the manlift said, including Song, and Preacher was happy. He considered much of his real work for the day already accomplished.

AT THE SIX West face, Petroski peered at the trio he'd split off from the others. "Song, Preacher, and Bum, you'll timber this morning. After you're done, shovel out the gob back at the entry. It's starting to get real deep back there. I want every bit of it gone before the day's out."

After Petroski was gone, Song asked Bum, "Where did you go yesterday? I had to drag and stack all these posts by myself."

Bum leered at her. "Why do you ask? Did you want to get me off in the gob somewhere, maybe lie down beside old Bum?"

"I would sooner lie down with a flea-bitten dog," she assured him while Preacher chuckled.

"Don't you laugh at me, you hypocrite," Bum raged at Preacher.

"It was funny the way she said it, that's all," Preacher replied amiably. "I apologize if I've offended you."

"Yeah? Well, here's something really funny." Bum smacked the preacher on the side of his head, knocking his helmet off. Then, when Preacher bent over to pick up his helmet, Bum put his boot on Preacher's backside and shoved him down. "One word about this," Bum snarled, his light flashing from Preacher to Song, "and I'll kill you. You hear me, girl?"

"Bum, don't talk like that," Preacher said from the gob. "We're not going to turn you in. Let's just forget it and go to work."

Bum's gap-toothed attempt to grin split his evil face. "Shut up, Preacher. You know what, girl? The day is coming when you and me, we're going to lay down together because you want to." He gave his privates a squeeze with both hands.

"You have to feel around for those little things to make sure they're there, Bum?" Song asked sweetly.

"You got a smart mouth, lady."

"And you've got a dirty one. Did you ever consider brushing the few nasty teeth you've got left in it?" She turned away from him and helped Preacher up. "Are you all right?"

"Better than all right," he said. "Please, children. Let's go to work."

"Please, children. Let's go to work," Bum mocked. "You two go ahead. I'm gonna take a crap first." He moved off into the darkness.

Song and Preacher, relieved that Bum was gone and hoping he wouldn't come back, started putting in the new posts. "I don't understand why Cable doesn't fire that fool," Song said.

"They were born about the same time and raised up in Highcoal," Preacher said. "I was a little younger, and the truth is both Cable and Bum were my heroes. They kind of ruled the roost of boys. Later on, they were on the high school football team together, both linebackers. Bum's daddy was killed in the mine and it made him bitter. Cable's dad was killed in the mine and it made him determined to make something of himself, and come back here to keep miners safe. That's the difference between them. I think Cable hopes to save Bum from himself somehow. That's why he keeps giving him another chance."

Preacher stopped and wiped the sweat from his brow with a red bandana. "But some men can't be changed. They harden their hearts. The Bible says he who sows iniquity will reap sorrow and the rod of his anger will fail."

Song laughed. "I bet you have a Bible quote for everything."

"It is a fount of incredible wisdom."

"Maybe, but you have to know it was written by a bunch of desert nomads to explain things they didn't know, things that our scientists and psychiatrists have now fully explained."

Preacher lifted a post and placed it on the stone floor. "What was mysterious to those desert nomads thousands of years ago is still mysterious to us today, no matter what the scientists and psychiatrists may discover. The human heart is filled with contradictions—that is the struggle between evil and good. We are a universe unto ourselves, where each of us are charged by something we will never understand. It is our sacred duty to fight evil, and the Bible is our guide on how to do it."

"I didn't mean to start an argument, Preacher," Song said. She used the butt end of an ax to pound the shim in until the post was tight between the roof and the floor. "Forgive me?"

Preacher's light flashed across her face. "Oh, a friendly discussion helps pass the time," he said. "But now, let's work as hard as we can. Somebody once said there is no water holier than the sweat off a man's brow."

"Or a woman's," Song said, and with her sore muscles starting to loosen up, set about proving it.

BUM NEVER RETURNED that morning, and Preacher and Song still managed to install the new posts, have lunch, and then set about shoveling gob at the entry. Petroski passed by an hour before quitting time.

"I'd a thought you'd loaded more gob than this," he said. "Where's Bum?"

"Taking a break," Preacher answered.

"Where's his shovel?"

"Probably with him."

Petroski shook his head. "I can't believe a preacher would lie to protect the likes of Bum."

"He didn't lie, he just left some things out," Song said. "We haven't seen Bum all day."

"That lazy fool," Petroski growled. "You two keep shoveling." He crabbed off toward the face.

Shoveling gob required them to be bent over beneath the roof, push their shovel into the thick slurry of rock dust and coal on the floor, then toss the result into a mine car without hitting the roof with the shovel. This resulted in a contorted posture with a lot of the gob blowing back into their faces. When they took a short water break, Song discovered that if she spread her feet apart far enough, she could actually straighten her back with her helmet just touching the roof. A couple of yoga twists and her back felt a lot better.

It also felt good to remove the chafing paper mask from her face. She slapped it against her leg and marveled at the dust imbedded in it. "This could be in my lungs."

"That's why a lot of miners chew tobacco," Preacher said. "They say it catches the dust."

"And gives them cancer of the mouth. Great trade-off."

"They trust in the Lord."

"Then it's a misplaced trust."

Preacher shone his light at her, then away. "You don't want to hear a sermon, do you?"

Song shook her head. "I told Cable I was a Yogist. He couldn't believe it. The truth is I'm pretty certain there's some benevolent force in the universe. I just don't know if organized religion has properly defined that force."

"Faith defies definition," Preacher said. "But I'm not going to try to proselytize you, Song. You're smart enough to make up your own mind. But you sure are welcome in my church. I know God likes having you there too."

"Did He say so?"

"Well, let me put it this way. He sure seems to have steered you to it, hasn't He?"

Song gave that some thought. Preacher had a point.

Bum chose that moment to return. He had a shovel with him. Without a word, he began to toss gob into the car.

"Petroski was just looking for you," Song said.

"He found me. I was looking for my shovel."

"Sorry it took all day."

"You just shut up, girl. Don't you open your mouth at me neither, Preacher."

Bum kept shoveling. One thing about him, Song noticed, he was a strong worker when he tried. Soon the car was full. They pushed it away and pushed an empty one to take its place. Not too long after that, they heard the equipment at the face fall silent. The day was done. Song retrieved her dented lunch bucket— Young Henry had banged it back into shape—then walked with the other miners toward the manlift pickup point on the main line. Everyone was quiet, subdued. It had been a hard day but good coal was mined, Petroski announced. Song felt proud, even though technically she had not mined a single lump.

On the manlift up to the surface, she realized she had done nothing yet toward figuring out why Cable wasn't meeting his quota. She suspected it wasn't miners like Bum who crawled off and slacked off all day. If there were any more like that big lug, the foremen probably knew who they were, and put them on cleanup duties and not on anything that would directly affect production by much. When she and Preacher had taken a late lunch, they'd carried their lunch buckets to the face and watched the action. Song had seen nothing in how the coal was being mined, loaded, and moved to the main line that would account for any shortfall. Quite the contrary. It was an efficient operation.

Then what was the problem?

As the week wore on, Song was moved to other foremen, other sections, and other duties. Although she was still sore at the end of each day, gradually she could feel her strength increasing, especially with the help of Rhonda's nourishing meals and her yoga exercises, which she sometimes did inside the mine, to the amusement and astonishment of the black caps. At Four West, she was stationed at a conveyor belt and told to shovel back any coal that fell off it. There was a surprisingly large amount. Later, when she was sitting with the other miners in a lunch hole, the foreman, Duck Mallard, came by.

"How'd you like to operate a shuttle car?"

Song was eating an apple, the last food in her bucket. The two sandwiches and bag of chips and cookies were already devoured.

"Are you joking?" she asked, suspecting a trick.

Mallard's grimy face seemed sincere. "You worked hard all morning. I think you've earned a chance to see what sit-down work is like. Come on, give it a try. Bama, you come along too, help us out."

Bama was one of the shuttle car operators. He had been born and raised in Alabama, thus his nickname. Grinning, he closed his bucket and took a last swig of water. "Glad to, boss," he said.

At the shuttle car, Bama went over the operation details. "First thing, ma'am, don't lean out. You get caught between a buggy and a rib, it'll tear your arm off." After that cheerful insight, Bama continued. "The seat turns around so the buggy don't have to. You keep easing in behind the miner until you get the car full, then you turn yourself around, not the buggy but *yourself*, then drive it through that curtain and raise the boom and dump it into the bin that feeds the belt. That's all there is to it. Understand?"

"I think so," Song said.

"Okay, here's the switch to turn the buggy on, here's the lever that raises the boom and lowers it. There the pedal on the floor that makes it go, and a brake to make it stop just like in a car. All your power comes through that big electrical cable. Got it?"

"Got it," Song said. She was getting excited at the prospect of driving the huge machine. "Can I give it a try?"

"Sure. Your car's already full so all you got to do is dump it in the feeder bin."

Song sat in the hard plastic seat and eagerly put her hands on the wheel.

"Go ahead," Bama said. He backed away, getting well clear.

Song took a deep breath, then threw the switch marked ON/OFF. She could feel its power vibrating through her seat. "Here I go!" she yelled, then pressed the pedal down. The shuttle car lurched forward, way faster than Song expected. She found herself roaring toward a rib. Steering wildly, she swiped it, took out three posts, and plowed on until the brakes took hold. Bama and Duck came running.

"You okay?" Duck asked, his eyes white and wide in his coal-blackened face.

Song was trembling. "I-I th-think so," she stuttered.

Duck whistled at some miners who had jumped in a manhole to get out of Song's way. "Get them posts back up!" he yelled at them and they got busy.

"Use a little less gas next time," Bama suggested, patting Song on her shoulder.

"You're going to let me try again?"

"Sure. Go on. You'll get the hang of it."

This time, Song pressed lightly on the accelerator pedal. The huge machine trundled forward. She turned and then braked, all without hitting anything.

"Well done!" Bama yelled. "Now, take the coal to the bin."

Song turned the seat around and pressed the pedal again and rolled across the soft gob. The buggy picked up speed. She hit the brake just before she reached the ventilating curtain that guarded the conveyor belt, then rammed the rib beside it, backed up, snagged the curtain with the shuttle boom, then roared ahead, the curtain flapping from the boom like a big gray flag. Bama appeared beside her. He was laughing so hard, tears were carving streaks in the grime on his cheeks. "You might as well keep going," he said. "I don't think you can do much more damage to this old mine. I'll hang the curtain back up."

Song happily kept going, managing to swipe another rib before finally lurching up to the belt where she stopped just short of ramming it. She started the belt, and the coal spewed in a black torrent off the boom, most of it on the floor. She backed up and tried again, dumping the rest of the coal more or less into the bin. Song wiped the sweat from her face, which was split with a big grin.

"I did it!" she yelled while the miners watching her laughed, cheered, and applauded.

Song turned the seat around and powered the huge machine back toward the face, men scrambling to get out of her way. Bama finally waved her down. "I'll take over from here," he said, still wiping his eyes from his laughing fit. He handed her a shovel. "See all that coal you dumped into the gob? Use this to get it where it needs to go."

Song's lip went out. "You think I'm a bad driver, don't you?"

"Not a bit of it," he said. "For a first timer, you did great!"

"You really think so?"

"Absolutely."

"Can I drive it more today?"

"Well, maybe not today. Company rules, you know. A buggy operator is only allowed to knock down three posts and rip down one curtain on a single shift."

Song nodded. "How about tomorrow?"

Bama chuckled. "You're something else, lady. For now, let's see how well you operate that shovel." Bama pressed the accelerator pedal and trundled smoothly off toward the face.

Song walked back to the pile of coal she'd accidentally dumped, shoveling the last of it just as Bama returned. He drove the shuttle car to the feeder, stopped precisely, and loaded the bin without losing a single lump of coal. "That's how you do it, ma'am," he said, touching his helmet. "Next time you'll do it perfectly, I swan."

Duck came by. "You did good for a red cap," he told her. "Last one I let run a shuttle car almost turned the dang thing over. Keep shoveling. Every lump of coal mined should be a lump of coal sent out of here."

Song kept shoveling until a question occurred to her. "Duck, is there some place in this mine where coal could get lost?"

"Lost?"

"Misplaced. Or even stolen?"

Duck gave her question some thought. "Not inside," he said. "Up there." He raised his light toward the roof.

"What do you mean?"

"Well, think about it. Where does all the coal go after it leaves the mine?"

"I heard some of it goes to India."

"That's the last place. Before that, it has to be washed."

"Coal is washed?"

"In a manner of speaking. Sometimes the process is called cleaning the coal. It's where the coal is separated into different grades in big water tanks. Simplest way to explain it is coal with a lot of rock sinks, while pure coal floats. Washing coal is done in a preparation plant. Gosh-awful lot of coal can get lost in a preparation plant. If the washing's not done right, a lot of good coal gets thrown away." He thought for a moment more, then added, "Also, there's coal rustling."

All of Song's investigatory antennae were up. "Coal rustling?"

"Stealing coal. Some of that's been going on around the coalfields during the last few years."

"How do you steal coal?" Song eagerly asked. She was certain she was on to something. "And why would you want to?"

"How, I'm not sure," Duck admitted. "Why? Same reason you'd steal anything, I reckon. To make money."

Song gave that some thought. "Is coal worth stealing?"

"Metallurgical coal is, if you steal enough of it. That's expensive stuff."

"How much is it worth?"

"Well, a few years ago, you could get a ton of the finest grade of metallurgical coal for thirty, forty dollars. These days, it's more like a hundred. This special stuff the Indians are after, wouldn't surprise me if they were willing to pay even more for it."

Song was dubious. "It still doesn't sound like it's worth the effort."

Mallard shrugged. "Most of the coal trucks you see out on the road can carry up to thirty tons. If you find a buyer, one load of coal would bring you some good money. Steal enough loads, it adds up." He frowned at her. "You don't plan on rustling coal, do you?"

"No. I was just wondering."

"Well, wonder with that shovel in your hand and pick up the rest of your spilled coal," he said.

"Yes, sir, Duck."

Song got back to shoveling along the belt, but the foreman's words kept running through her mind: *Steal enough loads, it adds up.*

Back on the surface, she spotted Mole at his usual station, leaning in the doorway to the office, watching the miners come off the manlift. She went up to him. "Tell me something, Mole. Why does this mine keep missing its quota to that Indian steel mill?"

He cocked his head. "Who wants to know?"

"I do."

"And who are you to wonder such a thing?"

"Somebody who has a hundred dollars in her pocket."

"Do you have two?"

"No. Just one."

Mole put out his hand and Song gave him the money. "So what's the answer?" she asked.

He tucked the bills in his back pocket. "I have no idea."

"You took my money and that's your answer?"

Mole shrugged. "It's the truth."

Song tried another tack. "What would it take for me to look at the production data on your computer?"

Mole whistled low, then looked skyward, as if for divine inspiration. Finally, he said, "Cable wouldn't like that. Why, a man could get fired."

"I didn't ask what Cable would like. I asked you what it would take. How much?"

"One thousand dollars."

"I'll have it for you by tomorrow," Song said.

He touched the brim on his black helmet. "Have a great evening, ma'am."

Song turned for the bathhouse, her step surprisingly light. Her blisters were still there, but the poultices had worked and her boots were loosening up. Her muscles still ached, but she could almost feel them getting harder. She held her head high. A knot of miners at the manlift watched her as she passed by. One by one, they took off their helmets. Song nodded to them, then touched the brim of her red helmet in mutual respect.

Twenty-Six

The church in Highcoal was rocking on Sunday morning. Preacher preached a great sermon, and then Song sang a solo Preacher had picked out for her:

O for the wings of a dove!
Far away, far away would I rove;
In the wilderness build me a nest,
And remain there forever at rest.

As Song sang, she felt Cable's eyes on her. When she sat down, she bowed her head, lest she look up and find him still watching her. Afterward, when she was exiting the rear door of the church, he was there. He took off his hat. "I didn't know you could sing."

She stood on the steps. "Until I came back to Highcoal, I didn't either."

Cable slapped his hat against his leg, that nervous gesture of his, then put it back on. "Well, that's all I wanted to say." He turned to leave.

"How was New York?" she asked.

He turned back. "It hasn't changed much. I still have a job, if that's what you mean."

"Did your managers know they'd been bought?"

"Nope."

"Good. We're not ready to let it be known." She looked him over. He seemed somehow diminished, as if the weight on his shoulders had pressed him down. "Can I ask you a question?"

"I haven't signed the annulment papers, but I will. I was going to take them to New York but forgot them."

"That's not what I was going to ask. Are you going to marry the governor?"

"Where did you hear that?"

"Highcoal gossip."

"You're plugged into Highcoal gossip?"

"I certainly am. I gossip with the best of them now. So, what about the governor? Are you to be West Virginia's first husband?"

He studied her for a moment, then asked, "What if the answer was yes?"

"Then I would be the first to congratulate you."

"I see. Well, the answer is I don't know." He consulted his wristwatch. "Look, I'm headed for the mine, got to meet Bossman there. Ventilation on Six West needs work. We're going to pull out of there pretty soon. Getting too close to the old section that's filled up with water. That's going to take some planning."

Song studied Cable for a long second. "Is that all you want from life, Cable? Just this town and your mine? There has to be more."

"There is," he said. "Family, friends, people you love, someday maybe children. That's what life means to me. Or could with the right woman."

"Then why," she said, doing her best to hold her tears back, "did you choose me to marry, of all people? Why didn't you pick someone who would want the same things you do?"

He looked at her, his eyes searching hers. "I don't know, Song. I honestly don't know. I sincerely regret I married you. Is that what you want to hear?"

Song felt as if he had driven a roof bolt through her heart. She struggled to contain how she felt. She mostly succeeded, although her smile was a bit crooked. "Michelle Godfrey's not the right woman for you," she said firmly.

"Well, that's one thing we agree on," he said, then turned and headed for his truck. He drove past her, without so much as another glance. She felt her heart crack, joining all the other cracks he'd already put there.

AFTER EVERYONE HAD gone to bed, Song slipped into Rhonda's office and sat behind her computer. She tapped on the mouse and the screen came to life. She inserted the first disk Mole had given her. It was software called *ProdStat*, which stood, she supposed, for Production Statistics. The computer whirred and clicked, installed the software, and instructed Song to remove the disk. She did, inserting the second disk, and opened on an icon marked *SectProd*. Mole had told her that was the one that would show her the tonnage produced over the last three years, section by section. The numbers were interesting, showing that each section had increased its production and efficiency per miner. *Good management, Cable*, she thought.

She next opened a file called *MonOrders*. This one let her look at the orders that had come in to the mine from Atlas headquarters month by month. She sorted through them until she found the one marked *India*. That was the one she was interested in. She saw that the orders for India had increased until the past three months, when they had gone flat, perhaps leveling off because the mine had never met the previous orders. She next opened an icon marked *GradeProd*, which showed the monthly tonnage of the various grades of coal as they came out of the preparation plant.

She studied the numbers. What she needed, she decided, was a monthly comparison of the Indian-grade coal and the overall production. The software, however, gave her no way to get it. She realized that she would have to print out the results she had, then do the calculations manually, a tedious exercise.

Song did the printing on Rhonda's laser printer, then removed the disk, trashed Mole's software out of the computer, and put the computer to sleep. She folded the documents, then headed for her room. Tomorrow was a work day. She didn't have time to work with the numbers now, but she would get to it as soon as she could. Inside those statistics, she hoped, was the answer to the mystery of why Cable wasn't meeting his quotas.

Song undressed and climbed into bed and slid beneath the cool sheets. She found herself looking forward to going to work the next morning. It was hard inside the mine, but it was always challenging. She liked that her foremen all thought she was doing a good job, and the other men, even the veteran black caps, respected her. She went to sleep soon after, and it was the sleep of quiet satisfaction.

Twenty-Seven

Bashful's rig was on the back slope of Tucker Mountain, on the western end of Atlas Energy property. Using bulldozers, his crew had cut a road across the mountain and set up a drilling rig, but Birchbark, his straw boss, was not happy with the setup.

"There's old mine works below this spot, Bashful," he complained. "We'll punch into them if we drill."

Bashful put his hands on his hips, took a deep breath, and looked around the slope. It was a lovely spot. Clear-cut thirty years ago to provide timbers for the mine, it had grown back into an even denser forest. The only people who ventured into it were deer hunters. Since hunting season was over, Bashful's crew had the place to themselves.

"Quit your worrying, Birchbark," he said. "So what if those old works are down there? They abandoned them twenty-five years ago, and they're at least a thousand feet below us. My gut tells me we can make a big strike here."

"How do you figure?" Birchbark demanded. "There's old wells spotted all around this area. They've been pumped dry, far as I know."

"Maybe, but nobody's drilled at this spot. I like the looks of the geology. I think there's a big pool of gas right below us."

"Sounds like wishful thinking, Bashful."

"Well, you just let me do the thinking, wishful or otherwise," Bashful snapped. "Drill here and keep drilling until I tell you to stop."

Birchbark opened his mouth to argue, but it was too late. Bashful was already walking purposefully toward his ATV. He climbed on, then roared off. Birchbark shook his head. He didn't like the idea of punching into a sealed-off section of an old mine. He'd never done that before and he didn't know what might happen if he did. But orders were orders, and there were car and trailer payments to make. Reluctantly, Birchbark waved at his men to level the rig and start drilling.

MONDAY MORNING, BOSSMAN Carlisle came up to Song as she stepped off the manlift. "I'm putting you as a helper on a roof bolt crew today. Two East. Don't let me down."

The chief foreman kept moving, whistling and waving his arms at his black helmets, signaling them to climb aboard the mantrip. Justin had overheard.

"I'll probably just shovel gob all day," he said despondently.

"I'm sure you'll be doing something else soon," she said.

"I don't think so. Seems like whatever I do requires a strong back."

Song put her hands over her head and stretched. "Speaking of backs . . ."

"I feel like I'm stove up half the time," Chevrolet admitted, as he, Ford, and Gilberto joined their fellow red caps.

"I wonder how our town got its name," Ford said. "I surely ain't seen much high coal. I stay bent over beneath that low roof all of the time."

Gilberto rolled his head. "I spent all day Sunday in a hot bath. I kept running it to make it hotter. My bones still hurt."

"No dang wonder there weren't no hot water when I took my shower!" Chevrolet erupted.

"Try yoga," Song suggested.

"Twist myself around like a pretzel?" Chevrolet demanded. "That's the problem, not the cure!"

"You red caps gonna stand around yakking all day?" Bossman yelled. "Get to work!"

Song and Justin crawled into a mantrip compartment together. Two black caps were in there already asleep. The mantrip trundled onto the main line and picked up speed, the posts flying by in a gray blur. It all seemed routine for Song now.

"How are you doing, Justin?" she asked when she saw he was wearing a morose expression.

"I'm still off drugs, if that's what you're asking," he snapped.

"That wasn't what I was asking, but I'm glad to hear it, all the same."

Justin peered at her, then shook his head. "You ever done drugs?"

"Some men are like a drug," she answered. "So I guess we've all got addictions. But what happened? How did you start?"

He shook his head and turned away as if she was not worthy of an answer. But then he turned back to her. She sensed his need to explain.

"One semester in college and I came running back. I just didn't fit out there, but it didn't take too long before I knew I didn't fit here, either. The mines were mostly closed then, so there were no jobs. About the only thing left to do was to get high. Clarissa was a cheerleader in high school and tried college but came running back too. We got married when she got pregnant the first time. She lost the baby, then we both started on meth, oxy, uppers, downers, painkillers, even heroin. Whatever. We didn't care. We broke into houses, stole what we could. Did some shoplifting in Beckley or Bluefield. Clarissa worked as a dancer in one of those men's clubs. Anything for money so we could buy the stuff we needed."

"What about your son?" Song asked. "Didn't the drugs . . . ?"

"He's fine," Justin answered quickly. "That's the one thing we did right. When Clarissa found out she was pregnant, she laid off the stuff until she had him, but then went right back on. I took care of both of them, best I could. I mean except when I was high. One day I came home, she'd gone off somewhere. I asked around, heard she'd been arrested. I gave the baby to some friends and went on a toot myself, then tried to sell some dope. I was in jail when she committed suicide. Before the funeral, they took my boy away from me. I thought about killing myself then, my idea to join Clarissa, you know, but I didn't have the guts, I guess."

"But you're here now," Song said gently. "Trying to put your life together."

"Yep. Because of Preacher. They put me in a clinic to dry me out and Preacher came over and sat with me and started to explain how heaven and earth worked. He said the devil made me evil by luring me into drugs. He said the only way to get out from under the devil's spell was to get baptized in the Lord. So that's what I did. It worked too." He pondered the passing posts and cuts, then looked at Song. "You don't believe in all that, do you?"

"I believe Preacher knew you needed to believe in something," Song replied. "But I don't think you were ever evil."

"Well, that's where you're wrong!" Justin retorted. "I made straight As in school and I was the big football star. I thought I knew everything there was to know. But my teachers didn't teach me about what was good and what was evil. Oh, I knew what *felt* good, but that was all. If you haven't figured it out, let me tell you, there's true evil in this world and those drugs I took, it was drinking the devil's own piss."

"But you're all right now," Song insisted.

He shook his head. "You just don't get it. Once the devil has hold of you, he never lets you go. That's why I still want it, why I'd give anything, even right now, to get high. But I know it's the devil talking in my head, telling me to go on, it won't hurt anything if I just take another pill, just this one last time. Get thee behind me, devil, that's what I have to say every minute, every hour, every day." He looked away. "I'm sorry. I get a little worked up."

"It's okay," she said.

"I'm going to get my boy back."

"I hope you're right."

Justin took on a determined expression. "First, I have to wear a black cap, and then have a real responsible job, like operating a continuous miner or a shuttle car. Then I can tell that judge, hey, I'm somebody important in the Highcoal mine. You can trust me with my boy."

"If I can help, be a witness or something . . ."

He gave her a sharp look. "You can. Tell Mr. Cable to make the foremen let me do something besides hold a shovel."

Song shook her head. "That wouldn't work, even if Cable did what I asked. You have to earn your way down here. You know that."

"So you're not going to help me, right?" He shook his head. "You're like everybody else. Just talk." He turned away from her and pulled his helmet down over his eyes, feigning sleep.

Song sat back against the steel bench and allowed a long sigh. She thought over what Justin had asked. Of course, she could help him if giving him what he wanted was helping. After all, her father owned the mine and she could do whatever she wanted to do, even forcing Bossman and Cable to train Justin for a responsible job. But would that truly help the young man? She didn't think so. Maybe too many people had given Justin too much throughout his life. Maybe that was why he'd turned to drugs when his life hit a snag. No, the way things were done inside the mine, where a man—or a woman—proved himself, step by step, day by day, that was the right way to go.

Still, she would do what she could, within limits, one red cap for another. Justin, after all, deserved a chance. The steel wheels of the mantrip kept clicking on the rails, each click carrying them deeper into the mine while Song thought over what she could do.

AT THE FACE, "Brown Mule" Williams provided a prayer, and then called Song over and told her to report to the roof bolt crew.

"How about Justin taking my place?" she asked.

Brown Mule cocked his head. "That dopehead? I don't think so. He can shovel gob."

"But he's off drugs."

The foreman reached over and rapped her helmet with a knuckle. "When your hat's white, lady, you can put crackheads on heavy machinery. But right now, it's red. So here's your choice. Do what I tell you or get off my section. You got less than a second to decide."

Song saw he was serious. "I'll find the roof bolt crew," she said.

"Lucky Irvine's the leader. Get going."

Lucky Irvine proved to be a tightly wound little man who ran his team like a well-oiled machine. "You mess up once and you're gone," he told her, and Song believed him.

The first thing Song discovered about roof bolting was it required perfect teamwork. When the continuous miner moved out of a cut, the roof bolters moved in, first holding up the freshly exposed roof with a power lift, then operating a drill to punch a hole in the roof, then feeding the roof bolt into the hole. If everything wasn't done sequentially and efficiently, the entire shift had to stop. She felt enormous pressure not to slow things down.

Her assigned task was to look for anything left behind and to make sure nothing impeded the reentry of the continuous miner after the bolts were secure. When a wrench fell off the front of the drill mount, she scrambled after it, and Lucky started screaming. The roof bolter was shut down, Song was jerked back by her jumpsuit, and everything stopped. Brown Mule came running. When he saw the situation, he turned purple with outrage, though he allowed Lucky to provide the lecture.

Lucky spun Song around and demanded, "What did you just do?"

Song was a little breathless after she had literally been pulled off her feet and dropped into the gob. "I just picked up a wrench," she explained.

"Right. But where did you pick it up?"

"In front of . . . *oh*!" She knew now what she'd done wrong.

"That's right. You were inby, under an exposed roof."

Lucky took a slate bar and lightly tapped the unsupported roof. In an instant, a huge dome-shaped dense black boulder fell, striking the bottom with a solid thump.

"That's a kettle bottom," he said. "An old tree stump sitting there for millions of years just waiting to fall. We got more than a few of them on this section."

Song stared at the huge stone. It would have easily crushed her skull, helmet or no. Her wide eyes told Lucky he had made his point, but he pressed it home. "You do that again, and I will have you sent you out of this mine. Understand?"

"Yes, sir," Song replied meekly.

"Then get back to work."

During the last hour of the shift, Bossman came by. Song was operating the drill by then. As Bossman and Brown Mule watched, she used the slate bar to knock down some draw rock, then inserted the bit and fed it up through the roof. She chose the correct length of bolt, pushed it into the hole, and torqued it down. The lights of the foremen flashed over her, then turned away as they huddled, talking over whatever foremen talked about.

On the walk to the mantrip, Bossman came up beside Song and said, "Good job," and kept walking. Song was filled with pride, but tamped it down when she again found herself sitting beside Justin on the mantrip out.

"Shoveled gob all day," he said glumly, then pulled his helmet down and turned away.

Before supper, Rhonda beckoned Song into the kitchen where she pointed at a bathroom scale. "Step up, honey; let's have a look."

Song stepped up and discovered, as she feared, that she had gained weight. But why, she thought, did her jeans fit so well? "You've lost fat but gained muscle," Rhonda explained. "I can see it in your back, your shoulders, and your arms. You're what they call *ripped*, girl!"

It was true. Song even had a six-pack of abs.

"All right, muscle woman," Rhonda said, "get out there and put the feed bag on."

At the red cap table, Song couldn't hold back. She told them what it was like to be on a roof bolt crew and what Bossman had said about her.

Justin slammed his fist on the table, rattling the plates. "Why are you getting these great jobs? You still sleeping with Cable?"

Ford glared at Justin. "What's your problem, buddy?"

Justin stood up, knocking over his chair. "I don't have a problem. Everything is just freakin' awesome." He gave Song an angry glance, then stalked out of the dining room.

"What just happened?" Gilberto wondered.

"He's tired of shoveling gob," Ford said.

"Well, who ain't?" Chevrolet demanded.

"This is my fault," Song said. "I shouldn't have been bragging. If Justin doesn't get a good job in the mine, he's afraid he won't get his son back."

"What's that got to do with you?" Ford demanded.

Song shrugged. "Nothing. He's just frustrated."

"Let's all go up to his room and kick his butt," Chevrolet proposed.

Rhonda swung by. "Leave Justin alone. I'll call Preacher. That's who that boy needs to talk to right now." She raised an eyebrow at Song. "And, yes ma'am, your bragging could ease up a bit."

"Sorry," Song said in a voice as small as she felt.

AFTER EVERYONE HAD gone to bed, Song sat at the table in her room and laid out the printouts she'd made the night before. With a borrowed calculator from Rhonda, she began her calculations, comparing the tons of raw coal produced at the Highcoal mine month by month with the tons of the various grades that resulted after going through the preparation plant. When she got the tonnages, she converted them into percentages. When she was finished, one number instantly leapt out at her. She tapped her finger on it. "Right there is where it started," she said to herself. "April of this year."

She pondered the silent number, then went downstairs. She checked the parlor, the dining room, and the kitchen to make sure she was alone, then went into Rhonda's office and sat down at the desk. She slid the county telephone book across the desk, then opened it and began to scan its entries. Even though it was late, she needed advice on what to do next and she didn't think it should wait. She found the number and dialed. A woman's voice answered.

"I'm sorry to call so late," she said. "But I'm one of Square's red caps. Could I please talk to him? Yes, ma'am. It's very important."

Twenty-Eight

Song looked for Bossman and found him in deep discussion with one of his shift foremen. He turned toward her with a broad smile. "Song, good morning. I wanted to have a word. I've decided to let you be a continuous miner helper today on Brown Mule's section. You'll get some training time in the operator's seat."

Song was thrilled at the prospect and knew Bossman was doing her a great honor. But she had other business to attend to.

"I'm not feeling well," she lied.

Bossman raised his eyebrows. "Then why are you here?"

"Well, I thought I could work outside today."

"Outside? If you're too sick to work in, you're too sick to work out."

"I'd really like to work out, if you don't mind."

Bossman glared at her. "What's wrong with you?" he demanded. "It better be something serious. Do you realize most red caps would kill to get trained on a continuous miner?" When she didn't answer, he said, "That time of the month, is it?" He shook his head and spat a stream of tobacco juice into the gob. "Well, there's another reason I don't like women in the mine."

"It's not my time of the month," Song replied evenly. "Even if it was, I could work. Maybe I'm coming down with something."

Bossman's lips curled up in doubt. "I should make you go see Doctor K, get a health slip. Are you wimping out on me, girl?"

"No, Bossman." Song felt terrible for disappointing him, but she had no choice. And she definitely couldn't tell him the real reason. "I just need to work outside today."

224

Bossman shook his head. "All right, have it your way. Check with Buck Puller—he's the chief electrician. You'll find him over at the office. He's got some boys changing out some wire at a couple of fans. They can use a hand, likely."

Song steeled herself for more rebuke. "I'd rather work at the preparation plant."

Bossman peered at her with his bright steady eyes. "You asked for a job outside, I gave you one, and now you're telling me you want to do something else?"

Song plunged on. "Square said we red caps should work all parts of the mine. I haven't pulled any training at the preparation plant." She looked at him beseechingly. "Would that be all right?"

Bossman chewed a couple of half-hearted chews, then spat again. "All right, little lady. We'll do it your way. Tell Stan Stanvic I said you could help him today. Stan runs the plant."

"Thank you, Bossman."

His expression was layered with disappointment. "All I got to say to you is have a nice day outside. No, wait. Something else. I hope you like shoveling gob. You didn't level with me just now, and I don't trust any miner who tells me a lie. I surely ain't gonna let a liar sit in on a continuous miner."

"I'm sorry," she said.

"That don't change nothing."

"One more thing," she said, shrinking back a little.

"What?" he demanded.

"Could you, please, maybe, since I can't do it, let Justin be a helper on the continuous miner today?"

"That druggie? Not a chance."

"He's not a druggie anymore, Bossman."

"How do you know?"

"He told me, and I believe him."

Bossman harrumphed, then stalked off.

Justin swung by. "I acted like an idiot last night," he said. "I'm sorry."

"It's okay, Justin. I was stupid, bragging like that in front of you."

"You ready to get on the manlift?" he asked.

"I'm working in the preparation plant today," she said.

Justin nodded. "I worked in the plant the other day. It's pretty boring.

Mostly I helped grease rollers and such. There's a big console of computers and stuff you'll probably like, though."

"Can't wait," Song said, glumly thinking about the continuous miner and how much fun it would have been to work around it.

Song watched as Justin and the other red caps got on the manlift. Bossman was on it too. He turned his eyes toward Song just as the manlift disappeared beneath the ground. His eyes were not friendly.

SQUARE MET HER at the door that led inside the vast steel building that housed the coal preparation plant. She thanked him for coming in.

"I'm feeling better," he allowed. "It's good to get out and breathe in some good coal dust. Just what a man with black lung ought to do!"

"Don't make me feel any worse than I do already," Song pleaded, then told him about Bossman and the continuous miner.

"Do you realize what a chance that is for a red cap?" Square demanded.

"Yes, and please leave me alone about it. Look, Square, I need your help to understand how this plant works."

"Why, exactly?"

"After you teach me about the plant, I'll tell you."

"You're a woman of mystery, ain't you?" Square said with a twinkle in his eye.

"Just help me. Please."

Square nodded, then led her up steps made of steel grate and into a control room. At a console of video monitors and gauges, an obese man with a round face, angry eyes, and a pencil-thin moustache swiveled their way. "Song, meet Stan Stanvic," Square said.

Stanvic eyed her red helmet. "You working for me today?"

"I'm giving her a tour," Square explained. "Just wanted to check in, see if it's okay with you."

Stanvic peered at Square suspiciously, then shrugged. "Knock yourself out."

"Tell us about those monitors," Square suggested.

Stanvic looked peeved, then stood up and waddled out, saying over his shoulder, "You do it. I ain't no red cap teacher."

"Stan's always been cranky at work until he eats lunch," Square said, smiling. "He'll eat about three lunches before he's through. Tell you what. Let's first go out into the plant and have a look around. Then maybe all these monitors will make sense. Leave your lunchbox here."

Once outside the office, Square said, "In a nutshell, what this operation does is take the raw material that comes out of the mine and separate it into rock, bad coal, and good coal. Rock's rock. You know about it. Bad coal has enough minerals in it to make too much ash when it's burned. Some you can sell, like to certain steam plants that don't care how much they pollute, and some you can't. Good coal is pure enough to burn in the modern power plants that have pollution standards. Really good coal, the finest, is called metallurgical grade. That's what's used to make steel."

Song followed Square up a series of steps that provided a dizzying view all the way down to the concrete floor of the huge facility. At the top level, which was over one hundred and fifty feet high, Square pushed open a door and they stepped outside onto another narrow walkway of steel grate. Song gripped the rail with both hands. "Is this where . . . ?" she began.

Square answered before she could finish. "No. Squirrel Harper fell from that perch over there, beside the froth flotation jig. Never figured Squirrel to be the kind of man who'd fall. He always struck me as being sure-footed."

"Maybe it wasn't an accident," Song said, recalling the constable's concern.

Square made no reply, just kept looking out into the distance. Song caught the brittle aroma of wood smoke, probably from someone building a fire in their fireplace. It was cold enough, and she shivered as the wind worked its way through her loose jumpsuit. Every morning for the last week, there had been a heavy frost coating the porch and the grass in the Cardinal's front yard. She had already thought about purchasing a warmer coat from Omar's.

From their perch near the top of the preparation plant, she could see the mine grounds were tucked in a little hollow, and behind it rose the steep mountain that lay over the underground works. Song studied the mountain, wondering, among other things, how much it weighed. Whatever it was, it was all pressing down on the mine below and the men she thought of now as her friends and colleagues.

"They're talking about taking the top off her," Square said of the mountain.

227

"Who is?"

"Atlas Energy. I heard Cable worrying about it the other day. Test bores show there's a lot of coal inside her, and the Atlas president has proposed mountain-top mining to get at it. They'll bring huge machines in, Song, bigger than anything you can imagine. To get up there, they'll have to scratch that old mountain to pieces to build roads, then they'll dig down inside her, pull out her guts, and drop them down the side. Oh, they'll say some day after they're done, they'll fill her back up with the spoil. But it won't ever be the same. Everything will be destroyed. Cable knows that and hates the idea."

"Cable against mining? I can't imagine that!"

Square shook his head. "You really don't know the man you married, do you?"

"Clearly not," Song said. "I guess that's why we're getting an annulment." She turned away from the mountain. "Tell me about this plant, Square."

"All right." Square pointed out where the raw coal was brought out of the mine from a separate shaft from the manlift, where it was first stored in a big silo, and then transported by conveyor belt aloft to rollers where it was crushed. Then he pointed to a slanted shaft where a series of screens separated the coal by size. "The big stuff is mostly rock and it's dropped down there," Square said, indicating a pile of yellowish rock below. He led her back inside and took her along another scary catwalk until they reached a huge tank of swirling black water.

"This is a jig, a dense-medium separator that uses specific gravity to separate the coal. The better grade of coal floats; the lesser grades sink. The coal that's skimmed off the top is good quality and is mostly used for power plants."

The next stop was another black vat of water, smaller than the first. A sharp odor from it pierced her nostrils. "Cable's pride and joy," Square said, patting the tank. "You've maybe heard about that steel mill in India with a requirement for an extremely high grade of coal. The only way to get it is with froth flotation, which is what this baby does. The water in it is mixed with special chemicals that make air bubbles sticky. When coal is dumped into the water and air is blown into it, the froth that's created sticks to the purest coal and floats it to the top. The coal that comes out of this jig is worth a great deal of money. Everybody pays top dollar for it, especially the Indians."

Song looked over the equipment with interest. Square led her down the steps until they reached the floor, then walked her to a huge inverted cone. "This is a cyclone. After the coal has been washed in the jigs, it has to be dried. It works just like the spin dry cycle in a washing machine. The coal is spun and the water is pushed out by centrifugal force. Then the coal is fed into what's called a bed dryer, which burns natural gas to evaporate any water left. Then, and only then, is the coal ready to go to market."

"What happens then?"

"Trucks carry it to a railhead. In our case, we use the one over at Fox Run."

"Why don't they put in tracks and have the train come here? It runs through town already."

"A very perceptive question," Square said. "They used to but when the demand for coal fell off thirty years ago, they took that track out. Now it's too expensive to lay down again, at least for now. Trucks are a stopgap measure."

Song followed Square through a door where he showed her three tall silos. There were trucks lined up in front of them. "The coal goes here in these bins to wait for pickup," he said.

Song looked around. "Who operates the plant?"

"It's fully automated so it pretty much operates itself. Not more than a couple of men are needed, mostly for maintenance, and as long as things are perking along, they generally only come in on weekends. Stan's job is to simply monitor things."

"Who watches the trucks and what their drivers load?"

"Stanvic does that. Before the trucks leave the yard, he checks each one. At night, the gate is kept locked except when there're special orders. Then Stanvic or Mole comes in and opens up."

"Mole?"

"He has lots of jobs around the mine."

The tour ended back in the control room. Stanvic was there with his feet up on the desk in front of the monitors. When he saw them enter his sanctum, he snorted in disgust, picked up his empty lunch box, and trudged out. "Thank you, Stan," Square called after him, then chuckled. "Stan's usually pretty grumpy after lunch."

"When *isn't* he grumpy?"

Square shrugged. "Maybe when he's asleep."

Square went over the purpose of each monitor and gauge. "So that's about it," he concluded. "Anything else you want to know?"

Song got up and brought her lunchbox to the console table, taking out the printouts she'd made. "Have a look at this," she said. "This column is the raw tonnage the Highcoal mine produced monthly over the past year. As you can see, every month this mine has been producing more and more. But this column is the percentage of how much of that coal was low grade. The next column is the percentage that was high grade, and this last column is the percentage that was metallurgical. What do you think?"

Square studied the printout. "In April, the percentage of high-grade metallurgical coal to raw tonnage slipped and never recovered," he said. He looked up at her, his eyebrows raised, his eyes wide.

"That's right. But why?"

Square thought it over. "Maybe a run of dirty coal. It happens."

"Wouldn't the other percentages also change in that case?"

"You'd think so," he said.

"Then what happened to that high-grade metallurgical coal?"

She watched as her suspicions dawned on Square. "You think somebody's stealing it?"

Song nodded. "Is there a way to do it?"

"Sure. You come in with a truck and haul it away."

"Wouldn't somebody notice that?"

"You'd think so."

"What if it was done when nobody was here? Like on the hoot-owl shift?"

Square looked dubious. "I told you they keep the gate locked at night."

"Except when there're special orders, you said."

"But then Stanvic or Mole are here."

Song pointed out the obvious. "So if there's theft, either Stanvic or Mole would have to know about it."

Square drummed his fingers on the printout. "Or both of them are in it together. But there's another possibility. If, say, somebody had a key and drove a truck in during the hoot-owl shift, they could load up without anybody knowing it."

"Wouldn't that make a lot of noise?"

"Yes. But around two every morning, as you no doubt have noticed, there's a train that rumbles through town. It could be done then and nobody would hear a thing."

"Just for the sake of argument, let's suppose somebody did that. What would they do with the stolen coal?"

Square thought some more, then said, "If they had a buyer, it would be a pretty simple thing to carry it to them and transfer it to another truck. There are a lot of coal buyers around."

Song and Square looked at each other, the possibilities and probabilities of the situation coursing through their minds. Finally Song asked, "So how do we find out?"

"We play detective, I suppose."

"Are you willing?"

Square frowned. "One thing worries me. What if it's Cable doing it?"

Song was astonished at that idea. "Cable? Surely not!"

"If we're detectives, everybody is under suspicion."

"I've never known Cable to do the first dishonest thing. Stupid, yes. Dishonest, no."

"Cable's a very intelligent man. Surely he's also noticed the drop in the metallurgical percentage."

"Mole's computer can't track it," Song said. "Only the gross tonnage. I did these calculations by hand."

"So you're saying you saw something even Cable couldn't see? About his own mine?"

"Figuring out what's wrong with companies is my specialty."

Square smiled at her. "You are a piece of work, Song, if you don't mind me saying so." He paused, then said, "When Cable bought Hillcrest, everybody wondered how he could afford it."

Song made a dismissive sound. "He's got a big mortgage. At least, I think he does."

"He sponsors the Highcoal T-ball and Little League teams, buys their uniforms and everything they need."

Song started to argue, then something dawned on her as well. "His Porsche. How could he possibly own a Porsche?"

She and Square shared a glance. "We have our work cut out for us," Square said. "Let the detecting begin."

Song gulped. All of a sudden, her enthusiasm for detective work was waning. *Cable, guilty of stealing his own coal?*

But she'd gone this far. She had to keep going, no matter where the evidence took her.

Twenty-Nine

Square sat in his truck, far enough from the light poles that surrounded the Highcoal preparation plant to put him in the shadows. He was watching the gate that the coal trucks only rarely used, the one on the far end of the mine complex, hidden from the town by a hillock and a tall stand of pine trees. Square poured another cup of coffee from his thermos, then checked his watch. It was approaching two o'clock. Soon the coal train bound for Fox Run would be coming through. He yawned and stretched. It was probably going to be another night of detective duty without result. For three nights, since Song had told him her suspicions, he had driven to the preparation plant to watch it. So far, nothing unusual had occurred.

He heard the rumble of a powerful engine and turned toward it. On the access road was a huge black coal truck, without lights, slowly making its way. At the gates, the driver got out, unlocked them, pulled them open, then got back into the truck and drove it toward the silos. The driver was too far away for Square to make out his face, but he was a big man with wide shoulders.

Square got out of his pickup and slipped through the gate. He stayed in the shadows, working his way until he could get a clear view of the black truck. The driver stayed inside the cab. A few minutes later, the coal train rumbled through town, its long line of cars thumping and bumping, a crescendo of noise. That was when the driver hopped out of the truck and rigged the silo holding the highest grade of metallurgical coal. *Bingo*, Square thought. Song was right. And now Square had the culprit. Soon everything would be clear as to why the precious coal was being taken, and who was doing it.

Unheard within the raucous thunder of the passing train, the fine grade of coal slid down the chute into the truck. Square slipped around a stack of lumber, to get into position to write down the license number of the truck. He was disappointed. A stack of mine posts obscured his view.

The driver walked away while the truck settled beneath the tons of coal. He lit up a cigarette, producing a glow on his face, a face that Square now recognized. The coal from the chute stopped, the truck was fully loaded, and the man got back in the truck, started it up, turned it around, and headed toward the gate. Square ran after it, then slowed, clutching his chest. Black lung didn't allow many long-distance runners.

While Square labored to catch his breath, the truck roared out onto the highway, its lights blinking on. Square stumbled ahead until he reached his pickup. After taking several hits off a small green oxygen bottle, he gave chase. He had to get that license number. It was one thing to recognize the driver, another to have the constable find out who owned the truck. That would tell them so much more, and prove their case too.

It wasn't long before Square caught sight of the truck's tail lights. It was heading in the direction of Fox Run. That was no surprise. There were lots of buyers of coal in the county seat. Square began to relax as the oxygen accomplished its magic. He just needed to catch up, get the license, then perhaps keep following to see where the truck went. But he didn't catch up with the truck. Either it had turned off, or the driver was driving like a maniac at top speed with a full load. Square kept going, driving over the first mountain, and then along the narrow valley that led to the next. He rounded a curve and was surprised to see the black truck pulled over. He had no choice but to pass it by.

Square looked for a place to turn around but there wasn't one until he reached the top of the next mountain. He turned off and tried to decide what to do. He decided his best course was to slowly drive on to Fox Run. Maybe the truck would catch up with him, even pass him. He pulled out on the road just as the black coal truck crested the mountain. Without slowing, it slammed into him, the pickup's windshield shattering in a hail of glass, its airbag pounding Square in the chest. The coal truck kept ramming Square's pickup all the way through the guard rail and over the mountain. It landed hard on its roof, then began to roll, knocking down trees as it plummeted toward the valley far below.

Thirty

Doctor K, dressed in scrubs, came out into the waiting room. "He's still with us," she told the assembly, which included Hildy, Square's wife, and numerous children and grandchildren. Preacher, Constable Petrie, Song, and all the red caps were also there. Doctor K directed her comments to Hildy. "He has two broken ankles, a couple of cracked ribs, a broken arm, and probably a concussion. There were no internal injuries that we could find. His black lung is being a bad actor, so we have him on a respirator."

"Is he going to be all right, Doc?" Hildy asked. Song had been surprised to discover she was a fellow New Yorker and had grown up in Idlewild. Square had met her while he was in the navy.

"I hope so," Doctor K said. "He's in intensive care. He'll stay there until we get him stabilized."

"Can I see him?"

"Sure. But only you and the immediate family." She did a quick count. "Okay, the top dozen or so."

"How about Preacher?"

Doctor K smiled. "Sure. I guess Preacher is family too."

After Hildy and selected children, grandchildren, and Preacher were led by an ICU nurse through the double doors, the constable asked Doctor K, "Did Square wake up long enough to say what happened?"

"No. And the paramedics said he was unconscious when they pulled him out of his truck. He'd be dead if it hadn't lodged against a big oak tree. There was a cliff that was vertical all the way to the river after that."

"Who found him?"

"A miner going to work at the Fox Run mine saw where the guard rails had been knocked down."

"What I don't understand is why he was out so late," Justin said. Justin had spent the hours of waiting by regaling his fellow red caps with the story of how he'd helped all day with a continuous miner. He'd even been allowed to operate it for a brief period.

"Maybe Square has a girlfriend at Fox Run," Chevrolet proposed.

"Shut up, brother," Ford said. "That's not nice."

The constable scratched up under his cap and eyed Song. "You're being awfully quiet," he said. "Do you know anything about this?"

"No," she lied.

The constable squinted at her, but said nothing.

Doctor K said, "Well, I've got work to do." She eyed the red caps. "And I think you're supposed to be at work in a couple of hours."

Gilberto let out a tired breath. "Another day shoveling gob and greasing belts, this time without any sleep."

"What you have to do, Gilberto," Justin said, "is tell your foreman you want to do something else. That's what I did, to Bossman, and he let me do it. You can't hold back."

"Oh, *sí*," Gilberto replied dubiously. "Please, Señor Foreman, you let Gilberto drive the continuous miner today? Ho, ho, Gilberto! I don't think so!"

"Come on, boys," Chevrolet said, standing up and stretching. "Square ain't gonna get any better, us just sitting around here. Let's get some shut-eye."

Cable came rushing into the clinic. "I just heard," he said.

Song didn't even acknowledge him, just walked out with her fellow red caps. She heard him ask the constable, "How is he?" just as the clinic door closed behind her. She kept walking a few more paces, then stopped.

"Wait for me," she said to the red caps and turned around.

Cable and the constable were talking when she came back inside. They turned toward her. "Forget something?" the constable asked.

Song looked at Cable. "I ran the numbers, Cable. Last April the percentage of high-grade metallurgical coal compared to total tonnage at your mine suddenly dropped. It never recovered. Did you know that?"

Cable looked surprised. "What are you talking about?"

"Let me put it a different way. While all the tonnage for the other grades of coal increased, the high-grade coal you needed for India decreased."

The constable frowned. "I don't understand what you're getting at here."

"I do," Cable said. "And it's nothing I didn't already know. We've been going through some bad coal since last April."

"No, Cable," Song said. "I don't think so. I think somebody's been stealing your coal."

Cable laughed. "That's ridiculous."

"Is it? Square's been watching the preparation plant. I think whoever's been stealing your coal was there tonight and Square caught him. I don't know how he got pushed off the road, but when we drove here, I saw where he'd gone over and there was a lot of coal on the road. If you tested it, I bet it's high grade."

When Cable said nothing, Song asked, "You didn't have anything to do with this, did you?"

Cable didn't answer. The constable was looking at him. Song felt like crying but she didn't. Coal miners—and that's what she was now—didn't cry.

"You gentlemen know where to find me," she said, then walked out.

THE NEXT WEEK passed in a blur. Song was shifted around to different sections each day, spending most of her time shoveling gob. On Friday, she and Gilberto spent the day with two black caps, changing out track on an old section that was scheduled to be reopened. The spikes had to be pulled, then the heavy rails levered off into the gob, the old ties lifted and carried away, then replaced by new ones. It was a laborious, difficult job, made worse by the low roof. Most of the work was done on their knees, and Song was grateful when one of the black caps provided her with a pair of spare knee pads. That evening she went to Omar's and got her own. And a fresh bottle of ibuprofen.

The news from the clinic was not good. Although he had been moved out of the ICU, Square remained unconscious. Song had seen nothing of Cable or the constable. Before her shift started, she spoke to Mole, who had nothing to say. He just raised both of his hands and said, "You keep this up, woman, you're gonna cost me my job," and refused to say anything more.

She thought about calling her father and asking his advice, but decided that was no good. If he heard about what had happened to Square, he would order her home. She finally did call, but told him everything was fine. No, better than fine. She thought she might have found the problem and she'd be home soon. But first, she said, she wanted the chance to operate a continuous miner.

Her father had chuckled at this. "You've turned into quite the little coal miner, haven't you?"

"I love it, Dad," Song confessed with a frankness and ardor that surprised even her. "I look forward to going to work every day. I've been told that mining gets in your blood. Maybe it's true."

But, though Song was happy in the mine, her heart ached. She wondered what she had unleashed. Square was injured Cable was in trouble. She didn't mind showing him how smart she was, and brave, and how stupid he was for giving her up, but she didn't want to send him to prison. She studied Hillcrest from the Cardinal's porch, wondering if he was up there, perhaps with a lawyer trying to figure out how to escape jail. There had been no sign of Governor Godfrey. At least there was that.

The weather turned bitterly cold. The autumn leaves withered, then fell in a rush until the surrounding mountains were brown and gray except for splotches of green pine and cedar. Highcoal seemed to wither too, the people retreating indoors. Chimney smoke drifted across the town with the delightful aroma of seasoned hickory and oak. Song imagined what it was like at Hillcrest, with fires built in the fireplaces and the kitchen warm with cooking. She tried her hand at baking biscuits with Rhonda and discovered she was pretty good at it. There was nothing quite so enjoyable as eating something you'd cooked yourself.

But mostly she waited and wondered what was going to happen next.

She didn't have to wait long.

Thirty-One

It wasn't hard for Bum to find him. Stan hunted on Sundays, and Bum knew where, at the old farm that belonged to his family out by the lake. It was Stan's plan to build a big new house on his property as soon as he retired. Bum guessed Stan would be able to afford it, considering the risks Bum had taken for him.

Bum had worked himself up for a confrontation all morning, mostly by popping meth. He was vibrating as he got out of the truck. He slapped his arms and legs and did a little dance, as if he'd been attacked by fire ants. He had enough sense to know it was just the meth. The sores that had erupted on his back and buttocks were caused by the meth too, but he loved the feeling of energy it gave him. It also allowed him to work all day in the mine, then moonlight for Stan at night.

Bum followed the retort of rifle fire and found Stanvic near the lakeshore. Stanvic frowned when he saw him, and this made Bum angry. He took it to mean Stanvic wasn't pleased to see him. Since all this started, it had been Bum who had done all the heavy lifting, driving the truck at night to load the coal, then hauling it to the buyer in Fox Run. He didn't know how much Stanvic got, but Bum had always suspected his cut was only a small percentage. The way Bum saw it, that needed to change.

"What do you want?" Stanvic demanded as the muscled, wide-shouldered miner got closer. "It's not good for us to be seen together."

Stanvic's attitude made Bum even angrier. "You know what happened to Square Block? That was me who done it."

Stanvic nodded. "I figured as much. How come?"

"He saw me."

"You were careless then."

"Yeah. Just like you were when Squirrel heard you talk to your buyer. That makes two men I've had to kill because of your little scam."

Stanvic shifted on his tiny feet and moved the rifle he was carrying so it could be swung easily. He had his finger on the trigger. "Well, you're well paid," he replied.

"Hell I am. Not like you. Anyway, I think it's time to end this thing. Square's a big buddy of Cable's. I think he was over there spying for him."

Stanvic looked into Bum's eyes and saw that he was not only angry, he was also on drugs, probably meth. "Maybe you're right," he said to give himself time to think.

"You got rich doing this," Bum accused.

Stanvic rolled his eyes. "Rich? You think I'm rich? None of this amounts to that much money. We're just skimming off the top, that's all."

"I figure you made a couple hundred thousand a year off it. What did I get? Twenty thousand? It just ain't worth it. I got bills, you know."

"The only bills you got are the ones you stuff up your nose," Stanvic said.

Bum was not impressed with that argument. "You give me a hundred thousand, I'll go away. We'll pretend this never happened. Neither Cable or the constable can prove a thing."

"What about Square?"

"I plan on paying him a little visit at the clinic, just to be sure he never wakes up."

Stanvic knew he was in trouble now. The meth had caused Bum to lose all sense of reality. "Bum, listen to me. I can't give you that much money, but I'll scrape up what I can. As for Square, what I heard is he might not wake up, so just leave him alone."

Bum took a step in his direction and Stanvic defensively raised his rifle. "Get off my property. I'm warning you, Bum. I'll shoot you otherwise. You know I will."

"I want my hundred thousand dollars," Bum said.

"I said I'd get you what I could."

"I want it all!"

Stanvic knew what he had to do. He had to kill Bum. It would be reported as a hunting accident. Bum had no business being in those woods, sneaking around. Probably taking drugs or something. *I fired, thinking it was a deer,* Stanvic would tell the constable.

Stanvic raised the rifle but it was already too late. Bum was coming at him like a crazed locomotive. He knocked the rifle aside and bowled Stanvic down. Stanvic's head struck a stump and that was the last thing he ever knew. A dark crimson pool of blood leaked out of his head, soaking the roots at the base of the stump. Bum looked down at him. "Well, Stan, look what you've done to yourself now. You never could take a good hit on the football field neither."

Bum dragged Stanvic to the lake, then tossed him in, wiped off the rifle, and threw it in too. After watching the body float for a few seconds, he took a circuitous route off Stanvic's property and back to his truck. There were more pills there. He needed more pills, but not meth. OxyContin ought to do it. It always brought him down and leveled him out until he was ready for more meth. Though his eyes were jerking around and his head felt like it was about ready to screw itself right off his body, Bum managed to stay in his lane all the way home.

Thirty-Two

Monday morning found a foot of snow that transformed Highcoal into a pristine white wonderland. As Song walked to work, she heard the sounds of joyful laughter. The children of Highcoal, and not a few of its adults, were out with their sleds. The constable, the blue and red lights of his truck flashing, was at the main intersection, watching over things, keeping traffic moving into the mine parking lot. Most of the pickups carrying miners had chains on their tires.

Song went over to have a word with Constable Petrie. "Did you and Cable have a talk?" she asked.

The constable looked at her. There was no information in his steady eyes. "We did. It's always good to talk to Cable."

"What did you talk about?"

"That would be police business," he answered.

"I was the one who ran the numbers. If you have anything, it's because of what I gave you."

"Still police business, ma'am."

"My father owns this mine."

"Now, Cable did say something about that."

Song recognized the futility of trying to get any information out of the constable, so when he tipped his cap to her, she nodded and left him to join the crowd of miners at the manlift.

"You and me are with Vietnam Petroski today," Justin informed her. He lifted his chin. "He told me the other day I had the makings of a good coal miner and maybe some day I might even wear a foreman's white cap."

She smiled at him. "I'm sure of it, Justin."

Chevrolet swung by, his eyes lit up with news. "Did you hear about Mr. Stanvic?"

"No," Song said and wrinkled her nose at the thought of the grumpy, obese man. "What about him?"

"He drowned in Spivey Lake."

"What are you talking about?"

"One of the foremen said Mr. Stanvic was hunting squirrels over there and fell in. They found his body yesterday."

"That don't sound right, somehow," Justin mused. "You'd think a man that fat couldn't possibly drown. He'd float, surely!"

Chevrolet shrugged. "Maybe he fell in face down, couldn't get hisself turned over."

"Maybe that's the stupidest thing you've ever said," Ford remarked as he joined the group of red caps. "All a man would have to do is flop his arms and over he'd go."

"I heard Mr. Stanvic had a bashed-in skull," Gilberto said, "so I don't think he could flop his arms too good."

"How did he get a bashed-in skull?" Chevrolet asked.

"Got hit by something, likely," Ford answered.

Chevrolet looked at Ford, then shook his head. "Brilliant, brother. Sometimes I just marvel at how you put things together."

Ford blushed. "Well, I do my best, you know."

On the mantrip, Song thought over the news and the subsequent discussion. Stanvic dead and found with a cracked skull. She wondered if the two-plus-two that was going through her head was really four. Cable, not only a thief, but a murderer too? Was that possible?

After his prayer, Petroski had a surprise announcement. It was the last day of mining on Six West. To get any closer to the old section just north of them was too hazardous. It was filled with water, and if they dug into it, it might flood the entire mine. Tomorrow, he said, they would come back and start moving out the equipment. "Cable says we're good to go for one more day," Petroski said, "but listen to me, boys. If you see any water seeping in, give a shout and we'll shut down and get out."

"What'll happen to the section?" one of the black caps asked.

"It'll be sealed off," Petroski answered.

"Too bad. There's still some good coal here."

"That's right, there is," the foreman agreed. "So let's make it a good day. Let's dig out as much of it as we can."

Song was put on gob-shoveling duty for the shuttle cars, her job to toss any coal they spilled onto the conveyor belt.

As quitting time approached, Song's tight shoulders and stiff back protested with every monotonous sweep of her shovel. At least she was almost caught up with the spilled coal, mainly because the continuous miner was down for maintenance. It had lost a tooth on its rotating drum and the operator had replaced it, then taken a short break. The face was quiet. A light swept over her, then came back. It enlarged as someone crabbed over to her.

It was Bossman. "You ready?" he asked.

She leaned on her shovel. "For what?"

"You want to try your hand on the miner?"

Her aches and tight muscles vanished in an instant. "I thought you were mad at me."

"I was. But I liked that you stood up for Justin."

"I never thanked you for that."

"No need. He did a good job. Come on. Let's get you checked out."

Ten minutes later, Song was operating a continuous mining machine, the best job in the mine. She loved the feel of power and control as she pushed the giant machine forward, tearing into a piece of the world that had lain undisturbed for hundreds of millions of years. She was the first human to ever see it, and that in itself was thrilling. She quickly got the hang of the levers that raised and lowered the boom with its spinning cutting heads. It was pure fun.

When the operator tapped her on her shoulder to replace her, she sought out Bossman to thank him again, but her light instead fell on Cable, who was alone and apparently waiting for her. He was holding a manila envelope, and his expression was grim.

"I'd like a word if you don't mind. It will take a couple of minutes." He nodded toward the curtain that covered the opening to the main line. "I've got my jeep. The others can go on out. I'll take you to the manlift after we talk."

Considering that it was at least conceivable he might be both a thief and a murderer, Song wasn't certain she wanted to be alone with Cable. "Why don't we talk topside?" she suggested.

He shook his head. "Needs to be here and now. I'm doubling back. The evening foreman on Three East has the flu. I'm going to fill in for him."

"Can't it wait until tomorrow?"

"Let's just talk, Song. Okay?"

Song gave it some thought, then nodded agreement. After all, Bossman, Vietnam, and all the black caps on the section knew she and Cable were together. If he had in mind to hurt her, he wouldn't likely do it under those circumstances.

Would he?

The shift was over and Bossman and the day shift trudged off, their lights flashing until they'd gone through the curtain. Then it was dark, except for the glow of the two helmet lights left behind. Before long, the sound of the mantrip's wheels had turned into a low rumble, and then there was nothing but silence.

Cable sat down on one of the track covers of the continuous miner. "I saw you driving this monster. You did well."

Song sat beside him, carefully keeping some distance between them. "Cable, what do you want?"

He swept his light around the face area, then pushed his white helmet up with a finger, scratched under it, then pulled it back into place. Finally, he said, "I want to tell you something. I'm grateful for what you did. Your calculations, I mean. When I went back and looked at the numbers, it was like a hammer right between my eyes. Why didn't I think about somebody stealing the coal? It was so obvious."

Song aimed her light at him. "You're saying you had no part in it?"

Cable's light swung to her. "Do you really think me so low? I may be stupid, Song. No, I take that back. I *am* stupid. But I knew nothing of this. After you left the clinic, I explained to Constable Petrie what the numbers meant. He bumped it up to the state police, who called in the FBI. That's where I've been the last few days—in Charleston, talking to the feds. It turns out there's been an epidemic of high-grade metallurgical coal theft all through the region. They think it's mostly bound for Chinese steel mills, but nobody knows for certain."

"What's going to happen now?" she asked.

"The feds swooped down on an outfit called Atomic Coal over the weekend. Looks like those fellows have been buying up metallurgical coal from anybody who'd sell it to them, no questions asked. Based on tests, some of their stockpile came from this mine."

"Who sold it to them?"

"If the feds know, they're not saying, but it had to be somebody who knew all the ins and outs of this mine and was a bit underhanded. My first suspicion, naturally, was Mole."

Song shook her head. "Not Mole. He'd have never given me the production numbers if it was him." They fell silent for a moment, then Song said, "You heard about Stanvic."

Cable took a breath and let it out. "Yeah. I think Stan was the thief, but now he's dead, murdered the constable says. He also thinks there's a strong probability Squirrel Harper was murdered too. But who killed them? That's what we don't know."

"I bet whoever pushed Square off the road is our killer," Song proposed.

Cable thought that over, then said, "Look, I don't know how this is all going to end, but I guess it's not up to me. It's up to Constable Petrie and the state police and the FBI. They'll figure it out. It's not what I wanted to talk to you about, anyway. Song, I'm proud of you, working in the mine like you have. And I want you to know I know I was wrong about you. There's a great deal more to you than I ever imagined." He smiled, and for just a moment, she saw the dimple in his cheek that she'd nearly forgotten existed. "I'd say all that to you even if your father didn't own the mine."

"Working down here has taught me a little about you too," she answered. "You run a first-class coal mine, Cable, and I respect and admire you for it."

"Thank you," he said.

They fell silent until Cable asked, "Do you remember when we met?"

She smiled. "You picked me up at Times Square. In more ways than one."

"As soon as I saw you, I thought, here is a woman I'd like to get to know."

"Well, you were on the rebound. We both were."

"Those first weeks we were together . . . Song, they were like magic. I want to thank you for them."

"They *were* magic, Cable, at least for me. For the first time in my life, I felt like I was really needed by a man."

"It was true. I needed you. That's why I asked you to marry me."

"Cable . . ."

"I know, Song. I wish those days could have gone on forever." Cable looked down at his boots, his light playing across them while her light played next to his.

Song slid a little closer to him. Her heart was beating so hard, she felt as if it were going to come out of her chest. The truth had finally burst through all her protective layers. She needed this man. She *wanted* this man. It was time to stop denying it.

"Cable," she said. "Maybe if we . . ."

"No, don't say anything. You're right. I've been a fool. About you, about the mine, about everything. That's why I sent Atlas headquarters my resignation today. I don't deserve to supervise this mine."

Song's eyes went wide and she flashed her light onto his face. "You did not!"

Cable was wearing a sad little smile. "It was the right thing to do," he said, then handed her the manila envelope. "This is the right thing to do too."

She took the envelope. "What is it?"

"The annulment papers. I signed them, Song. This is a copy. I sent the originals to your lawyer. You're free."

PART 3
THE DARKEST PLACE

Although affliction cometh not forth of the dust,
neither doth trouble spring out of the ground;
Yet man is born unto trouble,
as the sparks fly upward.
—Job 5:6–7

Thirty-Three

His men were adding thirty more feet of pipe to the well on Highcoal Mountain, which worried Birchbark more than a little. He thought about telling them to stop, to give it a rest, but they were into it now, the work nearly done. Birchbark heard the rattle of an engine and rolled his eyes. Here came Bashful again, his four-wheeler slipping and sliding through the snow. Birchbark stuffed his hands in his coat pockets and looked away. He didn't like his boss much, but what was a well-digger to do? If he wanted to live in Highcoal, Bashful's company was the only one around. Birchbark had dreams, big dreams. He had been saving up, and when he got enough, he was going to apply to the Fox Run First National Bank for a loan. Then he was going to buy his own rig and go into competition with Bashful. With the cruddy old hardware Bashful kept patching up and shoving into the field, Birchbark figured he could give the man a run for his money, especially if he could snag even a little piece of the Atlas contract.

But what he was doing now, Birchbark thought, could jeopardize everything. He needed to stop it. Bashful, dressed in a parka, snow pants, and insulated rubber boots, climbed off the vehicle. He looked like an Antarctic explorer. "Didn't think I was going to make it," he said as he came up beside Birchbark. "How'd you and the boys get up here?"

"Hello, Bashful," Birchbark said tiredly. "We came in on one of your bulldozers. See it over there?"

"Yeah, I see it. You know how much diesel that old thing burns? Y'all gonna put me in the poorhouse."

"It was either that or shut down the rig."

Birchbark knew Bashful didn't really care about the diesel. He just liked to pull Birchbark's chain. Bashful proved it when he immediately changed the subject. "How deep are we?"

Birchbark kicked at the frozen mud around the rig. "Too deep. We're almost down to the abandoned part of the mine."

"No gas yet?"

"Not even a wisp."

"Keep drilling," Bashful ordered. "There's gas down there, I swan."

Birchbark kicked his boots against the rig to dislodge the snow from the soles. "There may be gas down there," he said, "but if there is, I'm certain it's below the mine. And if we go any deeper, we could knock the roof down when we punch through."

Bashful shrugged. "So what? What about *abandoned* don't you understand?"

"I'm worried about a fire."

Bashful laughed. "That doesn't make sense."

"Yes, it does and you know it as well as I do. When it's cold like this, and the air pressure's high, methane starts coming out of the coal in buckets. Might be a lot of it built up inside those old works."

Bashful slapped his team leader on his back. "You worry too much, son. That old section's closed off with concrete block stoppings. I checked it out with Mole. A fire would have nowhere to go. That's why they're called stoppings."

"What if Mole tells Cable what we're doing?"

"I gave him a couple hundred dollars not to. Everything's going to be fine. I'll take the responsibility if anything goes wrong, but nothing is."

Birchbark saw that his team had the new pipe down and were drilling again. "Any second now and we're going to punch through."

"Good," Bashful said, rubbing his hands together and stomping his feet to warm them up. "Then maybe you'll stop whining like some little girl. I bet in the next few hours, we'll make one of the biggest strikes on this mountain ever."

"Maybe so," Birchbark said, then took off his helmet and looked up at the sky. "Looks like it's clearing."

Bashful was about to reply when he saw the crew suddenly run away from the rig. Then he felt the earth trembling beneath his feet. "What's happening?"

he asked, but it was to empty air because Birchbark had joined his riggers, running for the safety of the bulldozer.

THERE WAS A rumble, and then everything at the face shook. Draw rock fell with a clatter.

At the sound of thunder where it never rained, Cable's head snapped up, his light flashing toward the crosscut ventilation curtain. A moment later, the curtain flapped as if a hard wind had struck it. He got to his feet.

"What was that?" Song asked. She was still sitting on the track cover of the continuous miner and clutching the envelope with the signed annulment papers.

Cable's voice was unnaturally calm, as if he had to restrain himself from yelling. "Do you know how to activate your SCSR?" he asked.

"Of course." She stood up. "But what—"

"Be ready to put it on when I tell you."

"Cable?"

"Just do as I say. And for once in your life, don't argue."

BUM LOOKED DOWN the tracks, then cursed. He'd fallen asleep and missed the mantrip out. Now he'd have no choice but to confront the foreman of the evening shift and confess what had happened. The foreman's name was Gibson, nicknamed Hoot. Hoot and Bum had never gotten along. Likely he was going to get a laugh out of Bum's predicament and would probably tell him to either work the shift or sit down until it was over. It was one more frustration on top of frustration that had started when Bum had seen Square Block sneaking around the preparation plant. Bum was still confused about that. Why was Square spying, and who sent him?

Of course, Bum had taken care of the old busybody by pushing him over the mountain, and then he'd taken care of Stanvic too. The next morning, after popping some OxyContin, Bum had dragged himself to work, lest anyone be suspicious why he wasn't there. He'd slept most of the shift and was still hung over.

Now, he dug in his pockets and felt three capsules of crystal meth. One would give him plenty of energy to walk out of the mine. He grinned his gap-toothed grin. Shoot, if he took all three, he could fly out!

Bum heard voices coming from the direction of the face. He assumed some miners were doubling back on the evening shift and were taking a break until the rest of the section got there. He started walking toward them and then came upon Cable's jeep. He stopped and listened again. Now he recognized Cable's voice, plus one more. He frowned. It was that girl! What were they doing?

Bum crept closer. To his surprise, he heard them talk about the coal thefts, and how the state police and the FBI were involved. Then he heard them agree that Stanvic was in on it and that his murderer was probably in on it too.

Bum scurried back to his manhole and sat down and tried to figure out what he should do. With the state and the FBI involved, he knew there was a chance they might look at bank statements, his included. He had some vulnerability there. He had not tried to hide the money he'd made on the purloined coal, his bank statements reflecting thousand-dollar increments every time he made a run for Stanvic. That had been stupid, and now there was nothing he could do to change it. He allowed a meth crystal to melt in his mouth and quickly felt its hot, white energy coursing through his veins. It was just what he needed. His mind went into overdrive.

I have to run, he thought, *just as far and as fast as I can*. Yes, that was what he would do, withdraw his money and head west, maybe even slip over the border into Mexico, then lose himself somewhere. He thought about Cable's jeep and considered stealing it but dismissed the idea. Cable would hear him and call ahead and Bum would be caught at the bottom. No, the best thing to do was to quietly sneak out of the mine, get to the bank, and get gone.

Bum began to walk out. He reached the turn for the main line and kept going, ready to jump into a manhole if he heard Cable's jeep coming behind him. He felt a tremor, then a blast of hot air struck him from behind, so powerful it lifted him off his feet—and Bum was flying! With the meth coursing through him, he had a brief moment of ecstasy before crashing headfirst into one of the cribs. Then he flopped into the gob while the furious exhaust of a mighty explosion roared over him and began to spread through the mine.

MOLE WAS IDLY watching the manlift from the doorway. He was waiting for his brother Clarence to replace him at the bank of monitors so he could go home to his wife and eight kids in the doublewide he owned on the slope of Harper's Mountain. It took a lot of money to keep those eight kids in shoes, not to mention baseball caps for them to wear backward and iPods to stick in their ears. He pondered the birthdays coming up. The kids having them would expect nice presents.

They had it so easy. When Mole was a kid, the mines were mostly all shut down, and his father, after years out of work, had gradually gone nuts until one day he'd hung himself from the limb of a big oak just behind the house. His mother had soon been packed off to the loony bin. Mole was only twelve then, yet it fell to him to take care of his two younger brothers and three younger sisters. The state tried to break them up, shipping them off to foster homes, but they always ran away and came back to Highcoal, sneaking into their abandoned house and living off squirrels, mountain cabbage, and creek water. Finally, Old Preacher, Preacher's father, took responsibility for them. It had been quite a family since Old Preacher had six kids of his own. Somehow they'd made do, and now every one of those kids had grown up to have good jobs, mostly out of state. There were a ton of grandkids too. Mole was proud of what he'd done to keep his family together, and it didn't bother him a whit to extort a rich woman like Song, or anyone else, for a little extra coin. To him, money meant more than buying things. It meant survival.

Day-shift black caps and one red cap, which proved to be Justin, stepped off the manlift. They were joking around, as they always did. Mole saw Justin grinning and knew the jibes were probably being directed at him, but they were apparently good-natured ones. Justin was going to get his black cap, and maybe that would allow him to get his son back. Mole approved. Cable would be happy for Justin too, and Lord knew Cable needed some good news, what with Square in the hospital and now Stan Stanvic drowned. The news had the entire town in an uproar. The telephone lines had nearly melted from the people trading speculation on what had happened. Of course, nearly everybody in town had called Mole. Since he was the mine clerk/dispatcher with an office beside the superintendent's, it was expected that he would know everything. But Mole didn't know a thing. What had happened to Square and then to Stanvic was all a mystery to him.

Mole felt a sudden jolt through the floor. Another pillar pulled too close, he supposed. But if so, it had been a complete collapse. There was a lot of energy in the tremor he'd felt. Maybe part of the old works had collapsed. That would make sense. Then he heard a steady beeping in the control room. At first, he didn't put the vibration in the floor and the alarm together. He suspected that a sensor in the mine was in need of calibration or had failed. But then there was another beep, and then another, and another, all joining in an irritating cacophony, demanding that someone come and see about them.

Mole hurried into his office and sat down in his chair to study the monitors. It took just an instant to see the carbon monoxide sensors were activated near Six West. One by one, other sensors were being activated along the main line return. He'd never seen anything like that before. There was also a red light on the seismic monitor. Mole studied a blip on the screen that was nearly straight up and down. He'd never seen anything like that either. A bump or a roof fall created a sharp spike, but not one that big. He reached for the phone and called the machine shop at the bottom. "Did you feel anything down there?"

"Yeah," a machinist named Mayday said. "What was it?"

"Check your detector for carbon monoxide," Mole said.

A moment later, Mayday came back. "All's normal. Wait a minute." Mole heard Mayday talking to someone, then he came back on. "A motorman on one of the mantrips said he heard thunder and the mine shook. What's going on?"

"I don't know. I just see CO sensors lighting up in the return. Is Cable or Bossman at the bottom?"

"Nope. Bossman's usually the last man out so he's probably somewhere back down the main line."

"If either Cable or Bossman show up, tell them to call me."

"Will do," Mayday said and hung up.

Mole stabbed the button for the pager on Six block. When no one answered, he activated its speaker to demand that somebody, anybody, pick up. But no one did. He tried pagers working back toward the bottom on both the intake and the return. There were no answers anywhere.

The carbon monoxide sensors continued to beep. Mole turned off their audio, then pushed his chair back and thought for a couple of seconds, then got up and went to the door. He was looking for a white cap. He spotted Vietnam Petroski, waved him over, and told him all that had happened.

"Doggonit!" Petroski exclaimed. "Sounds like methane has lit off somewhere back around Six block. Did you call Cable or Bossman?"

"Bossman should be on his way to the bottom. Cable's in the mine somewhere, but I'm not sure where."

"I do," Petroski said. "He was on Six block. He was talking with Song. They were still there when we left. Cable said he'd bring her back on his jeep."

Mole uttered an expletive. "That ain't good, Vietnam."

Petroski kicked at the dirt, then looked back at the manlift. The cables were vibrating, indicating more men from the day shift were coming up. That at least was good. But the evening shift miners were starting to cluster around the shaft to take the ride down. They would have to be stopped. "Did you call MSHA?" Petroski asked.

"Not yet," Mole said. "I wanted to talk to a white cap first. What do you think? Should I call?"

Petroski worried it over. "This is above my pay grade. Cable or Bossman should decide."

"Yeah, but they ain't here."

Petroski reached into his pocket and pulled out a pouch of chewing tobacco. He dug into it with his fingers, then pushed a huge wad into his cheek, took a chew, then spat the whole thing out and kicked dirt over it.

"Call MSHA," he said to Mole's back. The dispatcher was already on his way to the telephone. Petroski turned to tell the evening shift to back away from the manlift. They weren't going inside, not until Cable, Bossman, or MSHA said so.

Before Mole could call anybody, his telephone rang. It was Bossman. "I'm at the bottom," he said overly loud. "What going on? My jeep almost went off the track that bump was so big."

Mole quickly brought him up to speed, ending with what Petroski had ordered him to do. "You agree with me calling MSHA, right?"

Bossman hesitated. "That's a question for Cable."

Mole heard Bossman put his hand over the receiver, then a few muffled shouts. When he came back on, he said, "I was trying to find out if anybody had seen Cable or his jeep. Nobody has."

"So I call MSHA?" Mole pressed.

Bossman took a few seconds to think, then said, "Call their main number, then track down Einstein."

THE VENTILATION CURTAINS had ceased flapping. Cable read his gas detector, then tucked it back in its holder.

"Stay here," he said to Song. "I think there's been an explosion toward the main line."

There was no way Song was going to stay alone in the section. She followed Cable through the curtain into the entry. There was a wisp of smoke floating in the beams of their lights and the odor of something burning. "Carbon dioxide and monoxide levels are up, but not too bad," Cable said, checking his detector again.

"How about methane?" Song asked.

"Higher than it should be." Cable took a breath and coughed. The smoke, though thin, was acrid. "We'd better get our SCSRs on." He turned to help Song but saw she already had hers ready. "Square trained you well," he said. "Let's get to the bottom before this air gets any worse."

"I'm right behind you," Song replied.

They hurried to the jeep. Cable energized it and they climbed aboard and began to head out of the section toward the main line intake, which was the way home. The smoke thickened, burning their eyes. "Put your goggles on," Cable ordered.

The smoke was getting denser. Soon it was difficult to see more than a few yards ahead. Cable slowed the jeep while straining his eyes to see the marker that indicated the turn onto the intake. "Do you see the placard?" he asked.

"There it is, I think," Song said when she spotted a whitish smudge through the smoke.

Cable eased the jeep forward, then felt it curve to the right. He was relieved. It was the turn that would lead them to safety. There was also a pager there.

Cable stopped the jeep and felt his way to the manhole where the pager was located. He picked up the receiver and listened. There was no dial tone, not even static. He went back to the jeep. "The line's probably been cut somewhere up ahead," he said. "We'll keep going out."

"I'm having trouble breathing out of the SCSR," Song confessed. "The air's too hot."

"Slow down your inhalations," Cable advised. "Relax as much as you can."

Song did her best to take slow breaths and also to relax, but it didn't seem to help. The oxygen was still too warm to be comfortable. It caused her to start coughing. "Hurry up, Cable," she urged.

"I can't go any faster through this smoke," he replied, talking around his mouthpiece and breathing between comments. "This is the intake and the smoke should be blowing past us, but it's not. Something must be blocking it, maybe a roof fall. We don't want to plow into it."

A few minutes later, Song felt the wheels on the jeep rolling over something. Cable pushed the brake and the jeep ground to a stop. "It's what I was afraid of. Rock on the track. We're going to have to walk ahead to see if there's more of it."

Song climbed off the jeep and felt her way until she bumped into Cable. "Oops, sorry," she said.

Cable took her hand. "Stay close."

"Like glue," she answered.

They hadn't gone far before they ran into a massive rock fall. Their beams shot aloft and illuminated exposed roof bolts hanging like bizarre chandeliers. Cable climbed up on the rocks and tried to see over it. He came back down. "I think there's another fall in front of it." Cable consulted his detector. "Carbon monoxide is rising."

"Can we move enough rock to get through?" Song asked.

Cable played his light along the rock fall, then shook his head. "It's going to take some heavy equipment to clear this."

"So what do we do?"

"First, we don't panic."

"I'm not panicking, Cable," Song replied evenly. "I just asked you what we should do. You're the experienced hand here. I'm just a lowly red cap."

Cable gave himself a moment to think. "Petroski ought to be at the bottom by now and he knows where we are. I'm sure the carbon monoxide and methane sensors have gone off in Mole's office." He paused to take some hits off his SCSR to satisfy his oxygen debt. "The one good thing this rock fall has done is to keep the smoke from being pushed back into Six West. The air back at the face might still be clear. We'll go back there and barricade ourselves in."

"I don't like the sound of that," Song admitted.

"We'll be fine. There's a half-dozen SCSRs stocked near the entry. We'll pick them up and take them with us. If we ration our oxygen, we'll be okay for a day, maybe more."

Song eyed the wall of rock. "Are you sure we can't move enough rock to squeeze through?"

"I'm sure. Come on. We're going to be fine. Get back aboard the jeep."

Song climbed aboard the jeep while Cable again checked his gas detector. "Carbon monoxide's still climbing. Methane's up but still not too bad. Most of it got burned off, I think."

Song looked at the detector, squinting through the oily smoke to make out the numbers. "What caused this?" she wondered.

"Methane explosion, I'm pretty sure. If I had to guess, I'd say in the old works. It was big enough to blow out a stopper. Maybe more than one." Cable put the jeep in reverse.

"What would cause that?"

"I have no idea."

While Cable went after the box of SCSRs at the turn-in to Six West, Song peered through the smoke and saw lying in the gob what looked like somebody's cast-off shirt. She got off the jeep to take a closer look. "Cable, there's somebody buried over here!" she yelled.

Cable secured the box of SCSRs on the jeep and came over for a look. "You're right," he said grimly. He began to dig with his hands until he had enough rubble and gob removed to turn the man over. When he did, an all-too-familiar face was revealed. "It's Bum! What's he doing here?"

Song shook her head in disgust. "Probably fell asleep and missed the mantrip out. According to Vietnam, it wouldn't be the first time either. Nobody can figure out why you haven't fired Bum a long time ago, Cable."

"That's not entirely true. Most folks know why."

"Yeah, yeah," Song said, rolling her eyes. "Your old football teammate."

Cable took the SCSR off Bum's belt, opened it up, then tossed it away. "Empty. He's been taking hits off it, most likely." Cable leaned in to smell Bum's breath. "He stinks of meth too. Bum, you sorry sack of . . . I've done my best to help you, but this is the end of it."

"Hallelujah," Song said.

Cable chuckled. "I didn't know Yogists said hallelujah."

"Oh, we say a lot of things, Cable. For instance, this Yogist is kind of curious whether we're going to get out of this alive."

"I told you we're going to be fine."

"And I heard you. But can I believe you?"

Cable pointed at his helmet. "See this white helmet? You have to believe me. I'm your boss."

"I thought you resigned."

"It isn't official until the end of the week."

"Well, anyway, I own this mine, so I outrank you."

"No, you don't. Your father owns this mine. A subtle but important difference."

Song took a deep breath. The air out of the SCSR was still too hot. "Just keep us safe, Cable."

"That's what I intend to do."

Cable went to the jeep to get a fresh SCSR for Bum and a roll of duct tape. He activated the rebreather, strapped it around Bum's neck, then put the clips on his nose. He used the duct tape to hold the mouthpiece in place.

"Nice look for him," Song said. "Too bad you didn't just tape over his mouth and forget the SCSR."

"Let's put him on the jeep," Cable said, ignoring her suggestion.

"Are you kidding? He's got to weigh two hundred and fifty pounds."

"That's why I said 'let's,' as in let us."

Song took another deep inhalation, then allowed a long sigh. "All right, Cable. Let's save your little teammate."

She knelt and lapped one of Bum's arms across her neck. Using the muscles in her legs rather than her back, just as Square had taught, she stood up, dragging the big man to his knees. His head fell forward and his black helmet fell off.

"Hey, you're strong," Cable marveled, picking up the helmet and jamming it back on Bum's head.

"Coal mining will do that for a girl," she grunted beneath Bum's weight.

"What else does it do?"

"Makes her mean and lean, Cable," she growled. "Are you just going to stand there or are you going to help me with this ugly brute? Remember you said 'let's' as in let us?"

"Oh, yeah. Sorry."

Together, Song and Cable half-carried, half-dragged Bum to the jeep and stretched him out on it. Cable drove the jeep very slowly through the smoke, turning into the cut that led toward the face on Six West and, hopefully, clear air.

"Just about there," Cable said just before another huge tremor shook the mine. A crib collapsed, and the header it was holding fell, swinging in a vicious arc into the side of the jeep. Cable yelled something, then the jeep was battered off the track.

Song was sent flying, landing hard in the gob on her back beside the crib on the other side. After a few seconds of shock, she pulled herself up. Dust and smoke hung in the air. "Cable, are you all right?" she called. There was no answer. Then she heard a splintering sound. She looked up and her heart turned to ice. Through the acrid smoke, she could see cracks racing through the draw rock. "God, help me!" she heard herself cry. It was decidedly not a Yogist's prayer.

Then there was a noise that sounded like a gigantic plate glass window struck by a sledge hammer. Song's desperate prayer stuck in her throat. The entire roof was coming down.

BOSSMAN ENTERED MOLE'S office just as another blip appeared on the seismograph. Mole pointed at it. "It's bigger than the first one," he said in awe.

Bossman studied the jagged line on the monitor. Then he looked at the CO sensors. They were lit up to Three block on the return and to Five block on the intake. "Fire damp exploding," he muttered, using the old miner's term for methane. "But where's it coming from?"

Bossman's eyes shifted to the big mine map on the wall. "This doesn't make sense," he said to himself, although Mole was listening intently. "I fire bossed up on Six block myself and the methane level was normal." He pondered a little more, then asked, "How're the fans?"

"All operational," Mole said.

"Did you call Einstein?"

"Yeah, but I didn't talk to him. His voice mail said he's at the MSHA Academy giving a class for inspectors. I left a message."

Bossman picked up the mine phone and called the bottom. "I want everybody out of the mine," he growled. "Yes, everybody!" Then he called the lamp house. "When you think all the men on the day shift are out, let me know whose tags are still on the board. And tell any miner on the rescue team you see to report to the dispatcher's office."

Bossman hung up the phone and turned to Mole. "Call the rescue team."

"You think Cable and Song are still at Six West?"

"How the hell should I know? If they are . . ." He left the sentence unfinished, looked again at the mine map, then picked up his white helmet and plopped it aboard.

"Where you going?" Mole asked.

"Back inside."

"But you just ordered the mine evacuated."

"I know what I did. I also told you to call the rescue team!"

While Mole picked up the phone to make the calls, Bossman tore across the mine yard, waving at the manlift attendant to open the gate.

ON THE AIRWAY entry to Six West, Cable's jeep was beneath the header that had struck it and a pile of draw rock. On the other side of the entry, pressed against the crib that had saved her, Song lifted her head, then brushed off the fragments of the knife-sharp rock splinters that had fallen all around her. She played her light through the dust and smoke, saw the jeep, then crawled to it. Its motor was still humming. She fumbled with its controls until she had it turned off. If it was methane that kept exploding, she didn't want a sparking electric motor to set off more. She was just a stupid red cap, but she knew that much!

She heard Cable groaning and found him folded into the small space below the driver's seat. "I think my leg's broken," he said through gritted teeth.

Song's spot of light moved along his leg. The bend in it told her Cable's suspicion was correct. "Tell me what to do," she said.

"Help me out," he said.

Song did her best, but she couldn't get any leverage. Finally, Cable reached up and grabbed the header with both hands and pulled himself up. He gasped at the resulting pain, but he worked himself hand over hand until his upper body was hanging over the lip of the jeep. Then he lost his grip and fell, landing on his back in the gob. He shrieked, then subsided into moans.

Song worked her way to him. "Cable?"

Cable took a long, ragged breath through his SCSR. "How far are we from the face?"

Song flashed her light down the entry. "I think maybe another fifty yards," she said.

"Get me a crutch or something."

"Cable, there's no crutch except me."

He rolled himself over on his stomach, gasping as his broken leg flopped into the gob. When she put his arm around her shoulders and struggled to lift him, he said, "You can't take my weight."

"Yes, I can. I've had you on top of me before. Remember?"

Cable managed a smile. "Guess I'd forgotten, it's been so long." Then he added, "Too long, maybe."

"This is no time to get romantic," she chided, then lifted with all her strength. He grunted in pain, and so did she, but she managed to lift him until he could hobble along on one foot with her supporting him. It took what seemed hours but was probably no more than fifteen minutes before they got to their destination. Song let Cable down as gently as she could, then spat out the mouthpiece of her SCSR and took a quick breath. "I think this is good air," she said.

"We need to put up a curtain."

"I'll get one."

Song trotted off to where she knew the curtain material was stored. She unrolled the plastic sheet, estimated the length she needed, cut it off, and hung it where Cable told her to. For the moment, they were sealed off from the smoke.

Cable crawled to a rib, dragging his broken leg. He rolled into a sitting position, then wiped the sweat and grime from his face. "You hung that curtain like an expert," he marveled.

Song shrugged. "I had a good instructor."

"You wouldn't happen to have any morphine on you, would you?"

"I have a bottle of ibuprofen in my lunch bucket."

"Go get it. I've got to knock this pain down a little so I can think." Cable released the mouthpiece on the SCSR and took a tentative breath. "You're right. This air isn't too bad."

"Check your gas detector to be sure."

Cable did. "Acceptable," he reported.

Song soon returned with the ibuprofen. She also brought a bottle of water from the box Petroski always kept near the face. There were plenty of bottles, so water wasn't going to be a problem, at least not right away. Cable swallowed four of the tablets, drank the entire bottle, then asked, "Did you see Bum after we ran off the tracks?"

"No, but I didn't look for him either."

Cable looked grim.

"What?" Song demanded.

"Well, a miner never leaves his buddy behind."

Song peered at Cable in astonishment. "Bum is not my buddy. Nor yours, I might add."

"I know," Cable said quietly.

Song had a furious argument with herself, then said, "All right. I'll go get him."

Cable touched her arm. "No. Stay here where it's safe."

Song made a hopeless gesture. "I can't just leave a man out there to die. Not even Bum. What would Preacher say? What would the church ladies say? They'd call me a pure snotty little witch again and this time they'd be right."

Cable groaned as pain shot through his leg. He took a deep breath, then let it out slowly. "I'm sorry I made you stay behind with me," he said. "You'd be safe outside by now."

"Yeah, well, if pigs could fly and all that." She stood up. "Any advice before I go risk my life for—I can't believe I'm saying this—Bum?"

"Bring along the SCSRs on the jeep. There's also an extra light and a charged-up battery in a metal box behind the driver's seat. Bring them too."

Song nodded, then walked to the curtain and pulled it aside.

"Song?" Cable called after her.

Song turned. For some reason, the sound of her name on his lips made her think Cable was going to tell her something from his heart.

"Don't forget the light and the battery," he said.

"I'm a woman, not a mule, Cable!" she snapped, then angrily pushed through the curtain into the entry. The smoke was like a thick gray wall. She put the SCSR mouthpiece back in, snapped the nose clip on, and pushed into it.

Thirty-Four

Birchbark's crew were shoveling dirt into the open sore in the ground that had been created by the eruption from below. Bashful was pacing around them. "What happened?" he asked for about the tenth time.

Birchbark had already explained it, though it was clear Bashful didn't want to hear the truth. "We drilled into the old works and lit off the methane in there. Just like I told you would happen!"

"But how could it?" Bashful plaintively demanded. He knew he was in big trouble and his brain was working overtime to figure a way out.

Birchbark shook his head. "Maybe we hit an old roof bolt, made a spark. What matters is we did it. That spout of fire out of our hole is proof."

Bashful stopped his pacing. "What if we fill that hole up, then leave? Pretend it never happened."

"That's not possible, Bashful. We can't run away from what we've done. For one thing, the riggers know it and they'll tell everybody. Now, get hold of yourself. First thing we got to do is to stop up this hole. If there's a fire down there, the air going through our shaft is feeding it."

Bashful shook a cigarette out of a pack and, after several fumbles, managed to light it. "I don't know what to do," he said between nervous, jerky puffs.

Birchbark shook his finger at his boss. "Yes, you do. Call Cable!"

Bashful licked his lips. "He's going to be mad."

"No doubt. Likely, he'll want to kick your butt. But before that, he's going to need you."

Though he wasn't thinking straight, Bashful sensed his salvation. "Need me? Why?"

"Bore holes, Bashful. Bore holes."

"What are you talking about?"

Birchbark threw up his hands "Try to focus on what I'm telling you, all right? We've caused an explosion. It happened in the old part of the mine so maybe—and pray to God this is true—nobody's been hurt. The mine is going to be evacuated, in any case. MSHA will show up, which means Einstein. Einstein's a careful kind of fellow. He'll want to test the air before anyone goes back inside. Bore holes is the only way to do that. We're in the hole business, Bashful. Remember? After you call Cable and confess, call Lester and tell him to get the spare rig ready to go."

"So you're saying they need me?"

"Yes! Now, call the mine, then call Lester."

Bashful took a long drag off his cigarette, then threw it down. He went to his ATV, which was equipped with a mobile telephone. He picked up the handset and called Lester and told him to get the spare rig up to speed. Then he took a deep breath and dialed Mole's number. Mole was his connection to Cable. But all he got was a busy signal.

MOLE WIPED THE sweat from his brow with a red bandana. He was talking to Bossman, who had reached the bottom and called in on the wireless attached to his jeep. "I just talked to the lamp house," Mole said. "Cable's and Song's tags are still hanging on the board, so it looks like they're still inside. You know we should turn off the power. Otherwise, a spark might cause another explosion."

Bossman was quiet for a couple of seconds, then said, "Yes, but that means the fans will stop delivering fresh air too. Any sign of Einstein?"

"He's on his way. I expect him any minute."

Bossman flashed his light around the bottom. No lights flashed back. There were only empty mantrips. He had never felt so alone in the mine before. "All right," he said. "Here's what I'm going to do. I'm going to take my jeep and run down the intake and see what the situation is."

"Alone? Einstein is going to raise Cain if you do," Mole warned.

"So let him. How about the CO monitors?"

"CO sensor just activated itself at Two West return. The sensors up on Six block are dead. I think that last explosion knocked them out."

Bossman thought things over. Two West was about a mile from the bottom. The carbon monoxide monitors had been activated one after another down the return, starting at Six block. They'd lit up in a hurry at first, all the way to Three block. Now the Two block sensors were beeping, but it had taken a long time for the carbon monoxide to reach them. That probably meant the expanding gasses from the two explosions were running out of steam. If the fans kept going, and the intake and returns were not obstructed, the carbon monoxide might be flushed out of the mine within a few hours. After that, it would be a simple matter of going to Six block and bringing out Cable and Song, presuming they were still alive.

On the other hand, Bossman mused, if the explosions had occurred near Six West—and everything pointed in that direction—and the fans kept going, the intake air might draw smoke and gas back into the section where Cable and Song were probably located. Since Cable hadn't called, Bossman had to assume he wasn't able, either because he was injured or there was an obstruction between him and a pager, or the nearest pager to Cable was knocked out.

With the information he had, Bossman made the best decision he could. "Keep the fans on," he ordered Mole, then looked up as the manlift platform came dropping down. Two black caps Bossman instantly recognized got off. It was Blackjack Jemson and Shorty Carter. Blackjack operated a shuttle car on the day shift; Shorty was on one of the roof bolt crews on the evening shift. They were also rescue team members.

"We heard you were down here by yourself," Blackjack said. "So we came on."

"The other guys are getting the rescue equipment ready," Shorty reported.

It was good to see the two trained rescuers. Bossman rang Mole again. "Blackjack and Shorty are with me. We're going to travel up the intake to see what's what. If we can, I intend to go all the way to Six block and bring out Cable and Song."

"That's crazy, Bossman," Mole argued. "Everything up there is filled with carbon monoxide."

"Well, it may be crazy, but it's what we're going to do. I'll call you at each pager to let you know where we are. Don't leave the phone."

Bossman turned to Blackjack and Shorty. "We're going in as far as we can go," he said.

Blackjack frowned. "If this is a rescue, rules say we're supposed to wait for MSHA to give us the go-ahead."

"I know what the rules say, Blackjack," Bossman snapped. "This ain't an official rescue, not yet. And I, for one, don't intend to wait around when there's a chance we can just scoot in and bring Cable and Song out."

"Bossman's got it right, Blackjack," Shorty said. "At least we'll know if we got a clear path inside."

Blackjack gave it a short ponder, then nodded his agreement. Bossman's wireless beeped. "What?" he demanded.

It was Mole. "Einstein just drove through the gate. Anything you want me to tell him?"

"Tell him I just left, heading inside."

"He's going to go off like dynamite."

"Let him," Bossman snapped, then switched off and waved Blackjack and Shorty to the jeep.

SONG WAS BENT over, clutching Bum beneath his armpits, dragging him one excruciating step at a time. She had attached to his belt three fresh SCSRs, and the battery and lamp Cable had stored in the box on his jeep. She had the other two spare SCSRs clipped to her belt. She felt like a deep sea diver laden with lead.

The smoke was thick, her SCSR wasn't delivering much oxygen, she was hot and exhausted, and she ached all over. Her hands lost their grip and she fell backward into the gob, and there she lay, gasping for breath. When she sucked in and got nothing in return, she took her SCSR off, threw it away, then opened up a fresh one she took from Bum's belt. She also gave him another shake. "Wake up, Bum! I'm tired of dragging you!"

Bum didn't wake up. She had found him lying next to Cable's jeep, which had protected him from the falling roof. He had groaned a couple of times but that was all. "Why are you men so heavy?" Song griped, then grabbed his arms and kept pulling, the heels of his boots leaving wavy tracks in the gob until they passed through the curtain. Immediately, she dropped him, then knelt down and took several deep breaths. When she was revived, she looked around, her light flashing along the rib where she'd last seen Cable. He was slumped against it with his head down. She crawled over to him and gave him a good shake. "Cable! Come on! Get those eyes open!"

To her relief, he raised his head. "Sorry, jus' a nap . . . needed it . . ." His speech was slurred, and when he looked at her, his eyes were unfocused.

Song shook him again. "All the way awake, Cable. Come on!"

He blinked a few times, then seemed to climb out of whatever deep pit he had visited. "You made it," he said. He flashed his light around. "Did you get Bum?"

Song sat down beside Cable and took off her helmet and gave her head a good scratch, which felt good. "I got him, but I wore out an SCSR doing it," she griped. "I brought the spares, but I'm wearing one of them."

"You can stop breathing off it. The air in here is okay."

She unclipped her nose clips and sniffed, then coughed. "It doesn't smell okay."

Cable looked at his gas detector. "That's only the smoke. If it was carbon monoxide, you wouldn't smell it anyway."

Song flashed her light back at the curtain. "I think the CO is real high out there, Cable. The smoke is thicker too. I didn't think I was going to make it."

"I know Bum will appreciate you going after him," Cable said.

"Why do I doubt that?" She rested for a moment more, then asked, "How are you?"

"It feels like somebody drove a steel peg through my leg, but I'm hanging in there."

"What made you sleepy if the air's so good in here?"

"I didn't say it was good, just okay. The CO is getting higher. We're too close to the fresh air intake."

"Isn't that good?"

"Ordinarily it would be, but see your curtain flapping? That's bad air pushing in on us. With all that rock down on the intake, the air pressure is quite a bit less but it's still there, enough to suck the bad air in on top of us. We need to move. You know where you and Preacher put up those timbers? That would be a good place to go. There should be plenty of air in that cut and we can curtain ourselves off and wait it out."

Song was too tired to move. She slumped against the rib. "What happened, Cable? What caused this?"

Cable started to say something, then shrugged. "I don't know. I'd be guessing, so I'll just say I don't know."

"I don't think I have the strength to move you both," she confessed.

"You just have to move Bum. I'll crawl. But first, I want you to splint my leg."

"With what?"

"There should be some wedges around. Just two flat boards is all you need. You can use strips from the curtain rolls to tie them on my leg." He looked at his detector. "Uh-oh."

"What?"

"The CO is already a couple of percentage points higher. Get the splints, please. We've got to move right away."

Song took a deep breath that turned into a long sigh. "All right, Cable. No rest for this weary red cap. Hang on. I'll be right back."

BOSSMAN FINALLY ANSWERED the insistent pager at the intersection of Two block. Its light was flashing, and Mole was shouting over the speaker: "Anybody there? Anybody there?"

"I'm here," Bossman growled.

"Oh, hey, Bossman," Mole replied. "Einstein's here. He wants a word."

Bossman grimaced and prepared himself to get royally chewed out by the MSHA safety man. Surprisingly, Einstein's voice was modulated. "What's your situation so far?" he asked.

"Everything's open to Two block on the escapeway. CO's up a little but not too bad."

"Good," Einstein said. "Now, turn around and come out."

"What's that, Einstein? I can't quite hear you."

Einstein's tone turned edgy. "You heard me well enough. Get out of there. I'm killing power to the mine just as soon as you get off the manlift."

Bossman hung up the pager phone. "Lots of static," he said to Blackjack and Shorty, then checked his detector. The CO had risen considerably. "Put your SCSRs on," he ordered.

IN MOLE'S CONTROL room, Einstein hung up the phone just as Rabbit Cole, the lamp man, walked in. He was holding three tags. "Here's the ones still in the mine, not counting Bossman, Blackjack, and Shorty."

Mole glanced at the tags. "Well, don't keep me in suspense," he snapped. "Who do they belong to?"

"Cable, Song, and Bum."

Mole was incredulous. "Bum? He can't be inside. He just probably forgot to move his tag when he came out."

"I don't think so," Rabbit said. "I've looked for him everywhere, even called his house. Vietnam says he didn't see him on the mantrip and none of his other buddies on Six West said they saw him either. Matter of fact, they said they ain't seen him since lunch."

Mole thought it over. "Bum sometimes sneaks away in the gob, takes a nap. He's missed the mantrip out before."

Einstein glowered at the dispatcher. "You've got one lousy operation around here, Mole."

"It ain't, neither, Einstein. I mean Mr. Stein. Cable runs a good outfit. He's just sorta got a soft side when it comes to Bum. Bum takes advantage of it, that's all."

Einstein raised his eyebrows. "Well, now they've got themselves trapped in the mine together."

There was no argument against a fact, so Mole asked, "What do you want me to do?"

"Have you called in your rescue team?"

"Yep. Bossman's the leader. Him, Blackjack, and Shorty, you know where they are. We got seven other men on their way."

"Okay. Call Fox Run and get their team over here too."

"Already done it. They got six men on their way with their rescue gear. It'll take 'em about an hour."

273

Einstein went to the marker board and started a list. "We need drill rigs. At least three, I'm thinking. Two in the field and one as backup. We need GPS fixes for Six West. I want a hole into the section for an air sample."

"I got the GPS numbers already figured out," Mole said. "Come to think of it, Bashful's crew is out near there already. If I can get hold of them, what do you want them to do?"

Einstein's eyebrows lifted again. "What's Bashful doing way over there?"

Mole shrugged. "Drilling for gas like he always does."

"When and if you contact him, I would very much like to speak to that young man." When Mole hesitated, Einstein said, "Now, Mole, *now!*"

Mole picked up the phone and dialed Bashful's warehouse. He wasn't there, but Lester was and Lester happened to be Mole's brother-in-law. "You get hold of Bashful," Mole ordered him. "And don't give me a second's worth of crap. I want to hear his voice in five minutes. You hear?"

Lester heard.

SONG TIED THE last knot around the makeshift splint. She'd found some short planks, and they'd been the right length. When she pulled them tight around Cable's leg, he had nearly passed out from the pain. He worked through it, then wiped the sweat from his face with his shirtsleeve. "I'm going to start crawling," he said. "You pull Bum."

That was when Bum suddenly groaned and sat up, looked around, then tore off the duct tape that held his SCSR mouthpiece in place. He spat it out. "Pull me where?" he asked, rubbing his head. "What the hell happened?"

"How are you, buddy?" Cable asked.

"I've been better," came the sullen reply. "I asked you what's going on."

"I think there was an explosion toward the main line. Then a few minutes later, another one. We're going over to a crosscut and curtain up. Can you walk?"

"I reckon." Bum's light fell on Song. "Hey girl! What you doing down here, honey?"

"She saved your life," Cable apprised him. "And don't call her a girl. She's a coal miner, the same as you and me."

Bum laughed. "Says who?" He got to his knees and turned on his helmet light. "You and the girl can stay here, Cable, but I'm gonna walk out."

"You won't get far. The escapeway is full of smoke and there's a roof fall blocking the way."

Bum flashed his light back to Cable and then Song. "Females in the mine have always been bad luck. It's her what probably caused this."

"Don't talk like a fool, Bum. I told you Song saved your life. She put up that curtain behind you, then went out and pulled you in here."

The spot of Bum's light moved to Cable and played along his leg. "What's wrong with you?"

"He has a broken leg," Song said. "Too bad it wasn't yours."

Bum ignored her. He swiveled his light around, studying everything.

"You should turn your light off when you don't need it," Cable said.

"You sure like to give orders, don't you, Cable?" Bum sneered. "How about you, girl? You want to tell me what to do?"

Cable put the spot of his light into Bum's eyes. "Leave her alone, Bum."

Bum insolently flashed his light back into Cable's eyes. "I ain't never gonna take no more orders from you. I quit your stinking mine, Cable. What's your detector say, anyway?"

"CO's rising; methane is within limits. Now, listen, Bum. You've quit and that's fine. Resignation accepted. But until rescue comes, we'll need to work together."

Bum took a breath, then moved his light out of Cable's face. "Beat up as you are, I'm the one who ought to give the orders."

"So what do you think we ought to do?" Cable asked.

Bum crawled over and took the detector from Cable's hand. He studied it, then handed it back. "Well?" Cable demanded.

"We should curtain up at that crosscut you said," Bum answered contritely. He felt along his back. "I'm pretty stoved up, though. Not sure I can curtain much."

Cable and Bum put their lights on Song. She knew what that meant. "Well, if you two strong, tough men will let me," she said, "I'll drag you both to the cut, then hang the curtain. Then I'll sweep up the gob and maybe polish the floor. Or how about I do the laundry?"

Neither man answered. Song shook her head and said, "Come on. Let's go find some fresh air."

THERE WERE TEN men on the Highcoal rescue team. Three of them—Bossman, Blackjack, and Shorty—were already in the mine. The rest crowded into Mole's control room. Einstein got off the phone and addressed them. "I want you to stand by, gentlemen. Check your gear and be ready to go inside when I tell you."

"What's going on, Einstein?" one of the team members demanded. "We just heard rumors so far."

"I'll answer as best I can," Einstein said, crossing his arms. "There's been two explosions. What kind and what caused them, we don't know, so we're just calling it an event for now. Bossman, Blackjack, and Shorty are tramming into the escapeway to see how far they can get. I've ordered them out so I can turn the fans off, but as far as I know, they haven't turned around. That's not good. We might be pushing fresh air overtop the methane, which could set off another explosion. We have three miners unaccounted for. I think you all know them: Cable, Song, and Bum. We think they're in or near the Six West section. We're lucky the event occurred between shifts. We could have had dozens of miners trapped instead of three. But three or ten or twenty or a hundred miners, gentlemen, it doesn't matter. You know why you're here. After I get the situation stabilized, I'll be sending you in there to get them. Be ready."

The rescue team filed out, and Einstein turned to Mole. "Keep trying to get hold of Bossman. And what about Bashful?"

"Got a call in to Bashful, but his office says he's out in the field. They're trying his radio, and if they get through, they'll patch him in. As for Bossman, you see me here with the inside phone in my hand. I've been flashing the pagers up and down the line."

The outside phone rang and Mole picked it up, holding a receiver to each ear. "Hang on for Einstein, Bashful," he said and handed over the phone.

"Bashful, this is Mr. Stein. Where are you?"

Bashful was all innocence. "On the south side of Highcoal Mountain. Why? Anything wrong?"

"We think there's been an explosion in or near Six West section in the Atlas mine. You wouldn't happen to know anything about that, would you?"

Bashful was silent for a long second, then said, "Why would I know anything?"

"Listen, Bashful, I can hear it in your voice. You're many things but a good liar you're not. So what happened?"

Bashful broke down and started blubbering. "We didn't mean to do it! I told Birchbark we shouldn't drill through those old works."

Einstein glanced toward the mine map, his eyes traveling up the escapeway to the area he'd warned Cable about some months back. "Do you mean the old works up by Six block?" he asked.

Bashful confirmed Einstein's suspicions. "Yeah. Birchbark said it would be okay to drill there."

If it had been possible, Einstein would have crawled through the phone to choke the idiot on the other end. Instead, he remained outwardly calm. Bashful might be an idiot, but right now he was a useful one for what came next.

"Look, Bashful, let me explain it to you. It's cold and the barometric pressure is low. That means that old section was exuding gas at a high rate. When you punched through with that hot drill head, or maybe hit a roof bolt and made a spark, it blew. At least that's my working theory at the moment."

"I'm sorry, I'm sorry," Bashful sobbed. "Don't send me to prison. I didn't mean to do it!"

Einstein's tone was deliberately soothing. For now he had to keep the man together. He could send him to jail later. "It's all right, Bashful. Nothing's going to happen to you. Who's your rig team leader?"

"Birchbark. You want to talk to him?"

"Please."

Einstein waited impatiently until the team leader answered. "I told Bashful this would happen," Birchbark said.

"We'll figure all that out later," Einstein snapped. "Now listen carefully. I'm going to hand you over to Mole. He'll give you the GPS coordinates for Six

West. I want you to put a hole down on the entry and take a gas reading. Can you do that?"

"I can put the hole down, Mr. Stein, but I don't have anything to read any gas coming out of it."

"That's okay. By the time you punch through, I'll have sampling equipment in your hands. We can run the sample through our gas spectrograph here."

"Getting out here ain't easy," Birchbark said. "You'll need a dozer. Luckily we got one to drag our rig."

"All right. We'll get one. Hang on for Mole. He'll give you the GPS numbers."

Einstein handed over the phone to Mole, then went to the mine map and studied it some more. The inside phone rang and he answered it. It was Bossman. "Where are you?" Einstein demanded.

"Three block and we're turning around. CO is rising. We're getting a methane reading that I don't like either. I de-energized the jeep back on Two block. We'll walk back to it, and if the reading is low enough, we'll tram on out."

"You know what this means," Einstein said.

"Sure I do. There's likely a roof fall across both the intake and the return. Ventilation is fouled."

"Hurry, Bossman," Einstein said. "The fresh air that's getting in may cause another explosion at any time. We've got to get the fans turned off."

Bossman hung up. He waved Blackjack and Shorty back toward the bottom, toward outside, and toward safety.

Thirty-Five

Song finished hanging the curtain. She, Cable, and Bum were now sealed off in a hole that was clear of smoke. Cable was satisfied. "As long as we don't get any bad air pushed in here, we should be able to hold out."

Bum had not helped with the curtain. Rubbing his back, he'd sat down and not moved. "Nobody's gonna come get us in time and you know it, Cable," he said. "We're gonna die."

"Don't talk that way, Bum," Cable replied. "The rescue team is probably already on the way."

Song took a drink of water. She had carried every water bottle she could find into the curtained area. "How long will it take for them to get to us?" she asked.

Bum answered, "Too long, no matter what Cable says. Einstein ain't gonna rush in here. He's a 'by the book' fool."

Cable grimaced when a jolt of pain flowed up his leg. He waited for the torture to pass, then said, "Einstein's no fool, but you're right. He'll go by the book. The rescue team will set up a clear air base at the bottom and then move in with maybe other teams hopscotching along. Then they'll run into that roof fall. That will slow them down some."

"If I didn't have bad luck," Bum griped, "I wouldn't have any luck at all."

"We need to let them know we're alive and where we are," Cable said. "Use that slate bar, Bum. Beat for five minutes on a roof bolt, wait fifteen, then beat again. Remember your training."

Bum shook his head. "I can't. My back hurts and I'm starting to feel dizzy."

Song wearily picked up the slate bar. "All right, I'll do it," she said. She chose a roof bolt at random and hit it with the tip of the bar. It only made a dull thunk. "They'll never hear that through all the rock over us!"

Cable encouraged her. "Einstein has acoustic listening devices. He can hear it."

"He don't have one in his pocket," Bum grumped. "Them things are in Beckley. It'll take at least a day to get them over to Highcoal and get set up. Pound away, girl, but it won't do no good."

"Bum, will you just put a zip in it?" Cable demanded. "You haven't changed in all the years I've known you. You were a great linebacker, but when the other team got ahead, you just gave up."

Bum blazed back. "You're a liar, Cable! You're still blaming me for losing the championship game, ain't you? It wasn't *me* who lost it, it was *you*."

"We lost it together, Bum. We both gave up when that fullback came busting through."

"I thought you had him," Bum said.

"He was closer to you."

Song had heard enough. "Are you two football heroes done reminiscing? If so, I'll keep beating on this roof bolt while you sit there and do nothing."

"I don't care what you do," Bum grumbled. "We're as good as dead." He turned on his light and flashed it across the remaining spare SCSRs, then he turned it out again.

Song went back to beating the slate bar against the plate of the roof bolt. She soon developed a mantra. With each thump she thought, *Stupid men!* At least it kept her going.

THE BELL HAD not rung at the steeple. There was no need. The people of Highcoal knew where to go. They were gathering in the church and Preacher was presiding over them, not preaching from the pulpit, but walking along the aisles, putting his hand on the prayerful, which was nearly everyone in town who wasn't at the mine engaged in the rescue. It had been a spontaneous thing for them all to come to the church, to sit in the pews and pray for Cable and Song. As for Bum, well, he was a coal miner and that was enough to earn him prayers that he might be saved, and in more ways than one.

Rhonda, Rosita, and Young Henry came in with trays of food and set up a coffee station. It was likely going to be a long night.

Before long, the piano player showed up in her big red hat and the congregation rose to sing. Men from the mine rotated in and out, keeping everyone apprised of what was going on. The constable showed up too and took Preacher aside for a word.

"Square's awake."

"Hallelujah!"

"He had quite the tale to tell. It was Bum who pushed him over the mountain. Turns out Song and Square were trying to be detectives. When Square saw Bum stealing coal, Bum tried to kill him. It was also Bum who probably killed Stan. I got folks who saw Bum's truck out near Stan's property on Sunday."

Preacher's anxious expression reflected his concern. "And now Bum's inside with Cable and Song."

"Yep. I just wanted you to know so you could send up some prayers that are specific-like. I'm going to tell Bossman and Einstein now, though there ain't a thing they can do about it."

"They can pray too, Constable."

"Well, you're right about that, Preacher," the constable said and then headed for the mine.

THE MEDIA WAS moving into Highcoal. A trickle of satellite trucks at first, then a flood of them. It was all going out live. Once again, miners were trapped in a dirty, stinking coal mine. Since there were only three miners trapped, the big-time reporters hadn't flown in, at least not yet. The networks were depending on the local talent from Charleston, Huntington, Bluefield, Beckley, and Roanoke. It was a Beckley station that first interviewed Governor Godfrey after she roared into Highcoal with a state police escort. She took the microphone away from the young reporter and started to explain everything about the Highcoal mine. She was an instant hit. Soon, nearly every reporter was clamoring to have her on the air.

Omar's was opened to sell candy bars, crackers, and coffee to the always-hungry reporters at only a moderately inflated price. The governor commandeered a back room in the store and was soon holding forth. Dressed in a revealing jump suit and wearing a white helmet, she demonstrated before a phalanx of television cameras how an SCSR worked, what a gas detector did, and drew on a marker board a layout of the mine. "Rescue teams set up clear air stations," she explained authoritatively, "then move forward, keeping communications open."

The governor was having a fine time, although, at appropriate intervals, she carefully wiped away a tear before it had a chance to spoil her perfect makeup. Someone asked her if she knew any of the miners inside. "Oh, I know them all," she said. "The mine superintendent, his estranged wife, and his faithful companion Bum. We are very good friends."

This aside created an explosion of interest. A miner and his *estranged* wife were together and trapped in the mine! Now, there was a story. The top network and cable reporters received the word. *Get down to West Virginia now!*

MOLE'S CONTROL ROOM was packed with foremen and engineers. Einstein had called them in to apprise them of the situation. "Each of you has expertise I might need," he said. "So what I want you to do is to keep yourself available. You can set up camp in Cable's office or you can be at the church. Just as long as I can track you down in a hurry. First man I'd like to talk to is you, Vietnam. I want to hear everything you know about Six West, what equipment is in there, where the curtains are hung, anything you can tell me."

"Bossman's made it outside, Mr. Stein," Mole reported.

"How about Blackjack and Shorty?"

"Them too."

"Good. Shut the power down. Everything."

Mole picked up the phone to make the call.

A few minutes later, Bossman clumped in, his face grimy with sweat and dust. He looked a bit sheepish. "Well, here I am," he said.

"Glad to see you're okay," Einstein said, but there was no trace of gladness in his voice.

"You have a right to be mad, Einstein," Bossman said, taking off his helmet and giving his bald head a good scratch. "But I needed to see what the situation was."

"And what is the situation, Bossman?"

"Well . . ."

"Did you find a roof fall?"

"No. But I didn't feel the air moving either. There must be an obstruction."

"But how much and what kind—you have no idea, do you?"

"No, I don't."

Einstein jabbed his finger at Bossman. "From here on, we're going to do this by the book and only by the book. You understand?"

"Sure. But that's Cable in there, Einstein. And Song . . . well, everybody in Highcoal's crazy about her. And Bum, though he's a rat bastard, he's one of ours too."

Einstein raised his eyebrows. "You think I don't care about them?"

"I didn't say that. It's just that you're so cool and collected about everything."

"What I am is unemotional, which is a good thing to be in a situation like this. Now, get over to the bathhouse. Your rescue team is there. Check them out. Make sure they're ready. I'm going to put a bore hole down on Six West return to test the air. I've got another rig putting a hole into Five block intake to test the air there too. When I get those readings, we'll know better what to do next."

Bossman nodded agreement. "Just don't wait too long, that's all I'm saying. You know what happened at Sago."

Einstein knew very well. At the Sago mine in 2006, with thirteen miners trapped after lightning had set off a methane explosion, incessant delays had followed, all perfectly explainable and by the book, but twelve men had died who might have been saved if the rescuers had gone directly to them.

"All right," Einstein agreed. "I'll remember Sago. You don't forget Brookwood or Crandall Canyon."

In 2001, at an Alabama mine named Brookwood, a dozen rescuers had rushed inside after a methane explosion. They had inadvertently sparked another detonation, killing them all. At the Crandall Canyon mine in Utah, three rescue works had been killed while desperately trying to burrow through to trapped miners.

Einstein and Bossman stared at one another, at an impasse because of these contradictory events. You had to be safe, but you had to be quick too. Bossman blinked first. "All right, Einstein," he said while putting his helmet on. "But just remember, those three miners down there can't breathe a book."

Bossman went out the door, heading for the bathhouse. Watching him through the window, Einstein saw the constable stop the top foreman and lean in for a word. The constable continued on toward the office and came inside.

"Got a minute?"

"Make it quick."

"Sure. Here's quick. Bum shoved Square off the mountain and murdered Stanvic. Some kind of coal rustling scam. I need to arrest Bum."

Einstein shook his head. "Constable, we don't even know where Bum is."

"Well, when you find him, let me know. I got a pair of handcuffs for him. Consider him dangerous."

The constable left, while Einstein processed this new wrinkle. "What's the status of that air spectrograph?" he demanded, just to break the silence that had enveloped the office. Everyone in it had heard the constable. The news would soon be rippling all over Highcoal.

Mole looked up from his console. "It just arrived, Mr. Stein. I told them to set it up in the red cap classroom."

"I told you to keep me apprised of these kinds of things," Einstein griped.

Considering he'd just learned of the spectrograph's arrival from the contractor who had delivered the thing, Mole started to snap back at Einstein, but then thought better of it. He held his peace. The MSHA inspector was under a great deal of stress. Mole saw no good reason to add to it.

SONG DROPPED THE slate bar and sat down beside Cable. "I'm beat." She emptied the water from a plastic bottle, then tossed it away. She looked at the roof, listening, but there was nothing going on up there as far as she could tell. She looked around. "Where's Bum?"

"I don't know. The way he's been guzzling water, maybe he had to take a leak."

"I don't trust him, Cable. I think . . . wasn't Stanvic on your football team too?"

"The center."

"So he and Bum knew each other very well, right?"

"Of course."

"Can Bum drive a coal truck?"

"Sure. He drove one for Fox Run for a while before I hired him on."

"Listen, Cable," Song said urgently. "I think it was Bum who pushed Square over the mountain and I think he probably killed Stanvic too. He's capable of it. He's always angry, he's violent, and he sleeps on the job. Maybe that's because he works at night hauling coal that's not his, then takes drugs to try to stay awake."

Cable went over the accusations, which matched what he already thought. "I guess right now, it doesn't matter," he concluded. "We're going to have to depend on each other, including Bum, to get out of this."

"But that's my point," Song argued. "We can't depend on him. Do you see how he keeps looking at the fresh SCSRs? And drinking all our water? He's planning on being here when the rescuers come, Cable, but I don't think he cares if we're here or not."

Song jumped when there was a roof fall not far away. "It's okay," Cable said. "It wasn't big,"

But then they heard screams. It was Bum. "Oh Lord, I'm covered up! Please help me!"

"Bum!" Cable yelled. "What happened?"

"I was looking for food for us," Bum shouted, then his voice trailed off into a whimper. "Top fell on me. I'm all busted up. Please help me."

Cable turned to Song. "I can't ask you to go after him again."

Song took a breath, then slowly climbed to her feet and picked up the slate bar. "Yes, you can. You just did. And I'm going."

Thirty-Six

10:32 p.m., Tuesday

Einstein walked into the bathhouse where Bossman was going over the layout of the mine with the rescue teams from Atlas and Fox Run, plus a team from the Amalgam mine who had come up on their own. All three teams had their rescue apparatus neatly laid out on the concrete floor, including stretchers, first-aid kits, gas detectors, and self-contained closed-circuit air packs, each weighing thirty pounds and providing four hours of oxygen under normal load. The air packs were full face-mask units with speaking diaphragms. Each team was also equipped with portable hard-wired mine rescue communication systems. Their equipment was state of the art.

Einstein addressed them. "People, I recognize most of you. You've competed against each other in the rescue contests at the MSHA Academy when I've acted as a judge. I know you're all good men, and you know what to do. Now, I'm in charge of this mine rescue. We've established a fresh air base at the bottom and that's where we'll begin. Whatever happens, don't forget your training. Test the roof from rib to rib if you see anything that looks suspicious. Team captains, test for carbon monoxide, methane, and oxygen deficiency at each stop or if you have the slightest suspicion of bad air. Also, test at entrances to sections, faces, walls of overcasts and undercasts, stoppings, ventilation doors, barricades, and seals."

"What's been tested so far?" asked Joe "Cotton Eye" Robinette, the team captain from Amalgam. He was a wiry, hard-looking man with a gleaming eye. The other he kept squinted, a scar above it the apparent result of an old injury.

"Assume nothing's been tested," Einstein replied. "You know the drill. For methane, hold your detector at eye level or higher. Carbon monoxide at chest level, oxygen below the waist. If you see anything out of limits, stop and communicate with the fresh air base at the bottom. Bossman's going to be in charge there."

"What about curtains?" the Fox Run captain asked.

"You'll carry curtains and brattices with you. When you curtain up, or change the ventilation in any way, be sure to mark what you did with chalk, including the date and your initials."

"Any sign of a fire?" one of the rescuers asked.

"Not yet, but we're not discounting it. We've got bore holes going down that should tell us."

"Well, let's get going," Cotton Eye said, and all the rescuers nodded agreement.

Bossman held up his hands. "Boys, I know you're impatient, but hold on. Shorty Carter here—you all know him—is our team captain. When the time comes to go in, he'll lead our team to the first block, then stop and check the air quality. If the air is clear enough, and methane levels are permissible, the Fox Run team—Pritha Mahata's the lead—how do, Pritha—will follow. We'll keep hopscotching teams. At each block, everything stops until we take stock of where we are and decide how to push on. Any questions?"

There were none, except more general grumbling that it was time to get on with the rescue. "Listen to me, men," Einstein said. "You're not going to do anybody any good if you rush inside and get yourself killed. Just follow the plan, and stay in communication with your team and the fresh-air base all the way."

"All right, Einstein," Mahata said, speaking for the others. "We hear you very well. We shall proceed slowly and with care."

"Thank you, Pritha," Einstein said. "Now one more thing. One of the men inside—he's known as Bum around here—is wanted for questioning in a murder case. We don't know if he's dangerous or not."

Shorty looked around the rescuers, then spoke for all of them, "Don't matter what he's done on the outside, he's still a buddy of our'n. We're going to go get him."

Einstein allowed a subtle smile while Bossman said, "I want you boys to know I'm grateful you're here. There ain't no men in this world better'n miners, and there ain't no better miners than them on the rescue teams."

With a whoop of enthusiasm and confidence, the best men in the world picked up their rescue gear and headed for the manlift and whatever waited for them below. Unnoticed, four more men, also dressed in rescue gear, appeared out of the shadows of the bathhouse and joined them.

THE AIR WAS still clear outside the curtain, though Song could taste smoke on her tongue and feel it in the back of her throat. Her light flashed around the entry. "Bum?" she called. "Where are you?" She heard nothing but the flapping of a distant curtain.

Song looked into the first cut where a continuous miner sat, empty and abandoned. Her light played across it and then the face, the raw coal sparkling back at her. Bent beneath the low roof, she walked to the next cut, then the one beyond, which she noticed had not been pinned with roof bolts. She supposed Vietnam Petroski had seen no reason to do it, since the section was going to be shut down anyway.

There was still no sign of Bum. "Bum, call out!" she yelled.

Still nothing. She clutched the slate bar, ready to use it as a weapon if Bum was pulling some trick. Her light flashed over a second continuous miner and two shuttle cars. She walked between the shuttles, then let her light sweep along the rib to the curtain that fed the air off the face into the ventilation return. Thin smoke drifted by. The roof was higher here, so she was able to straighten up. She decided to walk to the beltway to see if Bum was there. "Bum? Where are you?" she called.

Then Song heard footsteps. While she was trying to determine their direction, she was violently tackled and her slate bar went flying. When she crawled to her knees, Bum's light was shining in her eyes. He was holding the slate bar. He didn't say anything. He turned the bar around to its sharp point and jabbed it viciously at her chest. She dodged, the point just missing her. Then she leaped to her feet and started running. There was a curtain blocking the entrance to the beltway. She threw herself through it, rolled, got up again, and kept running. Bum careened through the curtain, the slate bar snagging it and pulling it down on top of him. While he was fighting to get free of the plastic material, Song was stopped by the sudden failure of her SCSR. She spat out its mouthpiece and cautiously inhaled the open air. It was foul and she coughed, but at least it seemed to have some oxygen in it. She crouched behind the beltway and turned off her light. Hiding was all she could think to do.

Bum threw off the curtain and then aimed his light at the beltway. His voice was a maniacal warble. "Come out, come out, girlie girl, wherever you are."

Song crawled beneath the belt's rollers and came up on the other side. Her hand found a cardboard box. Inside it were plastic tubes. Lubricating grease for the rollers.

Bum walked along the belt, his light flashing across it. "Come on out, girl," he called again. "I was just funning. Don't mean nothing. We need to go back and help Cable." He climbed up on the belt and began to crawl along it, his light flashing from side to side.

When he got to where she was hiding, Song jumped up and squirted grease into Bum's eyes. He yelled, dropped the slate bar, and began to paw at his face. Song snatched the bar, clambered over the belt, and ran back to where the curtain was lying in the gob. Bum, still wiping at his face, ran clumsily after her. She kept going, ran to a shuttle car, and crawled up on its boom. It was turned toward the third cut in the section, the one unpinned.

Bum saw where she'd climbed and laughed. "Get off that boom, girl," he said. "You could fall and hurt yourself."

"Stay away, Bum, or I'll use your head for batting practice," Song warned, holding the slate bar like a baseball bat.

Bum laughed all the more, then strolled around the shuttle car, contemplating the situation. "Too bad there's no power," he said. "I could raise the boom and smear your girl guts all over the roof."

Song didn't say anything. She just watched as Bum stopped beneath the unpinned roof. She turned off her helmet light so Bum wouldn't notice where she was looking.

"Well, that's a stupid thing to do," Bum said, misinterpreting her purpose. "I already know where you are."

In the darkness, Song visualized the draw rock that made up the surface of the unpinned roof. It had a crack, a place where the tip of the slate bar might fit. She recalled her training. *Don't pry down with a slate bar. Pry up.*

She thrust the flat end of bar toward the crack. It caught. Then she levered up.

"Hey!" Bum yelled, just as the roof came crashing down on top of him. When it stopped, there was no sign of him, just a pile of sharp-angled brown rock. A grave of rock, Song hoped.

She crawled off the shuttle boom, then poked the pile of draw rock and sandstone with the slate bar. There was no sound from within.

Then she heard something she hadn't heard before. She crept to the curtain she'd hung at the entry. As soon as she pulled it back, a spout of black smoke rolled inside. She dropped the curtain but not before she saw something that looked like a gigantic bright orange and red snake. But it was not a snake. Song recognized it as the worst thing that could happen in a coal mine. She ran back to Cable, pushed through the curtain that still sealed off the little manhole, and found him asleep. She shook him awake.

"The mine's on fire!" she gasped. Then, as her message sank into Cable, she said, "That's the bad news."

"What's the good news?" he asked, still groggy.

"Bum."

Cable blinked a few times. "What about him?"

Song smiled a grim, satisfied smile, then proudly said, "I killed the son of a bitch!"

Thirty-Seven

11:02 p.m., Tuesday

Trailing their portable communications phone wire, the Highcoal rescue team stopped at the entry to Two block. The team leader called Bossman, who was in charge of the clear air station at the bottom. "CO and methane levels are good in the intake," Shorty reported. "I poked my head through the mandoor return and took a reading on the beltline. The return has some smoke in it. CO is elevated, but within limits. Methane is acceptable too."

Bossman called Einstein and reported the information. "I'm going to send the Fox Run team forward, if you agree," Bossman said.

Einstein was in Mole's control room. "I agree," he answered.

Bossman called over Pritha Mahata, the Fox Run captain, and gave him the order to move up. Mahata nodded and waved his men on. Bossman noticed one of the Fox Run men wore coveralls of a different color and wondered what kind of specialty that indicated. Fox Run was a big operation and its miners were known to put on airs. Bossman didn't ask. He had better things to worry about.

"WHAT'S THIS ABOUT a fire?" Cable asked. He was fully awake now. "Tell me what you saw."

"In the intake entry. Like a snake. It was crawling around the roof. I think the headers are on fire too."

Cable was quiet for a moment. "A fire will slow down the rescue," he concluded.

"Not to mention it could burn us up," Song pointed out.

Cable nodded, then frowned at Song. "Was I dreaming or did you say you killed Bum?"

"You weren't dreaming. He tried to kill me first."

Song explained how she had levered the roof down at the unsupported face.

"He was a sorry excuse for a human being, but he was a friend once," Cable said. "I just couldn't abandon him."

Song was too tired to hold back how she felt. "After I left Highcoal, you abandoned me quickly enough."

Cable didn't respond. Instead, he just kept looking thoughtful.

Exasperated, Song pressed her aching back against the rib, then slid down it until she was sitting beside him. "That's right, Cable," she said bitterly. "Don't talk about what happened to us. Don't even think about it. After a while, you'll forget all about your short-lived, terrible marriage to that runt half-Asian girl from New York City."

Cable let out a long breath. "Song . . ."

"What is it?"

"I could use some more ibuprofen."

She shook her head. "Nurse Song to the rescue." She dug inside one of her pockets, pulled the bottle out, shook out four tablets, and handed them over along with a bottle of water. After he swallowed, she asked, "What's going to happen to us? I mean the fire . . ."

Cable wiped his mouth with his shirtsleeve, then finished off the water. "I won't lie to you. If the fire gets to us, we don't have anywhere to go. Let's just hope it stays where it is. By now, the fans should be off so there's nothing pushing it our way."

"How's our air?"

Cable checked his detector. "Carbon monoxide is up a tick. We'll have to go on the SCSRs again soon. But not yet. Are you feeling sleepy?"

"No. But I've been a little busy, so I guess I'm pumped full of adrenalin."

"How about banging on the roof bolt again?"

"Yes, sir, Mister Superintendent. Oh, I forgot. You quit."

"Not until the end of the week," he reminded her again.

Wearily, Song picked up the slate bar and started thumping it against the metal plate. She did it for as long as she had the strength, then sat down again. "If they heard us, how would they let us know?"

"They're supposed to fire three surface shots as a signal. Then I would expect to hear them drilling a bore hole down to us. That would be to get air into us and possibly a microphone."

"Oh good. I'll sing 'Destiny.' Jim Brickman would like that."

Cable smiled. "I sure do like his songs."

"You have no clue when I'm being ironic, do you?"

"When you're being what?"

"Thought so."

Song leaned against Cable's shoulder. "Now I'm feeling sleepy."

"Breathe through your SCSR. Get some oxygen in your lungs."

"What I really need is a cup of coffee."

"Fresh out, I'm afraid." He shook his head, trying to clear his thoughts. "What's next for you?" he asked. "Where do you go from here?"

"Besides heaven? Or, since I killed Bum, hell?"

"You're not going to hell. You're not going to die either. At least not for a long time. What I mean is where are you going after Highcoal? Back to New York?"

Song stared ahead. "I don't know. Considering our situation, you may be surprised to learn I sorta like mining coal."

"Good thing you own a coal mine, then."

"No, it isn't."

"Why not?"

Song shook off the cobwebs that seemed to be slowly covering her thoughts. "I need a mine superintendent. The one I had quit as of the end of the week. You wouldn't happen to know good one, would you?"

"Are you being ironic?"

"No. I'm too tired."

"Well, I'll keep my eye out," he said. He studied her. "You're trembling. Are you cold?"

"No, I'm mad."

"What about?"

"You. Me. Everything."

"I think you're cold." He put his arm around her shoulders and drew her in. "You feel good," he said.

"I'm filthy and I stink."

"You smell like a coal miner. I like that in a woman."

She put her hand on his chest, then looked up at him. "How's your leg?"

"It hurts like the devil, but I still want to kiss you."

"No, you don't."

"Yes, I do." And he proved it.

Song met his gritty lips with hers. As exhausted as she was, kissing him was still wonderful. "Cable . . ."

That was when the curtain was drawn back. A helmet light flashed across them. Bum, carrying a shovel, walked bent beneath the low roof of the little hole.

"Hidy folks," he said, grinning his awful grin. "I'm *ba-a-a-a-a-ack*. And this time I'm in a really bad mood."

Thirty-Eight

12:21 p.m., Wednesday

F ox Run is at the Three block entry," Mahata reported.

"How's the air?" Einstein asked.

"The smoke is a little thicker," the Fox Run team leader said. "Methane percentage is steady, and the carbon monoxide is acceptable."

"Okay, tell Highcoal and Amalgam to move up."

"They have already started."

"That's not by the book," Einstein sniped. "Each team is supposed to wait until I tell them to move."

Mahata clicked off the phone and looked around at the rescue teams. He hadn't been entirely honest with Einstein. The hopscotching had stopped and all three teams were together, acting now as one unit. "I fear Einstein will not be pleased with us," Mahata said in his clipped Indian accent.

"Screw Einstein," somebody replied.

Mahata peered at the team member who'd made the comment. He was in rescue garb, but his heavy tan coveralls did not match the others. The Fox Run team wore smart navy blue coveralls with an American flag stitched to their shoulders. The Highcoal team wore forest green; the Amalgam team were in red. This man's tan coveralls looked somehow retro, as if they belonged to a rescue team of twenty years ago. "You are not a member of my team," Mahata accused. "Or any of these teams. Who are you?"

"I'm on my own team," the man said.

"Raise your helmet," Mahata demanded. "Let us get a look at you."

When the odd rescuer hesitated, Mahata took a step toward him. "All right, all right," the man said and raised his face plate, revealing the face of a skinny young man with a GI buzz cut.

"Who are you?" Mahata demanded.

"Chevrolet's my name, rescue's my game," Chevrolet said.

"All right. *What* are you?" Mahata demanded further.

"My buddy's in there," Chevrolet said.

"What do you mean?"

"The woman. She's a red cap and so am I."

The Fox Run team members stared at the young man, then started to laugh. "Whoa, son, you got some brass," one of them said.

The other team leaders discovered the disguised red caps on their teams too. There proved to be a total of four. "Mine's a Mexican!" Cotton Eye reported with some astonishment.

"*Sí, señor,*" Gilberto said. "But I have my green card."

Cotton Eye scowled at him. "Like that makes any difference!"

Ford and Justin were pushed out of the gathering to stand beside Gilberto and Chevrolet.

"Where did you get your equipment?" Mahata demanded.

"Highcoal has a lot of retired rescue miners," Chevrolet answered with a shrug. "Our daddy, God bless his soul, had an outfit at our house. We borrowed the others, sort of, when their owners weren't looking."

"The oxygen bottles? Where'd you get them filled?"

"Quick trip to Bluefield took care of that."

Mahata called for a conference of team leaders. "What do we do?" he asked Shorty and Cotton Eye.

Shorty shook his head. "We can't send them back by themselves. They're red caps. They're liable to get lost."

Chevrolet was listening in. "We ain't gonna slow you down. Our equipment's good," he said.

Cotton Eye reached over and slapped Chevrolet on the side of his helmet, then laughed. "The boy's right, Pritha," he said. "Let's keep going. We can kick their red cap butts later."

Mahata gave it some thought. "All right, if we all agree. I am assigning one of my men to watch our foolish little red cap. I suggest you do the same with yours. Let us go ahead."

"I got something else to say," Shorty said. He flashed his light over his team members. "My boys and I think we need to ditch the book. We've only got about three hours of oxygen left in our packs. At this rate, we'll never get up to Six block. We got to get moving. Let's shotgun it. Straight ahead, fast as we can go."

Mahata looked at the roof immediately overhead, then flashed his light down the escapeway. "The roof seems good," he mused. "The air quality is not that bad."

"I agree with Shorty," Cotton Eye said. "Let's make a run for it."

"Einstein will go very much insane," Mahata worried. "He is also certain to levy a fine upon us."

"If we bring them back alive," Chevrolet interjected, "who gives a flying you-know-what?"

"You will please be quiet, red cap," Mahata interrupted. "You do not have a voice here. And kindly do not use profanity. Yes, yes, I know you didn't say the word, but you thought it. That's the same thing. It's bad luck."

"The next red cap says a word, he's going to get his butt kicked," Shorty growled. "Butt ain't profanity, is it, Mahata?"

"It is not to my way of thinking," Mahata replied.

"All right," Shorty said, "let's take a vote. Red caps, you don't get one."

The rescue teams huddled. One by one, through their faceplates, their eyes met. Every man nodded an affirmative. Chevrolet, Ford, Gilberto, and Justin stuck their thumbs up, even if they didn't count.

The decision was made. The rescue teams were through with Einstein's book. "Let's move, you smoke-eaters!" Shorty yelled, and every man cheered.

WHEN AN AMBULANCE arrived at the Highcoal Church, reporters and television personalities rushed it, thinking that somehow they had missed news of a rescue. The doors were opened and they were disappointed to observe an old man on a gurney, who was soon off-loaded. Still thinking there had to be a story, they stuck a microphone in the man's face. It turned out to be Square Block.

"Why are you here at the church, Mr. Block?" a personality named Geraldo demanded.

"I trained her," Square announced. "I trained Song. She's one of my red caps!"

"Red cap? Is that some kind of bird?" an anchorman asked. The breeze coming down from the mountains was ruffling his toupee.

"No, you idjit! She wears a red helmet!" Square roared. "And she's a dang good miner too!"

"What did he say?" a reporter from the *Washington Post* asked a reporter from the *Washington Times*. The *Times* reporter frowned at the *Post* reporter and said, "You guys haven't had a decent story since Watergate."

"Well, you've never had a decent story at all," the *Post* reporter sputtered.

"Take it outside, gentlemen," Geraldo said.

"We are outside," the *Post* and the *Times* replied in unison, at least agreeing on something.

Then the doors to the church swung open and Square was wheeled inside. As the doors closed, the journalists heard the voices within rise in strange jubilation.

"Does anybody have a clue what's going on?" Geraldo demanded.

"Let's go ask the governor!" a reporter shouted and a stampede began toward Omar's, where the voluptuous chief executive was still holding court.

"WAIT! BUM! LISTEN!" Cable demanded. "Don't you hear it?"

Bum's expression was odd, his features contorted, and Cable knew he must've sniffed more meth up his nose.

Song was staring at the roof. "I hear something too!" she cried.

There was no doubt about it. It was the sound of drilling.

"Put the shovel, down, Bum," Cable said. "They're probably drilling into the escapeway to see what the air quality is first, then they'll be right along."

Bum lowered the shovel, but he still had a wild-eyed look. He shifted his weight from foot to foot and his arms were trembling. He pointed a shaky finger at Song. "She tried to kill me!"

"Because you tried to kill me," Song retorted. "I guess that makes us even."

Bum slowly dropped to his knees. He put down the shovel and held his head in both his hands. "This sure ain't been my day," he muttered.

"It's going to be okay, Bum," Cable soothed.

Bum looked up with his sad, mad, contorted face. His mouth was all twisted. "No, it ain't. I pushed Square over the mountain, then I killed Stan. Oh, I'm so filled with sin. I'm headed down to the hot place, sure."

Cable and Song exchanged glances. Then Cable asked, in a soft voice, "Why did you do all that, Bum?"

Bum's lips were trembling. He pawed at his face as if something was crawling on it. "Square saw what he shouldn't have seen," he whined. "Stan, he wouldn't give me my money. He even tried to kill me. It was him who came up with the plan, the rat bastard."

"What plan?"

"To steal fine-grade coal. Stan had a dummy corporation." He huffed out a mirthless chuckle. "He called it Coal-ron."

"You and Stan really shouldn't have done that," Cable said. "I thought you were my friends. We all played football together."

"We didn't steal that much. Just enough to make it worth our while."

"Any amount was too much. But stealing's one thing, murder's another. You were brought up better than that, Bum. What would your mother say?"

Bum rocked from side to side. He slapped at his arms. "There's bugs on me," he whined.

"It's only the meth," Cable replied.

"My daddy was killed in this mine," Bum wailed. "Then Mama got cancer. What chance did I ever have?"

Cable's tone was firm. "You had the same chance I did. I went into the army, got the GI bill, and went to college. You went straight into the mine. There's nothing wrong with that except you got bitter about it. Then you got on drugs."

"Nobody ever gave me a break. My whole life."

"I did. Truth is, I should have fired you a long time ago."

Bum stared at Cable. "You know what I'm thinking? I'm thinking I should go ahead and kill you and the girl. You got to know that, yet there you are, sitting with your busted leg, saying mean things about me. Sometimes you ain't very smart, Cable, not nearly as smart as you think you are."

"You're not going to kill anybody ever again, Bum. Rescue is coming. Just sit down and breathe easy."

Astonishing as it was to Song, Bum seemed to acquiesce to Cable's advice. He crawled to a rib and sat against it, then turned off his light. Song kept listening to the distant drilling. It was the sound of hope and life. But then she felt Cable sag against her. "No, Cable, don't fall asleep. Please."

"Umph," he responded, but it was obvious he was sliding away.

Bum suddenly jumped to his feet. He slapped at his arms and legs and did a nervous dance, his boots shuffling in the gob. He turned his light back on. "Well, I made up my mind," he said. "I'm gonna kill you both. You see, I have to 'cause you know too much. God knows why I confessed to all that, but I did and that's the long and short of it."

Bum picked up the shovel and turned toward Song. "You first, girl. Say your prayers."

"I've said them, you moron," Song said, then summoned up all her strength and launched herself helmet-first into Bum's stomach. Caught by surprise, he doubled over and staggered backward. She snatched the shovel from his hands and swung it, just missing his head. He squalled in rage and fear and scrambled away on his hands and knees. He stopped long enough to pick up the last two fresh SCSRs and then disappeared through the curtain.

Song looked unhappily after him. "I just can't seem to kill that man," she muttered. She knelt beside Cable and shook him.

"Wake up, Cable! Snap out of it! Don't you leave me!"

Cable's only response was to mumble something incoherent. Song realized she was starting to wane too. She looked at the gas detector and saw why. The CO level was in the danger zone. She sat down and sucked into the mouthpiece of her SCSR, but there was little oxygen coming out of it. Her eyelids fluttered, and she felt consciousness begin to slip away. "No, must stay awake," she said to herself, or somebody, and then she felt like she was falling through a warm and comfortable and endless void.

"**WHAT IS IT?**" Einstein barked across the phone line.

"We've punched through, Einstein," Birchbark replied. "We put down those sensors like you said. They're reading hot, real hot. There's black smoke coming out of the borehole too. I'd say the mine's on fire."

Einstein grimaced. This was the worst possible news. "All right. Cap it off and move your rig five hundred yards to the west. I want to see if the fire is going that way."

"What does it matter?" Birchbark demanded. "You know they're good as dead down there. There's no way to put out a mine fire, not without foam, lots of men, and lots of time. And you ain't got none of that."

"Just do what I tell you!" Einstein demanded.

Birchbark was quiet for a few seconds, then said, "All right, Einstein. I apologize. You ain't giving up, so me and my boys ain't, neither. We'll have that hole dug in a couple of hours."

"Got Shorty on the black phone, Einstein," Mole reported.

Einstein put down the outside phone and picked up the inside one. "Where are you?" he asked.

"Five block," Shorty answered sheepishly. "But we've stopped now. There's been a roof fall here across both the intake and return entries. We're going to need to bring up a scoop loader to clear it."

Einstein simmered. He knew the rescue teams had ignored his careful plan and had simply lunged as deep into the mine as they could go. Shotgunning was what they called it. Einstein called it stupid, but he'd deal with their misdeed later. "Listen to me," he said. "There's a fire on Six block. How big I don't know, but you know what that means. How's the air where you are?"

"Carbon monoxide is high, methane okay; oxygen is below twenty percent. There's smoke, but not too bad. All this rock is probably keeping it from getting to us."

Einstein processed the information, then said, "Get back to Three block. I'll send fresh air packs to you there."

"What about the scoop loader to move the rock?"

"Can't do it. You open up a hole, the fire could spread through it."

"That fire's got to be put out," Bossman said. He'd been listening in from his station at the bottom.

Einstein knew fires in coal mines were all distinctive beasts, requiring different ways to put them out. He needed more information. "I'll get back to you when I learn more," he said.

Shorty turned to the rescue teams, including the red caps. "Boys, I'm sorry," he said. "We've got to turn around."

SONG WAS STARTLED awake. She'd been dreaming. Something about a great white bird. It had picked her up in its talons and lifted her out of the void, then dropped her from a vast height over the mountains. She had fallen and fallen. Just before she'd hit the ground, she'd woken up. She had no idea what it meant, or if it meant anything except oxygen starvation in her brain. She turned on her light, then leaned over and shook Cable. She was relieved when he groaned.

"Not now, honey," he said. "Let's just sleep in."

"You better not add 'Michelle' or 'Governor' to that line, buster," Song muttered.

"What's happening?" Cable asked, suddenly alert.

"Bum took our fresh SCSRs."

"Where'd he go?"

"How should I know?" she snapped. "He's gone. That's all I know. Hopefully, he'll stay gone."

Song looked at the gas detector in Cable's lap. "Put your mouthpiece in and breathe, Cable. The CO is in the danger zone." Her eyes were watering. "And the smoke is getting thicker."

"Because the fire's getting closer," he said.

She listened. "The drilling's stopped."

Cable took a deep hit off his SCSR. "They probably punched through," he said. "Maybe into the fire. It won't give them much hope for us."

"What can we do?"

Cable said nothing, which also appeared to be his answer.

"There has to be something we can do," she insisted. "We can't just give up."

She thought for a moment. "There're fire extinguishers on the miner and the shuttle car."

Cable managed a small shrug of his shoulders. "You can't put out a fire that's consuming an entire entry with a couple of fire extinguishers. It would take ten thousand gallons of foam to do that."

"Come on, Cable. I'm depending on you!" she raged, shaking him. "There has to be a way out of this!"

Cable lowered his chin, a gesture of defeat. "When the fire comes, try to find another hole. Keep moving away from it."

"I'll take you with me if I have to carry you every step of the way," she declared.

"No. With this leg, I'm not going anywhere, but you can. Just promise me to never give up."

"Why not?" she demanded. "You have! Just like you gave up on us!"

"I didn't give up on us," he said. "*You* gave up on us."

Song wanted to argue the point, but she didn't have the energy. She sank back against the rib. "We both gave up," she sighed.

Cable nodded. "You're right. We both gave up."

They fell silent until Song said, "I'm thirsty." She looked around. "I see Bum stole our water too."

"I'm sorry about all this," Cable said.

"Is that all you can say? Think, Cable! Think! You're supposed to be this all-knowing mining man. Get us out of this!"

Cable fought through the cobwebs in his brain. He was trying to put a cogent thought together. Then an idea formed. "Water," he said. "We need water."

"Yes, Cable," Song replied tiredly. "I just mentioned that."

"But would it work?" Cable asked.

Song peered at him. "What are you talking about, Cable? Would *what* work?"

"It might be too dangerous," he said.

Song thought Cable had slipped into delirium. "We're about to get burned up in a mine fire," she said. "How could *anything* be more dangerous than that?"

His hand found hers and gave it a squeeze. "I have an idea that might save us."

She looked into his eyes. They were bright, alive. "Really?"

"Really."

"Let's hear it!"

"I don't know, Song. It's kind of nuts."

"Cable . . . me wearing a red helmet and working in a coal mine. That's nuts. Nothing else comes close."

Cable told her his idea. "I may not be thinking straight, Song. And you'd have to go back out there to get what we need."

Song gave Cable's idea some quick, sequential thought. She concluded it was indeed nuts and it also had nearly zero chance of working. On the other hand, it was better than giving up. "Bum's out there," she said. "How can I get past him?"

"I keep forgetting about him," Cable confessed, then took a drag off his SCSR.

Song climbed to her feet. She was still game even if half her blood was bubbling with carbon monoxide. "All right, Cable. It's our only chance. I've got to try. Tell me again what I need to do."

"Are you sure?"

"Tell me before I lose my nerve!"

Cable nodded. "All right. You work your way past my jeep to the fourth crosscut on the right. There's a manhole there. I'm sure that's where the shot fireman left his box. It's plastic and it's yellow. His name's Rimfire Jones and he has his name stenciled on it. After we pulled out of Six block, he had a work order to knock down enough rock to seal it off, and then we were going to build a ventilation overcast there."

"How much does the box weigh?"

"About thirty pounds, I think."

"And tell me again what's in it?"

"High explosives and everything you need to detonate them." Cable took his SCSR off and handed it to her. "Here. Take this as a backup. It's still got a little juice."

"No. You need it."

"I'll hang on. I swan."

"You sure?"

"Yes, now get going. Bum's probably curtained himself off, breathing the SCSRs one after another. But keep an eye out for him."

"Got it. Pick up high explosives, avoid bad air, and keep an eye out for a hopped-up murderer. No problem." She clipped Cable's SCSR to her belt.

"Put your goggles on."

"Okay."

"Whatever you do, never cross in front of a mine fire. The heat will melt you. I'm serious."

"Okay."

"One more thing. There's something else I want you to know. I love you."

"Okay." Song headed for the curtain, then stopped. "What was that last thing you said?"

"I love you."

Her light played across his face. "I love you too, you idiot. I never stopped loving you, even though I really tried."

"I think you're a great coal miner."

"Is that why you love me?"

"Call it a bonus. Why do you love me?"

"I have a weakness for mine superintendents."

"That's too bad. I quit, remember?"

"Well, Cable, you can just be the superintendent of my heart."

Cable chuckled although it turned into a cough. "Go. And whatever you do, come back. If I have to die, I want it to be in your arms."

"You're not dying in anybody's arms, not today."

Song pushed through the curtain and into the smoky dark to begin her battle against the all-consuming fire, to save herself and the man she loved.

Thirty-Nine

1:14 a.m., Wednesday

At the Highcoal Church a television reporter, a lovely young redhead in a pantsuit, was doing her best to get a story. She held a microphone toward Young Henry, who was on the church porch, sent by his mother to keep any and all media representatives from entering. Backing up the pretty correspondent was a man holding a big camera on his shoulder. He kept swiveling the lens from her face to Young Henry's.

"Sorry, ma'am," Young Henry said. "Highcoal families only."

Her big blues batted at the boy. "If you would let me in, I would be like a mouse."

"Sorry. Mama would whomp me if I let you in."

"What's your name?"

"Young Henry."

"Such a marvelous name! Are you sure we can't come inside? I want my viewers to see what the inside of a West Virginia church looks like."

Young Henry remained firm. "Well, if that's all you're after, ma'am, there's a couple more churches right down the road in Fox Run, and a bunch more on the roads to Beckley and Bluefield."

She touched his arm. "Please, Young Henry. Just for a few seconds?"

Young Henry, flattered as he was, wasn't fooled. "What you really want is to see people praying and crying for those trapped below. I guess I understand that, but I just can't oblige you. I'm sorry."

"But if reporters like me don't tell this story, who will?" she asked. "Is your daddy a coal miner? You want me to tell about him, don't you?"

"He was a coal miner, yes ma'am. But he got killed in the mine."

"Then let me tell his story."

Young Henry scratched his head, then said, "Ma'am, here's the way I see it. You want to tell the story of coal miners? They don't need nobody to do it, nobody on television or the newspapers anyway. Their story is told every time you turn on your light switch, or watch television, or wash your clothes or your dishes or yourself. Their story is told in every building that uses steel to hold itself up, and every time you ride in a car, a truck, a train, or an airplane. Tell the story of coal miners? Heck, ma'am. It's told everywhere, if you'd just listen to it."

The television woman glanced over her shoulder at her cameraman. "Did you get that, Bobby?"

Bobby said he did. She smiled at Young Henry. "I think I have my story, Young Henry. I'm going to go do a wraparound and it'll be ready to go national. You're going to be famous!"

The boy lit up. "Really?"

"Really."

She handed her microphone to the cameraman, then gave Young Henry a big hug and a kiss on his cheek. Young Henry's face turned a brighter pink and his ears looked like they were on fire.

SONG WAS THANKFUL she hadn't encountered Bum. Cable was probably right. He had taken his SCSRs and curtained up somewhere. In the entry, the smoke was oily and dense, her light only able to cut through it a few feet. The threads of fire she had seen on the headers were still there, but did not seem to be getting any bigger. At least the headers were holding. She turned to follow the rails toward Cable's jeep. There was an orange pulsating glow up ahead.

When she reached Cable's jeep, she began to feel the heat from the glow. There was no doubt about it. This was the main part of the fire. She could even hear it, a groan like a chorus of anguished demons. Cable had told her to count four crosscuts past his jeep, then look in the fifth one for the shot fireman's box of explosives.

Song plunged on into the oily smoke, the heat rising with every yard of progress. She passed the first crosscut, then the second. It was at the third opening she encountered the devil's maw, a ferocious mouth agape with flames. It roared at her, puffed fire in jagged flames, and seemed to be daring her to approach its evil majesty. She recalled Cable's admonition. *Never cross in front of a mine fire.* The fire belched hot gas across the entry, subsided, then threw flame across it again like a giant, black dragon.

Song thought of all the prayers she had heard in the mine. She decided maybe it was all right to add one more. "Lord, I am not a Yogist, I swan. I'm just a coal miner. I think, I hope, that makes me one of yours. Let me get through and I promise . . ."

She stopped and thought some more. She and Preacher had shared a moment after choir practice one evening. He'd asked her if she had recently prayed. Song had confessed all her prayers were impromptu, usually to keep herself or her fellow red caps or the other miners safe. Preacher had nodded in satisfaction. "Those are good prayers, Song. And don't think they don't work. God is listening all the time."

"Then why doesn't He answer all our prayers, Preacher?" Song had demanded.

"What we don't see," Preacher answered, "are the ripples that happen every time anything happens. They're like stones dropped in a pond. Even bad things that happen have a purpose. We don't know what their purpose is, but it's for something." He'd smiled at her. "It takes faith to believe that in the end, goodness triumphs through adversity. Everything good, Song, takes faith."

Now Song had no choice but to have faith. "All right," she said. "Lord, here's my prayer and I've got a reason for it You might like. I need to get across this fire and then I need to get back. Why? Because the man You gave me to love is back there and it's the only way to save him. Is that good enough?"

Song didn't expect an answer except by results. She took a deep breath, lowered her head, and ran. She struck the scalding air, then threw herself across it, landing, rolling, and then she was on her feet again. She smelled something burning and realized it was her hair. She took off her helmet and slapped at the embers until she was sure she'd put them out. She took stock and realized she was alive. She looked up at the roof and silently voiced her thanks. One more cut to go.

"WHAT ARE WE going to do, Einstein?" Bossman demanded. He dropped into a chair beside the MSHA man.

Einstein had a telephone to his ear. "All right," he said into it. "Keep me apprised." He hung up and looked at Bossman. Einstein's face was drawn and desperately fatigued. "That was Birchbark. He thinks he should punch into Six West soon. If anybody's alive there, we can communicate."

"What do you mean *if*? You think they're dead, don't you?"

Einstein sat back and rolled his head, the bones in his neck crackling like tiny firecrackers. "Two methane explosions, a roof fall, and a mine fire are tough to survive. Yes, I think they're probably dead."

Bossman started to argue, saw the futility of it, and took off his helmet and threw it across the room. It landed hollowly, then rolled until it finally came to rest next to the door. "What do you think happened?"

"An investigation will determine that, but I think we'll find it was Bashful's drilling into the old works that started everything. It set off a methane pocket that blew, then probably started some old timbers burning. When they burned through a crosscut or maybe an old mandoor, they set off a second pocket. That one in turn started the fire on Six block."

"Of all the things to happen, I would have never guessed this one," Bossman said, lowering his head in fatigue.

"That's why the mining industry has to be eternally vigilant, Bossman," Einstein said grimly. "It's a never-ending job."

Bossman struggled to his feet and staggered over to Mole's coffee pot to pour himself a muddy cup of joe.

Einstein watched him. "How can you stand to drink that stuff?"

"I called Atlas headquarters," Bossman said, waving away Einstein's question. "They've started the ball rolling to put the fire out. It'll be an expensive proposition. If past fires are any guide, it'll take weeks. Our miners are going to be out of work for a while."

"Out of work miners are nothing new," Einstein said, yawning, and stretching. He looked up in surprise as there was a sudden commotion outside and the door flew open. A distinguished man with a silver mustache entered the room. He had an authoritarian presence. "Where is my Song?" he demanded. "Where is she?"

Mole jerked awake and stared at the intruder. "Who are you?" he, Bossman, and Einstein all asked at once.

"Who do you think?" the man bellowed.

Now they knew.

Joe Hawkins had arrived in Highcoal.

Forty

Her arms loaded with a big yellow box, Song stumbled through the curtain, then sprawled into the gob. When she looked up, she saw Cable was passed out again, his head lowered. She crawled to him, then shook him by his shoulders. Finally, and with what seemed immense effort, he opened his eyes.

"I got the shot box, Cable!" she yelled into his face, trying to get him to wake up. "And look what else!"

Song held up a fresh SCSR. She activated it and slipped it over his head, inserting the mouthpiece in his mouth and clipping his nose. "There were two of them attached to the shot box."

"God bless Rimfire," Cable mumbled. He took several deep breaths, coughed, then took several more. He looked at his detector. "I should be dead," he marveled.

"I prayed you'd be okay," she said.

"You prayed?"

"Hey, I'm in the church choir, aren't I?"

"Did you see the fire?"

"I had to cross in front of it."

"That's impossible."

"I know, but I'm a stupid red cap, so I did it anyway. That required another prayer. I'm getting this praying thing down to a science, I'm telling you. Funny thing too. So far, it works! Preacher may be on to something. Now, tell me what to do with this stuff."

Cable nodded toward the shot box. "Slide it over. Let's see what you got."

Song opened the box and he ran his hand through the packages. "This ought to do it," he said.

"So what do we do?" Song asked eagerly.

"We blow a big hole out of the third cut. Vietnam and I both noticed moisture seeping out near it. That's why I decided to close the section down. Part of the old works we abandoned years ago is underwater. If we blow a hole in the right spot, there's a good chance we can flood the section and put out the fire."

"Okay. But then what do we do? Grow gills?"

He smiled affectionately at her. "It won't stay flooded long. The main line drops toward the bottom. The water should drain away from us."

"How long will that take?"

"I don't know. Anyway, we have no choice. You ready to make some noise?"

"I've never even lit off a firecracker."

"Well, honey, we're about to explode the equivalent of ten million firecrackers."

"Then let's do it."

He smiled at her. "You are truly a wonderful woman."

"I know, Cable. But let's save this lovey-dovey stuff till later, okay? We've got work to do."

He turned all business. "You're right. Carry the shot box to the face, then come back for me."

Song took a deep breath, then another. "Next time I'll break the leg, you do all the heavy lifting."

After hauling the box to the face, Song returned and helped Cable to it. He started removing the short, cylindrical sticks of powder, along with several coils of wire. "We usually drill holes to put these in," Cable advised, holding up a cartridge. "But we don't have anything to drill with. Go find a slate bar or a shovel. We need to dig as deep a hole as we can."

"We?"

"All right. *You*. While you dig, I'll set up the blasting battery and the wires. We'll only need to detonate one stick. It will set off all the others."

"How many are you going to use?"

"All of them."

"Is that a lot?"

"You bet it is. We're going to make a very big hole, Song."

Song looked around until she found both a slate bar and a shovel, then came back and began to attack the face. She kept hacking and digging until she had excavated a small hole. The results were not impressive. "I don't think I can get much deeper," she said.

"We'll need to put something heavy on top of the charges," Cable said. "Otherwise the blast might not get to the water."

Song looked at the unpinned roof. "I could knock down the draw rock on top of the explosives. I did that once already when I thought I killed Bum."

He mulled the idea over. "Okay," he said. "But cross your fingers the rock doesn't cut the firing wire."

Song inhaled but not much came through. Her SCSR was starting to fail. She sat down. "I'm bushed."

Cable dragged himself and the shot box until he could pack the sticks of powder inside Song's small excavation. Two wires were attached to one of them. He crawled away, grunting in pain, while spooling out the wire. When he got clear, he said to her, "Knock down the roof, Song. Be careful not to get under it."

"I've already been under it, digging out your precious little hole."

"Oh yeah," Cable said. "I forgot. Sorry."

Song looked at the roof. She'd been afraid to look at it before or she wouldn't have been able to work beneath it. Now she was astonished at what she saw. "Cable, there's a kettle bottom here. No, there's two!"

"You're kidding. Did you pray for another miracle?"

"No. Did you?"

"No. But I bet they're praying a lot right now in church. Guess we're getting the benefit. Go ahead. Knock them down."

Song took a step back and struck the kettle bottoms with the slate bar, then did it again. Though she managed to scar their bottoms, they didn't move. "Great. Any other time, they'd have fallen on my head."

"Pry the rock from around them," Cable advised.

Song pried and some draw rock fell. Still, the kettle bottoms stayed stubbornly clinging to the clay and rock that encased them. She sat down again, shaking her head, trying desperately to suck a little oxygen out of her SCSR. "It's no use. We need a *real* miracle this time, Cable."

Almost as if on cue, a sound like a hive of mad hornets suddenly filled the air, then both kettle bottoms and a huge load of rock broke free, falling in a heap on top of the charges. Song was only able to scramble out of the way at the last second.

Moments later a spinning drill head poked through the collapsed roof and whirred to a stop. Then it disappeared back up through the hole to be replaced by something cylindrical and black. "Hello," a voice called through it. "Anybody there?"

"We're here!" Song and Cable cried out in astonishment.

There was a pause. Then an excited voice came back. "What's your situation?"

"We're alive!" Cable croaked. "Is that you, Birchbark? We're about to blow the face. We're going to try to flood the section."

Birchbark's voice was incredulous. "What did you say?"

"I said we're blowing the face! We're going to flood the section with the water from the old works. We've got a fire to put out."

"Did you say you're going to flood the section?"

"Just tell Bossman and Einstein!"

"Okay! Okay!" Birchbark yelped, the message finally sinking in.

"We've got to get to some place as high as we can," Cable told Song.

"The shuttle car in the entry," Song suggested. "It'll put a pillar between us and the face. And we can get up on its boom."

"I like it," Cable agreed. "Let's go."

Cable crawled through the gob, the wires spooling out behind him while Song tried to keep them from getting tangled. They made the turn toward the entry, but when they got ten yards from the shuttle car, Song felt the wires go taut. "They won't reach," she said.

Cable sat up and thought for a second. "All right. You keep going to the shuttle. I'll blow it from here."

Song sat down beside him. "No, Cable. You can't move fast enough. You go on. Crawl up on the shuttle. Let me know when you're there. I'll blow it and then join you. I can beat the water. I'm fast. Track team in college. Sprinter. Bet you didn't know that about me, did you? Thought not. Go ahead. Attach the wires to the blaster and then get clear."

Cable rigged the blaster. "When you're ready to blow the face, yell 'Fire' three times before you turn the key," he instructed.

"Why do I have do that?"

"Because that's the proper way to do it. You're still a red cap. I'm educating you."

"You're nuts, Cable. That's another reason I love you."

"There are too many reasons for me to count why I love you."

"Awww . . ."

Then came a dull roar and Song was astonished to see the curtain that led to the beltway suddenly catch fire. A hot wind blew past its remnants. Black smoke billowed around them. "Get going, Cable," she urged. "I'll be right behind you. Go!"

Cable crawled to the shuttle car and dragged himself up on it. He struck his splinted leg on the frame and stifled a scream. Then, inch by inch, he pulled himself up until he was on the boom. "Ready!" he called out.

Song knelt and steadied the blaster in her hands. Her helmet light was dimming, its battery dying, its yellow glow just bright enough for her to see. She was so intent she didn't hear the heavy boots behind her, but she did feel the kick of one of them in her back. She was slammed face-first into the gob.

"Hey, girl!" Bum yelled maniacally. "How ya doin'?"

She'd dropped the blaster. Song reached for it. Bum, holding a number four shovel in his right hand, stepped in front of her and picked it up first. "What were you going to do with this?" Following the wires, he walked around the corner of the entry, then walked back. His body was twitching.

"How much meth have you taken?" Song asked.

"Enough to keep me high and alive, girlie girl," he said. He walked around the pillar until the spot of his light landed on Cable stretched out on the shuttle boom. "Hey, Cable, old teammate. You don't look so good. What's the plan?"

"There's about ten million gallons of water behind that face, Bum," Cable said. "If we blow it, there's a good chance we can put out the fire."

Bum began to laugh. He kept laughing until he had nearly lost his breath. He beat on his legs and shook his head. Finally, he said, "Aw, we don't need to do that. They'll pump down foam to put it out. Probably in, oh, I don't know, a day or so. Good thing I've got lots of SCSRs. I found a whole cache of them. Looks like Petroski and his boys been squirreling them away."

"The fire's coming this way," Cable said, keeping his voice calm and modulated. "It'll kill you before anybody can get in to put it out."

"I'll take my chances. At least until I see you and that girl die. Ever since I met her, she ain't been nothing but trouble, just like you."

"Bum, think about it. All I've ever done is be good to you. Why would you want to see me die?"

"Are you asking me why I hate you? Well, let me see. Maybe because you gave me a job, a job where you could lord the fact you're the mine superintendent over me for the rest of my life? Just like you made all-county linebacker while all I got was kicked in the butt?"

"High school was a long time ago, Bum."

Bum disconnected the wires from the blaster, then tossed it down. He walked beneath the boom and shined his light up at Cable. "Tell me about it. I'll think about you when I'm old, Cable, and you're dead."

Cable tensed, readying himself. "Blow the face, Bum, or you'll burn up with us."

"I don't think so. I'll find me a little hole somewhere. Are you suffocating, Cable?" Bum giggled and did a little dance. "Oh, I'm going to tell everybody how sorry I was that you died. Maybe I'll write a book, be on *Oprah*. Oh, gol-l-lee, Oprah, if I had only known where my old buddy Cable and his stupid little wife were holed up, I'd have brought them an SCSR. I'll even shed a tear on national TV for you two."

Cable pushed himself off the boom and landed on Bum. Bum grunted, staggered, then fell with Cable on top of him. "Blow the face, Song!" Cable yelled while desperately trying to hold his old friend down.

Song crawled to the blaster and found the wires. She attached them, then twisted the key, but nothing happened. Desperately, she looked over at Cable and Bum. Bum had managed to roll Cable over and was sitting on his stomach. Bum's fist was raised to smash into Cable's face. "Say good night, Cable," he said.

With the last ounce of her strength, Song picked up the shovel Bum had dropped, then walked over and hit him as hard as she could in his face. Bum flopped over and went very still. Song kicked him for good measure, then stripped him of his SCSR, and handed it to Cable. "Get up on the boom again," she commanded, too spent to be polite.

Song went back and picked up the blaster, unscrewed the terminals, pulled the wires loose, and ran the ends through her mouth. Spitting out gob, she reconnected them. She turned to see that Cable was back up the boom. "How many times am I supposed to say fire? Oh yeah. Three times. Here goes. Fire, fire, *fire!*"

Song turned the key.

THE FLOOR TREMBLED in the control room. "What was that?" Joe Hawkins demanded.

Einstein and Bossman exchanged glances while Mole raced to the seismograph. "Another explosion," he said, after a cursory inspection of the screen. "Afterwards, a tremor, like a little earthquake."

"I think they just did what Birchbark said they were going to do," Einstein said.

Hawkins stood up. The miners in the room were surprised to see that he had his chin up and was grinning. "Gentlemen, I'll tell you who did it. My Song!"

IN THE EBONY depths, a small spurt of water began to grow. Then, with awesome force, a wall of water erupted like a gigantic geyser that turned into a monstrous wave. A tide of black water roared forth, first encountering a continuous miner, which it swept aside as if were a toy. It rolled on until it struck a shuttle car and flipped it over and over. The miner and shuttle car, tangled together, became wedged, creating a partial dam. Diminished only slightly, the great black wave turned the corner and raced toward the second shuttle car where Song desperately clung to Cable's outstretched hands.

Forty-One

Mole made the announcement. "Birchbark says all he's getting is steam out of the entry borehole."

"Is that good?" Hawkins demanded.

Einstein pulled the telephone away from Mole. "What about the borehole at the face?" He listened, then said, "Let me know if it changes."

"What's going on?" Hawkins demanded.

Einstein turned toward Song's father. "The entire end of the mine is flooded."

"I'll ask you again. Is that good?" Hawkins demanded.

What passed for a joyful expression on Einstein's face faded until it had returned to its usual grim countenance. "I don't know," he confessed. "If they were able to get above the water and hang on, maybe . . ."

THERE WAS A FRENZY around the governor, who had made herself available just outside the mine office. "Is it true?" the media demanded. "Is the fire out?"

Governor Godfrey, having just consulted with Einstein, allowed as how it might be.

The reporter named Geraldo had been doing his homework. "Governor, over the last hours, and I mean no disrespect, I assure you, we've heard all about the love story between Cable Jordan and Song Hawkins. But isn't it true that you and Mr. Jordan were also romantically, even sexually involved?"

318

The governor glared at Geraldo until he seemed to melt. "That is certainly not the truth. Cable and I are friends. That's common knowledge and everything else is mere gossip. After my dear husband passed on, Cable was nice enough to squire me around to a function now and again, but our relationship was always entirely proper. We were more like . . . cousins. Yes, that's it. When I saw Cable and Song together, I recognized instantly they were meant to be together. It is so saddening to me that they opted for annulment. I tried to talk them out of it. If this situation unfolds as I hope, I pray we will see these two fine young people back together."

A few of the West Virginia media people applauded the governor. They had never heard such an astonishing story told so convincingly. One nudged the other. "Never let the truth get in the way of a good story, eh?" There was a subdued ripple of laughter that neither the governor nor the national media caught.

Joe Hawkins came out on the porch, and the media spotted him and came running. They thrust their microphones in his face. "One at a time, boys, and ladies," the old pro said. "I will answer your questions gladly. Just don't yell them at me all at once. The only thing I want to say is I love my daughter. She is strong, very strong, and I believe she is still alive."

Hawkins looked up and found his eyes landing on the face of the governor of West Virginia. Her eyes were as blue as the Caribbean and he found himself falling into them.

"Excuse me, fellas," he said, coming off the porch and pushing through them. "There's someone I would like to meet."

ON THREE BLOCK, the combined rescue teams got the word that the fire was out. They cheered. Fresh oxygen tanks had been brought up. They were ready to go, including the red caps, now accepted as part of the crew.

"Holy smokes!" Mahata cried out as he aimed the beam of his light toward Four block. A river of water was coming their way. There was no time to run. In seconds, they were up to their knees in it. They held hands to stabilize themselves and leaned against the force of the flow. After a few minutes, they saw with relief that the water wasn't getting any deeper. Shorty called Einstein and told him the situation. "Can we get that scoop loader now?" he asked.

"When the water goes down," Einstein said.

Shorty looked around his group and they looked back. "There's a scoop loader on Two East," Shorty said. "That section's higher than the main line and the return. It should be dry."

"I'll get the dang thing," Blackjack said.

"We also need Doctor K," Shorty advised.

"The power's off," Mahata said. "How could she get down here?"

Shorty thought it over, then gave Einstein a call. "What now?" he demanded.

"We need Doctor K down here," Shorty said.

"When we turn the power on, I'll send her down."

"Einstein, every second counts. Just turn the power on to the manlift long enough to get her down here. That's all I'm asking."

Einstein was silent for a while, then said, "All right. That makes sense. But don't go any farther than you are right now unless I give you the word."

Shorty crossed his fingers. "Oh, don't worry. We wouldn't think of it."

Shorty hung up and looked around the rescuers. He chose Justin. "Justin, go to the bottom, then escort Doctor K back here. Can I trust you to do that?"

"You bet you can!" Justin took off.

"That's a good boy," Shorty said.

"No, that's a good man," Mahata said. Shorty had to agree.

THE WATER LEVEL kept dropping. Cable and Song clung to one another. "You did it," Cable said.

Song's SCSR was gone, ripped from her face by the flood. She hacked and coughed until Cable stuck his mouthpiece into her mouth. "Come on, baby. Breathe!"

Song had nothing left. She was completely spent. She took several breaths from Cable's SCSR, then spat out the mouthpiece and put her head down to sleep. "G'night, Cable," she said. "I love St. John, but I don't want to snorkel any more."

"We're not in St. John, Song. We're in the mine. Wake up. We've got to find Bum's stash of SCSRs."

She blinked awake when he pushed the mouthpiece back between her lips. "They had to be washed away," she said around it.

"Not if they were in a manhole. Go look for them."

"Leave me alone, Cable. You're a terrible boss. You keep making me do things I don't want to do. I'm going to take a nap. I deserve it." She let the mouthpiece fall out of her mouth again.

Cable stubbornly pushed it back. "Don't give up, Song. Please. We're going to get through this. I've always known we would. It's our destiny."

She opened one eye. "My favorite Jim Brickman song."

"And he wrote it for us, even though he didn't know it at the time."

Song tried to look at Cable, but his face was blurred. Her eyes were failing her, she thought, but then she remembered she had on her goggles. She pushed them onto her forehead. "I think I've changed my mind," she said groggily. "I don't like being a coal miner any more."

Cable tried to chuckle but he didn't have the strength. "Too late," he said. "You're trained now." He took off his helmet, unclipped the battery from his belt. "Here, I sill got some juice in my battery."

"No, Cable. I haven't earned a white helmet. I want a black one."

"Take it. You own this mine. I guess that gives you the right."

Song took off her helmet and handed it to Cable. "Don't lose it. It matches my lipstick."

"Song?"

"Hmm?"

"We're breathing a lot of carbon monoxide. Go after the SCSRs."

"Slave driver."

"I thought I was the superintendent of your heart."

"Same thing."

"Bum probably holed up around the belt. Look for the SCSRs there."

"All right, Cable. I'm going." She thought to kiss him, but didn't have the energy.

Song crawled down off the boom and into the mud. She was shivering from being wet. She looked around for Bum, hoping that she wouldn't have to see his body. She saw no sign of it, probably flushed away by the awesome torrent of water. She headed for the belt, but the going was slow, the sticky gray mud sucking at her boots with every tortured step.

When she finally reached the belt, she began to search the manholes. She was surprised and delighted when she found the sodden box of SCSRs in the first opening. She fired a fresh one up for herself, clipped two to her belt, put a couple more under her arms, and headed back to Cable.

"Not so fast, girlie girl." Rising up out of the gloom like a black goblin was Bum. "Thought I'd drowned, didn't you?"

Song aimed her light at him. Bum's face was bloody, his nose smashed by the shovel when she'd struck him. He also sported a broken-toothed grin around his mouthpiece, and his eyes were wild and crazy. He was also holding a slate bar. "You know, I'm going to have a little fun with you before I kill you," he said. He grabbed his groin. "Gonna join the mile down club, you and me are."

Song tossed down the SCSRs and backed away. "We're only eight hundred feet deep, Bum."

"All right. The eight-hundred-foot club. What does it matter?"

Song turned out her light and ran. Bum laughed and shot the beam of his light after her. "You can only go so far, girlfriend," he sang.

Song ran until she found herself beside a scoop loader. She climbed aboard and settled into its seat.

Bum laughed. "Stupid red cap. That loader's been underwater. It won't start."

Song looked up at the roof. "Well, Lord, here we go again," she said. "This one's for me and for Cable. Same reason as before."

Song pushed the start button and the dashboard lights flashed, dimmed, then brightened. She pushed the throttle forward. Bum saw the big machine groan, its tires tearing out of the mud, and then trundle in his direction. He ran. Song turned and twisted with him, catching him just as he came to rest with his back against a rib. She lowered the bucket and roared straight at him, stopping just short of running its sharp edge into his chest. "Don't kill me!" Bum screamed. "Please! Oh, have mercy!"

"Crawl into the bucket," Song ordered.

"Why?" Bum asked, wiping his shattered nose with the back of his hand.

"I'm not going to tell you again, Bum. Crawl into the bucket or I'm going to cut you in two."

Breathing heavily, his face wreathed in fear, Bum crawled inside the bucket. "What now?" he whined.

"This," Song said and pulled the lift lever to the stops. The bucket slammed into the roof, trapping Bum within a prison of steel and stone.

Song de-energized the scoop and climbed off it. She walked until she found the spare SCSRs and came back. Bum was scrabbling inside his cage and screaming. "You can't leave me in here!" he wailed. "I'll suffocate!"

"Tell it to someone who cares," Song muttered, and kept going.

THEY FOUND SONG and Cable beside a shuttle car. They were sitting in the muck, leaning against one of the big tires. Cable had his arm around her and Song was snuggled against his chest. Inexplicably, he was wearing her red helmet and she was wearing his white one. She had the mouthpiece of her SCSR in her mouth. He didn't.

Doctor K took their pulses, then touched Song on her shoulder. When Song didn't react, the doctor lightly shook her. Song's eyes slowly opened. She blinked a few times, then, as Doctor K watched, light and life came back into her eyes. A small smile formed on her lips.

"Doctor K. You're here." She looked up and saw the rescue team members standing around, then picked out Chevrolet, Ford, Gilberto, and Justin among them. "Hi, fellas," she said sleepily.

Song turned and looked up into Cable's face. His eyes were closed. "Cable? Look who's here. They've come for us at last."

"Song . . . ," Doctor K began.

Song moved her hand to touch Cable's cheek, the one with the dimple. "Cable?" she asked. "Cable?" she demanded.

"Come help me with her, boys," Doctor K said to the red caps. "Quickly now."

"No, please," Song said, running her hand across Cable's mouth. "Breathe, sweetheart."

"Stay back," Justin warned the rescue team members who were crowding in too close.

"Please, Cable," Song begged.

"We love her," Chevrolet explained to the others. "She's the best of us."

"Please, no. Oh, God," Song cried.

"We'll take care of her," Gilberto said.

And they did.

Forty-Two

It was a story that had briefly captivated a nation, but now it was at an end. Three weeks had passed and most of the reporters, anchors, correspondents, stringers, and strap-hangers of the media were gone from Highcoal, much to the relief of the little mining town. The satellite trucks, generators, trailers, and vans that supported them were gone too. The tale of the mine explosion, fire, and underground flood beneath the winter-bare hills of Appalachia was but one of a never-ending reality series reported by the American media for urban dwellers who were gratified to discover there were still real people in the heartland accomplishing real things.

The ratings reflected the interest, and they were huge. On the morning when the rescue teams and the town doctor (a woman!) reached the trapped trio, there were shouts of joy and hymns of salvation sung throughout the land. When the manlift rose from the darkness, the television cameras, one of them even belonging to Al-Jazeera, moved in for a close-up, and print reporters and famous anchors crowded in just to hear a single word from the adorable female miner. They were disappointed. She stayed silent, her head turned away, as two of her rescuers carried her in a stretcher to a waiting ambulance. Beside her walked her father, Joe Hawkins, his silver-maned head held at an attentive tilt.

The woman's husband, the man named Cable, had already been brought out and taken away.

The next manlift brought out the murderer named Bum, and beside him stood the town constable and more rescuers. Bum hung his head and wept tears of shame and meth as he shuffled to another ambulance. Constable Petrie climbed aboard it with him, and then its siren shrieked as it rolled out of the tipple grounds and through the gate. Bum was also headed for the clinic, before being transferred to the county jail at Fox Run.

And yet, even then, the story was not over.

A star had been born by the events deep in the Highcoal mine. Governor Michelle Godfrey had talked the nation through it as the tragedy unfolded. She had proved to be witty, articulate, always informative, confident, and sexy, a potent combination. She had worn her miner's jumpsuit and a white helmet as she demonstrated how an SCSR worked, talked learnedly of the problems of mine ventilation, and even put on a rescue pack. In the days that followed the rescue, there was an intense media interest in her involvement with the silver fox himself, billionaire widower and very eligible bachelor Joe Hawkins, who also happened to be the father of the courageous woman who'd been trapped and apparently had a hand in her own rescue. The governor and the billionaire had been seen together a few times since, in New York as well as attending the West Virginia Symphony in Charleston. The liaison with such a rich and powerful man only added to the governor's star power. There was talk of national office. A woman like that was too large in life to stay at the state level. Dick Morris called. So did James Carville. Several times.

The near-calamity produced another star, a twelve-year-old Highcoal boy, amusingly named Young Henry. His speech on the steps of the Highcoal Church about the importance of coal and the men and women who mined it had delighted viewers with its stirring simplicity. Governor Godfrey soon made an announcement that Young Henry was the new co-poet laureate of West Virginia (joining Irene McKinney), although he had not written poetry at all, just told the truth as he saw it. Young Henry was on David Letterman and Jay Leno, and all the morning shows, his big ears bright red from the attention. He did well on television, to the relief of his mother, and was adored by everyone. Despite his acclaim, his teachers did not let up on his homework and he got a B in English for the semester.

And still the story was not complete.

At the Highcoal Church of Christian Truth, they held a ceremony for Song and her fellow red caps to accept them into the fraternity of miners. For this event, the television cameras returned, and the nation tuned in as the five red caps were individually called forward by their instructor, a proud and beaming man named, even more improbably, Square Block. As each received their shiny new black helmet, Square took the scratched and battered red helmets and reverently placed them on the altar. In the choir pews, the choir and Preacher watched with benevolent satisfaction.

Song was the last red cap called forward. She took off her red helmet and solemnly put on a black one. Square hugged her for a very long time. She needed it. Her legs felt weak. Her whole body, mind, and spirit felt weak. She briefly wondered if she could go on, then she did.

Preacher rose and crossed to the pulpit. "Song," he whispered to her, "you should say a few words. The people expect it."

Song stepped into the pulpit. As she looked out into the congregation and the cameras, her eyes betrayed her fatigue. She had not slept much since her return to the surface. And tears came when she thought there surely were no tears left. She told herself to stand straight and proud, as Cable would want, as her mother would have required, as her father wanted now, as the world, always questing a hero, seemed to demand.

"I am proud to be here today," she said, her voice catching momentarily. "I am proud to be associated in any way with these men, my dear friends and fellow red caps, Gilberto, Justin, Chevrolet, and Ford, and our instructor, Square Block."

The ex-red caps all grinned encouragingly at her. The light from the winter sky poured through the church windows, burnishing their gleaming new ebony helmets, which they did not seem inclined to remove.

Song, however, took off her helmet and held it up, presenting it to the congregation and, some said later, as an offering to the God of all coal miners.

"I am proud to be accepted into the brotherhood and sisterhood of the men and women who mine the deep coal," she said. "I sometimes didn't think I would make it, but I did. To Square, Preacher, Bossman, Vietnam, and all the foremen and miners who helped me through my training, I cannot possibly express my gratitude adequately, except to say thank you from the bottom of my heart. You are the best people I have ever known."

Song took a ragged breath.

"Cable . . ."—she swallowed, and started again—"Cable used to tell me not to make easy things hard. I told him that there were no easy things, just things that seemed easy but weren't."

She put her helmet on. "I know now he was right, because there was a very easy thing I kept making hard, and that was loving him. Cable was the easiest man in the world to love, yet I kept making it difficult. It was not his fault. It was mine."

She looked down, as if gathering her strength, then lifted her head. "I was like the continuous miner operator who keeps digging into the roof, rather than into the rich, good coal. I was like the shuttle car operator who runs over his own cable or swipes a rib when he is turning. In love, I was just a red cap, uncertain what to do next, afraid to ask, certain I was going to mess up if I tried. Oh, for an instructor in love as good as the one I had in coal mining!"

Song smiled, and the people of Highcoal looked back at her with complete devotion.

"When we were trapped," Song said, "I learned what I would do to protect my husband. I would have done anything. I only wish I had done a better job of it."

Song slumped, and her shoulders shook, and copious tears came again. Preacher rose and went to her, and put his arm around her to hold her up. "Song," he said gently, "you must know there's someone else here."

"Yes, Preacher," she said. "You don't need to tell me. I feel God here, just as I felt Him in the mine as I passed before the fire."

"Yes, He is, child," Preacher said, "but there is someone else here too."

She sagged against him. "Not the one I want, Preacher," she whispered.

"That," he said triumphantly, "is exactly who I mean."

The door that led to Preacher's office opened, and when Song looked, there stood Cable. He struggled ahead on crutches, his rugged face fixed with determination. Doctor K and a paramedic hovered alongside, ready to catch him.

But he did not falter. Nothing was going to stop him.

"He came out of his coma this morning," Preacher said to Song and to everyone. "And he wouldn't listen to reason. He insisted on coming here."

Song hugged Preacher, then ran from the pulpit to hold Cable.

"I love you, love you, love you!" she cried as the congregation cheered, hugged one another, and wiped tears away. He took her in, held her in the way only he could. She could feel his renewed strength.

Doctor K drew her aside for just a moment. "There's no damage from the CO poisoning we can find. Cable's got a good heart, and apparently he had brain cells to spare."

Cable overheard. "I guess that surprises you, huh?" he asked Song.

She grinned at him. "That you had brain cells? Pretty much."

"You look good in your helmet," he offered.

"All women look good in black," she replied. Then, glancing at Doctor K, she said, "You said yesterday you were going to keep him under for another week."

Doctor K shrugged. "He started struggling to come awake on his own last night. His brain scans were perfect so we decided to bring him along. When he came awake—well, same old Cable."

"I'm not the same, Doctor K," he said. "I'm better." And then he grinned and there was his endearing dimple. Song's heart soared. She had never felt such joy. She wanted to hold Cable forever. She wrapped her arms around him again.

"Let me go, honey," Cable said gently. "I've got something that needs to be said."

"No, you have to rest. Go back to the hospital and I'll be along."

Cable insisted, and with an iron will, he struggled into the pulpit and gripped the sides to steady himself. The governor was sobbing quietly and Joe Hawkins had his arm around her while wiping away his own tears. The television cameras zoomed in on the power couple, then back to Cable.

"I want to express my thanks to each and every one of you here today," he said. "You fought for Song and me, each in your own way, and you brought us out safe. You even brought ol' Bum. If you pray for anyone, pray for him. He did evil things, but even he is not beyond salvation and God's mercy."

A few "amens" were heard, though they were faint ones. Preacher looked dubious, then shrugged and nodded agreement.

Cable looked across the congregation and saw Einstein, Bossman, Mole, the rescue team leaders, and the other rescuers. "Thank you, gentlemen, for your courage and your tenacity. You are the best of the best, and I'm proud there are such as you still in these United States."

Cable looked at each of the former red caps. "You new black caps deserve your honor today." He began to waver on his crutches, and his face went pale, the blood drained away. Song rushed to him, put his arm around her shoulders, and held him up. He had enough energy to say one more thing. "Square, good job, old son."

Square nodded his gratitude. "It were a pure pleasure, Cable."

To applause, cheers, and whistles, Cable came down from the pulpit, and Song helped him to the door. Outside, Doctor K and the paramedics put Cable aboard the ambulance. Song climbed in with him, and the ambulance pulled out. There was still a long recovery ahead for Cable, but that didn't matter. Song was going to be there with him every step of the way.

But that was still not the end of the story.

A little more than four months later, the sun was warm, the sky was blue, the women were in sundresses, the men in suits, the children in their Sunday school clothes on the same lovely beach where once Song and Cable had been married, and were about to be again.

Nearly all of Highcoal was there, all expenses paid, courtesy of Joe Hawkins: Chevrolet, Ford, Justin with his son, Tommy, Gilberto and Rosita, Rhonda, Young Henry, Preacher's family, Mr. and Mrs. Omar Kedra, Square and Hildy Block, Bossman and Mrs. Carlisle, the Petroskis, the Williamses, all the foremen and every miner who wanted to come. Over four hundred men, women, and children of Highcoal were there on the island of St. John—Love City.

Preacher, barefoot in a suit and tie, said the words. Cable and Song said them back, and the rings were exchanged once more. They were both wearing red helmets, symbolic of their recognition that they were yet students of love. "I now pronounce you wife and husband, coal miners both," Preacher said, and the marriage was sealed.

The reception that followed was grand, and the food, the drink, all were astonishing in their bounty. Even Jim Brickman made an appearance, singing "Destiny" for the once-again newlyweds. "*You* were our destiny," Cable told him, proposing a toast to the musician. Brickman happily lifted his glass to his new friends. Bossman came over and vowed that when they got back to the States, he was going to take the singer-pianist on a tour of the Highcoal coal mine, which was scheduled to be opened within a few weeks. Brickman agreed to go into the deep darkness. Maybe, he said, he'd even write a song about it. Bossman offered him a chaw of tobacco.

While the party was still going strong, Song and Cable slipped away aboard a small sailboat and, a couple of hours later, were in Sir Francis Drake Channel between St. John and Tortola. Above them, the stars were spread like a blanket of diamonds on a black velvet sky. The moon was bright and full, and the deck of the boat was made luminous by its milky light. The sea was luminescent. It was magical.

Song took off her wedding dress and put on a loose sarong. When she appeared on deck, Cable, who had stripped down to shorts from the first moments aboard, whistled. "Second honeymoons are great, aren't they, honey?"

Song sat down and watched him at the wheel. "Well, Cable, what do we do now?" she asked, her tone strictly business.

"Uh-oh," he said. "Are we having a meeting?"

"We are."

"What's the subject?"

"What do you think? You. Me. Us."

He frowned and said, "There you go. Making easy things hard again."

"There are no easy things," she snapped, "just those that seem easy but aren't. It seems to me, as sweet as all this is, we're back to square one."

"How can you say that, after all we've been through?"

"Because, Cable, darling sweet man, we still haven't settled where we are going to live."

Cable frowned. "We haven't? I thought you loved mining coal. You can't do that in New York, you know."

"True, but I also love my job. My *other* job. The one I do for my father."

Cable made a hopeless gesture, then shook his head. "You're right. Here we are again."

Song looked toward the bow pushing forward into the night. "But if we love each other enough, isn't it possible to figure out things like geography and time? Can't we do that, Cable?"

"If you love someone enough," he said thoughtfully. "I guess so. And I love you enough. For you, I'd live at the bottom of the sea."

"Then what are we to do?"

A small smile appeared. "Already done it."

Song turned her head toward him. "What have you done?" she demanded.

"I had a talk with your dad. Bossman is going to be the new superintendent

of the Highcoal mine. Management at Atlas has been shuffled off and I'm taking over. I'm going to be responsible for three coal mines, not just one. That
ought to be enough coal mining for any man. I'm going to modernize all of
them. My base of activities will be in New York, but I'll spend plenty of time
underground. It's going to be fun!"

Song rose and stood behind him, wrapping her arms around his chest and
resting her head against his bare back. He felt cool to her cheek and he smelled
so good too. *Eau de Cable.* "That's sweet, Cable, but I can't let you do it. You
love Highcoal too much. No. Here's my decision. We'll live in Hillcrest. I'll do
my work on the computer and the Internet. I talked to Mole. He has a sister
who works for the phone company. She's guarantees a clean line into Hillcrest."

"How much did that cost you?"

"Don't ask."

He pushed his ridiculous fedora back on his head. "Looks like we're on oppo-
site sides of the drift again. Now you're going to live in Highcoal and I'm going to
live in New York. Lady, I don't know if we're ever going to figure out this business
between us. But our meeting is temporarily adjourned. There's our mooring."

Cable pulled the boat into a pretty little lagoon, tied off on a float, and took
the sails down. Then he held out his hand to her. "Let's go below," he said. "After
all, we have a honeymoon to attend to."

Song settled into bed and held out her arms for Cable. Instead of getting in
with her, he said, "We'll share our time between New York and Highcoal.
Simple. That's a hard thing made easy."

She looked at him, blinked several times, then said, in some astonishment,
"Why didn't we think of that before?"

"Because we were being selfish," he answered.

She opened her arms even wider. "Let's not be selfish any more, not about
anything."

He climbed into bed and let her take him in. "I want to die in these arms,"
he said, nuzzling her.

"You almost did," she whispered. "Those weeks while you were in a coma, I
almost went out of my mind."

"But I'm here now. So, past and present and future Mrs. Jordan, what are
you going to do about it?"

She touched his face, stroked his cheek, then held his chin so he couldn't look anywhere but into her eyes. "I'm going to do what any bride does on her wedding night. And maybe one thing more."

He drew back a little. "Not another complication! And what would this one be?"

She kissed him and said, "I'm going to try to make a baby. But you have to help."

He grinned as big a grin as she'd ever seen, with his amazing dimple deeper than a coal mine. It was certain that Cable liked the sound of what he'd just heard and, in its way, it was the end of the old story and the beginning of a new one.

Song and Cable got busy.

It was the easiest thing in the world.

Acknowledgments

I am indebted to many men and women in the coal mining industry, state agencies, and the federal Mine Safety and Health Administration (MSHA) for their expertise and assistance during the writing of this novel. Among them were Mike Rutledge and Gilbert Randy Whitt of the West Virginia Department of Mines, Don Hager of the Consol Energy Company, and Pat Brady, Yvonne Farley, Becky Farley, and Ron Minor of MSHA. Guy Harman of Safety Source, LLC, teaches red caps in the Virginia and West Virginia coalfields, and was especially helpful by making some significant and important suggestions during the writing of the manuscript. Billy "Willie" Rose, a fellow Coalwood Rocket Boy and a great mining engineer, also assisted along the way. My thanks also include my uncle, Harry "Ken" Lavender, who is always willing to give me coal mining advice. Of course, any errors within the novel are entirely my own.

Linda Hickam read the first drafts of this novel and their later refinements and gave her usual astute advice for improvements. I am also grateful to Ami McConnell, the brilliant editor for this novel, and Rachelle Gardner of TheWordStudio.com, who did a magnificent job pitch-hitting for Ami during her maternity leave. Allen Arnold, *Red Helmet*'s publisher, is a true gentleman and a man I fully respect and admire who shepherded this novel through several ups and downs. He was responsible for all the ups and I was responsible for all the downs.

As always, I am indebted to my literary agent, Frank Weimann of The Literary Group and his associate, Neil Reshen. Agents do many things to support their authors. In my case, I am fortunate that Frank and Neil are also my friends. Burke Allen, a fellow West Virginian, of Allen Media Strategies, has also recently accomplished some remarkable marketing of my work. This is a very good thing. I would also like to thank Jim Brickman, my friend and a great entertainer, for the use of the lyrics to his ballad "Destiny." It was the perfect song for Song and Cable. Thanks as well, Jim, for your sense of humor and for allowing me to put you in the story.

Sago Miners Memorial Remarks

by
Homer Hickam
January 15, 2006

Note: On January 2, 2006, an explosion occurred in the Sago coal mine in Upshur County, West Virginia. Thirteen miners were trapped. For two days, the nation and the world were riveted by around-the-clock television reports on the attempts to rescue them. Despite the best efforts of all involved in the rescue, only one miner survived. Homer Hickam, author and West Virginia native, was asked to deliver the keynote address during the memorial services for the Sago miners on January 15, 2006, at West Virginia Wesleyan College. What follows are his remarks that day.

Families of the Sago miners, Governor Manchin, Mrs. Manchin, Senator Byrd, Senator Rockefeller, West Virginians, friends, neighbors, all who have come here today to remember those brave men who have gone on before us, who ventured into the darkness but instead showed us the light, a light that shines on all West Virginians and the nation today:

It is a great honor to be here. I am accompanied by three men I grew up with, the rocket boys of Coalwood: Roy Lee Cooke, Jimmie O'Dell Carroll, and Billy Rose. My wife, Linda, an Alabama girl, is here with me as well.

As this tragedy unfolded, the national media kept asking me: Who are these men? And why are they coal miners? And what kind of men would still mine the deep coal?

One answer came early after the miners were recovered. It was revealed that, as his life dwindled, Martin Toler had written this: *It wasn't bad. I just went to sleep. Tell all I'll see them on the other side. I love you.*

In all the books I have written, I have never captured in so few words a message so powerful or eloquent: "It wasn't bad. I just went to sleep. Tell all I'll see them on the other side. I love you."

I believe Mr. Toler was writing for all of the men who were with him that day. These were obviously not ordinary men.

But what made these men so extraordinary? And how did they become the men they were? Men of honor. Men you could trust. Men who practiced a dangerous profession. Men who dug coal from beneath a jealous mountain.

Part of the answer is where they lived. Look around you. This is a place where many lessons are learned, of true things that shape people as surely as rivers carve valleys, or rain melts mountains, or currents push apart the sea. Here miners still walk with a trudging grace to and from vast, deep mines. And in the schools, the children still learn and the teachers teach, and, in snowy white churches built on hillside cuts, the preachers still preach, and God, who we have no doubt is also a West Virginian, still does His work too. The people endure here as they always have, for they understand that God has determined that there is no joy greater than hard work, and that there is no water holier than the sweat off a man's brow.

In such a place as this, a dozen men may die, but death can never destroy how they lived their lives, or why.

As I watched the events of this tragedy unfold, I kept being reminded of Coalwood, the mining town where I grew up. Back then, I thought life in that little town was pretty ordinary, even though nearly all the men who lived there worked in the mine and, all too often, some of them died or were hurt. My grandfather lost both his legs in the Coalwood mine and lived in pain until the day he died. My father lost the sight in an eye while trying to rescue trapped miners. After that he worked in the mine for fifteen more years. He died of black lung.

When I began to write my books about growing up in West Virginia, I was surprised to discover, upon reflection, that maybe it wasn't such an ordinary place at all. I realized that in a place where maybe everybody should be afraid—after all, every day the men went off to work in a deep, dark, and dangerous coal mine—instead they had adopted a philosophy of life that consisted of these basic attitudes:

We are proud of who we are. We stand up for what we believe. We keep our families together. We trust in God but rely on ourselves.

337

By adhering to these simple approaches to life, they became a people who were not afraid to do what had to be done, to mine the deep coal, and to do it with integrity and honor.

The first time my dad ever took me in the mine was when I was in high school. He wanted to show me where he worked, what he did for a living. I have to confess I was pretty impressed. But what I recall most of all was what he said to me while we were down there. He put his spot of light in my face and explained to me what mining meant to him. He said, "Every day I ride the mantrip down the main line, get out and walk back into the gob, and feel the air pressure on my face. I know the mine like I know a man—can sense things about it that aren't right even when everything on paper says it is. Every day there's something that needs to be done, because men will be hurt if it isn't done, or the coal the company's promised to load won't get loaded. Coal is the life blood of this country. If we fail, the country fails."

And then he said, "There's no men in the world like miners, Sonny. They're good men, strong men. The best there is. I think no matter what you do with your life, no matter where you go or who you know, you will never know such good and strong men."

Over time, though I would meet many famous people from astronauts to actors to presidents, I came to realize my father was right. There are no better men than coal miners. And he was right about something else too:

If coal fails, our country fails.

The American economy rests on the back of the coal miner. We could not prosper without him. God in His wisdom provided this country with an abundance of coal, and He also gave us the American coal miner who glories in his work. A television interviewer asked me to describe work in a coal mine and I called it "beautiful." He was astonished that I would say such a thing, so I went on to explain that, yes, it's hard work, but when it all comes together, it's like watching and listening to a great symphony: the continuous mining machines, the shuttle cars, the roof bolters, the ventilation brattices, the conveyor belts, all in concert, all accomplishing their great task. Yes, it is a beautiful thing to see.

There is a beauty in anything well done, and that goes for a life well lived.

How and why these men died will be studied now and in the future. Many lessons will be learned. And many other miners will live because of what is learned. This is right and proper.

But how and why these men *lived*, that is perhaps the more important thing to be studied. We know this much for certain: They were men who loved their families. They were men who worked hard. They were men of integrity and honor. And they were also men who laughed and knew how to tell a good story. Of course they could. They were West Virginians!

And so we come together on this day to recall these men, and to glory in their presence among us, if only for a little while. We also come in hope that this service will help the families with their great loss and to know the honor we wish to accord them.

No matter what else might be said or done concerning these events, let us forever be reminded of who these men really were and what they believed, and who their families are, and who West Virginians are, and what we believe too.

There are those now in the world who would turn our nation into a land of fear and the frightened. It's laughable, really. How little they understand who we are, that we are still the home of the brave. They need look no further than right here in this state for proof.

For in this place, this old place, this ancient place, this glorious and beautiful and sometimes fearsome place of mountains and mines, there still lives a people like the miners of Sago and their families, people who yet believe in the old ways, the old virtues, the old truths; who still lift their heads from the darkness to the light, and say for the nation and all the world to hear:

We are proud of who we are.

We stand up for what we believe.

We keep our families together.

We trust in God.

We do what needs to be done.

We are not afraid.

Reading Group Discussion Questions

Note:

You are invited to http://www.homerhickam.com for lots more information on Homer Hickam and his writing.

We hope these discussion questions help you enjoy *Red Helmet*.

Synopsis:

Song Hawkins is a young, beautiful, and tough New York businesswoman who thinks she's found the man of her dreams in Cable Jordan, the manager of a West Virginia coal mine. But when they marry and travel to Cable's Appalachian hometown, Song is troubled by a people who love coal mining and mountains, who can't imagine a Sunday without church, and who cling to the rough ways of their ancestors. Since she can't live there and he can't live in New York, their marriage seems doomed. Then, in an astonishing turn of events, she decides to descend into Cable's mine and wear the red helmet of a new coal miner. In the deep darkness, Song has to use everything she's learned to save herself and the man she loves. *Red Helmet* is a stirring and unforgettable story of a proud people lost in the cracks of American society, told by the author born to write it. With the talent of a master storyteller, Homer Hickam delivers another exciting page-turner.

Below are some ideas for discussion in your group. Please contact Homer at http://www.homerhickam.com to let him know when you're meeting. He might even be able to answer your questions via telephone!

1. Song and Cable seem to believe it was their destiny to be together even though the circumstances were difficult. Do you believe in destiny in terms of romantic relationships? Or is it all luck and circumstance?

2. How do you see Song changing throughout the novel? How about Cable? Did he change very much or did Song have to do the changing?

3. Song's mother died trying to climb a mountain while Song was still an infant. How do you think that affected Song's attitude toward life?

4. When Song looked out at Highcoal for the first time, she instantly disliked it. Why do you think she had that opinion?

5. Why did Song's first visit to Highcoal go so wrong? Was it her fault? Cable's? Or did the people of the town not give her a chance?

6. What do you think would have happened if Song had not returned to Highcoal for Squirrel's funeral? How would Song and Cable's story have played out?

7. What did Song learn about herself when she took her red cap training? What did she learn about Cable? The people of Highcoal?

8. Could you go into a coal mine? How do you think you would feel? Did you get a sense of what it was like by reading this novel?

9. What do you think happened to Song and Cable after the end of the novel? Would you like to read a sequel?

10. Other than Song and Cable, who was your favorite character in the novel and why?